MY

Tragic

LIFE

NECIE NAVONE

Brothers
of
Camelot
prequel

My Tragic Life

Book Two in My Life Series

by Necie Navone

Copyright 2018 by Necie Navone

Cover Design: RMGraphX

Stacey Debono Editing & Graphic Design

My Editor and friend with an enhancing eye:

 Michelle Luxembourger

Final Eyes Editor: Katy Nielsen

Formatting & Graphic Promotional Design: Kaila Duff

ISBN: 978-0-9997235-5-5

Table of Contents

Dedication:

This book is dedicated to all of "YOU" who are reading this and supporting me. I graciously appreciate it.

And to my husband for being so supportive and allowing me to follow my dreams.

Chapter 1

CAPO LEARNS OF MY TALENT AND MY TRUE VALUE

It's been nine months since I got slapped, or 'beat up' as some like to call it, by my Capo. I don't like to think about it. The Capo's been around a lot more though, and I only speak to him when he says something directly to me. Otherwise, I ignore his presence in my life, and I don't share anything about me. He's a lot nicer to Mom and very chatty with Nonna. Heck, he and Mom have even gone out on a few dates and some overnight trips, just the two of them. It makes her happy, so I'm happy for her. She seems calmer, more at peace with her life, which lifts a huge weight off my shoulders.

One night at dinner, I overheard Uncle Louie tell Capo to just give me time. I laughed inside at that. There is nothing that my Capo could ever do to repair the damage he's wrought. It's not that I'm rude to him... just distant. The needy little girl who would have done anything for his attention died that night in his office. A small part of me still loves him, but now that I know I'm just his property, a pawn to use as he sees fit, I'll never be able to love him unconditionally like I love Uncle Louie.

Training with Luigi and my uncle has continued. Most of the time, they don't take it easy on me. They use their full set of skills and size against me. Rarely do I get the upper hand, and when I do, they quickly reverse it on me. I hate the fact that just because I'm a girl and much smaller, they can take me out if they really want to. Thankfully, they show me all the dirty tricks and how to use leverage against a larger opponent in case I have to actually protect myself.

On the other hand, no one can hold a candle to my knife and gun skills. I dominate all challengers when it comes to weapons. Sometimes, for the Family men's delicate male egos, I make it look like they could beat me, deliberately missing the actual target, but then hit what I aim for. Uncle Louie caught me one time when I was up against Lefty and purposely aimed a little low. He gave me a wink. Luigi out and out laughed. They both know no one can beat me... not with knives, swords or guns of any kind. I can load and shoot faster than anyone. There isn't a weapon I haven't mastered.

Luigi is my dance partner during my dance classes. He acts like he hates it, but I think he secretly enjoys our dances as much as I do. Come on, what girl my age wouldn't love dancing with an extremely hot guy like Luigi? I only see Lefty occasionally now, as he's been assigned as Nonna's full-time bodyguard. He drives her everywhere and is her shadow. I'm fine with that, she needs protection, and I feel more comfortable with her safety knowing how skilled he is in any situation.

Today, Uncle Louie is taking me out to one of the Family's shooting range. This one is bigger than ours back at the compound, so we can use higher caliber guns. He told me yesterday that he "wants to show me off." My uncle is incredibly proud of my skills and wants everyone to know it. He said to not hold back, to hit every target.

Uncle Louie feels that if the Capo and the rest of the men see me in action, I would gain respect and be trusted more like some of the younger men in the Family. This test is important, but I'm not as nervous as I thought I'd be. I have trust in my skills and steady hand. There isn't a man in this Family that can outshoot me. I'm a bit excited to show up some of the arrogant men surrounding me. Ha! I hope I get to go against Antonio. Knocking him down a peg would be amazing!

Standing in front of the mirror, I start pulling my hair back into a twist. Dropping my hands, my hair flutters around my shoulders to the small of my back.

"No," I say to the empty room. "I don't know why the Capo insists my hair be up in a twist." It's not practical for today, especially with the little wisps that'll blow into my face on the open gun range. Anyway, I like it down. "You're growing up too quickly, Princess," he always tells me.

Gah, like I, can stop growing. Placing my hands over my double D breasts, I lament the fact that I can't tell them to stop growing. They get in the way sometimes. Jeez, I'm bigger than my mom, and all of my friends too. At fifteen, I could pass for a fully-grown woman.

"You take after your Auntie Elena," Mom said one night, "she had large breasts too. You think your Papa is overprotective now, just you wait." Like I can change the genetics they gave me. I'm so tired of being made to fit into their mold of who they think I should be.

Because of the importance of today, I don't want to look like I'm young, or to have the men look at me and think, "Oh, she's just a fifteen-year-old little girl." I want to look like a girl on the verge of womanhood, because, darn it, I am. I want to prove myself to them, and I want them to see a young woman, worthy of responsibilities and respect.

I also want to have a little freedom from Uncle Louie and Luigi's constant guard duties. Sheesh, I can't even use a public bathroom without one of them "checking and clearing it." I'm losing more and more freedom by the day… maybe I'm just noticing it more.

God, I wish I'd been born into a normal family. I don't want to be the protected, coddled Princess of a Family, destined to take over one day. I just want to be ME. This life feels like a prison, run by an evil dictator. My dreams are to be free, an average, normal girl, living in America... and of being reunited with Grayson.

With that thought in mind, I reach for a pair of chestnut brown dress slacks and tug them on. Carefully, I situate my ankle holster, loving the loose leg of the slacks. I pull on a cream blouse and tuck it in, adding a thin, gold belt and matching flats. French braiding my long hair is a feat, but I think it looks pretty good twisted into a bun at the nape of my neck. Making sure to secure it with extra bobby pins, I give my head a good shake to double check that it won't fall out.

Grabbing my Family necklace from its custom box, I put it on and let it nestle on my cream blouse. Once I pull on my blazer, I take one final look in the mirror. Yep, I definitely look professional and grown up.

My bedroom door suddenly opens, and I whirl around. Nonna and Camilla, my nanny, hover at the threshold. "You look lovely, young lady. So, grown up. Are you going to tell us about your secret meeting? " Nonna, asks curiously.

Camilla approaches and circles me. "You did a great job... but you were supposed to wait for me to assist you. I won't tell if you don't," she winks.

"I've made sure your mom is busy," Nonna announces, "so we can talk. You know how she worries."

Smiling, I nod. "I can't say anything yet, but if it goes well I'll tell you all about it when we get back, I promise," I vow, crossing my finger over my heart.

"Okay," Nonna shakes her head, "but I'll be

questioning both you and Lou when you get back. You'd better have your stories straight."

"Be careful, whatever it is," Camilla adds with a smile. She knows Uncle Louie, and I don't keep secrets from Nonna.

With a final smile, I head to the front door where I know Uncle Louie and Luigi are waiting for me, as usual. "Very good, Little One," Uncle Louie says after inspecting me from head to toe. "You'll impress those egotistical assholes." He leans into the room, and calls out, "See you later, Mama." He lingers for a bit, turning his head slightly towards Camilla's direction. Hmm… Wonder what that's about.

As we turn to head to the stairs, Nonna calls, "I mean it. A full report when you get back!"

Within short order, we're in the SUV and off to the shooting range. It's deep in the hills, surrounded by acres of Family property. This range is where the men gather for challenging each other's skills, and I'm sure, to have some drinks and cigars when they're done with their pissing contests.

Luigi parks the car and Uncle Louie hands me my purple grip Sig Sauer P238, which I tuck into my ankle holster. Uncle Louie opens my door, and I slip from the SUV to a huge audience of men. All men. I'm the only female here. Ugh, I hoped that someone would have brought a girlfriend, but nope. Just me. Everyone is dressed in black, from suits to turtlenecks and slacks. Great, another reason for me to stick out like a sore thumb.

All in all, there are about a hundred men. Some have shoulder holsters hanging from their bodies, having removed their jackets already, holding cigars and chatting with each other. There's still more cars arriving as we move toward our Capo. Just how many people are coming to this thing? God, there's already more than I expected, and the cars just keep coming.

Excitement courses through my veins as I feel all eyes on me. Uncle Louie and Luigi flank me, half a step behind me. Some give me a nod, the younger men openly check me out and even wink. It's a little gross, but I ignore it as best I can. Holding my head high, I project confidence and pride into my steps as we make our way through the crowd.

"You sure she's ready for this?" Capo asks Uncle Louie, ignoring me completely.

"Yeah," he answers confidently, "very sure. I don't think there's a man here that can outshoot her. She's unbelievable."

"Are you nervous, my little Princess?" Capo asks, finally acknowledging me. He takes a long draw from his cigar.

"No, sir," I answer, smiling with confidence. "In fact, I'm excited to show you just how good I've gotten."

Capo throws his head back, laughing loud and deep, silencing the crowd. He doesn't laugh like this, ever. People turn, staring at him. Uncle Louie ignores the stares, reaching for a slice of bruschetta from a passing server carrying a tray laden with appetizers.

"Laugh now," he says and pops the food into his mouth. "You'll be eating crow later. She has every reason to be confident in her skills."

The server is just about to move on, but my uncle stops him. He grabs a shrimp wrapped in prosciutto and devours it quickly. The poor guy shrugs, adjusts his hold on the heavy tray and stands there to be Uncle Louie's personal server. He leans toward me and offers me my choice, which I decline. My uncle grabs some apple slices and cheese, giving the server a head nod, acknowledging he made the right choice.

Capo smiles and shakes his head at Uncle Louie's antics as he grabs an artichoke heart dipped in pesto. "Nice of you to wait while my brother eats all the appetizers," he says to the server. "As for your boasts Lou, we shall see just how good she is very soon."

My mind wanders, getting bored of the chit-chat. People have returned to their chatting, ignoring our huddle. Some are just engrossed in the food and drinking, obviously not taking part in today's shooting challenge.

Surveilling the crowd, I watch as a man steps out of the tree line. He's about fifty feet away, and I don't recognize him. As he moves towards us, there's something off about him. I realize it's his sunglasses. They're mirrored, which no one in our Family wears.

He leaves the shadows of the trees and, when the sun hits him, I notice his suit isn't the uniform our men wear. The Family tailor didn't make it. Its store bought, not tailored to fit his frame. I know, to my toes, that he isn't one of our men.

The man increases his pace, almost running. Reaching into his jacket, he pulls out a Glock. Instinct takes over. Grabbing the tray from the server, I dump the food and hold it in front of my Capo's chest with one hand. My other slides along his waist to the holster in the middle of his back. Pulling his gun free, I flick off the safety and take aim at the man who is raising his gun to aim at my Capo. He squeezes the trigger, and the bullet hits the tray, sending vibrations up my arm. I return fire, shooting twice. My first shot lands right between his eyes, the second lodges into his heart. The man falls, landing face first onto the concrete.

Those three gunshots shatter the calm of the late morning. Men pull their guns out, some aiming at us, some at the man sprawled lifelessly on the ground. A puddle of blood grows larger around him. Frozen in shock, I watch several men walk over to the body and kick his gun clear. They flip him over and see what I already know. My aim is incomparable.

They tuck their guns back into their holsters, a clear sign that the man is no longer a threat. The crowd does the same... except me. I continue scanning everyone, pointing my gun at each of them, looking for a store-bought suit, still holding the tray in front of my Capo.

"Little One," Uncle Louie says cautiously. "You did good. You saved your Papa... our Capo. Can you hand me the gun? All the men here are Family."

My eyes slide to Uncle Louie, finding warm concern reflected back at me. Papa slowly places his hand over mine and flicks on the safety. He pulls the gun from my hand and tucks it back into his holster.

My arms fall, the tray clattering to the ground, still staring at Uncle Louie. "He... he walked out of the trees. His sunglasses were wrong, and his suit. It wasn't made by our tailor. It was boxy, not fitted right. Mirrored sunglasses..." I trail off.

Uncle Louie grabs me, pulling me into a tight hug. My eyes close as love, protection and security wash over me. He knows how much his hugs mean to me, how much they can heal. Taking a deep breath, I inhale his cologne and steady myself.

"It's Dino Caza," one of the men announce. "We've been looking for him for a while. Thanks to the Princess, he's dead. What do you want us to do with him?"

"Get rid of him. I want no remains ever found," Capo declares.

Uncle Louie releases me and holds my face. "Are you okay, Little One?" he asks.

"Yes, I'm fine," I nod. "I just needed, well, that." I smile, and he smiles back knowing I'm referring to his bear hugs that heal.

"I needed it too," he whispers. "I'm so proud of you. No one noticed what you picked up on so quickly. You, *you*, Alessandra, saved our Capo today. I couldn't be any prouder." He kisses my forehead and gives me another quick hug. Feeling a hand at my back has me turning to look up at my Capo.

Papa puts a finger under my chin, looking into my eyes. "Not a tear in her eyes," he announces. His hand slides along my neck, pausing at my pulse point. His eyebrows shoot up in surprise at my slow pulse rate. Finally, he reaches for my hand. "Look at her hand," he says loudly. "It's steadier than mine right now."

Pride and wonder suffuse his voice. "I'm truly blessed. I have the best daughter a man could dream of having. She is strong and capable. She acted on instinct, better than *any* of us did today. Did you see her accuracy? A headshot and a heart shot! The Princess took down our enemy today!" There are a few cheers, but others stare at me in silence.

"I was only doing what I've been trained for all my life... to be aware, to protect myself, my Family and my Capo. It's just luck I was looking toward the trees."

Capo shakes his head. "No young lady. No one but *you* saw that man. No one but *you* noticed the difference in his suit and glasses. No one but *you* saw him coming out of the tree line. *You did*, and you responded instinctively, saving my life."

"And to you, Lou," he says, reaching for my uncle's

hand. "I owe you my life as well. Once I questioned your training of Alessandra. Never again. She proved me wrong, along with anyone else who has ever doubted that she can fulfill her role in this Family. Thank you, Lou."

My eyes wander to where the body was, but it's already been removed. The blood is being cleaned as men pour bleach on the ground. Several men approach me and shake my hand, others just give my shoulder a squeeze as they pass, thanking me.

Pride suffuses my soul as I realize what's happening. The men's opinion of me has changed. They now look at me with respect, and even with a little awe. They realize my worth. The crazy thing is, I don't regret it. I don't regret ending a life. It was either him or my Capo. Am I so cold-hearted that, at fifteen, I can take a life without a second thought?

"Someone grab that tray," Capo announces, breaking my reverie. "I want it engraved with today's date next to the dent from the bullet and hung in the clubhouse. I want it displayed to remind us all of the Princess's skill and abilities."

Lorenzo grabs the tray from the table and takes it to the Capo's car. Wow, he wants it hung in the clubhouse. This is not an honor bestowed often.

"Come here, Princess," Papa calls. "I would like another display of your abilities."

Uncle Louie winks at me, his eyes flashing with humor. He continues chatting with some men as I walk toward the firing range.

"Is there anyone who would like to challenge my daughter?" Papa calls loudly. Several men laugh as some hands raise. "Antonio," he chooses. "Let's see what you can do."

I hadn't noticed Antonio was here before that moment. He struts over, smiling at me. I return his smile, and he winks.

"Okay Antonio," Papa says in loud, clear voice, "everyone knows you're interested in my daughter. If you can outshoot her, I'll promise you her hand in marriage... when the time is right."

Hoots and catcalls sound from the watching crowd, cheering Antonio on. He smiles huge, giving me another wink. I roll my eyes dramatically, making the men laugh. As we approach the shooting line, Uncle Louie attaches a target to the clips hanging from the wire. He turns and hands me my ear protection and a box of bullets. With a bit of show, I slowly bend over and retrieve my gun from my ankle holster. I pop the clip and check that it's loaded.

"Here's your chance, Little One," he says quietly. "This is the moment you've been waiting for. Hand him his balls and take no mercy. You can do this."

"I'm planning on it, Uncle Louie. Don't worry. Now that Papa's put my future on the line, I'm not about to let him win."

"You ready to become my wife-in-waiting?" Antonio calls from his lane. "After I school you, that is."

"Ha! I'm going to hand you your balls and prove I'm the better man," I answer, loud enough for the other men to hear. Throwing my head back, I let out a dramatic laugh. Unable to resist teasing him further, I shoot him a cocky wink, which replaces his smile with a look of grim determination.

Vito, standing with Antonio, glares at me as Papa laughs at my words.

"Did you hear what she said? She just told him

she's about to hand him his balls!"

More men join the crowd, laughing right along with my Papa. "That's my little Princess! You keep telling him how it is." He gives me a look of pride, adding in a low tone, "You show him, Little One."

"Like her little purple gun can actually hit anything," Antonio says, trying to save face.

Luigi and Uncle Louie chuckle. As I pull on my ear protection, I wink at Luigi who is controlling the electronic target lines. "You know what to do."

He returns my wink. "Your call, Princess," he says with a secret smile.

With my ear protection in place, all sound fades away. Taking my gun into my hand, I find a good stance. Once the target hits the end of the line with a jolt, I fire in quick succession. After six shots, I return my gun to the stand in front of me and pull off my ear protection. Luigi pulls the targets in for a better look.

"Antonio," Luigi calls, laughing, "how come you only fired three times?" I snicker at the question.

Uncle Louie pulls my target off the line as Vito does the same with Antonio's. Both of them smile with pride as Vito hands the target to Papa, who inspects it.

"Not bad Antonio," Papa says, patting him on the back. "One shot to the head and two shots to the center of the chest. This man would be dead."

My father turns, taking the target from Uncle Louie. I haven't looked at it. Don't need to. I know what I hit. I give Antonio a smirk as Papa bursts out laughing. He turns, lifting the target up for the men to see. "Look," he laughs. "Our Princess just handed Antonio his balls! One between the eyes, one in the heart and a little curve, cupping Antonio's balls!"

Vito's hand flies up, smacking the back of Antonio's head. He jerks forward, his chin hitting chest. The men are still laughing at our Capo's words as I watch Vito berate and abuse Antonio.

"Great job, Little One," Uncle Louie says, congratulating me.

"Guess Antonio has to wait a few more years and work a lot harder for the Family to earn you," Papa says, putting his arm around me. I lean onto my toes, getting close to his ear.

"Papa," I plead. "It's not fair for Vito to be so angry with Antonio. He can't take me either. I can't stand watching him hit Antonio. Please grant me one favor. Let me challenge him. Let him know what it's like to lose to a girl. Let me put him in his place. Please?"

His head turns toward Vito, who is still yelling at Antonio. He turns back to me with a puzzled expression. "You sure, Little One?"

"Absolutely, sir," I nod. "Who protected you today? Your right-hand man, or me, your daughter?"

Papa looks down, shaking his head. "Alright, Little One. You earned this. But be careful not to make too many enemies today."

"I don't care. Vito shouldn't punish Antonio for losing a shooting challenge when he failed to do his job today."

"Men!" Papa turns, getting everyone's attention. "My little girl wants to challenge Vito to a match."

Men gasp as Vito's head snaps around, pinning me with a nasty look. He's not happy I'd challenged him. Crossing my arms, I return his glare. Vito marches up to us, Antonio trailing behind. I give Antonio a little smile, hoping he isn't too upset at losing to me.

Vito steps up to Papa, almost getting in his face.

"Your little girl grow some balls I didn't know about? First, she shows up my son in front of the men, and now she thinks she can challenge me?" he asks, getting heated.

"Yes, Vito. She wasn't happy with you scolding Antonio and hitting him when he did his best." He pauses, giving Antonio a slight nod. "He's just not as good as she is." Papa lowers his voice, leaning into Vito, "Besides, she made a good point about having to do your job for you." I watch as Vito's neck turns bright red with the Capo's final words. Uncle Louie steps up behind me, putting his hands on my shoulders.

"Everything all right over here?" he asks, growling.

Papa steps between us, saying, "Everything's fine. Luigi!" he calls. "Get some more targets set up. Our Princess is challenging my right-hand man!"

Papa grabs Vito's shoulder, giving him a firm shake. "Now, if my little girl beats you, I don't want to hear another word about it. No rematch. Do you agree?" At his nod, Papa continues, "And no more hitting your boy. Antonio is twenty and needs to be treated like a man."

Vito smiles, giving me another mean look. "We have an agreement. Let's sweeten the deal. If I put your daughter in her place, she becomes Antonio's wife on her eighteenth birthday... none of this wasting time in university bullshit." Papa agrees and shakes Vito's hand, pissing me off.

"Excuse me, but this is my challenge," I announce.

"You're right, Princess. Would you like to accept his bet?" Papa says, giving me a wink.

"Yes, sir," I answer and step up to Vito. I shake his

hand, squeezing it firmly. "Challenge accepted."

Uncle Louie wears a mischievous smile. "Do you want to use your Sig or do you want to use my Beretta to hand Vito his ass?"

Smiling, I hold out my hand. Smoothly, in front of Vito, I pop the clip and check that Uncle Louie's M9A1 is fully loaded with thirteen rounds. Replacing my ear protection, I head back to my booth and Uncle Louie tucks my Sig into his holster. Vito rolls his eyes as he heads towards the booth Antonio used.

Luigi sets the targets and flips the light to begin shooting. I pop off thirteen rounds, taking a little over twice as long than when I went against Antonio. Pulling off my protection, Luigi announces, "Vito shot ten to the Princess's thirteen." Waiting for the targets to come in, I pop the clip and replace it with a full one my uncle hands me and return his Beretta to him. He hands me my Sig, which I casually clean as Papa inspects Vito's target.

"Nice job, Vito. Five to the head, five to the body," he comments.

Uncle Louie hands Papa my target as I begin filling my clip. Again, I don't need to look at it. I know what he'll see.

"At least she didn't cup your balls!" Papa laughs. "Three to the head, three to the chest, with a heart around it." He looks at me with pride and puts his arm around me. "Great job, *Piccola*," he says and kisses my temple.

With a little trepidation at what I'll find, I force my eyes to Vito's. He smirks and offers his hand to shake.

"You won this round, Princess," he concedes. "Just means Antonio and I will be spending a hell of a lot more time on the range. Probably won't be the only ones either."

Relief floods me at his words as I smile at both of them. Antonio winks at me, *again*. For some unknown reason, this time I blush, feeling my cheeks heat.

Papa pats Vito's shoulder, joking, "Looks like my little girl still gets to go to university like I plan. Don't worry, your boy isn't out of the running yet." He leans closer, whispering to Vito, "She only challenged you to protect Antonio, after all."

I roll my eyes, having heard him. Luigi comes up, saying "Hey, don't go giving her away before the rest of us have a chance to throw our hats in the ring."

God, I have to be bright red in embarrassment. Turning, I punch Luigi's shoulder hard. He grabs it, play-acting that my punch hurts him more than I intended.

"Is this what we have to look forward to?" he asks Antonio. "Her beating on us while we try to court her?"

In a flash I'm on Luigi, punching him repeatedly as he laughs and tries to fend me off.

"If I had known," Papa says, "you were interested in her, I'd gladly put you back on the short list."

Both Luigi and I freeze. I stare at my father in abject horror. Luigi stutters, mumbling, "Oh, ah… No, sir. You don't need to add me to the list. Um, it's just something Princess, and I joke about sometimes. I'm, uh, just teasing her. I'm unworthy to be on that list. Don't think she wants me on that list either."

"I think we've had enough excitement for one day," Uncle Louie interrupts, saving us from this embarrassing moment. "Are you ready to head back to the compound?"

"Yes," I answer in appreciation, "Nonna was already grilling me with twenty questions when we left. I don't want to worry her."

"Okay," Papa says, his eyes bouncing between me and my uncle. "It has been a big day for you, Princess. But Lou, I want her at the Family meeting next week, to witness the men taking their vows into the Family. She needs to get used to seeing this too, just as the men need to get used to seeing her in her position in the Family."

"Really?" I ask excitedly. "You want me to be a part of it?" From the corner of my eye, an impish smile flashes across Antonio's face.

"Yes, Little One. You proved yourself ready more than once today." He gives me a side hug and kisses the top of my head. "I'll see you at home, Princess."

Feeling like I've accomplished something huge today, I smile and return his hug. "Okay, see you at home," I say, pulling away.

When we turn to leave, I find that the men have formed a line from us to the SUV. As we pass each man, they kiss my hand. Some congratulate me on my shooting, and some thank me for saving our Capo. I just smile and nod with each kind word from their mouths.

As soon as my uncle closes his door, he turns to me, asking, "Do you need a hand wipe for that overly kissed hand of yours? Maybe some hand sanitizer?"

Laughter fills the car as Luigi puts it in drive. Our laughter fades as we get underway. So many thoughts dance through my head on the way home. I killed a man today, to protect my father. I realize with a start that I'm calling him Papa again, after months of calling him nothing but Capo. Huh.

An odd feeling settles over me. Not like I'm upset, but odd… maybe it's a comfortable feeling. I don't like it, not one bit. I don't want killing someone to be *normal* to me. But if I hadn't killed that man, my father would be dead right now… and I don't want that either.

Has being a part of this Family, seeing so much violence, made me numb to such an atrocity? Can I ever be that normal girl I dream of becoming? Could I escape one day to Switzerland or London? Wait, no… I already decided on America.

But, if I do pull off an escape, could I ever fit in with normal people? Could I hide who I really am? I know I can never come back to this life if I leave. I don't want to marry Antonio or any other man in the Family. I have to prepare to escape.

I don't want to be a murderer. I don't want to be the Family Queen, selling guns and drugs, running prostitution rings and strip clubs and who knows what else. I don't want to have to watch my back and constantly looking over my shoulder, hoping to stay one step ahead of the other Families wanting to take me out, not to mention the police and international intelligence services.

No. That's not what I want for my life. But how do I convince Nonna and Uncle Louie? How do I leave Mom? It would kill her. I have to wait until university to attempt it anyway because if I don't want this life, I must escape somehow and that'll be the best time.

Pulling up to the front door, Nonna throws it open. She probably told the security detail to let her know as soon as we pulled up the driveway.

She opens my door and practically hauls me out. "Are you okay, Little One? What happened today?" She crosses her arms over her chest as Uncle Louie and Luigi join us. "Okay, you two. Start talking."

"Can this wait until we get up to her room? No one else needs to hear what happened today. She's okay, as you can see," Uncle Louie answers her. He leans close, whispering, "Sophia can't hear this. It'll upset her."

"Okay," Nonna nods. "Dinner first, then we talk."

Having finally eaten dinner, Uncle Louie and I head to my room and wait for Nonna. She wants all the details, and she'll get them. She was a Capo's wife and knows the score. Patiently, my uncle and I explain what happened today. When I tell her about killing a man, she looks at me, inspecting my face. I can tell she's a little unsettled that I'm okay with what happened. Eventually, it hits her that her son was the target of yet another assassination attempt.

"Thank you," she sniffs, holding onto me, "for saving my son. Even, after all, he did to you… thank you, my precious granddaughter."

Reassuring her, I tell her the truth. "Nonna, no matter what he's done, he's still my Papa, too. Naturally, I'd protect him. Today, I just acted on instinct. I'd never let anything happen to *anyone* in this Family."

"Alessandra, you're becoming such an outstanding young lady, with so many hidden talents. You're such a wonderful granddaughter. I'm overjoyed to hear about all you accomplished today."

She pushes my hair out of my face and smiles mischievously. "Sweetie, not only did you put Antonio in his place but Vito too!" She shakes her head, looking serious. "You watch your back when it comes to Vito. It's been a long time since I've trusted that man. I fear his only thought is gaining power through marrying Antonio to you, and nothing else."

"I showed them both up, Nonna. I have no fear of Vito. I can take him out if I have to. Even though he didn't say it out loud, I know he has a newfound respect for my skills," I answer her seriously.

Uncle Louie laughs, nodding his head in agreement. Nonna finally relaxes, and we both laugh with my uncle.

Once they both leave my room, I lay back on my bed deep in thought. The next few years are going to go by so fast. I've got so much I still need to learn. So many things… I've got to be prepared, but it can wait a little while.

Reaching over and pulling Fluffy into my arms, I inhale my uncle's smell. I just need to hold him. This bear has always been my go-to for comfort and safety. He brings back so many memories of fun times with Uncle Louie, from tea parties to building forts. He's like a substitute for my uncle, especially since I sneak into Uncle Louie's room occasionally to give Fluffy a spritz of his cologne.

Closing my eyes, it dawns on me. I know I'll keep Fluffy with me now and forever. When I leave for good, I'll be talking him with me then too, even when I go to university, along with a bottle of Uncle Louie's cologne. That way I'll always have a part of him with me.

Lying here, my mind wanders. What is Grayson doing now? Is he thinking about me? I can picture him perfectly in my mind's eye. His black hair and dark purplish-blue eyes still strike me, even months after our first meeting. The way his smile would stop the world, and his twin dimples, gah, they make my stomach flutter.

My hand slides to my stomach like I can control the roller coaster I'm feeling. The way his hand engulfed mine... As much as I hate to admit my weakness, this is how I fall asleep most nights, remembering all that happened between Grayson and me. I pray that fate will bring us back together one day.

With a final glance out of my bedroom window, I look at the stars and remember Grayson's words... *Every night when you lay in bed and look out your window at the stars, just remember I'm somewhere looking at those same stars and making a wish that fate will bring us back together again someday.* God, please let him be looking at these same stars, thinking of me.

Chapter 2

TAKING MY PLACE IN THE FAMILY

A little over a week later, I'm woken up to Nonna walking into my bedroom carrying a large, long garment bag. Mom's right behind her.

"What's going on?" I ask, sitting up and rubbing my eyes.

"Well young lady, remember early last week your Papa asked your mom and me what size dress you wore and your measurements as well? We had no idea what he was up to, until this morning." Nonna gives me a huge smile.

"He came in early this morning with this garment bag. He told us he wants us to get you ready for tonight, then he handed me this, saying everything should be in it. He told us to get Camilla to alter it, if it needs any adjustments before tonight. We haven't even looked at the dress yet." Curious light shines from my grandmother's eyes.

Mom takes the bag from Nonna and hangs it on the hook on the door to my dressing room.

"He told us to help you style your hair for tonight… and to leave it *down!* Why does your Papa want your hair down? He said we can pull some of it back, maybe 'fluff the top' if we need to. What in the world has gotten into him?" Mom turns wide, shocked eyes to me. "Little One, we're both as shocked as you are."

They giggle, and Mom continues. "We're sure your Papa realized our shock because he started laughing. Laughing! Your Papa! I haven't heard that in more years than I can count. He's so excited for tonight."

Nonna sits on the side of my bed and takes my hands, "Tonight is the Family Initiation Dinner. It's very important to your Papa, but also to you. He wants you perfect, and not just because you're our Princess but because *no* other woman has ever been invited to one of these events. Not only are you going, but your Papa said you're taking part in it. I have no idea what goes on at these events, I've never been. I do know that the men pledge their lives to the Family, dedicating themselves to the Capo."

"*Piccola,*" Mom says leaning over from her chair beside my bed, "this is *big*. Your Papa has gone to a lot of effort to make this special for you. This is incredible. You must be on your best behavior… pay close attention and follow directions to the letter."

Nonna nods, adding, "Your Papa also said that Uncle Louie would instruct you about certain things you should know beforehand. Both he and Luigi will be here at quarter to five, sharp, to pick you up and you aren't to be a second late."

Nonna continues, but my mind screams, *What the heck?!* I'm going to the Family Initiation Dinner? What is going on? What am I supposed to do? What does that dress look like? Papa's allowing me to wear my hair down? Papa hates my hair down! No one outside of us have ever seen my hair down… my mind races, bouncing from thought to thought.

Nonna clears her throat, getting my attention. "Little One, listen up. Your Papa wants you by his side tonight as the Family's Princess. You're to start learning more about your role in this Family and what's expected of you. But first, you have to look the part! And to do that, we need to see if this dress needs altering. Camilla will be here any minute with her supplies. Get up and go hit the bathroom. Hurry, *cara.*"

Leaping from the bed full of nervous excitement, I do as my Nonna instructs and rush through my bathroom routine of brushing my teeth and washing my face. Why tonight? I know tonight is the night Antonio is taking his vows to the Family. Will I be a part of that?

Opening the door, I hear gasps as I walk through. Hovering halfway in between my room and my bathroom, I freeze as I see the most beautiful dress I've ever seen. It's a deep and rich ruby red with a black, iridescent sheer overlay, and is absolutely stunning. The sweetheart neck is covered with the same sheer fabric that covers the rest of the dress, but I can tell that a lot of my chest will be exposed.

Directly under the bust is a thick band of black crystals that trickle off as it flows down the skirt. The sleeves are the same sheer fabric as the neckline. The wrists form a point that will rest on the top of my hands. Oh, Saints, this dress is gorgeous. My Family Necklace will look stunning. This is more of a dress for Mom, not me…

"Well?" Mom asks, noticing me. "Come here and try it on. What do you think?" Her voice is excited, but I'm so overwhelmed by it all.

"It's black and red…" I murmur.

"Of course, child," Nonna chuckles. "Everyone will be wearing black tonight. Your Papa didn't want you to stand out in a light pink dress."

I giggle, picturing the day at the gun range…

"You're a young lady now," Nonna continues, "and your Papa recognizes that. This doesn't mean you get to wear black and red all the time, only occasions like this. Besides, this is what your Papa chose, even had it made just for you. I think it'll make you look far too old, but who am I to say?"

24

Finally, I move to Mom and Camilla. Camilla carefully lowers the dress to the floor.

"Step in," she instructs. Once I'm in, her and Mom pull it up, and I slide my arms into the sleeves. Camilla holds the front up while Mom zips the back. Carefully she snaps the two closures holding the sheer fabric covering my breasts.

Slowly, I turn to face my full-length mirror. My mouth falls open.

"Wow," I breathe. "I do look all grown up. I never thought I could look like this."

"A bit too old, I think," Mom says, meeting my eyes in the mirror. "What is your Papa thinking with this dress? I need to talk to him about this." She walks around me. "Uh, if a man is this close to you, he can see quite a bit of cleavage. What do you think, Mama?" she asks Nonna.

"Oh, I agree. This is far too old for her. Camilla, pull her hair down. Let's see if that helps."

Camilla talks as she gets to work on my hair. "I agree, too. It fits like a glove and shows every curve of her body. I always thought our Capo wanted to keep her covered, not put her on display like this. This dress gives everything away. Lou will have a conniption."

"That's it! I'm texting Lou." Mom giggles. She pulls out her phone and starts texting my uncle.

Nonna walks around me slowly as Camilla mists my hair with hairspray and scrunches it to show off my big, natural curls. My hair hangs all the way past my bum, and I've always loved my thick, wavy curls. Camilla pulls a section from each side of my head. She braids them loosely and pulls them to the back of my head, combining them into one, all the way to the end. She's so talented when it comes to my hair.

25

Mom fishes a shoe box from the bottom of the garment bag. She opens it, revealing three-inch black heels with red soles and a red bow on the back of the heel. Kneeling before me, she holds the shoe out for me to slip my foot into. I pull up the gown and carefully slide my foot in. She repeats the process with the other shoe while I hold onto Nonna's arm.

"These are lovely, but far too old for you. But hey, at least you're only a few inches shorter than my five six." Mom giggles at her own joke while Nonna shakes her head. I smile, happy to see her acting normal, something I don't see often.

"Thanks, Mom," I answer, playing along with her jokes. "You do know I'm still growing. I could end up taller than you!"

"I'm sure you might," she smiles still teasing, "but with the way you take after Elena, I wouldn't be surprised if you stop at five two. Don't be too disappointed if you're pretty much done."

There's a swift knock at my door before it slowly opens. Uncle Louie's arrived. In the mirror, I watch his face. My uncle's jaw drops. The vein in his forehead pulses as his jaw ticks.

"Holy shit! What in the Hell is he thinking?" Uncle Louie moves closer, instructing me, "Alessandra, turn around slowly."

Doing as he asks, I slowly turn around and look up at him. He isn't looking at my face. His eyes travel my dress, looking like he doesn't even see me. He stumbles back, and Camilla reaches for him.

"God," he mutters grabbing Camilla's arm. "She looks just like Elena." His eyes plead with her. She nods, giving his arm a squeeze.

Uncles Louie's eyes fly to Nonna. "What the fuck

is he thinking? Cut off two or three feet of her hair, give her some heavier makeup… Jesus Christ. This is not a dress for a fifteen-year-old, especially not in front of a bunch of men!"

"Couldn't agree with you more," Nonna replies.

"If I didn't give birth to her myself more than five years after she passed," Mom adds, "I would honestly swear that Aless is yours and Elena's daughter. She's beautiful. My baby girl is growing up."

My uncle pulls his phone from his pocket and angrily stabs at the screen.

"Get your ass up to Alessandra's room and see this dress. What the Hell are you thinking?" he growls into his phone.

Ah, he called Papa. Uncle Louie is quiet while he listens to my Papa's reply.

"Yes, she has the dress on right now!" he practically screams into the phone. "No, it absolutely does *not* need to be taken in. Hell, it needs to be let out, more fabric added."

He turns from us, hunching over his phone. "Al, it fits like a fucking glove. Is your goal with this to have every man thinking of fucking your daughter? Because they will dammit! It's the only thing they'll be thinking about tonight!"

Uncle Louie listens for a minute. His voice is calmer when he answers my Papa. "Okay, see you in five minutes."

The second he hangs up, Mom throws questions at him. "What did he say? Is he upset that we're questioning his judgment?"

Uncle Louie's brow wrinkles as he looks at her. "No, the asshole laughed. But, he is coming up here.

27

Says he has something to add to the outfit. I'm hoping it's a large fucking coat."

We watch the door, waiting for him. Uncle Louie doesn't disappoint us. He starts his 'I'm pissed off' pacing. Every so often he glares at my dress as he walks back and forth. Turning, I glance at myself in the mirror, wondering if Uncle Louie sees me, or does he see Elena when he looks at me?

Five minutes of watching Uncle Louie pace, mumble and scowl at my dress pass before Papa walks into my room. He stops a few feet away.

"Turn around for me, Princess," he instructs me. Slowly, I turn around again until I'm facing the mirror and my back is to him. He walks up behind me, looking me in the eye in the mirror.

"I think you look stunning. You are, by far, the most beautiful young lady I've ever seen. And yes, all the men will want you, but none of them can have you. That's what makes this so much better. Every man will work harder for the Family, in the hopes that I choose them for you."

Nonna gasps at my side, but Uncle Louie growls… yes, growls.

"Yes, she looks a lot like Elena. This dress isn't as bad as you're all making it out to be. We have kept her dressing young and modestly, and we'll continue to do that." He turns to me. "The only time, and I mean *The. Only. Time* you dress like this is for special Family meetings… when you have *me* by your side. Not to mention Lou, Luigi, Vito, and Lorenzo. You will be surrounded at all times. *No one* will get close to you. There have been two things missing for a while from this Family. And I'm about to change that."

Looking at Camilla, he instructs, "Can you make her hair a bit more mature? Undo those braids and pull it back, give the top that puffy thing women do to their hair."

Nonna hands slam onto her hips. "Al, I don't like this. First, this dress and makeup... *and* you want Camilla to tease her hair?"

Papa snaps his head to his mother. "Yes, Mama. I have a very special reason for her hair to be more grown up."

He places a square, black velvet box on my dressing table. I didn't even see it in his hands. "Every Princess needs a crown. This isn't like the tiara that you had to wear everywhere. This is only for events like tonight. I want everyone to remember who you are when they look at you and give you the respect you're due."

He lifts the lid, revealing a delicate gold tiara covered in rubies. From the center of the tiara, a single tear-shaped black sapphire hangs, suspended from an intricate chain. Gently, Papa lifts the tiara and places it on my head, centering the sapphire over my forehead. Camilla had already finished with my hair while he was talking. She secures the tiara, adding bobby pins to the ends and covering it with my hair.

Turning, I look in the mirror again. God, I feel like Miss Universe of the Criminal Underworld. Standing taller, I smile at my Papa in the mirror. "Thank you, Papa. It's gorgeous."

He chuckles. "Turn around, Alessandra. I have one more thing to finish off this outfit. This one you are to never take off."

Turning around, I watch Papa pull a small ring box from his pocket. My eyes fly to his face to find him wearing a smile I've never seen before. He opens the box, exposing a feminine version of his Family ring, resembling the ring every man in the Family wears. Mine and Papa's are different. Ours have a square cut ruby with two golden swords crossed over it, all held in place by two gold banners. The top one is etched with 'Canzano,' the bottom with 'Family.' The rest of the men's rings don't have a ruby.

Sucking in a breath, I stare at the ring, then at my Papa. Finally, he says, "Yes, I had Enzo DiCello make you a Family ring of your own. As of tonight, I will show and teach you more of your role in this Family. I will begin training you to one day, to take over and run this Family, hopefully many, many years from now. In the years to come, I will tell you so much, show you so much. I believe you will be more than capable to take over one day. You more than proved that last week." Papa pulls the ring from the box and places it on my right ring finger, then kisses it.

"Her dress is beautiful and perfect," Papa announces to the room. "Yes, it fits her like a glove, but nothing indecent is exposed. Yes, it shows off my daughter's beautiful figure, the figure that we've carefully kept hidden, but all men have wondered about. I also know that no one will get the chance to look down her dress to see her cleavage. Most of the night, she'll be up on the stage anyway."

"This is yours and Luigi's job," he says, turning to Uncle Louie. "Make sure none of the men get close enough to steal a peek. Can you do that?"

"You're damn straight. No fucking one will get anywhere near her in that dress tonight," he answers instantly.

"Now," Papa says, chuckling at my uncle, "Mama, it's yours, Camilla's and Sophia's job to make her look her best. Not too much makeup. I don't want her looking like a painted whore. I want her to look sophisticated and mature. Yes, I want to show off her beauty, her figure, and that hair. I want *every* man in that room willing and wanting to work hard for this Family in the hopes of winning her.

"She's not playing dress-up. She's showing the men in this Family that she's a beautiful young lady. She's also letting them know she's their Princess and will one day be their Queen, their Capo, she will rule over them. This subject is closed." Papa bends, kissing me on the forehead. Turning on his heel, he exits my room, leaving everyone stunned.

No one is happy about Papa using me this way. I was feeling beautiful and cherished a few minutes ago. Now I feel like an expensive virgin prostitute, going to the highest bidder. That's exactly what my father's doing with this farce. Looking down, I inhale and exhale slowly. Uncle Louie's hands slide onto my shoulders, and I look up at him in the mirror.

"I'll live," I say, giving him a small smile. "It's just, I suddenly feel like an expensive call girl… maybe like a piece of meat for the highest bidder."

He gives me his fake smile. "I know. But Luigi and I will be by your side all night, and it's only one night. I vow to you that this subject isn't over between me and Al. I'll be talking with him about this again. I don't like this one bit, Little One. Neither does anyone else in here. This isn't settled, no matter what your Papa thinks. Let's just get through tonight, okay?"

Nodding, I look down at my feet, hating my life more than ever. At this moment, I feel dirty and disgusting… not at all like the Princess, I felt when I first slipped on the dress. Releasing a sigh, I accept my fate for today.

Chapter 3

FAMILY INITIATION DINNER

*A*s required, at quarter to five I'm ready. My hair is in big, soft curls down my back, all fluffed up. I've tried to get past what Papa's plans are for me tonight, to appreciate how grown up I look, but I just can't. Sure, I feel grown up and mature, but I can't see how beautiful everyone says I look. I still feel like a prize to be won.

"Little One," Nonna says catching my attention, "be careful tonight. Stick close to Lou and Luigi. I don't even want you going to the bathroom alone. You'll be the only female there. Keep in mind the men will be drinking, okay?"

My nod is stopped mid-movement when there's a knock at my door, which opens immediately. Uncle Louie steps over the threshold, followed by Luigi.

They're both decked out in the standard men's Family formal wear, looking great in their fitted black suits with white shirts. What surprises me is instead of the standard black tie, they're wearing blood red ties that match my dress perfectly. Whoever made this dress made those matching ties.

Walking over to Uncle Louie, I finger his tie and tease, "Wow... nice tie."

He chuckles, taking the tie from my grasp and tucks it back into his suit. "Thought you might like it. All five of us will be wearing the same tie tonight."

"Five?" I ask, shocked. "You mean Lorenzo, Vito, and Papa will be wearing this, too?"

From the corner of my eye, I see Luigi shake his head as if to clear it. I feel his eyes travel up and down my body. I'm sure he's trying to find something sarcastic to say.

"Umm, I feel like we're in a wedding or something. Capo gave us these ties an hour ago, saying that Vito, Lorenzo and the two of us have to wear them. He already had his on."

Luigi's eyes are still glued to my body as he shakes his head one more time. "But seeing you in that dress, I get it now." His eyes travel the length of me one more time and a cocky smile breaks across his face, making his dimple pop. "Damn... you look absolutely gorgeous in that dress. Wow."

Uncle Louie's head snaps to face him. "Okay Luigi," he growls. "Roll your damn tongue back into your mouth and let's get a move on. Just a reminder, don't forget she's only fifteen." Uncle Louie whacks Luigi in the shoulder, breaking his trance.

"Hey," Luigi defends. "I'm only stating the truth. She doesn't look fifteen in that dress. And man, we'll have our job cut out for us tonight."

"I'm almost sixteen," I argue. "My birthday's only a couple of months away. You know that, right?"

They both stare at me for a second before Uncle Louie grabs my elbow and turns me to the door. Luigi follows behind, as he always does.

"Lou," Nonna calls as we reach the door, "keep her close to you tonight. That goes for you too, Luigi. I told her she's not even allowed to go to the bathroom alone. Keep your eyes on her and let *no* man close enough to look down that dress! They get to see enough of her figure as it is."

Uncle Louie pauses, looking back at Nonna. "Mama, she's not getting more than a foot away from either of us tonight. That starts the moment we walk out this door," he nods at my bedroom door with raised eyebrows.

"Are you trying to make me more nervous than I already am?" I ask, shaking my head.

Uncle Louie takes my elbow again as we make our way to the stairs. "Little One, I'm fully aware you'll be sixteen much sooner than I'd like. But you'll be just fine tonight. There's nothing for you to be worried about. All the men are a part of the Family. I don't think any of them will do anything inappropriate in front of the Capo and us."

"Alessandra," Luigi asks, "are you telling me you're actually nervous about tonight when less than two weeks ago I watched you, cool as a cucumber, kill a man to protect your father?"

"That was different, I acted on instinct. I'm at a loss with tonight. I don't know what to expect," I mumble in response.

"You'll be just fine, Little One. Relax, learn, and enjoy. Don't worry. If anyone is out of line, one of us will shoot him in the balls," Uncle Louie says, causing Luigi to crack up behind us.

As we leave the house, I pull my hair over my shoulder to hang in front of me. I knew if I didn't I'd be sitting on it once I climbed into the SUV and mess up my curls. When Nonna, Camilla, and Mom were working on my hair, Mom teased that she just wanted to lop it off, but she was afraid Papa would blow a gasket. Papa only let her cut my hair once when I was very little, I don't even remember it, but I've seen the pictures.

After Mom cut my hair, it grew back in huge, luscious curls, more suited for a grown woman. That's when Papa had Camilla start braiding it, or put it in ponytails, always with pink ribbons, to make it look like it belonged on a toddler. He laid down the law that day. I'm not allowed to cut my hair until I'm married. Period, end of discussion.

Luigi closes the gap between us, walking right on my heels. It feels like if I stopped suddenly, he'd bump right into me and knock me down.

"You know," I say, looking over my shoulder at him, "you don't have to walk so close to me on our own property. It isn't like someone's going to jump out here and grab me right in front of you two."

I giggle at the thought, shaking my head. Uncle Louie glances back at Luigi. His head lowers, like he's looking down my back. He does that stupid chin lift thing. I look back at Luigi with wide eyes, then back at Uncle Louie.

"Why do I feel like you two are talking about me without saying a word?" I ask.

"Oh, that's because we are," Uncle Louie chuckles. "We don't need words to get our point across."

Men are so strange. It's like they're aliens from another planet with their weirdness.

Reaching the SUV, Luigi steps in front of me and opens the back door. I get in, double checking that my hair isn't going to be crushed under me. Luigi hands me my seatbelt, and I buckle it. Uncle Louie takes his seat riding shotgun, and Luigi hops in the driver seat. I'm still pondering their silent communication. What in the world were they saying?

Unable to let it go, I ask, "Okay guys, you need to tell me what happened. What were you talking about without words? I know it was about me, and it's rude not to tell me."

Uncle Louie looks at Luigi and smiles. Luigi just shakes his head.

"Come on, guys. What's going on? What did you say?" I plead.

"Go ahead and tell her," Uncle Louie says. "We both know she won't shut up until she knows. I still have other things I need to tell her about this evening before we get there."

Luigi lowers his sunglasses and looks at me in the rearview mirror, with a smirk on his lips and a playful light flashes in his eyes.

"Are you sure you want to know, Alessandra?" he asks, replacing his glasses.

"Yes," I answer firmly. "Yes, I want to know."

"Okay," he smiles on a shrug. "I wanted to make sure Lou saw that ass of yours, the way that curve-hugging dress clings to your sweet ass." Luigi shakes his head again. "When you pulled all that luxurious hair over your shoulder... damn, girl. You have a fine, tight, full, heart-shaped ass. I don't mind admitting it either. However, I'd rather not get my balls shot off by our Capo, or your uncle walking around with a hard on. Nor do I want to have to beat the shit out of one of my brothers because of it being on display. Believe me, it's a distraction. Keep your hair to the back when we arrive, let it hang like a curtain to hide your ass."

Heat works its way from my neck to my cheeks. In embarrassment, I hide my face in my hands, laughing nervously. I can't believe he said all that in front of Uncle Louie!

"That was *not* nice, Luigi!" I scold him. "You're not supposed to be looking at my bum. And you're not to think like that either!" Nervous laughter bubbles from my lips, ruining my scolding.

"Babe," he says, tipping his head, "I'm only

human… a very *male* human. I happen to have a thing for a sweet ass. I will look. I don't care who it belongs to. If it deserves to be admired, I'll damn well enjoy admiring it."

"Okay, that's enough," Uncle Louie says, delivering a swift swat to Luigi's shoulder. "I'd rather not think of you admiring Alessandra's ass, thank you very much. Fuck, I may have to kick your ass now. I'll make sure she keeps her hair back to cover it."

I'm still beet red, trying to compose myself from Luigi's words and to recover from the shock that he actually said them. Uncle Louie clears his throat, getting my attention. He's turned in his seat, facing me.

"Alessandra, tonight is a first for the Family. No woman has ever attended a Family meeting like this. Usually, we mingle for a bit, chatting and catching up. Luigi and I will move you through the men, to the stage, as quickly as we can. That's our number one priority. We'll have a big dinner, and afterward, the men who've been chosen to be initiated will come forward to take their vows.

"You'll stand with your Papa. Luigi, Vito, Lorenzo and I will surround you. Each man will stand in front of you and our Capo, pledging their life to the Family, reciting the vows. They will bow and kiss our Capo's ring. They'll have to do the same with you, since you are the next in line. All you need to do is meet their eyes and give a small nod of acknowledgment.

"Now, this is a big one. Once they take their vows, they will receive their Family tattoo, somewhere on their upper body. Usually, it's on their chest, over their heart. In the past, some have requested full back pieces, so they start with just the outline to finish later. Either way, the tattoo is put on their body tonight. After the tattoos are done, they parade around, showing it off to the Family. The men have been known to get rowdy during this time. There's been pushing and punching, even full-blown fights.

"Listen carefully. While the initiates are receiving their tattoos, the men will be drinking and smoking cigars. There will be a lot of swearing and a lot of vulgar talk amongst the men. If anyone says anything to you, do not respond unless your Papa or I give you a head nod. We're hoping they'll remember how you proved yourself with your shooting skills and be aware that their position in the Family is directly linked to how they treat you, the heir. If they do say something inappropriate, it will be dealt with severely."

"What?" I ask unable to resist teasing him. "Why can't I be involved in the punching and name calling? Can I at least scratch my imaginary balls and act like the rest of the men?"

Luigi's laugh escapes as Uncle Louie tries hard to contain his. There's a big smile on his face as he answers me. "No, Little One. You cannot scratch your 'imaginary balls.' Not in that dress. Hell, you aren't allowed to touch any part of your body."

Luigi and I both crack up. However, the closer we get to the clubhouse, the more serious the vibe in the car becomes. The joking and teasing helped relieve some of my tension, but now it's ratcheting back up.

As soon as Luigi parks the car, Uncle Louie hops out. I wait for him to open my door, turning in my seat, ready to climb out.

"Hair," Uncle Louie says quietly once he opens my door. I'm already one step ahead of him, having already tossed the length of it over my back. Once I'm on my feet, he's at my back and arranging my hair to make sure my bum is covered. He tucks my hand into his elbow and Luigi takes his position at my back, a foot behind me.

Together, we move to the front door, ignoring the looks of the men standing outside. One rushes ahead and opens the door for us. As we pass him, I give him a slight nod in acknowledgment. He's young, probably taking his vows tonight, but I don't recognize him.

Inside the dining hall, the sounds of conversation, shouts, and noise falls off as my presence is noticed. All the men stare, most with shocked expressions, and a few with pride. I feel like I'm walking in naked as a jaybird with all the ogling eyes on me. Squaring my shoulders and checking my breathing, I stand tall and follow Uncle Louie's lead. I don't want to show my nerves or any sign of weakness.

I avoid making direct eye contact with the men and instead run my eyes slowly over the crowd with a small smile. As we pass, some men welcome me, saying things like "Good evening, Princess," or just nod their head. A select few even bow. However, I feel eyes running the length of my body. I've never felt so uncomfortable with attention aimed my way. I'm determined not to let my feelings show, though.

Papa notices the room's volume has dropped and turns from his conversation with Vito and Lorenzo. He spots me approaching and moves to intercept Uncle Louie and me. He takes my hand from his brother and tucks it into his elbow. Uncle Louie falls back, standing next to Luigi at my back.

"You look just beautiful, Princess. I'm so proud of you. Pay no mind to the men and their stares. They all want you, and that's just what I want them to think."

My stomach roils at Papa's words, but I nod, keeping pace with him. God, how sick is it that my own father wants his men to want me? I feel dirty all over again. Like a high-priced escort or a prostitute. I don't like feeling this way, not at all. I feel so gross.

Knowing I have a role to play, I return the nods

I receive, all with a pleasant smile on my face. Papa leads me up on the stage and to my seat at the head table. Sitting down, I'm relieved to put an end to being paraded in front of the men. I'm beyond thrilled to be able to cover at least part of myself with the table.

Surreptitiously, I watch the dining hall. There are close to two hundred men gathered here tonight. They range in age from thirteen to over eighty. I'm surprised there are kids so young here, though. I guess it's better to train them young before their mothers have too much of an influence on them. As I run my gaze over the hall, I spot a few scowls, mostly from the older men. They don't appear very happy at my presence, other than being able to check out my body.

God, I have no idea what Papa is thinking with this stunt. Yeah, it's a good idea for the men to get used to the idea that I'll one day be their leader, but why dress me up like a whore?

Papa stands behind his chair to my left, Vito and Lorenzo on his left stand behind theirs. Uncle Louie is to my right, with Luigi beside him. Quickly, men find their seats and stand behind their chairs. I feel like I did something wrong, sitting here like this, and I glance at Uncle Louie. He gives me a slight nod. As one, the five men on the stage with me take their seats. As soon as Papa pulls his napkin from his glass, the men in the hall take theirs.

Looking over the crowd, my eyes find Antonio, right in front of me. He gives me a wink. Ugh, every time I look up from my plate, I'll be looking right at Antonio. He doesn't take his eyes off of me. I feel them follow my every movement, making me uncomfortable. I just want to poke his eyeballs and demand he knock it off.

Uncle Louie leans into me, whispering, "I think I might have to kick Antonio's ass before the night is over. If he keeps looking at you like that, he *will* regret it. You won't mind, will you?"

"Can I at least get a good punch in?" I ask, giggling.

"We'll see, Little One," he chuckles. "Glad to know you're not crushing on Antonio like every other girl in the Family."

"Ugh," I mumble, scrunching up my nose. "Never." Uncle Louie laughs hard, drawing attention to us yet again.

Papa stands, pick up his glass of wine, and waits for everyone's attention. Within moments, the room quiets, and all eyes are on my father. He smiles, giving them a slight nod. My eyes wander the crowd, and I silently laugh that all the men are wearing the standard uniform of a black suit and white shirt. What surprises me is that most of the men are wearing a red tie. Papa must have sent out a memo, which a few men didn't get because they're wearing the usual black tie. I'll have to ask Uncle Louie about this later.

"Tonight is a very special evening. I'm proud to be joined by my beautiful daughter, our Princess and my heir."

The men applaud, a few adding catcalls and whistles. I'm not surprised at their behavior, but it does make me smile a real smile. I give them a small nod to acknowledge their welcome.

"My daughter, as you all know, is the first woman to ever attend one of our meetings. She is the first to take part in an initiation ceremony. Alessandra will be joining us from now on. I believe she's earned her place here after proving her skills and defending my life. It's time for her to learn more about the Family and the way things are run since she will one day take over when her time comes, along with the man I choose for her."

My stomach rolls and twists as Papa nods at Antonio, Stephen, and a few other young men. I cringe with the last person he looks at. Luigi. Oh, no way. That's not going to happen... ever. My hands clench and unclench in my lap. I despise every moment of this.

"The plans for tonight will be as usual, we'll have dinner and then the oaths, not only to me and the Family, but the Princess as well. The new initiates will then receive their Family crests, so we can see who the real men are."

Lifting his glass, he finishes his toast. "To our Princess and our new initiates. Welcome to the Family. Salud!"

"Salud!" everyone responds, taking a drink from their wine glasses. I reach for my glass, ignoring the decorum of not drinking to my own toast. The way I feel right now, I'm hoping I'll be allowed refills tonight. I might just need it.

Chapter 4

THE FAMILY PLEDGE AND ME

*A*fter dinner and dessert I'm feeling a little more relaxed, thanks to the extra half glass of wine Uncle Louie snuck me. I watch the men chat and laugh, smoking their cigars and cigarettes. The air is thick with the smoke. All I can think is that I hope the cleaners can get the smoke odor out of this dress.

When the tables are cleared, the men get to work moving the tables in front of the raised platform where we are sitting. Staff move our table back as others bring Papa's wing back Capo chair to the front of the stage. To my surprise, they also bring a smaller version of his chair, probably made just for me. The men place it to the right of Papa's chair.

Papa takes my hand, leading me to the front of the platform.

"Men," he announces. "It's time."

The room quiets again as ten young men walk to the foot of the stage and stand in front of us. They wear solemn expressions, not smiling. Both Antonio and Stephen are in line to take their vows. They stand tall, shoulders back, feet shoulder width apart, and hands clasped behind their backs.

"We are ready to hear what you have come to request," Papa says in a clear voice. I stand beside him, wearing a neutral expression.

The first man, Salvatore, unclasps his hands and steps forward. He holds his hands firmly to his side and looks Papa, or rather, our Capo, in the eyes.

"I want to join the Family."

"Are you ready to pledge this with your life?" Capo asks, his voice firm.

"Yes, Capo," he answers in an earnest voice.

"State your pledge," Papa replies.

Salvatore lifts his right fist and holds it out to our Capo before bending his arm at the elbow and slamming his fist into his chest, over his heart.

"I swear this pledge with my heart and soul, to you and this Family. I vow to always listen to your guidance and follow the rules with my life. I will shield and protect it and shed my life's blood for it. Nothing and no one will come between this Family and my pledge of devotion to it. Nothing, save my death, will take me away from it."

He drops his arm to his side, and Papa gives him a nod. Salvatore steps forward.

"You are accepted into this Family," Papa starts. "With my strength, pride, and power, I accept your devotion. Nothing, save your death, will take you from it. This Family is now your Family."

Papa extends his hand, and Salvatore takes it and kisses Papa's Family ring. Salvatore steps to the side, standing in front of me. I copy Papa's movements and extend my hand. Salvatore takes my hand and kisses my ring.

"I devote myself to you as well, to guard and protect you with my life," Salvatore pledges, looking me in the eye. He nods, and I return it. Finally, he steps back a few paces, returning to his spot in the line.

The next seven men repeat the process, with no variations. They all maintain their solemnity and Papa's face remains impassive for each of them.

Finally, there are only two people left. Stephen steps forward, and a smile breaks across Papa's face. No, oh no. Stephen cannot be on Papa's short list. I can't do that to Annalisa, my best friend. She's crushed on him all her life. It would destroy her, and our friendship. I have to get him off that list. I don't care that Papa says I have no choice in who he picks for me. I'll be talking to him about this very soon.

Before I know it, Stephen is lifting my hand, and while looking me in the eye, he softly kisses my ring. He gives me a quick wink, then pledges, "I devote myself to you as well, to guard and protect you with my life."

Stephen steps back, giving me an odd look. Maybe he feels the same way about this as I do. It might be better to discuss this with him first after I convince Annalisa to confess her feelings to him.

Antonio is the last to take his pledge. My mind is racing, and I barely pay attention to the words that he and my father exchange. It's just a repetition of what I've heard nine times already. I wonder if Papa had talked to any of the others, aside from Antonio and Stephen about me. I can't believe each one of these men are so willing to give up their own lives and their free will to devote themselves to the Family.

Antonio pledges with his life to follow the rules and listen to our Capo. If Papa tells him to marry me, would he still put aside his free will and do everything Papa requests of him? Would he obey me, as head of the Family? Antonio finishes his pledge and moves to stand in front of me. Antonio takes my hand and recites the same pledge everyone else has said. I watch his face and know without a doubt every word out of his mouth comes from his heart and soul. Not only will he obey Papa, but me as well.

My heart pounds in my chest. It's so loud, I fear

45

Antonio can hear it. As he bends his head to kiss my ring, he looks up through his thick lashes and gives me a flirtatious smile. After he delivers a kiss to my ring, his mouth travels to the back of my hand where he gives me a quick kiss, taking me by surprise. He's the only one who's done that. My eyes fly to my Papa's face to find him watching us with smiling eyes.

Antonio straightens and gives me a wink, along with his signature smirking smile. Slowly, he steps back, never taking his eyes off of me. I know, without a doubt that if things don't change, Papa will choose Antonio to be my husband. After tonight, my planning for an escape will start in earnest. No more thinking about it. I have to escape this life. I'll never be able to take the pledge Antonio, and the others just took. My best chance for escape is when I'm off at university. Somehow, some way, I have to get away from this insanity.

I'm startled out of my thoughts when Papa's hand settles on my lower back. Glancing at him, he smiles down at me.

"Princess, would you like some entertainment before the men receive their Family brand?" Papa asks in a loud voice.

"That sounds nice," I answer. What entertainment? Uncle Louie didn't say anything about entertainment.

"When your Nonno was Capo, men didn't receive tattoos. They received brands of the Family crest from a hot iron over their heart. Several of the older men here tonight still carry their branding with pride."

Several men call out, raising their fists in the air. Papa nods to them and continues his explanation.

"Now though, we allow the men a choice to get a tattoo somewhere on their upper body, as long as it's as big, or bigger than the brand. They must endure the pain of a tattoo as we watch, to see their worth as a man."

"Yeah, Princess, you'll find out who the pussies are!" someone shouts. Several men laugh and cackle.

"This is how we separate the boys from the men! Let's see if anyone cries out for their mama!" Papa shouts.

Papa nods at Uncle Louie and Luigi, who are already laughing. Uncle Louie winks, mouthing, "Have fun and enjoy the show, Little One."

The men in the crowd begin cheering and getting rowdy as Papa shouts over them all.

"Gentlemen, you've been staring at, and admiring my daughter all night long!" Papa shouts to be heard over the cheering crowd. "Now it's time for her to have something to stare at and admire. Remove your shirts!"

Luigi presses the play button on the stereo, and I crack up at the first notes. The jazz-influenced "The Stripper" by David Rose and His Orchestra echoes off the walls. This is the quintessential stripper song, with its prominent trombones and bassline.

Salvatore's head whips toward my father, a look of confusion on his face. Antonio locks his eyes on me, making sure I'm watching him as he unbuttons his suit jacket.

"Take it off!" someone shouts from the crowd. Jeers and catcalls follow the demand.

As the ten men in front of me start to take off their clothes, I can't help but laugh. This is so ridiculous, almost comical. This ludicrous song and these men, none of whom are more than twenty-five if I'm a day, trying so hard to impress me. Some look over their shoulders, smiling at me. Others face me, slowly sliding their jackets off. The third guy, though... he's having fun, playing up the funny. He snaps one side of his jacket open to the beat of the song and closes it, just like a classic striptease. Covering my face with my hands, I peek through my fingers at them, laughing hard. I cannot believe this is Papa's idea!

I find Antonio, who's still staring straight at me. As he slowly takes out his gun from his holster, he turns around doing a little booty shimmer as he sticks his gun in the back of his pants. I do have to admit, it's a nice one. A blush creeps up my cheeks. Slowly, Antonio slides his holster from his shoulders, letting it drift down his arms with his head tilted down and to the right, trying to look sexy.

The whole thing is hilarious, I'm laughing so hard I have to sit down. Tears fill my eyes, but I wipe them quickly, so I can keep watching. Stephen twirls his holster on his finger, then drops it to the floor. He dramatically throws me a kiss. I reach out, grabbing the kiss. Theatrically, I bring my hand close to my face and stop inches away. I shake my head vigorously before throwing Stephen's kiss on the ground and stomping on it.

The watching men burst into laughter, cheering me on. The men enjoy my teasing of Stephen, who winks at me. Antonio still has his eyes locked on me. It's a little creepy the way he stares at me. The other men look at me, but they also feed off the mood in the crowd and play up to them.

"Are you enjoying yourself, Princess?" Papa asks, leaning down to be heard over the music and wolf whistles.

"Oh, yes, Papa! I can't remember ever laughing

this hard. Thank you!" I answer him, not taking my eyes off the display in front of me.

Papa kisses the top of my head and continues, "I saw how those men were watching you and thought turnabout is fair play. I also want them to be comfortable around you. They needed a laugh after you showed them up at the gun range. I want them to respect you and know you can easily take them out if they give you reason."

Nodding in response, I turn my head to Stephen, not wanting a serious discussion right now. He has his back to me, looking over his shoulder and hamming it up. His shirt is mostly off, but still around his wrists. He slides it back and forth on his wiggling bum. More peals of laughter break from my mouth. I can't help it, this is just too funny.

Guy number three, God I wish I could remember his name, is twirling his shirt over his head, snapping his hips to the beat of the music. I need to find out who he is, Gigi would love him. My eyes slide over the dancing men again, finding Antonio's eyes still locked on me. It's so creepy how he keeps his eyes on me. He slowly slides his shirt from his body, but I quickly continue my perusal of the other men.

I have to hand it to them, they're finely built and muscular. Unable to resist it, I whistle at them. "Shake it, but don't break it!" I yell through my laughter. I'm sure Papa and Uncle Louie would have a heart attack if they knew just how much I'm enjoying this. My eyes wander over the different men, their defined chests, muscular backs and nicely defined bums. Some even have a visible bulge in their slacks. I'm enjoying this in the naughtiest of ways. The men flex, showing off their muscles, to the crowd and to me. I've never realized a back could be so sexy.

Antonio's still watching me. He has his shirt off

49

his shoulders and walks slowly to the bottom of the stage. Looking up at me, he slides it down his arms and straddles it. Holding it in his hands, he rubs it up and down his crotch, grinding his hips.

My eyes roam over his body, taking in his defined chest. He has those V cuts at his hips and a trail of dark brown hair from his navel to his waistband. He chuckles, watching me. My eyes fly to his face, and he smirks. God, I just want to slap that smirk off his face. He continues dancing, riding his shirt.

Looking away, the others are still flexing and showing off. Some have dropped to the ground, doing push-ups of varying types some one-handed, and others show off with a clap after pushing up. Salvatore's, though, are the most impressive. He pushes up, spins on his toes while clapping his hands behind his back and ends in the pushup position. Sweat beads on their well-defined muscles. Gah, it's so *hot*!

"Woohoo!" I scream, laughing. I'm definitely enjoying this mini workout! Like Uncle Louie and Luigi, these men take good care of their bodies, working out regularly, I'm sure. It is one of the Family rules, though. Enforcers and guards must be in fighting shape at all times.

Turning my head, I find Uncle Louie watching me. His eyes dart to Antonio, and I know he's fully aware that Antonio's been watching me intently this whole time. Uncle Louie nudges Luigi, and the music fades. Within seconds, Uncle Louie is behind me. Antonio, still standing in front of the stage, swings his shirt over his head, rotating his hips in time to his swings. Releasing it, he sends it flying at me like I'm a panting fangirl at a concert.

Catching his shirt, I laugh at him. I wad it up and throw it back in his face.

"Thought you might want a souvenir, Princess! Keep it, and sleep in it while you dream of me!" he yells, tossing it back at me.

"You thought wrong," I laugh at him and return it yet again like we're playing hot potato. "I don't want your nasty shirt! Besides, we can't have one of our newest initiates catching a cold on their way home."

The crowd roars with laughter at our banter. Antonio shakes his head. "I watched you check me out. You don't have to lie, it's okay to want me," he says flexing his pecs, making them dance.

"You weren't the only one I was checking out," I shout back, amusement in my voice. "Nor were you the only one I was admiring! It has nothing to do with wanting you. Keep your shirt."

Uncle Louie squeezes my shoulder, chuckling at our bickering. Papa places his arm around me and speaks to the men, "Okay, the male revue is over. I've never seen my daughter laugh so much." He turns to me, asking, "Did you see any potential husband material tonight, Princess?"

My head falls back as I howl in mirth. Opening my eyes, I find Antonio still watching me, his cocky smirk on his face. Just one chance, I want just one chance to smack that thing off his face.

"Oh my goodness, no!" I cry. "My future husband is *not* in this group!"

The crowd hoots and hollers, teasing the initiates. Some even throw punches, hazing them. Antonio receives the brunt of the punches. Does the rest of the Family think we're a good match too? Ugh.

"Glad to hear that," Luigi appears at my side and whispers loudly, like he's trying to be heard by everyone. "Does that mean I'm still in the running?"

He winks as I deliver a swift elbow to his ribs. From the corner of my eye, I see Antonio give Luigi the *Malocchio*, or evil eye. Good thing Luigi wears his cornetto to ward off the evil eye. The men around us laugh at his reaction to the competition.

Two tattoo chairs have been set up on my left, and another two on my right... or at least, I'm assuming they're tattoo chairs. Four elders of the Family have their jackets off and are rolling up their sleeves while their apprentices prepare the tools they need to tattoo the Family crest on tonight's initiates. They quickly snap on blue surgical gloves and take seats on rolling stools.

"Alright!" Papa calls. "Who's going to be the first victims, I mean, recipients, of their crests tonight?"

As one, the initiates step forward, ready to receive their tattoos.

"Antonio, Stephen, Salvatore, and Diego, come on up," Papa instructs. Oh, that's right, that's his name, Diego. I can't wait to tell Gigi about him.

Stephen and Antonio take the chairs to my left, Salvatore and Diego, to my right. Stephen looks a little nervous as he straddles the chair, presenting his back to Franco.

"So, boy... which shoulder do you want the crest on? Or do you want a fullback mural?" Franco asks on a smirk. Stephen flinches at the idea, and I giggle at him. "Right shoulder, sir," he answers.

"Right shoulder it is," Franco nods, slapping his hand on Stephen's back, causing him to jolt. "You want something to bite on, boy? You're a little jumpy," he jokes.

The men gathered around the left side of the stage laugh and howl.

"You want your mommy?" someone calls. "Need me to come hold your hand?" another shouts. The name calling begins calls of "Pussy," "Little baby," and "Don't be a bitch!" ring out. The men are so harsh, I feel a bit bad for Stephen.

I walk between the stations, seeing where the initiates are having their tattoos placed. Salvatore chooses to have his placed between his shoulder blades. Antonio wants his over his heart.

"Antonio," I taunt, "do you need Uncle Louie to come hold your hand?"

"Why don't you come do it?" he teases back with a half-smile.

"Nope," I answer, shaking my head. "I think you got this. You're a big, tough guy," I say, my voice laden with sarcasm.

I laugh again, Uncle Louie joining me. "Hey, pretty boy!" he calls. "You want the Princess so much, why don't you add her name to your crest?"

"Don't give him any ideas," I poke him in the side.

"What a wonderful idea!" Antonio says. "She is our Princess and will one day lead us. Can you add her name underneath the crest, in a girly script, maybe add a banner? I want something that represents Alessandra."

"Dammit, Uncle Louie," I hiss. He just keeps laughing. The other men all speak up, requesting the addition of my name. UGH!

"This is perfect since it's her first initiation dinner. What a great idea," Stephen says.

"Look what you started," I loudly whisper at my uncle. He's too busy laughing to answer me. "This isn't funny. That's permanent! What will Annalisa think when she sees my name not only on her brother, but also the man she's been crushing on for forever and a day?!" Exasperated, I throw my hands in the air.

"Look, Little One," Uncle Louie says, recovering from his mirth. "You should feel honored. Besides, any woman they one day marry will know who you are because you'll be their Princess, too."

"I still don't like it," I whisper, leaning into him with my arms crossed over my chest.

Hours later, I'm sitting in my chair waiting for the last two initiates to receive their tattoos. These shoes, no matter how gorgeous they are, are killing me. All of them have opted to have my name added in some form or another. I can't wrap my brain around that. Huh… what will they do when I escape? Hopefully, it can be covered up later. My wandering mind is interrupted when Antonio and Stephen appear in front of me, startling me.

"You're not supposed to be up here," I scowl up at them.

"Thought you might want a closer look at my tattoo," Antonio flirts.

"I saw it when you were getting it," I answer him.

"It won't hurt to show you up close, I'm sure." Antonio smiles down at me.

"Still, I'll pass. Thanks though," I decline, looking around for Luigi or Uncle Louie.

Stephen comes a step closer, looking down at me

from his standing position. "If your Papa picks me as your mate, uh, husband, would you fight with me like you do Antonio?"

Shock hits me at his blatant question, and my eyes bulge. "Are you serious, Stephen? You want me to answer that?"

"I do," Antonio interrupts. "I want you to answer that."

"Look," I sigh. "I've known you both my whole life. Antonio, I'm sorry, but we bicker like brother and sister... All. The. Time. And Stephen, I can't marry you. Not with the way Annalisa feels about you. Sorry, but girl code. You're a great guy, but not the guy for me. My best friend would be heartbroken. And you'd better keep your trap shut about that!"

"Really?" he asks, his face lighting up. "I've got a chance with Lisa?"

"You tell her I said anything," I laugh, "and I will deny it to my grave. And I'll have to kick your butt too. You know I can and will. Don't tell her anything."

Stephen's smile is so big, his eyes crinkle. "You still have to get *his* permission," I nod at Antonio.

Antonio, who had been quiet during our exchange, comes back to life. "Bro, no. That's my baby sister. She's only fifteen. You touch her, and I'll cut your cock off and feed it to you."

"Hey, Antonio," I call, needing to add my two cents. "Your sister is two months older than me, and you're asking about my wedding plans... and besides, you can't tell me you're so oblivious that you've missed your sister's feelings for your friend. She's been crushing on him forever and a day. It's not like he's gonna run off and marry her tomorrow."

"You and I aren't talking about Annalisa," Antonio

retorts. "I'll deal with Stephen later about this. Much later. We're talking about you."

"Look, Antonio," I interrupt him. "I know more than half the girls you've already slept with. When will you learn that girls talk, and they talk a lot. I just don't see how we could ever work. You're a player. I don't want that."

Antonio smiles his cocky grin and tilts his head down, looking down my dress. I don't react, but it grosses me out. Shaking my head, I continue, "By the way, I'm not marrying anyone for a long time. I'll only be sixteen on my next birthday. I'd rather not think about marriage right now at all, if that's alright with you."

Antonio's silent, I think my breasts have put him in a trance. Finally, he shakes his head, clearing it. "Alessandra, I'm not giving up on you. I'll give you some space, but I'm not giving up. I'll be working hard to prove myself to our Capo. I know I'm at the top of his list. I'll treat you right, and I seriously doubt that I'd ever screw around on you."

Once again, Antonio's eyes wander to my breasts. God, I want to sock him in the face or fist-punch him in his family jewels. It would be so easy… He '*seriously doubts* he'd screw around on me'?! Please… I'll never give him the chance to find out.

From the corner of my eye, I see that we've gained the attention of Luigi and he's making his way to us. He grabs Stephen and Antonio by their shoulders and spins them to face him. "What the Hell are you two fucknuts doing up here?" he practically yells. "Get your asses off this stage and away from the Princess before I throw you off!"

Uncle Louie materializes behind Luigi, having heard him yelling. "Hey, Vito!" he yells. "You wanna get your horny son away from the Princess? I'll do some major damage to his pretty face if he's not out of my sight in the next three seconds. You know I'm not kidding."

"Hey," Antonio defends. "We were just talking."

"Okay, pretty boy," Luigi says. "Time to move along. No more standing there looking down Alessandra's dress. If I see your eyes try to check her out one more time, you'll never see another set of tits again. I'm not scared of your daddy, and I have no problem with plucking your eyeballs right out of your skull. Get. The. Fuck. Off. The. Stage." Luigi uses his three inch and twenty-five-pound advantage and physically backs him to the stairs.

Stephen, smart guy that he is, is at the stairs waiting for his friend. He grabs Antonio by the arm. "Come on, dude. Remember your place."

"This isn't over," Antonio vows. "You can have your space, for now, Princess." Before he makes it to the stairs, he gives Luigi another evil eye, risking his life.

Vito, at the bottom of the stairs, calls up to Antonio, "Tone, boy, get your ass down here. You can talk to the Princess the next time she comes over to visit Lisa. Now is not the time or place. You know no one was to get up on the stage. Breaking the rules like this just after pledging doesn't look good, *coglione*. Get down here before I help Lou and Luigi kick your ass."

"Sorry, Princess," Stephen calls as they descend the stairs. "Didn't mean to offend."

"You're fine, Stephen. Just remember what I said… you know nothing," I call back with a smile.

Stephen walks away on a wave, but Antonio moves to stand in front of me on the floor. "You happy now?"

he asks Luigi and Uncle Louie. "I'm at her feet."

"Stronzo," Vito says, thumping the back of Antonio's head. "Knock it off before the Capo sees you and you lose your top position on the fuckin' list," he hisses.

Nodding to his father, Antonio walks backward still facing me. He taps his eye then points at me, reminding me he's got his eye on me. Shifting his gaze to Luigi, Antonio once again tries to give him the evil eye, this one a little more impressive than his last two.

Luigi just flips him off. Pulling my hand into a fist, I tuck my thumb between my pointer and middle fingers and wave it in front of Luigi to ward off the evil eye. "Real mature. But, we can't have his evil eye affecting you. His last one was almost impressive. And thank you for rescuing me," I say batting my eyes up at him. He laughs, then acts like he's trying to look down my dress. Since he's standing in front of me, I thrust my hand out to punch him in the stomach. He jumps back, avoiding my fist. He always knows how to lift my spirits, to lighten my mood.

"You're welcome, Princess. Anytime I can help," he bows formally, making me laugh all over again. Luigi really is a great friend. I love his humor and playfulness.

I remain on the stage, so I don't have to talk with anyone if I don't want to. If I'm up here, I'm off limits unless I initiate the conversation, according to Papa... not that Antonio or Stephen followed that rule. Men walk by smiling at me, hoping I'll choose to talk with them. Instead, I just smile and give them a slight nod. Thankfully, they catch the hint and continue on their way when I look away. Some of the men stand about ten feet back from the stage, alone or in small groups, blatantly staring at me, checking me out. If I were to leave the stage, it'd be open season for the men to approach me. Looks like I'm stuck up here until the night is over.

Uncle Louie and Luigi have taken turns hanging out with me since the Antonio incident, joking and telling me stories of some of the men who walk by. I've had a blast finding out about what the men do within the Family and hearing funny stories about them. Occasionally, Uncle Louie would tease me, asking if I'd like to marry one of the men passing by. I'd laugh, answering with a firm 'no.' This has gone on for hours, and I'm more than ready for this night to end.

For now, Luigi's keeping me company. I made him sit in Papa's chair. It felt weird having him stand next to me and having to look up at him. I also didn't want him looking down my dress, either. Papa joins us, putting his hand on Luigi's shoulder. Luigi moves to stand, saying, "I'm sorry, sir. I'll get up."

Papa pushes him back down. "Keep your seat, Luigi. I like the way you look there," he winks at him and gives me a smile. I mentally roll my eyes, understanding what he's implying.

"I bet you're getting tired of sitting up here while the men ogle you, Little One. I'll go tell Lou you're ready to leave when he's finished shooting the shit with Lorenzo. You did great tonight, and you look so beautiful." He squeezes Luigi's shoulder again. "Doesn't she, Luigi?"

Luigi coughs. "Uh, yes, sir. She's incredibly beautiful. She also looks a lot older than fifteen. I have to keep reminding myself just how young she is."

They both chuckle. "I've heard nothing but positive comments from the men," Papa adds. "Some have even approached me to ask to be considered as her husband." He smiles down at Luigi, then moves to my side and kisses my forehead. "Goodnight, Princess. You've made me very proud tonight."

Papa walks away as I look down in embarrassment. "Luigi, I'm so sorry about that."

Luigi just chuckles, placing his hand on top of mine. He squeezes it, making me look up at him. His eyes are trained on our hands. "It's okay, Aless. The Capo makes no secret of who he wants on that damn list of his."

"Luigi, I want to ask you something," I say seriously. "Don't say anything, it's just something I want you to consider. Let me explain myself, but keep it tucked into the back of your mind. Please don't answer me right now. You'll know when the time is right if you need to act on my request, okay?"

He tilts his head, watching me with curious eyes. "Okay, Princess, I promise. I'll just sit here and listen."

Taking a deep breath, I lean closer to speak quietly. "Okay, here goes. First, let me say I'm not in love with you. But if I'm forced to marry someone in this Family in like five years…" I pause, closing my eyes to collect my thoughts. Opening them I flick my eyes to Luigi, finding surprise on his face. I can't continue if I keep looking at him. He squeezes my hand encouraging me to continue. With another deep breath to fortify myself, I keep going.

"If you don't find the love of your life in the next five years…" I trail off, my heart pounding a staccato in my chest. "I mean, don't stop looking. I'd be so happy to see you find true love, that heart pounding, stomach dropping real love, really. But if you don't, and if Papa tries to marry me off to Antonio… please try to stop it for me. I'd be much happier, if I *have* to marry someone in the Family, if that person is you. We tease each other and have fun together. I think we'd have a better chance of making it work, more so than with any of the other 'candidates.'"

Shaking my head, I look down at my lap and continue with my request. "Since Papa won't give me the option of finding someone and falling in love on my own, and I'm stuck in this life, I'd rather be stuck with a good friend that could possibly turn into a loving relationship."

Taking another deep breath, I keep going. "Luigi, honestly, if I'm forced to marry Antonio, I'll end up killing him. Especially since he 'seriously doubts' he'd screw around on me. I love him like a brother. The two of us bicker more than him and Annalisa. Half the time, I just want to smack him upside his head. I also know he's screwed around with a number of girls I know. That just grosses me out. The idea of marrying him after he's slept with girls I know personally makes me sick to my stomach. I just can't do it."

"Please, Luigi. Just think about my proposition. And I beg you, please don't mention it or throw it in my face. Just keep it in mind. If you don't find love by then, and it's something you agree with, please ask Papa to put you at the top of the list if it comes down to it. I'm not going to say anything more, just leave you with the idea," I finish.

Luigi squeezes my hand, a silent acknowledgment of my request. I sit there, watching the crowd, letting him think about all I've said.

Luckily for me, Uncle Louie walks up, standing on the floor in front of us. "Are you two enjoying pissing off Antonio?" he asks. My eyes scan the room, finding him. His stare is fixed on us, his eyes hard. "He might just explode in a few minutes, his face is so red."

"Awww," Luigi chuckles. "Is wittle Antonio upset because I'm sitting in the Capo's chair, with the Capo's blessing? Or is it because I've been holding Aless's hand for the last five minutes?" He laughs, and Uncle Louie joins him.

"Are you ready to leave, Little One?" Uncle Louie asks when he stops laughing.

"God, yes. Can I take off my shoes? My feet are killing me," I request.

Luigi slides from his chair to kneel in front of me. He slowly removes my shoes, and gives my feet a quick rub, digging his thumbs into my arches. I fight to hold in the moan that wants to escape me. He hands my shoes to Uncle Louie and extends his hand to help me up.

"What are you up to, Luigi?" I ask him, taking his hand and seeing him smirk as he pulls me to my feet.

"Luigi!" I gasp. "I can walk," I demand as he sweeps me into his arms, holding me like a groom carries his bride over the threshold.

Uncle Louie laughs as Luigi makes his way to the stairs. "Oh, but Princess, you said your feet were killing you. I can't allow you to be in pain," he teases.

My uncle laughs harder, and I'm dying of embarrassment. Does he not care about my reputation? Ugh!

"Honestly," I whisper to Luigi, "I can walk." God, please let him put me down.

He squeezes my thigh, whispering, "Oh, but I enjoy holding you in my arms. If you'd rather, I could just throw you over my shoulder. It'll give me the chance to swat that ass of yours for not taking those shoes off hours ago, and the chance to give everyone nice show to boot."

"You wouldn't dare," I gulp, turning my head to face him.

"Oh but wouldn't I?" he teases.

He stalls, adjusting me in his arms. "Don't you dare. I will so kick your butt if you do this. Your family jewels will no longer be off limits," I threaten him.

He throws his head back, laughing. On a huff, I cross my arms over my chest and look away from him. My eyes land on Stephen and Antonio, who has a vein pulsing in his forehead. Huh, I thought that only happened to Papa. My father stands just behind them at the door. He holds it open for us, saying "It's nice to see you taking such good care of my daughter, Luigi. I know she's tired. Just don't drop her, or I'll have to shoot you."

Papa guffaws as Luigi pretends he's about to drop me. Squealing, I throw my arms around his neck and hold on for dear life. All the men laugh at me, making me growl in his ear, "Oh, just you wait. Payback will be mine."

As we approach the SUV, Uncle Louie opens my door. Luigi sets me down and hands me my seat belt. He's sporting a huge grin, making his dimple stand out.

"I hope you enjoyed yourself, sir," I huff at him.

He winks, closing my door. Luigi climbs into the driver's seat and looks at me in the mirror. "Oh, I had a blast watching Antonio suffer. I loved every second of it."

"I enjoyed it too, Little One," Uncle Louie adds from his spot in the passenger seat. "You should do that more often, Luigi. Some of the men were pissed off watching you carrying Aless, and extremely jealous." They both crack up as Luigi starts the car and puts it in drive.

"I'm not speaking to either of you. How do you

like that?" I announce in exasperation. I cross my arms, letting them know I'm completely serious.

They laugh harder in response to my statement. Ugh! Men. I bite my lip to keep from speaking. I will not give in and be the first one to break.

"Hmm... how long do you think she'll last, Luigi? Five minutes?" Uncle Louie asks.

Luigi laughs loudly. "I don't know, man. She's pissed enough she might, *might*, just make it till we get home."

They continue their laughter most of the way home. I'm proud that I don't break when we pull up to the house. Uncle Louie opens my door, and I give him a hoity head nod.

"See you in the morning!" Luigi calls, laughing at my retreating back. I don't answer him, I just continue on my way to my room. "Sleep tight and dream of me- unless you'd rather dream of Antonio!" His laughter trails off as I make my way down the hall to my room. It ends abruptly when I slam my bedroom door.

Finally, safe in my room, I let loose the laugh I've been holding in at thinking of how to get back at Luigi. Dream of Antonio?! Please... that will *never* happen. Unless it's dreaming of kicking his ass or kicking him in the ol' family jewels! That's one dream I'd definitely enjoy. Ugh, but dream of Luigi? After practically proposing to him tonight? I can't believe I actually said all that to him! He is really attractive... But, I'm still too embarrassed to let myself go there. Oh, vengeance will be mine for him teasing me tonight, that's for sure.

After a few minutes of struggling, I'm finally out of that dang dress, and it's safely hung in my dressing room. In my most comfortable pajamas, I climb into bed with Fluffy the Bear. There's a light tap on my door just before it opens. Turning, I find Uncle Louie standing in the doorway. I keep my lips pressed tightly as he enters my room.

"Just wanted to tell you I love you, Little One. I was just playing with you. You aren't allowed to go to sleep mad at me. You can be mad at Luigi all you want," he says quietly. He kisses me lightly on the forehead. "Are you still mad at me for teasing you?"

I sigh. "You know I can't stay mad at you," I giggle. "But I will be getting Luigi back for tonight. For carrying me out like a damsel in distress, and for even suggesting I dream about Antonio… he deserves a serious butt-kicking!"

He laughs, walking to the door. "I couldn't agree more. But does that mean you're okay with dreaming of Luigi?" He laughs harder as he walks through the door.

"Now I'm going to sleep mad at you!" I yell, throwing a pillow at the door. The door clicks shut, but I can still hear him laughing outside my room. I'm not really mad at him, and he knows it. I love him so much. He always makes me laugh and feel safe. Uncle Louie is my everything. However, I can't have him thinking I'm crushing on Luigi. I'll have to set him straight on that.

Rolling to my side, I look out my open window. The sheer curtains blow in the breeze, allowing me to see the moon and stars. Is Grayson looking at these same stars? Is he thinking of me the way I'm thinking of him? It's been months since our time together, since our passionate kisses and touches. Does he still remember me? He is probably already serving his role in the Army, after his training and boot camp. Is he okay? I wonder what he's doing as I rub my chest, hoping to remove the pain in my heart from thinking about him.

Closing my eyes, I say a prayer, *"Our father who art in heaven, hear my plea. Please, Father God, keep Grayson safe from all harm. Let him remember me, and please let fate bring us back together again."*

Opening my eyes as I gaze out my window towards the sky again, I watch a shooting star, and I make the same wish. Reaching over I pull Fluffy into my arms as I whisper, *"You're the only one I'll ever dream about Grayson,"* before drifting off to sleep so I can relive our precious memories over and over again in my dreams.

Chapter 5

FINDING OUT MORE FAMILY SECRETS

*S*itting on my window bench seat, I gaze out over our grounds. As always, several guards wander the yard, carrying automatic weapons. Off in the distance, our wisteria trees blow in the wind. I love those beautiful trees, especially when they're in bloom. They line the pathway on the west lawn that leads to the Family garden and mausoleums. The garden is one of my favorite places to sit and think. The guards tend to give me the space I need out there since it's so deep on our land. Mom and Nonna spend a lot of time out there too.

I'm a little melancholy today thinking about my sixteenth birthday, which is rapidly approaching. I'm not looking forward to the normal party here at home. No one will ask for my opinion, though... not about anything. My life is dictated to me, and I'm supposed to be overwhelmed with joy and gratitude. I'm not. I resent this life, even with the superficial luxury it affords.

My birthdays are never what I want. It's always what *they* want. I'd rather skip the big Family get-togethers and have something small and intimate instead. A few friends, my iPod on shuffle, maybe even a few guys... but that'll never happen, especially after the fiasco at my fifteenth birthday party. Mom enjoys decorating for large parties, and Papa says we need to be in the forefront of the Family member's minds. "We must maintain appearances, Princess. It wouldn't do for the Family to think we don't want them to be a part of our lives."

Ugh. I wish I could have a normal party, like Annalisa. She had her sixteenth about two months ago, and it was a blast. She invited people from her school and had music blaring from a stereo connected to her iPod. I got to dance with whoever I wanted, and it wasn't just Family members.

By far, I danced with Luigi the most, which was fun. Antonio glared at any guy I danced with, even taking a few of the non-Family members aside after they left the dance floor. I can only imagine what he said to them. Luigi would talk smack about Antonio while we were dancing, making me laugh. I couldn't help it, Antonio's face got redder the more fun I was having without him. Luigi was always there, ready to request a dance if I gave the slightest hint I wasn't comfortable with who wanted to dance with me, letting them know it was time to move on. It was impressive, the way he could read me. There wasn't one time he failed to save me.

I loved the casual atmosphere of my best friend's party. It was finger foods and appetizers, not sit-down meals and full bars. Just a bunch of kids my age having fun and dancing without a bunch of adults standing around drinking, chatting and watching our every move. It was *normal*. I have to admit, I was a little jealous.

Annalisa confided that she and Stephen have been hanging out more and more. I'm beginning to think they might just end up together after all. She shared with me that Stephen had kissed her after her party. I'm so happy for her... and relieved Stephen hasn't said anything. She swore me to secrecy about their kiss, especially to Antonio. As if I chat with him all the time. Even the thought of that makes me laugh to myself. Annalisa's been crushing on Stephen for as long as I can remember. She's falling in love with him already, and it's nice to watch her have a normal life, one I can only dream of. It was only a matter of time before Stephen opened his eyes. I just had to give him a little shove in the right direction.

I'm a little concerned about Mom, though. She was doing really well helping Gwen, Annalisa's mother, with the party, but when that ended she locked herself in her room. As the time for my party comes closer, Mom seems to be more of her cheerful self, but I worry that when it's over, she'll seclude herself in her room again. Probably rocking and singing to that stupid doll she has. It's like she lives in a fantasy world where my brother survived his birth, yet hasn't aged.

I know Mom suffers from depression, but this doesn't seem normal. I have no way of diagnosing her or even helping her. It's not like Papa would do anything to get her the help she needs, though. That would mean admitting there's something wrong with her, admitting he'd failed her. At times like this, I spend a lot of time reading in the bay window seat outside of her room. I've always loved this seat. It brings back good memories of when I was little, and she would read to me as I watched the wisteria trees outside. I feel better being outside her door in case she needs me or wants something.

One positive note, Papa's been spending more time with Mom. They've gone out, often just the two of them, and their guards. Annalisa told me they've come to her house a time or two and had dinner. Gwen and Mom are still best friends, just like Vito and Papa. Hopefully, this is a new norm for them. There are one or two nights a week where Papa disappears, though. Something about his nights away just doesn't feel right. I don't know why, it's just a feeling. Usually, my feelings are right. Glancing at my watch, I find I'm about to be late for my training.

Luigi and I have been practicing hand to hand

combat for an hour when both his and Uncle Louie's phones chime. I had just flipped Luigi over my shoulder for the first time and was doing my little happy dance when Uncle Louie called a time-out before Luigi could retaliate. This has never happened before. Everyone knows our training time is sacred so it must be an emergency. I watch them closely as they check their text their messages.

"I'll check with Al, see if he needs our help. I'm sure Little One will be happy to end the day with the victory of kicking your ass," Uncle Louie says.

"She just got lucky," Luigi defends.

"Whatever helps you sleep better at night. You're just mad that a five-foot-three-inch girl just flipped your ass. That's okay, I know you're tired," my uncle teases him.

"I took you down fair and square," I add, jumping in. "I can do it again, if you want," I say, pointing at the mat.

"Al," Uncle Louie says into his phone. "We're in Little One's studio, training. Do you need Luigi and me to come with you?" He pauses, listening to Papa's answer.

"Yeah, we can be there in fifteen minutes."

Papa says something before Uncle Louie answers him with a definitive, "Yeah, we got this."

His eyes flick to me, and I cock my head with a questioning look. Uncle Louie shakes his head.

"She'll be fine. We'll escort her back to the house…"

Papa must have interrupted him because his words trail off.

"Nah, she can handle it. She just flipped Luigi on his ass." He laughs, and nods.

Luigi just sighs, mumbling, "I'm going to shower and get dressed."

Bored with waiting to find out what's going on, I start climbing my silk ropes.

"Yeah, we'll see you in a few." Uncle Louie hangs up his phone and calls out to me, "Little One, you know the rules. No working out alone. We have to leave for a few hours. Get down here and get cleaned up."

I climb down. "Okay, okay. I'll just shower in the house and then call Annalisa." Glancing at him, I tease, "Unless you think you might need me... I'll gladly come help."

"We're headed to one of the clubs. They're off limits to you for now, and you know it," he laughs.

Grabbing my towel, I head for the door and call back to Uncle Louie, "You two enjoy the naked ladies!" He chucks one of the tennis balls at me, but I dodge it and take off running as I giggle.

Luigi and Uncle Louie get home right after dinner, saying it was a false alarm. They call it an early night and head up to bed. Hours later, I'm making my way to my bedroom and pass Uncle Louie's door. He's snoring louder than a chainsaw, even though his door is closed. It's well past one in the morning. I was on the computer downstairs and completely lost track of time. I didn't realize it was so late until I looked at the clock. Everyone in the house has to be asleep.

Walking into my room, I look for my book. After

ten minutes of searching, I realize I left it in my studio earlier. Dang, it! I really want to find out what happens to these vampires. What would it hurt if I snuck out to get it? I only have to cross the east lawn to get to my studio. I've done it before, and no one's ever found out. I can do it again.

Grabbing my navy sweats and hoodie, I pull them on quickly. I open my door and peek out. Slowly, I close my bedroom door, making sure it latches silently. On light feet, I run down the servant stairs at the back of the house. They lead to the kitchen and back door, which I exit just as quickly. Outside, I stick close to the house and shadows. At the corner of the house, I peek around the side to find the guards huddled in a circle, chatting and smoking. Staying low, I dart from tree to bush, praying they won't spot me and shoot me.

About twenty yards away from my studio, I hear muffled music coming from inside. It's got to be loud inside if I can hear it from this distance. I know the men take it over on the occasional Friday or Saturday nights to play poker, and sometimes have dancers come as so-called entertainment. Something else I'm not supposed to know about.

There aren't a lot of cars parked along the building, so this can't be a poker night. I spot Papa's car, along with a little convertible. I'm not sure what kind it is, but it's new and looks expensive.

Creeping to the side door, I keep low to avoid the windows. This close, I finally identify the song blaring from my sound system. "Pour Some Sugar On Me" by Def Leppard doesn't seem like a song Papa would listen to, let alone this loudly. Opening the front door, I find it's mostly dark, except near the stage where my ropes hang. Huh… maybe Papa is in the office up here listening to music with some of the men.

Getting up on my tippy toes, I peek into the window separating my studio from the hallway. My mouth falls open, and I stifle the gasp that wants to break free. Papa's in there, alright... but he's not in there with any of the men. No, he's in there with a woman. An unbelievably beautiful, curvaceous woman.

The woman uses the pole, *my pole*, to dance on. Holding onto the pole, she spins around, her legs in the splits. When her feet hit the ground, she lets one hand fall and smacks her bum. Her hips grind and rock into the pole. I flick my eyes to my father's face to find him staring in bewitched attention.

When the chorus hits, *"Pour some sugar on me..."* he motions the woman over to him. She approaches his chair slowly, her hips swaying and her hands cupping her breasts. She stops in front of him as he whips off her red and black push up bra, sending it flying. Her boobs, bigger than Mom's, bounce free. She's got to be at least ten years younger than Mom, too. Her panties, if you can call them that, are nothing more than a string up her bum.

With her next step, she gracefully straddles Papa's lap, her hands sliding into his hair. Papa slides his hands along her hips and tears her panties off, throwing them to the floor. His hands trail along her body, up over her chest and neck, into her hair. With his hold on her head, he leans forward and kisses her fiercely.

Suddenly, my mouth is covered tightly, and I'm lifted off the ground by an arm around my middle. My training kicks in and I start fighting to get free.

"Shhh," my attacker whispers in my ear. I freeze, knowing I'll have a chance to kick his butt as soon as he puts me down. He carries me out the door, being careful not to let it slam. Hmm, maybe it's someone who doesn't want me to get in trouble.

"What the hell are you doing out here?" Luigi growls in my ear, carrying me further from my studio. "You're not allowed to leave the house by yourself at night. You could have been shot by one of the guards with all your sneaking around." He stands me up and takes my arm, dragging me toward the house.

"We need to talk," I growl right back.

"Be quiet before someone hears you," he commands. "You'll get your ass in a lot of trouble if you're caught out here."

"We're talking," I whisper again, almost pleading. He gives me a slight nod as we walk into the house. Our trek up to my room is quiet. Once he shuts the door to my room, I whirl around to him.

"My father's having an affair with some *stripper!*" I hiss at him.

"First, tell me what in the hell you were doing out there!" He almost yells, but checks his voice, knowing we could be caught.

"Did you know? That my father was having an affair?" I ask, ignoring his demand. "Does Uncle Louie know? Do *all* the men know?"

Luigi scrubs his hand over his face and looks up at my ceiling, ignoring my questions and returning to his own. "First, I need you to tell me what the fuck you were doing out there, in the middle of the night, no less. My God, Aless, you could have been shot!"

He looks so distressed at the thought that I deflate. "I went to get my book. I forgot it when you guys had to leave for that emergency earlier. And when I got out there to get it, I had to watch some *stripper* have sex with *my father!* Now, can you answer my question?" I finish, with putting my hands on my hips, demanding my own answers.

Luigi's expression saddens, telling me everything I need to know. "Yeah," he answers softly. "But it's only the one girl. It's been going on for a couple of years. He's not going to divorce your mom, so don't worry about that. It would look bad for him, and he knows she isn't well."

"Like finding out about this won't push her over the edge… no, she'll be just fine with this." My voice is heavy with sarcasm.

"Aless," he says, grabbing my hand. "I'm sorry. I really am. No one ever wanted you to find out. Don't confront him. It'll just get ugly and end up hurting your mom."

"Thanks for being honest with me," I mumble turning towards my bed. Pulling off my hoodie, I climb in, not bothering to change out of my sweats. "And don't worry. I'll never say anything to Mom. I could never hurt her like that. And I won't say anything to Papa."

Luigi comes to my bed and tucks me in. "This just makes me hate my life even more," I whisper up to him.

"Come on, *cara*," he says. "It's not that bad."

"Luigi," I plead. "Every second of my life is dictated to me. I can't even do my own hair, let alone cut it. I can't go anywhere without a guard. I can't even have a casual birthday party with a few friends. Mom should be getting the mental help she needs, and Papa's having an affair. I'll be forced to marry someone I don't love when I graduate university. My life is crap." A single tear falls down my cheek.

"Scooch over," Luigi directs me. Doing as he bids, I make room for him. He climbs in after me and pulls me into his arms. Turning into his chest, I bury my face into him and hold on.

"If it means anything," he says quietly, "she's the only one. She's more than just a stripper to him. He's the only one she dances for."

"I'd rather not know anymore, thanks," I mumble into his chest.

My mind wanders over the sad state of my life. Does Papa love this woman? She's so young and beautiful. Does he still love Mom? How could he do this to her? Luigi is right, though. This would break her. Mom is still very much in love with Papa. Is he doing this because of her depression? What about that woman? Is she okay with being the second choice, knowing that Papa will always choose Mom first?

I know Mom will never be a normal mother. No one wants to talk about it or get her the counseling and help she needs. Her moods are swept under the rug with a "she's having a bad day." Someone takes her up to her room and drugs her. I can't count how many times I've seen her stoned out of her mind. I doubt she's even seen a real doctor about this. The Family doctor probably gave Papa sedatives for her, to make it easier and keep things quiet. Her bad days are outnumbering her good days more and more lately. Hell, she may even know about Papa's affair.

Lying in Luigi's arms, I realize he gives good hugs. So much like Uncle Louie's, I feel safe and comforted here. I've also come to the conclusion that there is no way I can escape this life, my tragic life, without taking Mom with me. I'd be signing her death certificate myself if I did. What am I going to do? I refuse to marry Antonio... maybe I should just marry Luigi and stay to protect Mom. But, is that fair to him? God, I hate my life.

Chapter 6

MY THOUGHTS AT 16

*I*t's hard to believe I'm sixteen today. The last few months have flown by. I've learned so much about the Family, met so many people. Papa includes me in Family meetings, talks to me more and more like a business partner and not a daughter. I keep storing all of the information I can get my hands on, hoping it'll come in handy one day.

As of today, I'll be allowed on what Papa calls "group dates." I'm not allowed any physical contact with any guy, so it's not really a date. It's just a bunch of people my age, half boys, half girls, going out on a weekend to a movie or some other date like activity.

Annalisa, Lola, and Gigi are to be a part of these dates. However, the no touching rule only applies to me. Luigi and Uncle Louie are to always accompany me, guarding me and my virtue, thus making sure I'm never allowed a second alone with my 'date' ... if you can even call it that. Honestly, I'm okay with it. I don't feel anything for any of the guys my age.

Antonio kissed me last week, and there was nothing like I felt with Grayson in America. There were no stomach drops, no tingles, no anything when I look at him. I just feel nothing for any of them. I've even tried once to see if I could get those feelings by letting one of them give me a quick kiss. You could say I planned it. I was in an elevator once playing a trick on Uncle Louie and closed the door before he and Luigi could get in giving me a full minute alone with a guy. Well, I felt nothing. In fact, I was slightly grossed out by it. I have felt nothing like those moments with Grayson from anyone else but him. I was beginning to think I never would.

(LAST WEEK)

I'm spending the night at Annalisa's, and it's late. My bestie's already fallen asleep while I stay up reading. My eyes are heavy as I set my book aside and reach for Fluffy the Bear. He's not on the bed with me… oh man, I left him in the playroom. I can't sleep without him, so I'm going to have to go get him.

Quietly, so as not to wake Annalisa, I slide out of bed and make my way to the door to her and Antonio's combined playroom. I slowly open the door and hear the TV playing softly. Looking around, I find what looks like Antonio sleeping on the couch.

I creep over to the love seat where I left Fluffy and grab him. Turning to sneak back out, I see Antonio sitting up, staring at me. His eyes are on my bare feet, and they slowly drift up my body, over my naked legs to my long t-shirt. His eyes pause at my breasts a moment before continuing to my face.

Being the smart-aleck, I am, I ask, "Like what you see? If I'd known you were awake, I wouldn't have even opened the door."

"I knew you'd come in here for Fluffy," he says standing up and coming toward me. "Why do you always have to verbally attack me the moment you see me? Is it because I've admitted I'm interested in you? I'd have to be blind not to be. You're beautiful… stunning in fact." His eyes don't leave mine, don't wander my body.

"You have been all your life. It's not just your looks, though. You're funny and a great friend to my sister. You have a heart bigger than life. I know all about you donating your things to girls who don't have much. Not just clothes, but toys, some that were practically brand new. You just gave them to the other girls in the Family. Most kids don't think that way, but you did… and still, do. You're a giver. I've never met anyone like you, Aless."

He stops, standing right in front of me. I ignore his words, stepping around him and walking to the door. I pause, my hand on the knob and look over my shoulder at him.

"Antonio, you're an attractive guy, but you know it. You use it to get what you want from girls. All the while, those poor girls are hoping to win your heart. But we both know that won't happen. I can't get past that. I know them, personally. I've told you that before. And well, I just don't get that *feeling* with you."

Taking a deep breath, I look down at my feet. "I don't get that tingle, that stomach dropping feeling when I'm around you. I get that cocky, big brother vibe. That's how I view us. I want more. I want *all the emotions* when I find someone… the heart pounding, the butterflies, the roller coaster of feelings. We don't have that chemistry."

He walks over to me. "Turn around, Alessandra," he instructs. For some reason, I do. I need him to understand. To know what I know. His hand cups my face, tilting it to look up at him.

"How do you know? How do you know if you don't let me get close enough to see you, to touch you?"

I look into his eyes, letting Fluffy fall from my hand. His eyes bounce between mine as I just watch him, waiting. Antonio bends, slowly pressing his lips to mine. I return his kiss, knowing he needs this to know we don't have that spark. His lips part and I follow his lead. His hand finds my neck and pulls me closer to him. Our tongues dance, circling one another. He's a good kisser, but the magic is missing. Can I get into this, enjoy it and let it go further? Maybe. Could I live with this for the rest of my life? No. Not without the love I know I deserve.

Antonio moans, and I know I have to stop this. The faces of his past conquests flash through my mind. Pulling away, I look into his eyes, then back down to the floor. I grab Fluffy and hold him to my chest. Reaching for the knob again, I look over my shoulder at a shocked Antonio.

"That never happened. You're a good kisser, skilled in fact. But there's nothing there, Antonio," I say quietly.

I leave him there, returning to Annalisa's room and shutting the door. I lean back against the door, hoping to hear Antonio walk away.

"What in the fuck?" I hear him grumble through the door.

I lock the door to make sure he doesn't try to come in and question me. That's not going to happen. I'll never give him the chance to talk about what happened. This just reinforced that there is nothing at all between Antonio and me. There never will be, either. We have *no* sexual tension. No chemistry. I may have just encouraged him to keep trying because I turned him down. I made *myself* a challenge, something he can never have or seduce.

It doesn't matter anyway. I'm still stuck on Grayson and my memories of us. When I can't sleep late at night, I pull them up. The memories I can't seem to let go of.

It's hard to believe it'll be a year, right after my last birthday. After all this time, just the thought of him makes my stomach drop. What's he doing right now?

He has three years left before he has to decide if he wants to reenlist. Does he like his assignment? What does he do? Is he safe?

As always, these thoughts bring me to pray, "Please Father in Heaven, I pray that Grayson is still alive, that he's doing well and is happy. Please help him to think of me and remember our time together as I do, and keep him safe from all harm. Amen."

Even if I do escape to America one day, how will I find him? That's it, I have to let him go. Reliving my moments with Grayson Riggs isn't helping me. I'll keep him for my dreams, because that's all he can ever be to me. If I can't have him, I still want the stomach dropping, heart pounding, uncontrollable desire I felt when I was with him. I won't settle for anything less. I need that chemistry. I *deserve* that chemistry.

Shaking my head, I clear my thoughts of last week. I take one last look at myself in the mirror, making sure not a hair is out of place. My hair is up in a messy bun, and I'm wearing a tank top with white trim, matching tan pants and white flats. Papa had some tailor make this and several other outfits for me. They aren't store bought, as there's never any tags. Also, they fit my curves just right, not too tight, nor too loose. The clothes are always flattering, and I love them.

The last thing I need to complete my outfit, sadly, is my ankle holster. I put that on, and push my gun into it, along with an extra clip. Grabbing my purse, knowing my Beretta and extra clips are in there as well. I sling the strap over my shoulder sighing to myself. I hate that this is a necessary fact of my life. I make my way to the door, knowing Luigi and Uncle Louie are waiting for me. I find them on either side of my door when I open it.

Uncle Louie bends, kissing my forehead. "Happy birthday, Little One. You look as beautiful as ever. You have your gun? You know I always feel better when you're carrying."

I nod, scolding, "We are *not* going to jinx my sixteenth birthday. Understand?"

"Understood," he chuckles.

Luigi hasn't said anything yet, and just stares at me.

"Is something wrong? Do I have something on my face?" I ask, concerned.

Luigi shakes his head as I try to check out my outfit. "No, everything's fine. It's just... you look great. Are you sure you're not twenty today? You don't look sixteen."

Relieved, I smile at him. "Yes, I'm sure. Thank you. As much as I wish I was turning twenty, everyone reminds me enough that I'm only sixteen. Come on, let's go. I don't want to be late," I finish, moving to the stairs.

Within minutes, we're in the SUV heading to the Family park and campgrounds. "There aren't any surprises planned for today, are there?" I ask Uncle Louie. "I've had this weird feeling that I can't shake for days."

He turns to face me in the back. "No ma'am, just a Family gathering with everyone. They'll be cooking the main dishes in the reception hall kitchen. Chef will be outside, manning the grill for the meats."

Uncle Louie chuckles. "I'm sure you'll receive some challenges from the men, which will lead to their embarrassment when you hand them their asses.

You've been to the grounds, there will be horseshoes, bocce ball, and games. Just a nice day of family fun. Al said, 'keep it casual,' which explains why you're wearing pants on your birthday."

I sigh, looking out the window. "I'm thrilled that my birthday is a casual thing. I just want everyone to have fun. I want today to be a day to remember, just a great Family get-together."

The whole way to the park, I try to shake the feeling that something bad is going to happen, but it sticks with me, getting more intense with every passing minute.

BIRTHDAY COOK OUT

The Family park and campgrounds are vast, including several playgrounds, a reception hall for weddings and private parties, basketball and tennis courts, and a camping area that the boys of the Family can use. There are picnic tables all over the place, most clustered in large groups, and some secluded for a little privacy. In the center of the grounds is a huge covered picnic area where the meal will be served.

Having my party here is such a great idea. No major stress, no being on display at a head table. Fun and games, with a little competition from the men wanting to see if they can best me - which they won't be able to do. I might, *might*, let some of the older, more respected members win, though. I can't wait to see what kind of challenges the younger men come up with. Papa must have chosen this outfit knowing the challenges were coming. I'm relieved he wanted to give me the best possible chance of winning, not being restricted in my movements or hindered by a dress.

The large, covered picnic area is already being set up with buffet tables and gift tables. But like always, there is our 'Family Table' up on a platform in front of everyone, facing them. Some things will never change. There is a huge banner over this area that reads, "Happy 16th Birthday, Princess!" Of course, it's pink with pink balloons. God, I hate that color. But Mom loves it, so I won't complain. Heck, she's probably wearing pink today.

The Family has grown large in the last several years. There's now over three hundred dedicated members. Including their families, there's got to be over five hundred people here today. I even spot some of our out-of-town Family members here today.

"Hey!" I shout to Uncle Louie. "I'm going to the playground to play with the little kids!"

He motions for Luigi to join me. "Go with her, I'll be up there soon." Luigi falls in step beside me.

"You are aware that this is *our* Family, right? Most of them are scared of me. I'm thinking it's safe to walk to the little kids' area and play with them. Unless you think one of them will attack me?" I gasp dramatically. "Do you think they want to take me out and take my place? Besides, I have my guns with extra clips because you never know when I might need it, right?" I shake my head, laughing at the absurdity of me carrying at a Family party.

"Come on, Aless," Luigi says as we walk up the small hill, "you know I have to follow orders. You also know how much I like to throw those kids around."

"More like scare those little kids," I taunt him.

Mom and Gwen approach us on the path to the playground. Mom's wearing a big smile and it makes me happy to see it. They both stop, giving me hugs.

"Happy birthday, *cara*," Mom says, stepping back. "You look lovely. That top looks so cool and comfy. I'll have to ask Al to get one made for me too."

"Thanks, Mom," I answer, smiling. "You look great as always. The white and pink always makes your light blue eyes stand out."

She smiles, pushing her hair back. "Thank you, *Piccola*. Where are you and Luigi headed? And where is Lou? I'm surprised he let you out of his sight."

"Well, he's here so he can play with the kids at the playground, under the pretense of escorting me. I'm going to have the kids attack him when we get there. Besides, there might be some leaping leprechauns waiting to ambush me," I joke with a playful smile and an elbow to Luigi. He just shakes his head.

"As for Uncle Louie, I'm sure his x-ray eyes are on me as we speak. Where are you two headed without your guards, Mom?" I ask her.

"Rocco and Lucca are carrying our stuff to the tables. We're popping into the kitchen to make sure the cooks have everything under control," Gwen answers.

"Okay," I nod. "We'll probably see you down there when it's time to eat."

They continue on the path that leads to the reception hall. Gwen stops and calls back, "Do me a favor, Aless. Remind Annalisa not to get dirty with all those kids. She's wearing light pink pants. She'll be a mess before the day is over, but I don't want her to look like a royal mess in the Family pictures. I tried to warn her about those light colors."

"Will do," I reassure her, laughing. Luigi and I watch them disappear down the path before continuing to the playground.

Once the play pirate ship is in sight, I take off running, play-yelling, "Help! Help me! The Wigi Monster from the sea is trying to get me!"

I hop over the low wall around surrounding the playground and climb onto the huge pirate ship play structure. Boys scatter, grabbing their play swords and run to Luigi, attacking him. He growls and roars, chasing them and deflecting blows from their swords.

I laugh, watching him pick up one of the boys and pretending to throw him on the ground. He stops just short and lays him down gently, then holds his foot on the boy's chest. He raises his arm over his head like he's the victor. Three more boys attack him, poking and swatting at him with their swords.

Once I reach the top of the pirate ship, I yell down to my heroes who now have Luigi pinned to the ground. "Thank you, thank you, you've saved your Princess from the evil Wigi Monster."

The boys cheer, continuing their attack on Luigi as Uncle Louie approaches the playground.

Waving to him, I call, "You might want to hurry up, or your right-hand man will be taken out by these strong, young heroes!"

He laughs, hopping the wall, and grabs two boys by their pants and lifts them off, Luigi. Turning, he crouches down and growls at them. The boys' laughter warms my heart. As one, they turn on my uncle and attack him as they did Luigi.

Standing on the top deck, I look around the play area. I spot Annalisa waving at me from the front porch of the playhouse. Several girls are having a tea party, with my bestie serving as hostess. I wave at Nonna on a bench, holding a little girl on her hip. She sings a silly song, giggling most of it to my grandmother who just smiles at her.

Not far from Nonna, Lefty stands with a line of little kids. He takes a child by the hands and steps back. The kid takes a running start, and Lefty starts spinning in a circle, causing their feet to leave the ground. I smile, remembering when Uncle Louie would play that same game with me. This is what life is about. Being normal and letting kids have fun.

"Hey," Annalisa calls. "Come down and join the tea party!"

"Ahoy, matey!" I shout back. "I'll be right down."

Chapter 7

FROM PARTY TO NIGHTMARE

*W*alking up to the playhouse, I spot a framed sign Annalisa, and I made many years ago. It reads "Girls Only" in a rainbow of colors, and the "R" is backwards. It makes me laugh, remembering tea parties Annalisa and I made Uncle Louie share with us, despite our girls only rule.

Glancing over my shoulder, I find Luigi and Uncle Louie have their own swords and are standing back to back, fighting off my rescuers. They're trying to commandeer the pirate ship as their own.

Something flashes to my right, catching my attention. Turning, I look to see what it is. There's nine men, crouched down and moving toward the playground, guns drawn, knowing instantly they aren't part of my Family.

"Uncle Louie!" I scream at the top of my lungs, keeping my eye on the men approaching us. I duck behind a boulder the boys like to climb and jump off and pull my gun from my satchel. I tuck my extra clip into my pocket. All I wanted was one day, one flipping day, where I could be normal.

I take stock of my Family. Lefty is urging the girls to lie down, squatting to the side of them as he pulls his gun. He waves to keep them down. Nonna opens the door to the playhouse and hurries the girls into it.

"Aless," Annalisa calls in panic. "Come on before you get shot!"

"No!" I call back. "Help Nonna get those girls to lay down, flat on the ground. Don't come out until I tell you it's safe!" Nonna grabs her by the arm and pulls her into the house.

Uncle Louie and Luigi are getting the boys onto the pirate ship when I hear a bullet hit the rock in front of me, sending a spray of debris up into the air.

A switch flips inside me. They're firing at a playground. With children! Taking aim at the first man I see who's aiming at Lefty, I pull the trigger. The bullet finds my target, hitting him in the side of the head. He crumbles to the ground instantly.

Rotating around the rock I'm crouching behind, bullets ping off the playground equipment. Carefully, I peek around it to find a man shooting a Beretta ARX100 at the playhouse, blowing holes straight through it.

"NO!" I scream, abandoning my hiding spot and running toward him. Aiming at him, I shoot him in the head and chest. He falls to the ground as I leap onto the porch of the playhouse. "Stay down," I yell over the cries and screams coming from inside. Gunfire sounds throughout the playground, echoing off the trees in the distance.

My instincts are in control as I turn to the side of the house. A man steps out from around the corner onto the porch. I don't think, just point and shoot. His body hits the porch with a dull thud. I kick him off the porch with my foot, not wanting the children to see him. The girls inside cry out, hearing the gunfire so close to them must be scaring them to death. Nonna shushes them, saying "We'll be okay, just stay down."

"Nonna," I call, "there's at least six more men. Keep the kids down. I'll be back."

Taking stock of the situation, I see Luigi on the top of the pirate ship, shooting. He's found the perfect advantage of height to shoot down on our attackers. Uncle Louie has moved, taking my spot behind the boulder. He's aiming to the other side of the playhouse. Ducking down I creep to that side and peer around the corner. There're two men bleeding out on the ground before me. That's five down, only four more.

Looking over the lawn, I find the four men, spread out and shooting wildly. One aims in Uncle Louie's direction. Hell no, they aren't getting my uncle!

Standing, I aim at his head. With one shot, I take him out, but I've given away my position. The three remaining men turn, training their guns on me.

I leap off the porch and shoulder roll into the shrubs. Looking through the branches, I find one man shooting at the bush, but he's aiming too high to hit me on the ground. I aim at his knees and fire twice.

"Son of a bitch," he yells, falling to the ground. My clip is empty, so I pop it out and let it fall to the ground. I replace it with the one from my pocket.

"You low-life, pussy-assed mother fucker! You're shooting at kids!" I yell running up to him. "Today, you're going to hell, and I'm sending you there myself!" Standing over him, I shoot him between the eyes.

I crouch down, but the gunfire around us has suddenly stopped. There's a lot of noise coming from the picnic area and the reception hall. We have to get the children to the underground shelter. Now.

"Uncle Louie, Luigi, Lefty?" I call. "Check in."

"Here," Uncle Louie shouts and I breathe a sigh of relief that he's okay.

"Fine," Lefty calls.

"All clear in the immediate area," Luigi informs us.

Uncle Louie steps out from the side of the playhouse. Standing up, I start issuing commands.

"Luigi, bring the boys over here. Nonna, Annalisa, let's move the girls. We have to get them to the underground shelter right now. This isn't over yet."

Turning, I run to the dead men, gathering their weapons and clips as I go. "Lefty," I yell. "Mind the little eyes! Don't let them see!" I don't want to yell 'dead bodies,' so I hope he catches my meaning.

Uncle Louie stops me, catching me by the shoulders. He stares into my eyes, but before he can say anything, I speak. "I'm fine, no injuries. We need to get these children to safety. They're attacking the picnic area and the reception hall. Mom's there. I need to make sure she's safe."

"Okay, let's do this," Uncle Louie nods, like he's waiting for me to give him his next orders.

We move to Lefty and Luigi, finding they've both pilfered guns from the dead men. Hard to believe the four of us took out nine heavily armed men with just our handguns.

Glancing at the children, I see they're all terrified. Some are visibly shaking, some crying, others silent and staring at the ground. Nonna still holds the little girl from earlier, who is clinging to my grandmother for dear life. Annalisa has her arms around several girls who are hanging onto her legs.

"Any wounded?" I ask Nonna.

"Some scrapped knees, one bullet wound," she nods to Coco. In Coco's twelve-year-old arms is her little sister Liza. She has her hand clamped over her upper arm, blood seeping through her tiny fingers. Her eyes are wide, pupils dilated. Crap, she might be going into shock.

"Liza, honey," I say softly. Her head turns to me. "Can I see your boo-boo?"

"You're the Princess?" she asks, a small smile spreading across her lips.

"I am," I nod. "And you're Liza, a brave little soldier. Can I see your boo-boo?" I ask again.

She nods, lifting her fingers away. "You know, I was six years old when I was shot. And I'm perfectly fine. You'll be better before you know it," I say, inspecting her wound. It's a through and through in her upper arm. All meat and no damage to the bone. That's good.

I pull a brand new, clean scarf from my purse. Liza watches my movements carefully.

"*Piccola*," I say, getting her attention. "Your boo-boo is just like my Uncle Louie's. I'm going to wrap it with my pretty scarf. Keep it on until the doctor can look at it, okay? Hey, you have something in common with my big, bad Uncle Louie." I smile at her, trying to reassure her.

While I wrap her arm, Liza's head tilts back to look up at Uncle Louie, who, I'm sure, is smiling down at her.

"It only took him a week before he was good as new," I tell her before kissing her forehead. "I'll check on you later."

"Take care of your sister, sweetie," I instruct Coco.

She nods, answering solemnly, "Yes, Princess. I will. I promise."

"Nonna, take these kids and get them in the shelter. Now. Annalisa will go with you. Have you ever shot one of these?" I ask, holding out the ARX100.

"No, but your Nonno had me shooting the older version of this," she answers, reaching for the M4 Uncle Louie holds. "Just point and shoot, right?"

"Yeah, that's the basics, Mama," Uncle Louie answers.

I give Annalisa the ARX, knowing it's lighter and will be easier for her to carry. Hooking the strap over her arm, I hold it in front of her and explain how to use it. "This is the safety. Leave it off until you're in the shelter, in case you need to defend yourself and the kids. Once you're underground, switch it like this," I explain, flicking the safety to on. "The gun won't fire like this. Keep it away from the kids once you're safe."

Placing my hands on her cheeks, I turn her head to face me and rest my forehead against hers. "Annalisa, you need to pull on your big girl panties. You have a job to do, for the Family. This is one of the most important job you have ever been asked to do. You need to get all these kids underground and keep them safe until one of *our* men come and get you. If you see anyone in the woods, *do not* hesitate to put a bullet in them."

"But," she protests on a shaky voice, "what if it's one of our men?"

"Doesn't matter, if it isn't a woman or child, you shoot. If there's a man hiding in the woods, he's either our enemy or a coward and deserves to die. Listen, Annalisa. We are under attack. Our people are being murdered right now, and we have to go help them. You need to suck it up and get your ass in gear to protect these kids. Do you understand?"

"Okay," she nods. "I got this. Be careful. I love you, bestie."

Tears shimmer in her eyes as she reaches for me

and gives me a quick hug. A shiver works its way down her spine before she pulls away.

"I love you, Little One," Nonna says in my ear as she too gives me a quick hug. "You be careful. I don't want anything to happen to you. Go get your mom. Send her and Gwen to the shelter, they know where it is. Go now, okay?"

Nonna herds the kids toward the east path, whispering, "Come on, kids. We're going on an adventure. Everyone hold hands and hold tight. Let's move on quiet feet and hurry as fast as we can." They take off into the woods, and I breathe a silent prayer for their safety.

God, Mom! She has to be freaking out with memories of Uncle Louie and Elena's engagement party. I have to get to her. She was headed to the reception hall to check on the food. Passing one of the dead men on the ground, I spot a large knife on his belt. I pull the sheath off his belt and slip it in my waistband. I grab the last M4 laying on the ground and check the clip. Searching the dead man, I find two extra clips in his pants pocket and shove those into my purse, along with my Sig and the five remaining bullets in it.

Standing, I look up to find Luigi, Lefty and Uncle Louie heading towards the picnic area. "Hey!" I yell after their backs. "I have to get Mom!" The three of them stop and dive for cover. Shit, there's more attackers coming this way. I don't want to leave them, but I can't abandon her. They have this. She's freaking out, I'm sure.

I turn, taking off down the other path toward the reception hall. Gunfire from ahead reaches my ears, causing me to slow down. From my right, the sounds of a fight, of punches and cursing, overcomes the sounds of the gunfire. Creeping through the bushes,

I find Antonio fighting for his life with an attacker. Antonio's attacker turns, hearing my approach.

"Well, well, well," he says with a sneer as he reaches for me. "Look who came right to me. Is this your little Princess?" he taunts Antonio over his shoulder.

I dodge his grasp as Antonio yells, "Run, Alessandra!"

Antonio lunges for the guy, but he dodges him, causing Antonio to stumble. I find the knife on my waistband and pull it free, keeping it hidden from the attacker by using my sleeve to cover it.

"You don't want to do this," I say to him.

"Oh yes baby, I do," he smiles a creepy smile at me. "I want to do this and a whole lot more to you. We'll have a lot of fun together."

Antonio recovers and tries again to intercede, but someone comes through the trees and shoots at him. He dives for cover, luckily spotting the man as he aimed at him. Crap, I have to put an end to this skirmish and get to Mom.

Sliding the knife into my hand, I stab out, hitting the man in the lower stomach. With a quick jerk, I pull it up toward the man's sternum. Blood flows from the wound, covering my hand. The man gasps, reaching for his stomach as I shove him back with my free hand. Stumbling, he falls to his knees with a pained look on his face.

Knowing it'll be a matter of seconds before he dies, I turn to find Antonio's knocked the gun from the second attacker's hand. I leap onto the man's back, grabbing his hair in my fist to hold on and pull his head back. Quickly, I wrap my legs around his waist and hook my feet together to keep him from throwing me off. With my right arm over his shoulder, I press the knife against his neck by his left ear and slowly drag it across his throat. The knife slices through his neck as more blood coats my hand. The man tries to grab at me, trying to pull the knife away, but I pull the knife faster. He stumbles like the first man and falls to his knees, and I release my hold on him. Gracefully, I step off his back and onto the ground as he falls to his side, his life's blood gushing from the mortal wound I've inflicted.

The man's hands reach for his neck in a vain attempt to staunch the flow and save his own life. I step away, pulling one of the M4s from my shoulder, and hand it to Antonio. He stares at me, shock clear on his face.

"Antonio," I bark, pulling my Sig from my purse. "Snap out of it. You have to go help Luigi, Lefty and Uncle Louie at the picnic area. Keep the men away from the woods. Your sister and Nonna are heading to the shelter through the trees with the children from the playground. I'm going to get our moms. They went to the reception hall to check on the food."

"I can't let you go by yourself," he says, shaking his head.

"Are you kidding me?" I snarl at him. "We don't have time for your macho bullshit. I just took out two men in front of you. Get your ass in gear and go help my uncle, NOW!" He stares at me for a second.

"Antonio," I plead. "I've killed seven men today. I've got this. Please, go." I don't wait for him to follow my orders, I just turn and run. God, what has happened to me? I'm a killing machine. My instincts take over, letting me do what needs to be done to protect myself and my Family... without remorse, without regret. I'm not shaking, but my stomach is beginning to twist with worry. I have to make it to Mom before anything happens to her.

As I dash through the campgrounds, I wonder if Vito has gotten Papa to safety before things went to hell. Oh, he'd better have done a better job today than that day at the shooting competition. "Lord," I pray, "please protect Uncle Louie and the rest of the Family. Let no more harm come to them."

The reception hall comes into view, gunfire coming from the front of the building. I bound up the back steps and try to open the door, but it's locked. Peering in through the window, I see they've blocked the door with furniture for their safety, but dammit, it's preventing me from getting in.

Abandoning the back door, I jump from the porch and hide behind the tall shrubs that surround the building. Keeping low, I creep towards the front. The gunfire gets louder the closer I get.

Gwen's voice sounds out, over the din. Her voice is panicked. Mom cries out, pleading for her life. I hasten my steps, hurrying to find them. I stop at the front corner of the hall and look out to the front porch. Mom and Gwen stand there, a man in front of them is holding a gun out, pointing it at them. My view of him is blocked by a pillar that holds the porch up. Dammit, I can't shoot him from here.

"You're the Capo's whore of a wife!" the man rants. "You're the cause of this war! He was supposed to marry Olga and unite our Families. Instead, he *humiliated* her in front of *our* Family, to marry *you!*"

Before I can move to get a better angle, he pulls the trigger.

The world slows.

Time stops.

Mom grabs her chest and staggers back into Gwen, who struggles to catch her. They both fall to the ground, a red stain blooming on Mom's chest.

"Nooooooooooooo!!" I scream, jumping onto the porch. The man turns to face me, but I fire, unloading my last six bullets into him. His body falls, sliding down the stairs.

Running, I fall to my knees beside Mom and Gwen. Mom coughs and blood dribbles from her mouth.

"Elena," she whispers.

"No, Mom. It's me, Alessandra," I say.

"No, *cara*." She coughs again, more blood coating her chin. "Elena's here. I love you, Alessandra."

"Get some towels," I scream at Gwen, my voice shaky. "We have to put pressure on the wound."

Gwen slides out from under Mom. Lifting my hand, I push her hair out of her face, leaving a trail of blood on her skin. Blood from the men I've killed today. Quickly, I swipe my hand across my shirt in a vain attempt to clean it.

"Mom, you have to hold on. We're getting you help," I plead, staring into her eyes. "Stay with me and fight. Please, Mom!"

Mom smiles over my shoulder and nods, her glazed eyes find mine again. "Baby, you have to escape this evil Family. Promise. Promise me you'll escape. Find real love. Don't settle." She coughs again and blood leaks from the corner of her mouth. I help her sit up. "Find your own happiness. Out there, away from all of this."

Mom tries to take a deep breath and coughs again, a sickly rattle coming from her chest. "Honey, I'm okay. I've found peace. Elena's here and is going to take me to Junior."

"No!" I yell, looking for someone to help me. "No, you can't leave me! I love you, Mommy! Please, I need you here!" I beg and plead. Her eyes flutter, and then emptiness fills them. With one last rattling breath, her body stills and falls limp.

Pulling her slackened body to me, I kiss her forehead, knowing I'll never feel her kisses again. I bury my head into her neck and give her one last hug. My breath falters in my lungs, my throat tightens at the coppery smell. Pulling back, I look down at her upper stomach. The hole is huge, how did she hold on as long as she did?

She wanted to go... she had found peace, she said, and Mom wants me to escape. Oh, God. I'm so relieved she found peace. She wasn't scared, wasn't shaking.... Mom was calm.

Lifting my hand, I slowly reach up and close her eyes. "I love you, Mommy," I whisper. "I will escape this life. I promise. I'll find real love somewhere far away from all this evil." I kiss her bloody lips in one final goodbye.

Bullets crack through the air, breaking the silence. Looking up, I see Gwen standing near us, tears falling from her eyes. I grab her and pull her down. I take the last M4 into my hands.

"I'm going to get you out of here," I announce quietly, checking the clip. "Nonna and Annalisa are safe in the shelter. Do you know how to get there from the woods?" I ask her.

She nods, sniffling, and I lean forward to wrap my arms around her. Not only did I lose my mom, but she lost her best friend. They've been friends since they were young girls. They were in each other's weddings, were pregnant at the same time with Annalisa and me. They've been best friends forever.

Two men run up the steps of the porch. Shoving Gwen behind me, I take aim and fire, killing both men instantly. They didn't even have the chance to raise their weapons. Taking Gwen's arm, I duck behind one of the pillars.

"Gwen, we have to get you out of here. Just like I told Annalisa, you need to pull up your big girl panties. We have to move."

Reaching out, I grab the weapons from the two dead men at our feet. Another M4 and an ARX100. "Have you ever shot one of these?" I ask her.

"Maybe?" she answers, her voice breaking. "I don't remember. I just know it was brown and those are black." Did she really just say that?

I hand her the M4 and show her the basics, point, and shoot. Slowly, we make our way to the side of the porch. "We're going to jump down and hide behind these bushes, okay?" I whisper.

She nods, and I leap down, landing on my feet. Gwen follows my lead. "Remember," I say, "if you need to shoot someone, just point and pull the trigger. Don't let go until they hit the ground."

Again, Gwen nods her head. I pause for a moment, listening for the location of the sporadic gunfire. Some comes from inside the hall, but I'm more concerned about the picnic area where there's more. I have to get there and try to help.

Peering out from the bushes, I don't see anyone. "Ready?" I ask.

"Yes," Gwen answers. Taking her hand, I sprint to the trees. Surprisingly, we make it with no one spotting us. "Gwen, shoot any man you see out here in the trees. Tell Nonna and Annalisa I'm okay. I have to go check on my men and make sure they're okay."

"No," she begs, reaching for my hand. "You have to come with me."

Shaking my head, I pull my hand free. "No, Gwen. This Family killed my mom, my aunt, *and* my brother. This ends today. I will not stop until I put a bullet in the brain of their Capo. I've trained for this all my life. You just saw that I can take care of myself. Now go to the shelter."

She drops her arm, fresh tears forming in her eyes. Trying to reassure her, I say, "On my way here, I saw Antonio. He was fine, but he went to go back up Uncle Louie, Luigi, and Lefty. I have to go help them. I love you," I whisper, giving her a final hug. Turning, I head in the direction of the picnic area and my men. I don't look back, knowing she'll be okay.

Fire and determination flow through my veins. I'm going to kill every member of the Caza Family if I have to, to put an end to this war. I will avenge my mom. Approaching the playground, I find a few more dead bodies than when I left. The gunfire dies down as I make my way through the playground.

On the far side, I see one of our men, Giovanni Pompa, and his family being held at gunpoint. Before I can get close enough, the man holding them hostage shoots them, starting with my man. My heart lurches in my chest as he shoots the wife, then the kids. Finally, I'm close enough to kill the monster who shot those innocent children. Taking aim, I shoot him, a double tap to the heart.

Approaching the family, I hope they're still alive. Leaning down, I feel for a pulse on the little four-year-old girl. Dammit. This asshole just killed a man and his wife and their two children without a second thought. What is wrong with someone that they can do such a horrific thing? God, the mom, lays there, her children on top of her where they fell. Fury boils

101

my blood. I'm killing Pietro Caza tonight.

Abandoning the macabre death scene before me, I sprint toward the picnic area, passing more dead Caza men. Mere feet away from the main area, I find Lefty laying on the ground, his blank stare aimed at the sky. I skid on my knees, stopping at his side.

"I'm so sorry, Lefty. I wish I could have been here to help you. I'll remember you always. You were such a good friend and a loyal guard. You have a special place in my heart. I love you, friend." Bending down, I kiss his forehead and his still warm lips.

Standing up, rage and anger flood me. "Uncle Louie, Luigi?" I yell. "Where are you?"

"Princess!" they call, relief clear in their voices. "We're here, we're coming!" They run towards me, coming from the other side of the picnic area. I'm getting madder by the second. My chest hurts so badly. I thought my heart was going to explode from the anger.

I run toward them, meeting them halfway. Uncle Louie halts steps away from me, and I crash into him. With his hands on my shoulders, he pushes me back to arm's length, looking me over.

"Oh God, Little One! Are you okay, where are you hit?" he asks, fear in his tone.

For the first time, I look down at myself. My once tan clothes are stained with blood. My whole front is covered, from sleeves to knees. In my mind's eye, the faces of all the men I've killed today flash by. And Mom. God, Mom.

"It's not mine… but Mom is dead. They killed her right in front of me," I tell him in a small voice. "They killed Lefty, too."

Uncle Louie pulls me into a hug, wrapping his

arms around me tightly. Warmth replaces the cold I've felt since the beginning of this horrific nightmare. He holds me, safety and security filling my soul. With reluctance, I pull away and take stock.

Not hearing any gunfire, I ask "Where's Papa? How many did we lose?"

"What?" Uncle Louie asks.

"Where's Papa? How many did we lose?" I repeat.

"They took your Papa back to the compound and locked him in the safe room with Lorenzo. Vito came back to check on you and Antonio. They're around here somewhere," Luigi answers for Uncle Louie.

"Good. Now, where does the Caza Family hide their women and children during something like this?" I demand.

"What?" they ask in unison as Uncle Louie steps back.

"You heard me," I say. "I want an answer."

"Why?" Uncle Louie asks, confusion marking his face. "Why do you want to know where their women and children are?"

"Because," I say, staring into his eyes. All emotion I have has been squashed, retribution determined to find its path. "We're going there, now. I want to talk to Pietro Caza's wife and find out where he is. This ends today."

Luigi and Uncle Louie exchange glances. "Look, I watched them kill my mom on his orders. I watched them kill the Pompa family in cold blood. They shot poor little Rachel as her big brother tried to protect her, after killing their parents. That's why. This war ends *today*. That Family is evil, and this needs to stop. This has gone on long enough."

During my speech, Vito and Antonio suddenly materialized at my side. Vito watches me with a look I can't place. It might be pride.

"Where's your SUV?" I ask him. "I need someone to take me to where the Caza Family's women and children are hiding."

"The warehouse. Heard they keep them locked up underground there," he nods turning toward the parking lot.

"Let's go," I announce, following him. With no choice, Luigi, Uncle Louie and Antonio trail behind.

Chapter 8
THE END OF THE CAZA FAMILY

*L*oaded in Vito's SUV, he drives us toward the industrial part of town with Antonio in the passenger seat. Uncle Louie has chosen to sit next to me, with Luigi on the other side. The ride is quiet, until Antonio turns around.

"Alessandra, I'm so sorry about your Mom. I wish I would have gone with you. Maybe I could have helped," he says, regret lacing his voice.

"No, Antonio," I say, shaking my head. "I was too late. I was just too late."

"It's my fault," he interrupts me. "If you hadn't stopped to help me, saving my ass *twice*, you would have made it in time."

"You don't know that." Placing my hand on his shoulder, I give it a squeeze. "It's not your fault. The Caza Family has wanted my mom dead since Papa broke his engagement to Olga. Mom's executioner said it right before he shot her."

Sitting back, I look at my bloody hands in my lap. Antonio opens the glove box and hands something to Uncle Louie. My uncle takes my hand and starts cleaning it with some wet wipes, chucking them to the floor as they turn dark with the blood. Pulling out more, he continues working on my hand. I let him, it'll make it easier to hold a gun.

"Ton," he asks quietly. "You got a sweatshirt or something she can change into?"

"No!" I snap. "I want that woman to see the blood of my mother, and of her men that I killed today. She needs to see what I can do and what I've done. She needs to know I won't hesitate to kill her."

Uncle Louie stares at me for a second, then nods. I turn back to Antonio.

"Look, I didn't do anything today that any of our men wouldn't hesitate to do if they walked up and found you in that situation."

He hangs his head, saying, "Maybe, but I don't think any of our men would have been able to kill two men with just a knife as fast as you did. You saved my life. Thank you, Aless."

"It was just instinct, Antonio. Something inside me takes over and does what needs to be done. Please don't thank me," I finish quietly. God, I'm a trained killer. Is this what Papa wanted for me?

Shaking my head, I clear my thoughts and focus on what's about to come, what I want to accomplish. Vito slows down, turning down a long street with three buildings in a cluster at the end.

"There are a few men outside. I think they keep the women and children in the center warehouse, downstairs. Do you know what the wife looks like?" Vito asks, breaking the silence.

"Look here," Antonio says, handing me his phone. On the screen is a woman, mid-forties, with short black hair. She has light brown eyes that look sad. A prominent mole stands out on her left cheek, despite the heavy makeup she wears. Or maybe she accentuated it.

"Does she ever cover up her mole?" I ask.

Vito shakes his head. "No, she makes it stand out more with makeup. I think she likes it."

"She'll be easy to spot, then" I announce, studying and memorizing the picture. "Thanks."

Vito nods while Antonio tucks his phone back in his pocket.

"I'm going to drive right through the gates," Vito informs us. "The car is bulletproof, but once we open the doors, we'll be exposed. Wait until they stop to reload before getting out. I'm going to try to get us as close as possible to the center warehouse, so hold on."

Vito steps on the gas, pushing me back into my seat. The SUV crashes through the gates with a shower of sparks and the sound of metal scraping. Bullets ping off the windows and doors in a deafening cacophony as he steers the car to the rolling door of the warehouse. Without pause or hesitation, he crashes through that like a hot knife through butter.

Men run towards the SUV, firing at us. Vito, Antonio, Luigi and Uncle Louie jump out and return fire, using the doors as shields. Inspecting the interior of the warehouse, I spy an EXIT sign and know that it leads to a staircase down to the shelter.

I hop down and squeeze around Luigi, then take off toward my destination. Keeping low, I shoot any man who gets in my way. Bursting through the door, I run down the stairs. At the bottom, I find two doors, but the first one catches my attention. The sound of crying children and women doing their best to shush them comes from behind it.

I burst through the door, slamming it off the wall inside. The women jump, covering their children. Some scream. Feeling along the wall, I find the light switch and flick it on. Standing in the middle of the room is a boy about my age, who looks a lot like Lilith, the Caza Family's Princess. He's probably her younger brother, Pietro Jr. Lilith just started university. Pietro raises a gun shakily and aims it at me. Just behind him is the woman I saw in the picture. A little girl clings to her leg.

Hearing footsteps from the hallway, I turn and find a man trying to sneak up on me. Raising my gun, I shoot him between the eyes. The guard falls to a heap in the hallway. The children begin crying again, a few of the women scream.

"Be quiet," I order, lowering my weapon. "No one will be hurt as long as you're quiet." Pietro's handshakes even more.

"Do you want to die today?" I ask, nodding at his gun. "If not, I suggest you put that gun down and listen to what I have to say. I will not allow any harm to come to you."

Taking a deep breath, he asks, "You're the Canzano Princess, aren't you?"

"I am," I answer, looking into his eyes. "Now, put your gun down before I'm forced to do something I'll regret… in front of your mother and little sister."

He looks over his shoulder at Mrs. Caza, who has tears streaming down her cheeks. "Put it down, Pete. Put it down," she says quietly.

"I've never killed a woman or child. Please don't make me behave like one of your men. They shot at women and children today. They killed my mother right in front of me."

Slowly, Pietro lowers the gun to his side. I continue. "Not only did they kill my mother, but their first attack was on our playground. They aimed at a playhouse where little girls, just like her," I lift my chin to Pietro's sister, "were hiding. We were lucky your men have terrible aim. A five-year-old girl took a bullet to the arm. They also killed one of my guards. I've killed at least ten, or maybe more, of your men today. My men have killed every single man that was sent to attack us today. They're still fighting and killing upstairs. If you want to live, place the gun on the floor and kick it over here."

He crouches, placing the gun on the ground. "What do you want then?" he asks kicking it to me. "If you've killed all our men, what's left?"

I glance at his mother. "I want your Capo. He's been attacking my Family since my mother and father fell in love. Years ago, he killed my Aunt Elena at her engagement party and tried to kill my mother. Mom lost my big brother when she was seven months pregnant. She spent her life traumatized and in fear until they killed her today. This ends now. I'm putting a stop to this damn war."

"How?" Mrs. Caza asks. "How are you going to do that?"

"Pietro, take your sister," I instruct. "In exchange for letting you live, you promise that you'll never allow your Family to kill another child or woman again, except to defend themselves."

He nods eagerly. "I promise our Family will never do that again. My father is an evil man, hated by many. I'll be forever grateful if you succeed."

"Viviana, go to Pete," Mrs. Caza says, guiding the little girl to him. I motion for her to join me. She kisses both of her children then comes to my side.

"I swear to you," I vow to Pietro, "Once your mother brings me to your father, I will let her go. I will not hurt her as long as she helps me."

"Thank you, Princess," he bows his head.

I nod and turn on my heel. Mrs. Caza keeps pace with me. "Is there a way we can get out of here?" I ask her. "I need you to take me to wherever Pietro Sr. is hiding."

As we walk out the door, for my own safety, I fold

the padlock over the door and lock it. Knowing when Uncle Louie comes down here looking for me, he will open it. I turn to her and ask, "How can we get out of here? I want you to take me wherever he is hiding."

"Follow me," she says, taking the lead. "We'll take my car. It's in the underground garage. We'll exit from there."

I follow her lead as she approaches a wall and pushes on a brick. The wall parts, revealing a sleek Maserati.

"Get in," she instructs. "It's always ready with the keys inside."

The secret door closes as soon as we enter the garage. The garage door opens as we approach the car. Once inside, she starts the car and drives away.

Once we're on the main road, Mrs. Caza starts talking. "I've heard a lot about you. Well, about your abilities. I can see they weren't lying about it now. Your father has made sure everyone knows of your, let's say, talent. Rumor has it, you never miss a target."

"Where did you hear that?" I ask.

"They have Capo meetings a few times a year," she chuckles. "They all get together, try to discuss peace and alliances, chat, brag... Pietro always comes home, ranting about how Al brags about you. It makes the other Capos jealous, makes them want to take you."

She glances at me, lifting an eyebrow. "Not just to kill you either, if you catch my meaning. At the last meeting, Al was bragging about your marksmanship. All the men wanted to challenge you when Al reported it, to prove him wrong. That's probably why Pietro decided to attack on your birthday. Your Papa has a big mouth."

I sigh and change the subject. "Where are we going?"

"My house," she answers. "Pietro and his two guards are in the safe room next to his office. When we pull into the driveway, he'll see my car and know it's all clear. This is the signal we worked out for this particular attack. Luckily, he picked me this time. Last time it was the guard you shot. I'm supposed to pull into the driveway, drive to the garage and turn around, and they'll see it on the cameras. Then I'm supposed to head to the country house with the kids and the other women and wait for them to tell us to come home. Once he sees me, he'll know it's over, and they'll head to the warehouse to hear how the attack went. They'll leave the house through the tunnels to the garage."

God, is she setting me up? I don't think so. She knows my men are at the warehouse with her children. After about five minutes, she starts talking again.

"Pietro is an asshole. After hearing your story and knowing what I know, we'll all be better off without him. It's time for his just punishment. It's long overdue."

"Was your marriage arranged too?" I ask out of curiosity.

"I knew he was to be my husband by the time I turned thirteen. I had a huge crush on him. When we got married, I learned I was nothing more than a possession. He never loved me. He's had more mistresses than I can count. More importantly, though, you're right. He's an evil, vindictive man… a heartless son of a bitch. I'll owe you, if you come out of this alive."

"Don't worry about that. Pietro Caza dies today, along with his guards. I'll walk away untouched."

Mrs. Caza slows the car, turning down a street lined with nice homes. At the end, there's a massive fence. "Your father always says he'll be the one to pick your husband. Don't end up like me," she says ominously.

She pulls the car over. "Our house is at the end, behind those gates. Once I pull into the driveway, I'll make the U-turn near the garage. That's when you have to get out. It's the only blind spot for the cameras." She pauses and fishes in the cup holder. Handing me a gold key, she continues. "This key opens the side door to the garage. There are no cameras on that side, and it's not connected to the alarm, it's where his mistresses come in and where I sneak out when I need me time."

Her mouth hitches at the corner. "He's an arrogant bastard, so once he sees my car, he'll be excited to hear how you and your mother were killed. They'll rush to the garage and open the garage door before they are in the bulletproof SUV. That's your only chance. You have to get him before he gets in the car. Luckily, he's not as fit as your father. He's got a huge gut, and he'll be the last one to the garage."

She pats my knee and gives me a warm smile. "Good luck, Alessandra. When I leave, I'll return to the warehouse. I'm sorry for all of the horrible things he's done to you and your Family. I pray you can find peace now."

Taking a deep breath, she resumes her drive to the house. "Thank you. I wish you the best," I tell her, ducking down to avoid being seen on the cameras. "Hopefully you and your kids can find happiness without Pietro hanging over you."

I hop out as soon as she pulls to the side of the garage to make her U-turn. I close the door quietly and run hunched over to the side door. Sticking the key into the lock, I glance up and see the camera pointed upward and not at the door. A sigh of relief escapes me. Once the door is open, I walk in and shut it softly. I pause, listening for a blaring alarm. The garage is silent.

Surveying the garage, I find four cars. The SUV is closest to the house door. Knowing this is the car they think they'll be taking, I make my way toward it to pick where I want to wait for them. They'll be coming through the house door and won't be expecting an ambush here of all places. Several feet down the wall is the shadow of the SUV, I press myself against the wall and turn my face toward the door.

I slow my breathing, calming myself. This will all soon be over.

Moments later, excited chatter comes from behind the door.

"I bet not only is Al's whore of a wife dead," someone says as the door opens, "but that little bitch of a cunt daughter he loves to brag about is, too. Bet she can't shoot her way out of a paper bag."

The guards stop in front of me, turning back to look at Pietro. Taking aim, *bang, bang,* I shoot them in the back of the head in quick succession. They fall instantly, never knowing what hit them.

"Mother fucker," Pietro shouts as I train my gun on him. He reaches into his jacket, probably for his gun.

"Tsk, tsk," I say, shooting him in the arm. "Didn't your mother ever teach you not to use foul language?"

"You fucking little cunt," he growls. Blood pours through his fingers clasped over his arm. "How the fuck did you get in here?"

"Oh, you know," I say waving my hand not

holding the gun. "Just wanted you to see the face of the '*little bitch of a cunt*' that will be sending you to hell. That wasn't a very nice thing to say about a girl you've never even met."

His face turns red, anger and hatred filling his gaze. "You know," I taunt, "you killed my Aunt Elena who my Uncle Louie was in love with, at their engagement party. She was carrying his baby, too. Losing her sister caused my mom to lose my brother. She never got over that, carried that with her *every day*, suffered *every day*... until today, when *your men* shot her."

"At least my men got half of their mission accomplished today," he smiles.

I shoot his other arm.

"You bitch," he cries, trying to grab the wound.

"You're an evil man. You sent your men after me when I was *six years old*. You had your men attack children playing on a *playground*. You're a sick bastard. Your men killed one of my favorite guards today. But you know what, you've lost more. I killed over ten of your men myself today, I kind of lost count."

"You lie," he seethes.

Aiming my gun lower, I fire a bullet into his massive stomach. He falls to the ground, moaning in pain. Pietro curls into a ball, grunting, "You're a whore just like your mother."

"It seems like you haven't learned anything today. Let me fill you in," I say, stepping into the blood pool forming around his huddled form. "I may be a bitch, but I *am* your judge, jury, and executioner. *Your own son* wished me luck when I told him my plan, as did your *wife*. How does that feel?" I ask calmly.

His only response is a groan.

"I loved my mother very much," I say, kicking him in the stomach. He grunts, trying to protect himself.

"Let's see, what else," I say, tapping my finger on my chin as I watch him slowly bleed on the ground. "Oh yes, you said that I 'couldn't shoot my way out of a paper bag.' I couldn't resist showing you how wrong you were by dispatching your guards *in front of your fucking face!*" I scream, kicking him again.

"Did you know, I watched my mom die in front of me today? She took a bullet to the stomach, just like you. I thought turnabout would be fair play." I deliver another vicious kick to his stomach.

Pietro coughs, blood dribbling from his mouth. The blood surrounding his body turns dark as it soaks into the cement floor of the garage. I know it won't be long, and I have one more thing to add.

"Just so you know, every single one of your men who attacked my Family today... Every. Single. One is dead. You see, a few months back when I showed off my skills, it kind of humiliated my men. They trained every day since then to be better, so they wouldn't be shown up by a little girl again. They've become excellent marksmen."

Blood pours from his mouth. He coughs and tries to spit it up at me. Staring down at him, I watch his eyes flutter. I kick him again, and he tries to gasp.

"See you in hell," I say, shooting him between the eyes. I fire my last two bullets into his chest. Turning, I replace my clip and shoot his guards one more time each, just to be sure.

My breathing picks up, no longer calm and steady. I turn back to Pietro Caza and shoot him once more... twice. Again, and again. And again. I realize my clip is empty, but I keep pulling the trigger. My breaths saw in and out of my lungs.

Crap, I'm on the verge of hyperventilating. Bending at the waist, I take a deep breath and hold it for three counts. I slowly let it out. Once more… twice. Again, and again. And again.

Feeling slightly more in control, I grab a towel off a bucket in the corner by the door. As I leave the garage via the door I entered through, I carefully rub the towel to remove my prints from both doorknobs, then shove it into my satchel. I walk down the short path to where Mrs. Caza dropped me off.

My energy disappears, the adrenalin rush I was on crashes, leaving me fatigued and drained. I collapse, falling on my bum. I pull out the key she gave me and rub it obsessively on the hem of pants, once again removing the fingerprints. Not much I can do about the blood, though. I chuck it into the planter box at the corner of the garage.

Numb, I sit there. My hand slides into my satchel, looking for my gun. I find it, feeling slightly more secure, even though I'm out of ammo. My hand brushes my phone, and I pull it out. Scrolling through my contacts I find Uncle Louie and press his name, then put the phone to my ear. He answers on the second ring.

"*Princess, are you okay?*" he asks.

"Yeah," I answer on a sigh. "It's over, Uncle Louie. They're all dead." My breathing picks up again.

"*Don't hyperventilate on me, okay?*" He's breathing as heavy as I am, "*I need you.*"

Sighing again, I say, "I need you, too."

The sound of hurried footsteps comes through the phone. "*Okay, Little One. I'm on my way. Where are you? Tell me so I can come get you.*"

Taking a deep breath, I look around, realizing I

have no clue where I am.

"His wife took me to their home. I don't know where I am. She said she was going back to the warehouse to get the kids, though." I answer.

"*Luigi,*" Uncle Louie yells away from the phone. "*Find Pietro's wife, or someone who knows where they live.*" His voice returns to me. "*Okay Piccola, we're on our way. Stay right where you are, don't go anywhere.*"

"I need a shower," I whisper. "I just want a shower. I can't... I don't... I need a shower. I have Mom's blood on me. But I ruined it. That asshole's blood has tainted her pure, innocent blood. I need to get it off of me..." My voice fades as my breath hitches in my chest. God, I feel so dirty with Pietro Caza's blood all over me.

"*Little One,*" Uncle Louie says into my ear. "*I'm on my way right now. We'll be there real soon. Vito's SUV is a little beat up, but it still runs great,*" he chuckles in my ear. "*Where are you exactly? Are you in the house?*"

I shake my head.

"*Aless, where are you, cara?*" he asks again.

"I'm on the side of the garage, sitting on the ground. No cameras. Just sitting. Waiting for you."

"*Okay, Bella,*" he says, letting out a breath. "*We're almost there. Vito and Antonio will scrub the place of evidence, okay?*"

I nod.

"*Does that sound like a plan?*" Uncle Louie asks.

"Yeah," I answer. "Sounds good."

Uncle Louie continues talking to me. I tune out his words, just listening to the soothing tone and cadence of his voice. It's like a balm to my tortured soul, calming me, keeping me sane.

A short time later, a vehicle comes roaring up the driveway, almost breaking me from my trance. A door opens, followed by three more. Booted feet stand before me. Lifting my head, I find Uncle Louie's concerned stare focused on me. He bends, wrapping a blanket around me and sweeps me into his arms.

"Come on, *bamina*. Let's get you home," he whispers in my ear. "It's all over." With his arms wrapped around me, he carries me to the SUV.

"I'm taking Princess home," he barks out. "Luigi, drive me home. Vito, you'll have to take one of their cars to get you and Antonio home after you clean up here. Make sure to scrub the cameras and wipe everything down."

"I only used that side door," I whisper. "And I only touched the wall to the right of the door to the house. I never went into the house itself. I might have touched some cars, but I don't think so."

"It's okay, *Piccola*, we got this," he says softly, pushing my bloodied hair out of my face.

"Is she going to be okay?" Antonio asks. "Is she going to lose it like her mom?"

Pain lances my heart at the mention of my mom. "I'll be fine," I yell in a daze. "I just need a shower. Can I have a shower, please?"

There's a thump, like someone punched someone in the stomach. "If I *ever*," Luigi growls, "hear you say something like that again, I'll beat the living shit out of you. Do you understand me?"

"Yeah, man," Antonio coughs. "I hear you."

The door to the SUV opens, and Uncle Louie climbs in, still holding me tight. The door slams shut and another one opens before slamming shut quickly.

"Lou," Luigi quietly says, "let's get our Princess home so she can take that shower."

Curled in Uncle Louie's warm embrace, I'm in a foggy daze. I'm unaware of the passing houses or countryside. My chest hurts, and I feel numb to the world. God, Mom, saw Elena. She seemed so relieved at the end…

How many people did I kill today? Fourteen? Fifteen? Each man's face flashes through my mind. I count them. God, fifteen men. I don't want to be this person, this brutal killer. Something just takes over when people I love are threatened, and I become this killing machine.

The SUV stops, and I sit up a bit. Relief washes over me at seeing my home. Luigi jumps out and opens the back door. Uncle Louie helps me out, keeping the blanket wrapped around me. The front door opens, Nonna and Camilla burst through it, rushing to my side. They stop short, Nonna's hand covering her mouth on a gasp.

"She's physically fine," Luigi says. "None of it is her blood."

Her eyes fly from me to Luigi, then Uncle Louie, who holds me tight to his side.

Papa comes stands in the door, calling, "Come! Come on and tell me what happened today!"

I break from my silence, screaming, "Mom is dead!"

There's no reaction from my father. He simply nods. "I know, Princess. We've already contacted the Gentile family to prepare her. But I want to hear it first hand from you. No second or third-hand accounts."

My eyes bulge. Did he not love her at all? Does he even have a heart? God, I bet he wasn't even the one to contact the Gentiles. Probably had Nonna do it.

"Have you seen her?" I ask. "Have you even left this house to check on *your* men? Do you know who *died* today? For you… for me. How is little Liza?"

Turning to Uncle Louie, I beg quietly, "Please find out how she is. I want to go see her tomorrow."

Turning back to my father, I square my shoulders. "I'm not doing or saying *anything* until I take a shower. I watched my mother murdered in front of my eyes. I heard her pleas, her cries for mercy that were ignored. *I* held her hand as she took her last breath, and *I* brushed her hair out of her face as she told me she loved me. *I was there* when she told me Elena was there to take her away…" Uncle Louie squeezes my shoulder, making me realize I'm close to yelling.

Taking a deep breath, I feel the sting of tears filling my eyes. I shrug from my uncle's comforting hold and storm past Papa. Releasing the blanket, I let it fall to the floor. My shoes are tacky, sticking to the marble floors with each step and I know I'm leaving bloody footprints in my wake. I don't care at this point. I just need that fucking shower.

Nonna and Uncle Louie both reprimand Papa, whisper-yelling at him. I shake my head as I hit the stairs. My mind is blank, empty, as I make my way down the hall to my room. Placing a hand on my doorknob, I feel a hand on my shoulder. I whirl, finding Luigi looking down at me with concern.

"If you need anything, I mean *anything*, just call. I'll be there in seconds. Okay?"

I nod, giving him a half-smile. Looking down, I turn back to my door but freeze as my hand starts to turn the knob. Pivoting on my heel, I throw my arms around Luigi's neck. He doesn't hesitate, wrapping his arms around me tightly. I relish his hold, breathing deeply. It's peaceful in his arms, comforting, so I hold onto him. After several long minutes, I release him. Stepping back, I look down at his now bloodstained clothes.

"Oh, Luigi," I sigh, waving a hand at him. "I'm so sorry I ruined your clothes."

"They were already bound for the trash," he says, tapping my chin. "Remember, Aless. Anything you need, call me."

"Okay," I whisper.

Chapter 9

MY BREAKDOWN

*E*ntering my bedroom, I sigh. The sight isn't as relaxing as I'd hoped. Maybe it's the smell of blood permeating my clothes. Making a beeline for my bathroom, my eyes sting once again with welling tears.

Catching sight of myself in the mirror, I silently freak out at the image. Blood stains my face and hair. Whose blood is that? Touching my cheek, I ask myself, is it Mom's from when I hugged her after she died in front of my eyes? I blink and watch a tear roll down my face, trailing through the blood.

My heart races at the sight as a lump forms in my throat, making it hard to breathe. Quickly whirling from the gruesome vision before me, I turn the water too hot. I climb in and stand beneath the pulsing spray.

Pink droplets of water hit the tile walls, and I look down to avoid the sight. Red rivulets of water stream down my clothes. The beautiful clothes Mom loved, the outfit she wanted duplicated for herself, are ruined... utterly destroyed. Oh, God...

Reaching up, I pull the remaining pins still holding my messy bun in place and throw them out of the shower. My hair doesn't tumble softly around my shoulders like it normally does. It falls in stiff chunks, dried with blood and stuff I don't want to think about. Turning my back to the spray, I let the water flow over my hair. I grab my shampoo and pour a bunch into my hand. Rubbing and running my fingers through my hair, my hands become coated with pink bubbles. It's not enough. I rinse the bloody shampoo from my mass of hair. Grabbing the bottle again, I upend it over my head. Cold shampoo hits my scalp, coating my hair. I toss the bottle and reach for my hair once again. Using my nails and fingertips I scour my head, paying attention to the length. I check my hands and find the normal, clean bubbles and breathe a sigh of relief.

Standing under the spray again, I carefully rinse all the shampoo from my hair. Finally, the water runs clear of soap, and I gather it into a knot on the top of my head. Turning my attention to my soaking wet, stained clothes, I reach for my body wash. I pour the sweet smelling liquid over my clothes and begin to rub. I have to clean it, Mom loved it so much. I keep scouring the fabric, rinsing it to check and see if the blood is gone.

Maybe I should take it off… I rip the shirt over my head and shuck the pants, dropping them on the floor of the shower. Falling to my knees with a thud, I pour more body wash over the clothes. I scrub and scour the clothes, kneading and grinding the fabric against the tile. God, I need to get the blood out. Sitting back on my heels, water flows over the sopping wet mound of fabric, the water coursing from it is still tinged pink. God, I can't do this.

Leaving the clothes, for now, I stand back up, reach for the body wash again and clean my body. I take my time, making sure to get every centimeter of my skin. Rinsing off, I still feel unclean, so I reach for the bottle for a second pass. Grabbing my pumice stone, I cover it with soap and rub it over my fingers, getting the blood that has soaked into the grooves and lines of my fingers. It works, so I continue, rubbing it over my body in small circles. Every inch of my skin tingles as I rinse the soap off, raw from the pumice stone. Satisfied, I turn back to my bloody clothes.

God, why can't I clean it? Reaching down, I grab the tunic and bunch it into a ball and pour shampoo on it. I'd already used body wash, so this has to work. I squeeze and twist the fabric, working the shampoo deep into the fabric. Holding it up to rinse it, my hand shakes. I drop the outfit and watch my hands. They both tremble and shudder.

My legs shake too, and I lose my balance, falling into the wall. Sliding down to my bum, my breathing comes in quick, raspy pants. A tremor wracks my body, and I bury my head into my knees, curling into a ball.

Mom grabs her chest and staggers back into Gwen, who struggles to catch her. They both fall to the ground, a red stain forming on Mom's chest.

"Noooo," I moan. God, why did she have to die? Why did they hate her so much? My breathing hitches as the lump returns to my throat.

"Elena," she whispers.

"No, Mom. It's me, Alessandra," I say.

"No, honey." She coughs again, more blood coating her chin. "Elena's here. I love you, Alessandra."

Why did God take her from me? The one person who understood what I was facing, the one person who would have helped me plan my escape. "Why God?" I wail.

"Mom, you have to hold on. We're getting you help," I plead, staring into her eyes. "Stay with me and fight. Please, Mom."

She smiles over my shoulder and nods. Her glazed eyes find mine again. "Baby, you have to escape this evil Family. Promise. Promise me you'll escape. Find real love. Don't settle." She coughs again and blood leaks from the corner of her mouth. I help her sit up. "Find your own happiness. Out there, away from all of this."

Mom tries to take a deep breath and coughs again, a sickly rattle coming from her chest. "Honey, I'm okay. I've found peace. Elena's here and is going to take me to Junior."

My breath stutters in my chest. Mom's blue eyes flash in my memory, fluttering closed... Why?! Why did my mommy have to die?

"Mom!" I cry, my voice hoarse. "I love you so much." I wail. Tears flow over my cheeks, combining with the spray of the water. My body shakes and trembles as I hug my knees. My throat closes, and I can't swallow. Grabbing my head, I curl tighter into a ball.

God, Mom... I know you're in a better place now, but I miss you so much. I know how much you hurt, how much you missed Elena and Junior. Please God, please, let her be at peace, with Junior in her arms and Elena by her side.

I start rocking, tears streaming faster from my eyes. My breath stutters more, I can't get enough air. God, why couldn't I save my mom? I'm a trained killer. Why couldn't I save her? Why? Why wasn't I good enough? Why? Why wasn't I fast enough? Why? Why, why, why?

Nonna's voice calls to me quietly, but I ignore it, lost to my pain. Her heels click across the tile as she walks into the bathroom.

"Oh, sweetie," she cries near me. "Come on, let's get you out of there before you catch cold."

I don't respond, *can't* respond. My world has crumbled, leaving me without my mom. Why?

"Lou," she yells. "Come here. She needs your help! Hurry!" Nonna shuts off the water, leaving me colder than I already am. She pushes my hair back and wraps a towel around me. As I glance up to her,

I'm unable to see her clearly through my tears or catch my breath. My whole body is trembling, as I look away and see the window, I notice how dark it has gotten, and I can see the moon in the sky from the window in my bedroom.

"Oh, Little One," Uncle Louie says softly. "Come here, *carissima*. I never should've left you alone." His big, strong arms lift me, and Nonna wraps another towel around me. He carries me from the bathroom, sitting on the corner of my bed.

He holds me like a baby in his lap, his arms wrapped tight around me. My head rests on his broad shoulder. "It's okay, *cara*," Uncle Louie whispers. "I've got you. It's going to be okay, I promise. We'll get through this together. I'm here, I've got you. It's okay to cry. Tears are just your heart leaking the love it's lost."

His voice cracks, and I take a deep breath. Blinking my eyes, I look up at his face and watch tears roll down his cheeks. Nonna rubs my back, sniffling quietly.

"I can get dressed," I say, my voice quivering from my tears. "I'm sorry for crying and freaking out." I don't think I've cried like this in my life. I don't even remember crying as a child. These feelings and emotions are new to me… and so overwhelming.

Uncle Louie puts his free hand on my face and locks eyes with me. "Listen to me, Little One," he says firmly. "You don't have to apologize for crying. You lost your mom, it's normal to cry. Remember that you're not alone. I'm here, and I love you. I'll always be here for you. Okay? And never, ever say you're sorry for being sad, for showing emotions."

Nodding, I spot Camilla coming to our side. "Let's get that wet hair of yours dried or braided, and get you dressed. I'll go get you some jammies," she says softly turning away, wiping her eyes on her way to my walk-in closet.

Uncle Louie shifts and sits me on the bed. He stands, saying, "I'll be back in a second, okay? I need to change."

I open my mouth to apologize, but he stops me by placing a finger over my parted lips. "I just told you, no saying sorry. I'll be right back." He kisses my forehead and leaves.

Camilla approaches as I lean into Nonna who sits beside me. She carries a light pink nightgown and dark blue silk night shorts.

"No," I whisper, curling into Nonna. "No pink… I just can't."

Camilla spins on her heel. "No pink got it."

She quickly returns with the nightgown that matches the shorts. They help dress me, moving my legs and maneuvering my arms. I'm shocked at how weak I am, barely able to lift my limbs. Is this what emotions do? If it is, I want nothing to do with them.

Uncle Louie returns, wearing pajama pants with polar bears on them and a t-shirt with a polar bear on it. It reads, "Bear hugs are PAWSOME." My heart warms at seeing Uncle Louie wearing the gift I got him last Christmas.

"Thought you said you'd never wear those," I say, giving him a sad smile. "Glad you changed your mind."

"I thought you might like them," he answers, smiling warmly at me.

I reach for a tissue from my nightstand and blow my nose. Grabbing another, I wipe the tears from my face. My breathing is still shaky, but a little better. Leaning against the pillows, I close my eyes and try to regain control of my lungs.

My door opens, and Papa walks in. Luigi is hot on his heels.

"Tried to stop him, Lou," Luigi says. "He said he'd shoot me, so I backed off. Sorry."

Uncle Louie waves his hand, forgiving Luigi. Papa surveys the room, a scowl growing on his face.

"I thought my instructions were clear," he says. "I wanted to speak with my daughter after her shower. What is she doing in bed?"

"And we told you," Uncle Louie says, marching up to Papa, "that she needs time."

Papa looks around my uncle and points at me. "I will not allow you to be as weak as your mother."

My uncle knocks his hand away, growling, "Al, hallway, *now*."

Luigi moves to Uncle Louie's left, and Nonna stands to his right, pointing at my door.

"Alessandro Dante Canzano, you *will not* speak that way to your daughter about her mother. Not now, *not ever*. Get your ass out of this room before I have these two men remove you from it. Do you hear me, young man?"

My eyes bulge as my mouth falls open. Papa turns his glare on Nonna, beyond pissed. However, he holds his tongue and moves around my trio of protectors and approaches my bed.

"Sleep well, Princess," he says and kisses my forehead. "We'll talk tomorrow. Your bulldogs don't think now is the right time."

He turns and stalks to the door. "Good night, Mother," he says, pausing in the doorway.

Luigi moves to the wall by my bed, leaning against it. Papa watches him but doesn't say anything. He turns to Uncle Louie, asking, "Do you still wish to speak with me?"

He nods but pauses to have some silent eye communication with Luigi. Luigi tips his chin and hurries after my father.

"I'll be back in a few minutes," Uncle Louie says softly. "I sent Luigi to get you food. You haven't eaten all day and are suffering from one hell of an adrenaline crash. It's past nine o'clock. Please try to eat something, okay?"

I nod, knowing when to keep my mouth shut and when I can talk back to my uncle. I don't think I can stomach any food right now, but no way I'll tell him that right now. Uncle Louie comes to the bed and leans down, whispering, "Don't worry. I won't kill him." He straightens a bit and winks. "I may have to knock some sense into him, but I won't kill him."

He leaves my side, pausing at the door, calling out, "This time."

Uncle Louie is so much more than my uncle. He's more of a father than my own father. Papa didn't care that I haven't eaten all day. No, he just wanted all the gory details of how I killed fifteen men today. He probably doesn't even care how Mom died. God, Mom... I roll to my side and grab Fluffy, burying my head into his chest.

Chapter 10

SETTING MY BROTHER STRAIGHT
(LOUIE)

*A*s soon as I shut Little One's door, I grab my brother by his collar and shove him into the wall opposite the door. My anger builds as I stare into his heartless eyes.

"No one's here to stop me tonight. They're home taking care of their own families. They're good men, counting themselves lucky that they were able to walk away from today's attack. We lost *eighteen* men today; twenty-nine are wounded. Fuck, one child took a bullet to the arm, and two were shot in cold blood. *And that little girl watched her mother murdered in front of her eyes.* Listen and listen good. Now is not the fucking time for this."

Al's eyes narrow as the vein in his forehead becomes more prominent, pulsing in time with his heart rate.

"Am I going to have to kick your ass? If you don't let me go right this minute, I will," he growls, his face growing red.

"Ha," I laugh in his face. "You've never been able to kick my ass, and as pissed as I am right now, going a few rounds with you might just cheer me up."

Al smirks. Swiftly, he lifts his knee, smashing it into my stomach. Fuck, that hurts like a son of a bitch. I retaliate, delivering an elbow to his chin. His head snaps to the side, and I let him go. Unable to maintain control of his body, Al falls to the ground.

With a smirk of my own, I pick him back and shove him into the wall again, this time harder.

"Have you had enough?" Spittle flies from my mouth as I growl into his face. "Are you ready to listen to me? Like you said one time, I can keep this up all night."

Al licks his busted lip. Seriously, how stupid is it to attack the man who's done nothing but train his daughter to defend and protect herself for nine years? He's out of shape, pampered and protected by his guards all the time. Shit, Aless could kick his lazy ass. He'd better straighten up, or she might just do it. The thought makes me laugh inside.

"What? What the fuck do you have to say that's so fucking important that you attack your Capo?" Al bites out.

Letting him go, I take a step back, but keep my eyes on him. "Look, Al… your little girl in there," I point to her bedroom door, "isn't a little girl anymore. She turned sixteen today, but she also became a lethal weapon. A killing machine. From the second she saw that first shooter to the time she killed Pietro Caza, she was led by instinct. She took charge in an instant, issuing orders and directing the men, including me. Shit, she didn't even bat an eye. Alessandra was strong and firm, telling *your* men what to do. And they didn't argue. Me, Lefty, Luigi… fuck, even Vito listened to her. She handled the children with grace, first directing them to hide and then getting them to safety after. The thought of her going to the shelter with them didn't even enter her mind."

Taking a deep breath, I remember watching my niece with a little awe and a lot of pride. "Her main priority was to protect the Family. She watched her fucking mother murdered right in front of her eyes. She didn't fall apart then like any woman would. No, not for a second. She moved on, killing the fucker, then she got Gwen to the shelter. After that, she tracked down her men and *demanded* to be taken to the Caza shelter. She killed at least fifteen men today, Al… two with a fucking knife.

"God, Al, she simply stated Sophia was dead, like I would say the sky is fucking blue. She closed Lefty's eyes when she found him at the picnic area. She didn't cry, or scream 'Why?' No. She fucking demanded to be taken to Pietro Caza's wife. She said, 'This ends today.'

"I still don't know how she got Pietro's wife to take her to their home where the asshole was hiding with his guards. Your little girl convinced the wife of a Capo, an evil, malicious Capo, to help. She even got a key from the wife to sneak into the garage. After, *after*, she killed Pietro is when she broke. After she avenged her mother, her aunt *and* the two innocent children we lost today. And she didn't just end him quickly. She spent some time with him. He had a bullet wound in each arm and one in the gut. She ended him with a shot between the eyes, Al. I'm sure after he was dead she put a couple more bullets in him just for the fuck of it. That's when she fucking lost it.

"God, her voice when she called me. I could hear her shaking. Her voice had a tremor I'd never heard from her. You saw her, she was covered in blood, from head to toe, and not just the blood of our enemy. She carried her mother's blood on her clothes. All she wanted was a fucking shower. Could you not give her that?"

Footsteps echo up the stairs. We watch, waiting for Luigi to appear. His head crests the top of the stairs and his eyes survey us.

"Is that Little One's dinner?" I ask, nodding to the tray he carries and the basket he has tucked over his arm.

Luigi nods. "You need any help out here after I

132

deliver this to Aless?"

"I got this," I answer, opening the door for him. "Make sure she eats. Work some of your Luigi magic and try to get her to smile… or cry. Okay?"

"I prefer to make her smile," he says solemnly. He walks into her room, and I close the door behind him.

Al lifts an eyebrow. I shake my head, knowing that he's thinking Luigi is into Little One. I sigh. "They're close, but nothing's going on. They don't see each other like that. Sure, they tease each other in a flirty way, but it's a huge joke to them. It's not the way she bickers and fights with Antonio."

Al smiles. "Both have good potential. I'm leaning toward Luigi right now. I'm liking what I see."

I shake my head. "Back to my point. Aless has had a tough day. After all, she went through today, the moment she walks into the house, you want to interrogate her. You broke her heart, not showing any emotion at all about Sophia. You told her the Gentile family were tending to her mother like she was nothing more than an obligation. You didn't even see your only child was hurting, was in pain."

Al looks down, probably trying to find a way to defend his actions today. "I just don't want her to break down like her mother did. Sophia… she was a weak woman. She was never the same after losing Elena and Junior. I don't want that for Alessandra."

"Yeah well, you didn't see her today. She didn't shed a single tear. Not one. Not after seeing her mother murdered, not after witnessing an entire family shot before her eyes. *We* saw that. *We* dealt with that. Where were you? You were locked up, safe and sound. You didn't have to see even one dead body today. She was strong, calm and steady until it was over.

"It wasn't until she got here, until she was in the shower, safe and alone, that she began to break. God, she was crying and shaking. Fuck, Al, she lost her mother! Thank God you and I have no idea what that's like. She couldn't even catch her breath. She needs to mourn her mother's death. She is allowed to mourn!

"Is any of this penetrating? She loved her mother. They were close. This does *not* make her weak. It makes her human. Something I doubt you are anymore. You lost all sense of humanity when you took over for Papa. It's like you turned off your heart. I don't know what happened to my brother, but this isn't the actions of the man I once admired."

Al crosses his arms and rubs his chin. He paces, thinking. I wait, wondering what the fuck will come out of his mouth next. I know he's going over everything I just told him.

Finally, he stops and raises his eyes to mine. "Fine, I won't crowd her for now. I'll give you tonight. But... tomorrow, I want to talk to her, hear her side of the story," he says firmly.

"No. We'll see how she is in the morning. I know she wants to go visit Liza and the families of those who lost someone today. If, *if*, Mama and I think she's okay, *and* she wants to, you can hear her side."

"Hmmm," Al ponders. "She really wants to go visit our people? She's better at handling that than I've ever been. I hadn't even thought about that."

"Al," I pause, collecting my thoughts. Taking a deep breath, I push through. "Look, when it comes to Sophia's funeral... she might cry. How are you going to handle that? You cannot call her weak or broken. Do you understand?"

"Yeah," he answers. "I got this. Believe it or not,

I hurt too. Sophia was the first woman I ever loved. At one time, she was my everything. I tried so hard to help her. She just couldn't let it go. She will always have a place in my heart. But the woman who died today was not the same woman I fell in love with when we were young. She was so happy and carefree back then. The world was before us, ready for us to explore and enjoy together. She... we were never the same after we lost Junior. She became lost and broken. If he'd lived, she might have been able to get over losing her sister. I'm relieved she's at peace now. Don't get me wrong, I'm not happy about her death. I wish I was the one who administered this justice to Pietro Caza, for all the damage he caused her." Al looks down, shaking his head.

"Yeah, I was there, Al. You weren't. I saw how a part of her died with Elena. And when Junior died in her arms two days later, I watched her lose the rest of herself. Every noise frightened her. She was scared of her own shadow. When you emerged from your sulking and vengeful thoughts, you expected Sophia to just snap out of it. Aless isn't like her mother at all, but she loved her wholeheartedly. You need to give your daughter time to heal, give her time to grieve. She needs that."

Al exhales loudly, nodding. "Okay, I'll leave the next few days for you to decide. But when she goes to visit the families, I'd like to join her... if she'd like. It'll be good for us to be seen together, unity in loss and all that shit."

"I'll talk to her," I agree. "But for now, I'm starving. I'm going to go grab a sandwich then check on her. Do you want to join me?"

"Sounds good," he smiles.

With one last glance at Little One's door, I know she's in good hands with Mama and Luigi then I lead

my brother away from his daughter to get some food...
and hopefully, talk about anything but her and today.

Chapter 11

LUIGI TRIES TO LIFT MY SPIRITS

*L*uigi walks in, carrying a basket over his arms and a huge tray in his hands.

"Luigi," I say, "please tell me that's not all for me."

"No, madam," he chuckles. "This is dinner for two... or maybe more," he says, looking at Nonna and Camilla. "That is, if you two fine ladies would like to join us for pesto pasta or chicken pesto sandwiches. I might even have some cake in here." He cocks his head and gives me what could be called a devastating smile.

Nonna and Camilla smile, coming to help relieve him of his burden, setting it up on the foot of my bed.

"Let's see what you brought," Nonna says with a smile. She pulls the lids from the plates as Camilla pulls a wine bottle and glasses from the basket. The smell of pesto fills my room when Nonna reveals a huge platter of pasta. Next, she lifts the lid off a plate of chicken pesto sandwiches. Camilla pulls a plate of my favorite strawberry cake from the basket, and I gasp softly at the sight.

"Look," Luigi smiles at me. "I got a reaction out of her! I know it was the cake." He hangs his head, sniffing and acting like he's wiping away imaginary tears. "I'm heartbroken she didn't gasp like that when I came in." He kicks the floor with the toe of his shoe like a little boy. A small smile creeps across my lips, despite my broken heart.

"Get over here, you big doofus. Grab a fork and help me eat this pasta. Did you remember the parmesan cheese?" I ask.

He smiles and toes off his shoes. With a running start, he leaps onto the bed beside me, causing Nonna and Camilla to chuckle at his antics. Camilla places a small tray table between us and Nonna puts the plate with pasta on it, then hands us each a fork.

"Eat up, kids. I want that plate clean before either of you get any cake," Nonna announces. She gives me a sweet kiss on my forehead.

"Sure thing," Luigi says as I nod. Nonna and Camilla each take a small sandwich. Camilla sits on the bench at the foot of my bed, and Nonna rolls my chair over from my vanity.

"I'm just saying," Luigi mumbles around a full mouth, "if you ladies can't eat all those sandwiches… well, I'm a growing boy and will gladly help you out."

Nonna laughs. "Go right ahead, you bottomless pit. I'm sure there will be plenty left over for that growing body."

Camilla sets her plate aside and pours four glasses of wine. She hands me and Luigi a glass. Closing my eyes, I take a long sip and enjoy the taste, a comforting warmth spreading through me. Luigi's already shoveled a quarter of the plate into his mouth, and I'm praying he'll eat more. I'm more playing with the pasta, sliding it around than actually eating it. Thankfully, Luigi's so busy devouring his food that he hasn't noticed that I keep pushing more pasta to his side.

Unfortunately, I'm not that hungry. The food tastes like cardboard and sits like lead in my stomach. I force myself to have a few more bites. My hand still has a slight tremor as I lift the fork to my mouth. Luigi has abandoned the pasta, having stolen a slice of cake. He grabs a piece with his fork and ponders it. Then he turns and directs it toward me, making airplane noises.

"Here comes the airplane… open the hangar doors," he instructs in a sing-song voice.

My eyes warm, and I do as he tells me. Again, even though it's my favorite food in the whole wide world, I have to force myself to swallow the normally delicious cake.

"I can feed myself, Luigi," I protest trying to force a small smile on face, unsuccessfully.

"Nope," he shakes his head. "Not today, sweetheart. I'm having too much fun."

Nonna and Camilla giggle at his silliness as he steers another bite to my mouth.

"It's nice to see you know how to feed a toddler," Camilla comments. "Shows you'll be a good papa someday." Her eyes sparkle with mirth and playfulness.

Luigi coughs, almost choking on his bite of cake. A genuine laugh bursts from my lips.

"Aww," I say. "How sweet. I know you'll make a very good daddy one day. You should have seen him at the playground with the kids today, Camilla."

Nonna joins us in teasing him. "I like this side of you, Luigi, so soft and tender."

Nonna and Camilla giggle, but I yawn in exhaustion. He hands me my fork on a huff. "You're on your own for the cake. And for your information, nothing about me is soft."

Camilla about falls off the bench because she's laughing so hard.

"I don't know what you ladies are laughing about. I don't see anything funny," Luigi protests, crossing his arms over his chest. Nonna cackles with glee. A warm feeling spreads through me, and a small sense of peace settles in at seeing them happy.

Their laughter dies down, and sadness overwhelms me. I fidget with my blanket. "That's fine, Luigi. I'm full, so don't worry. Can we watch a movie? I'm really tired."

Nonna and Camilla spring into action. "You two go ahead and watch the movie. We'll take this downstairs and be back in a bit."

Luigi rolls over and grabs my controller from the nightstand. "Okay, Little One," he says on a shimmy, shaking the bed. "You get comfy and I'll pick the movie." He throws some pillows behind him and gets to work picking something out.

Crap, I hope he doesn't pick a war movie. I can't deal with that right now. I don't say anything though, just watch as Luigi flips through the channels.

"I know the perfect movie, one we'll both enjoy," he says, stopping on *Crazy, Stupid, Love* which just started.

"Perfect," I smile. "Thanks for picking something embarrassingly funny. It's just what I need." Fluffing my pillows, I lean back and get comfortable.

Luigi elbows me. "Hey, this movie has it all! A nice sappy romance for you, some good Bromance for me, and come on, isn't that the funniest fight scene you've ever seen? Now let's watch our movie."

He climbs from the bed and turns off the lights, except the one on my nightstand. Thirty minutes into the movie, I start to doze. Luigi slides his arm under my head and runs his fingers along my arm. I turn into him and snuggle close.

(LUIGI)

Aless curls into me and I let out the breath I've been holding. She's been so strong today. The girl thinks she's so smart that I didn't notice her pushing the pasta to my side of the plate. At least she ate something. God, I hope she can pull through this better and stronger than ever, after all the tragedy she's endured. She's impressive, though. The memory of her asking me to step in if Al picks Antonio to be her husband flashes in my mind. Shit, I know we get along amazingly well, and she has a-rockin' body. It might not be so bad…

"What the hell are you doing?" Lou whisper-yells, breaking me from my thoughts and making me jump. Aless snuggles into me deeper, making this look worse.

"Shhh," I whisper, looking up to find Lou and his mama, Alexa, glaring at me. "We were just watching a movie."

"What are you doing in bed with Little One?" he asks threateningly. "Why is she pressed up against you? Do I need to kick your ass?"

I can't help it, I chuckle. "Look, dude. We were just watching the movie. Aless fell asleep and curled into me. I wasn't about to push her away when she was actually able to get some sleep."

"Lou," Alexa says, "lift her up. Be gentle and try not to wake her. Luigi can slide out, and I'll replace him with Fluffy."

Aless stirs as Lou does as he's told. Quickly, I slide off the bed, and Alexa puts Fluffy in the spot I vacated.

"Nooo," Aless mumbles in her sleep. "I want firm Fluffy, not soft Fluffy. Firm Fluffy smelled better... he was warmer."

Shit. Lou thwacks the back of my head.

"Oww," I complain.

"Good night, Luigi Bear," he growls, pointing to the door.

Ignoring him, I lean down and kiss Aless's forehead. "Sleep tight, Little One," I whisper.

Alexa follows my lead, kissing her granddaughter, then tucking the blankets firmly around her. Standing, she points to the hall. She and I move to the door while Lou kisses his niece and whispers to her.

Out in the hall, Alexa says, "Lou, keep your door open. I'll do the same. Just in case she has a nightmare or needs one of us."

"Yeah, good idea," he mumbles, looking back at Aless's room. "I was planning on doing that anyway. I want to be able to get to her quick if she needs us."

"Good night, Luigi," Alexa says softly. "Thank you for cheering her up and staying with her. I think Aless just needed a friend."

"Yeah," I agree. "I was really worried about her. Good night." Turning to leave, my thoughts return to Alexa and Camilla teasing me about being a good papa... Do I want that? Could I have that? With Alessandra?

Chapter 12

FACING THE DAY AFTER

*A*fter that crap-tastic day and adrenalin crash, I thought I'd be able to get some sleep. I was wrong. I laid in bed, sleeping intermittently, awake more than asleep. Now it's six in the morning, and there's no way I can get anymore shut-eye. I crawl out of bed and take another shower. Someone cleaned my bathroom during the night, removing my clothes and getting rid of the blood stains, for which I'm thankful.

Freshly showered, I towel dry my hair and toss it into a messy bun. Mom loved my hair like this. I move to my closet, hoping to find something black, which I know is futile. Papa won't allow me to wear anything black. I finally find a navy pencil skirt and matching blazer that will have to do. Searching through my blouses, I spot a light pink one Mom picked out on our shopping trip. I dress quickly, then move onto makeup. My skin is blotchy, and I have bags under my eyes. Ugh. Seriously, emotions can take a freaking hike if this is the end result. I carefully conceal them, but make sure to keep my makeup light and fresh. Closing my waterproof mascara, I give myself one final look in the mirror. Grabbing my ring, I shove it on my finger, hating everything it represents. My Family Necklace, though, I handle with more care, knowing Nonna picked this stone for the crown.

On my way to the door, a picture of Mom and me catches my eye. It was taken last year on our trip to America. We're on the ferry, and you can see the Statue of Liberty behind us. She looks so happy and carefree. I'm so glad we got that time together.

"Mom," I whisper to the picture. "I know you're finally happy… at peace. I *will* keep my promise to you. I'll escape this Family. One day. I'm so sorry I couldn't protect you." I kiss the picture and put it back on my dresser.

Taking a deep breath, I walk to my bedroom door. Pausing with my hand on the knob, I whisper, "Okay, it's time to pull up your big girl panties, Aless. Time to face the day." Opening the door, I'm surprised and relieved to see the hallway is clear. I only have a few moments before facing a million questions, and I can only pray that I'm able to keep it together.

Walking down the stairs, Papa and Uncle Louie's deep voices float up to me. Of course, they're discussing me and my plans for the day.

"I'd like to join you when you visit the families, Lou," Papa says. I pause, waiting outside the room, to see what my uncle has to say about that.

"I know, Al. I told you yesterday I'd talk to Aless. If she wants you to come, you're more than welcome," Uncle Louie answers. I shrug to myself. It doesn't really matter to me, and I guess it would be good for him to come. Taking a deep breath, I decide it's time to make my presence known.

"Good morning, everyone," I say, walking into the dining room. "Is there any food left for me?"

All heads swing to me, and Chef nods with a slight smile. He gets to cracking eggs and whisking them in the small omelet bar he has set up. Luigi and Uncle Louie jump up, coming to my side.

"How are you doing, Little One?" my uncle asks, a soft smile in his eyes.

"Here, Princess, have a seat, and I'll get you whatever you want. Bacon omelet?" Luigi asks on a wink. "By the way, you look beautiful."

"Thank you, Luigi. That's nice of you. And I feel a bit better this morning, Uncle Louie," I say, sitting in the chair Luigi holds out for me. Silly man, trying to take care of me. Luigi swiftly moves his plate and silverware to the seat next to me.

"Luigi, I could have just sat over there," I say as he grabs me a fresh set of utensils.

"No, no," he says, shaking his head. "You belong right there, between your uncle and I... unless the Capo requests something different."

Uncle Louie bends and kisses the top of my head. "You really do look beautiful this morning. Now, what do you want Chef to make for you?"

I give Chef a small smile. "I'd love some scrambled eggs with a bit of cheese. And some toast. And maybe orange juice?" Chef nods, pouring the eggs into the pan.

"Bring some strawberry jam for her toast, Chef," Uncle Louie calls as he regains his seat. Chef winks, acknowledging my uncle's command.

"Thank you," I whisper to Uncle Louie.

"Good morning, Papa," I say, turning to him now that the hoopla that surrounded my arrival has died down. "I hope you slept well."

He nods, smiling. "And you, Princess, how did you sleep? I expected you to sleep until noon after last night."

"I've slept better, but today is a new day, and there's a lot I want to do anyway. I didn't see a reason to stay in bed and stare at the ceiling."

Papa nods, leaning back in his chair with his coffee. He takes a sip, observing me. "You do look nice this morning, daughter. If it's okay with you, I'd like to join you in your visits. I've been informed," he raises his eyebrows and points at Luigi and Uncle

Louie, "by these two, that you must agree to it…even though *I'm* the one who appointed them to be your guards."

I smile, looking between my two heroes. "Thank you, both of you, for being so fiercely protective of me. I really appreciate it. But I'm okay this morning. Yes, I still hurt, but… Mom's at peace and in a better place. I'll love her forever, as well as honor the promise I made to her, but I will persevere. She'd want that for me."

I blink my eyes, making sure no tears form. Chef places a tall glass of freshly squeezed orange juice and a cup of coffee in front of me.

"Thank you, Chef. You know me so well," I say looking up at him. Lifting the juice, I take a big sip, hoping to clear the huge lump that's formed in the back of my throat. The coffee looks perfect, with just the right amount of cream. Chef coated the rim of the cup with extra sweet cocoa, just how I like it. Once I put down my juice, Chef presents my plate of food, which looks amazing as always.

"Let's finish breakfast. We have a busy day ahead of us," Papa instructs.

Surprisingly, I'm really hungry. Thoughts of my Mom pass through my mind. God, I'll never have another breakfast where I see her smiling face. My fork clanks heavily against my plate, and I wonder if I'm really ready to face the Herculean tasks of visiting little Liza today. What about those who lost someone yesterday, like me?

Eventually, the breakfast dishes are cleared, and we sit, drinking our coffees. The men chat, and I try to pay attention, but my mind keeps wandering.

"*Lou! Lou!*" Nonna calls. Her voice is far away and holds a hint of panic. Uncle Louie abandons his seat and rushes out the door.

"*Lou! Little One isn't in her room!*" she cries louder.

"*Calm down, Mama. She came down to breakfast thirty minutes ago. Come see for yourself,*" my uncle says calmly.

Within seconds, she rushes into the dining room, Uncle Louie trailing behind her with an indulgent smile on his face. I giggle at the sight before me. Nonna isn't even dressed, she's still in her robe and slippers.

"Oh, thank God," she mutters, crossing herself. She comes to my side and kisses my forehead. Placing her hands on my face, they tremble slightly as she inspects my eyes.

"You didn't get enough sleep last night. There are bags under your eyes. Are you sure you want to want to go visiting the families today?" she asks with concern.

"Yes Nonna," I nod with a smile. "I got this. I know the next few days will be rough, but we'll get through it together."

"Yes, we will, sweetie," she says, rubbing her thumb along my cheek. "Now, I have to go get ready for the day, too."

Turning, Nonna spears Luigi and Uncle Louie with a look. "I don't want either of you to leave her alone for one second. Do you understand me? Not one second. If someone is near her, you are next to her. If she needs the bathroom, you wait right outside that door until she is done. Do I make myself clear?"

"Yes, ma'am," they answer in unison, nodding.

"Good morning, Mama," my Papa says.

"Good morning, my son," Nonna answers him.

"If you do one thing that upsets my granddaughter in any way, you'll answer to me. Capisce?"

Papa chuckles. "Yes, ma'am," he answers, saluting her.

All three men laugh quietly as Nonna leaves to get dressed.

Our first stop is little Liza's house. I'm a bit nervous, but on the surface, I know I look calm and composed. My stomach is a huge knot, but my hands are as steady as a rock. Papa is by my side as we ring the doorbell, Luigi and Uncle Louie a step behind us.

Elizabeth, Liza's mom, fawns over us, directing us to the living room. She smiles profusely, apologizing for the mess as she scrambles to straighten up.

I stop her, grabbing her hand. "Your house is fine. We came to see Liza, make sure she's okay. Is she awake, or is she still in bed?" I ask on a smile.

I realize, belatedly, that we probably should have called beforehand. It's just after ten in the morning, and they had an eventful day yesterday. However, I didn't want stress Elizabeth out or feel like she had to play hostess and entertain us.

"Oh, no, no. Liza's downstairs, watching a movie with Coco. I'll go get her. The room is small." Elizabeth says.

"Thank you. I promised to check on her yesterday, and I wanted to keep my word," I say, trying to help Elizabeth relax.

She freezes, her eyes filling with tears. "They weren't making it up…" she whispers. "You did take care of my little girl yesterday."

"No ma'am, they didn't make it up," I reply quietly. "We were at the playground when the attack started. Annalisa and my Nonna got the girls into the playhouse and Uncle Louie, and Luigi got the boys into the pirate ship. Lefty had the other girls lay down in the field."

Elizabeth swipes at her eyes. "That was your white scarf? And you told her about you and your uncle being shot? You took the time to check my baby's arm, wrap it and send them to the shelter?"

"I just did what needed to be done," I answer, still whispering.

She rushes to me, enveloping me in a crushing hold. "Bless you, bless you, child," she gasps into my shoulder as she cries. "May God watch over you and bless you all the days of your life. A night will not go by that I don't remember what you did for my precious daughter and pray for your safety and happiness. Thank you so much."

Hesitantly, I hug her back, patting her shoulder. "It was my honor. It really was. Can I see Liza, please?" I ask quietly.

"Oh, yes. Yes, of course. Let me go get her. The doctor came by yesterday and stitched her up and gave me medicine for her."

Elizabeth leaves the room, her steps quick and hurried. "*Liza, Coco!*" she calls as her steps echo on the stairs.

Minutes later, Coco comes in, carrying Liza, who's wearing a huge smile. Coco settles her sister on the couch and sits at her feet. I smile, joining them, kneeling in front of the couch facing Liza.

"How are you feeling, Miss Liza?" I ask, taking

her uninjured hand in mine. Her other arm has a wrap around the upper part.

"I'm better today, Princess," she says shyly. "As long as I don't move my arm too much, I barely even feel it, just like you said."

Smiling, I brush her hair out of her face. "You, little lady, are special to me. I want to give you something very dear to me. My mom gave it to me on my sixth birthday, and now I want to pass it on to you."

Liza's eyes grow wide, and her mother gasps behind me. Reaching into my purse, I pull out a little black jewelry box. Liza watches my every move as I open it. I retrieve the necklace, a small teardrop ruby pendant with a gold bow that hangs from the delicate chain. Opening the clasp, I say "Sit forward for me." Liza does as I ask, and I put it on her little neck.

"My mom gave this to me when I was shot. She said the red teardrop ruby represents the blood I shed for the Family, and the tears I no longer need to shed."

Smiling, I admire the pendant laying against her chest. Liza tenderly lifts it with her tiny fingers and looks down her nose at it. "Your Mama really gave this to you? And you're giving it to me? But... but my Mama told me your Mama died yesterday."

"Yes, my Mama died yesterday," I say sadly. "But I know she would want you to have it, since I can't wear it anymore. I have a new Family necklace that I wear."

She looks at my neck, lightly fingering the large ruby. "Wow," Liza breathes. "That's really big... and really pretty."

"Thank you, Liza," I say, trying to keep the amusement out of my voice. "This necklace will help remind you what a strong young lady you are." Liza straightens on the couch as best she can.

"Look, Mama," she cries, looking over my shoulder. "Look what Princess gave me!"

Elizabeth appears at my side, and I scooch over to make room for her. She bends, looking at the necklace. "Liza dear, this is a very special necklace. You must take very good care of it. It's not a toy, but a real, grown-up necklace. No taking it off unless I help you. We can put it in Mommy's jewelry box to keep it safe when you need to take it off. Okay?"

She claps excitedly. "Yes, Mama. I'll take the bestest care of it! I promise," she says in a sing-song voice.

Standing up, I catch sight of Papa sitting in a wingback chair. He winks, nodding his head in approval.

"Liza, sweetie. I have to leave to see other people who were hurt yesterday. But make sure you do what your mommy says, and take your medicine so you can get all better, okay?"

She nods solemnly and reaches her good arm up to me. I bend down giving her a hug. "I love you, Princess," she whispers in my ear. "I'm sorry you lost your mama yesterday."

Her words strike my heart like a dagger. "Me too, *bambina*, but I'll be okay. Thank you," I choke out around the lump that swiftly appeared in my throat.

Outside on our way to the car, Papa puts his arm around me and kisses the top of my head. "I'm so proud of you, Princess."

"Thanks," I say looking up at him with a small smile. "Mom would be happy that I gave the necklace to Liza. I can picture her smiling down at me right now."

Luigi opens Papa's door for him as Uncle Louie opens mine. "You're right, *Piccola*. Your mom would be so proud of you. Just like Elena would be, as well. I know she's been watching over you since the day you were born. I know they'll both watch over you together."

My eyes sting with tears, but I blink them away. I'm done crying. Nodding, I climb into the SUV and Uncle Louie shuts the door. Luigi turns slightly, looking at me from the driver's seat. "Good job, Aless. You handled that perfectly."

I give him a small smile from my seat beside Papa. Knowing we have a lot of visits to make today, I try to prepare myself for the hardest ones, for the families that lost loved ones in the attack yesterday. It's going to be a long day.

It's dark by the time we finish with the last of the visits. I'm emotionally, physically and mentally drained. Visiting Lefty's mom was the hardest one for me. She managed to gather herself a touch when she opened the door to find us on her porch. Clasped tightly to her chest was a picture frame, probably holding a picture of him. Her eyes were red and never stopped leaking tears.

I sat with her on the couch, hugging her for a good, long time. During our hug, Uncle Louie shared how Lefty was playing with some of the girls, throwing them into the air, when the attack started. I told her that her son protected each and every one of them.

Luigi volunteered stories about how he helped train me.

"We all loved and adored Lefty," I told her. She gifted me with a sad smile that reminded me of my own loss.

"Olivia," Papa said quietly. "Lefty was a valued soldier, protecting not only the Princess at times, but was on my Mama's detail. He made the Family proud. Your son will be honored with a plaque in the Family hall. On his last day, he protected those little girls and fought to save many more. You won't want for anything. The Family will take care of you from this day forward."

Papa sealed his promise with a kiss to each of her cheeks. She seemed to be a little better by the time we left. Luigi and I promised to send her pictures from the first day I officially met Lefty, as well as some from our trip to America, Paris, and Venice. Her eyes grew bright with fresh tears as she thanked me repeatedly. Her gratitude put a lump in my throat, but I managed not to cry… barely.

In comparison, the rest of the visits were a lot easier, though still hard. Mostly, they were thrilled and thankful that we would visit them personally. I sigh in relief as we pull up to the house, knowing the hard part of this long day is over.

Entering the house, I vaguely notice the furniture in the front rooms has been moved, and folding chairs have replaced them. That means there's a Family meeting later. Great, just what I want… to see more people. I can only pray that I won't have to attend, that it'll be a men-only meeting, but I know that wish is futile at this point.

We finally make our way to the dining room, where Nonna and Camilla greet us with warm smiles.

"How are you doing, sweetie? I'm sure it's been a rough day for you. Many have called the house, wanting to thank you for your visits. It meant so much to them that you would do that. You are very, very much loved by the Family," she whispers, enveloping me in a warm hug. She kisses my forehead and then pulls away. "Now, everyone must be hungry. Let's sit down and enjoy a meal together."

Camilla gives me a quick hug, whispering, "Your mom would be so proud of you, *cara*. You're a wonderful, strong young lady, mature beyond your years."

Papa pats my back, "Yes, let's eat our dinner. We have a big night ahead of us, and, if I'm not mistaken, there's something for you to try on after dinner," he says, cocking an eyebrow at Nonna.

She nods but looks like she tasted something sour. "Yes, a young woman," she says with derision, "brought over several outfits for Little One. They're in her room."

My eyes bounce between Nonna and Papa, trying to figure out what the issue Nonna has is. Camilla shakes her head sadly. What is going on? And what young woman would bring me clothes? And from where?

After dinner, Nonna, Camilla and I head up to my room to see these mysterious outfits. Camilla goes straight to my closet and returns, carrying four garment bags. She hangs them from my armoire door and unzips the first one. I'm shocked to see a black shift dress. A pink belt hangs from the hanger, with a bow at the closure. Removing the dress from the bag, Camilla also pulls out a matching blazer and holds it up, spinning it on the hanger. There's a little strap at the small of the back, to make the jacket lay tight against my waist and bum.

"That's a black dress," I say, looking at Nonna. "Not navy... black."

"Yes, sweetie," Nonna laughs. Camilla chuckles into her shoulder. "It's only proper for you to wear black while in mourning. And I think, your father is lightening up on some of his rules for you after this past year. You've long since proven you're no longer a little girl."

"I like it," I say, taking the dress. "How did he find a black dress with a pink belt? Where'd it come from?"

Nonna and Camilla glance at each other. "Well," Nonna says hesitantly. "Your Papa found a new tailor to create your outfits. He didn't think the Family tailor would dress you properly. Let's forget about that and see what else she put together for you."

Camilla opens the next one, revealing another basic, black dress, several belts in different widths and colors, silver, pink, gold along with matching purses and low heels. The next two garment bags contain black suits. One is black slacks and a blazer with a light pink blouse with a thin, feminine neck tie, almost ribbon-like. It looks like a feminine version of the suit the men wear while working for the Family or at meetings. The other is a skirt, with kick pleats at the knee, a flowy, light pink blouse with fuchsia rose buds on it. The jacket has a fuchsia rosebud on the lapel.

"Come on, Little One. Try them on. You need to decide what you want to wear to your mom's services tomorrow," Nonna instructs me.

I quickly try them all on. Whoever made these

outfits for me knows my body really well. They all fit like a dream. I have to meet her one day to thank her personally, because if what Nonna said is true, I'd like to ask her to make me something in denim. I chuckle lightly at the thought.

"What's so funny, Little One?" Nonna asks. "They all fit you perfectly. She does have good taste, I have to admit. I don't think your Papa would refuse anything she designs for you."

"Why is that?" I ask, a little confused. "Have I met her? I thought all the Family tailors were men. It's obvious whoever is designing my clothes is a woman. Who is she?"

Nonna and Camilla give each other another odd look. What is going on? What is it that they're keeping from me?

Nonna changes the subject, none too subtly. "Sweetie, you have some options for tomorrow. You need to decide what you want to wear."

Well, I guess that's that. I won't be getting any information out of them, but I will find out more. Their behavior has aroused my interest.

There's a knock on the door and Uncle Louie saunters in.

"Wow, don't you look nice," he says, his face lighting up. "That's perfect for this evening. I'm here to escort you downstairs."

"Fine, let's get this over with. Do I need to know anything about this meeting?" I ask him.

Uncle Louie shakes his head. "I don't even know what this meeting's about. I'm just as much in the dark as you are."

Nodding in understanding, I link my arm with

his, and we head to the door together. I halt at the door and turn back to Nonna and Camilla.

"Thank you… both of you. Without you, I wouldn't be able to make it through this. I love you both," I say seriously.

Camilla crashes into me, wrapping her arms around me. "You can't say something so sweet without getting a hug," she breathes in my ear. Nonna is right behind her, wrapping her arms around us both. I give them both kisses and turn, again, to go to this meeting with my uncle.

Chapter 13
A NIGHT TO REMEMBER

*T*he deep rumbling sounds of men chatting floats up to us as we descend the stairs. There's got to be a full house. Judging from the number of chairs I saw earlier, I think every able-bodied man in the Family will be here tonight. At the bottom of the stairs, Luigi stops us. He wraps a pink armband around Uncle Louie's arm, then does the same with mine. Looking down, I make out the words "In Loving Memory of Sophia," in a flowing script. I look up to see every single man here wearing the same armband. My chest feels heavy, and I blink to clear the tears forming in my eyes.

The moment we're spotted, it's like a wave. Every man in the rooms falls to one knee and starts rhythmically pounding their right fist over their heart, with their heads bowed. It's like a building crescendo as it gets louder. I gasp almost frozen in surprise, but Uncle Louie pulls on me as we continue our walk to the front of the room where Papa stands waiting. I try to motion the men to stand up, but Papa quickly walks over to me and takes my hand.

"No, Princess," he says quietly. "They do this of their own free will, to show you respect and honor."

As the men continue their rhythmic pounding beat as I look over to see, even Lorenzo and Vito are on bended knee as well. Papa takes my hand, linking our arms together. As he leads me to the raised platform, the men pound harder and harder on their chests, the thuds echoing through the room.

Vito stands, grabbing me into a tight hug. He squeezes me so tight, it makes it hard to breathe. This is so out of character for the usually stoic man. His breath stutters and a tremor wracks his body. Is he crying? I hug him back tightly, shock riding me hard.

"I owe you my life," he says quietly in a shaky voice. "You saved my whole family yesterday. Gwen told me what happened, how you protected her and got her to safety. I'm so sorry you lost your mom and had to witness that. Thank you for saving my wife. You were so brave and courageous to continue as you did yesterday. Annalisa told me about the playground, about how you told her to get to safety and how you gave her the strength to get those kids underground." He pulls away, tears glistening in his eyes. "And you saved my son, killing those two men with only a knife. I know he mentioned it in the SUV yesterday, but it didn't sink in until we came together as a family and recounted what happened. Thank you so much, Alessandra, my Princess."

He closes his eyes and takes a deep breath, probably trying to compose himself. I try to say something, but he speaks again. "You made Antonio go help the others instead of going with you. You are, by far, the strongest woman I've ever known. I am forever in your debt."

Then he drops back down to his knee, taking my free hand and kisses it before returning to the pounding over his heart in unison with the other men. We step up on the platform and make our way to the chairs and stand before them. The men continue kneeling, still pounding their fists in unison, over and over. The sound is like a war drum, thundering through the room. Feeling a tad uncomfortable, I shift on my feet.

"When will they stop?" I whisper to Papa.

"When they are ready," Papa says proudly, his head held high.

The pounding stops seconds later, and again, as one, they lift their heads and lock eyes on me. "I pledge," someone calls out.

Uncle Louie and Luigi both drop to a knee beside me. My eyes fly from them to Papa. He nods and takes my right hand in both of his and places it over his heart. Papa's eyes water as he watches me.

"*I swear*," Papa starts, and all the men join him in unison, "*this pledge with my heart and soul, to you and this Family. I vow to always listen to your guidance and follow the rules with my life. I will shield and protect it and shed my life's blood for it. Nothing and no one will come between this Family and my pledge of devotion to it. Nothing, but death, will take me away from it.*"

My eyes survey the room, the men kneeling before me and pledging their lives to me. My mind races. How will these men feel when I make my escape? How will they react? My stomach flips, twisting into knots as I fight tears of my own.

The men finish their pledge simply by standing and dropping their hand to their side. I'm overwhelmed by the devotion and love illuminating from them. Feeling the need to say something, I pull my hand back from Papa's hold and square my shoulders.

Looking over all the men standing before me, I pledge, "*You are Family, with our strength, pride, and power. There is nothing and no one that will take you from this Family, but death. This Family is your Family. We devote ourselves to each other, to guard and protect each other with our lives.*"

Papa nods in approval and turns to the men. "Let the meeting begin," he says loudly.

Papa walks me to my chair. I sit as Luigi and Uncle Louie take their spots on either side of me. As soon as I'm seated, the men follow suit and take their seats. Papa takes his seat next to me, and Vito nudges him. He turns to Vito, and they talk in hushed tones.

My thoughts turn back to my pledge. Thankfully no one picked up that I said, "We devote ourselves to each other…" and not to the Family. I just can't bring myself to devote myself to the Family… and I certainly won't pledge my life to it.

In the front row, Antonio and Stephen watch me. Stephen gifts me a chin lift, and Antonio winks at me. This one is warm and lacks his usual flirtation. I smile in return, feeling slightly more relaxed.

As I wait for Papa to begin the meeting, my thoughts turn to Mom's service tomorrow and my promise to her. I have to come up with a foolproof plan to escape. Can I make my dreams come true? Can I find true love? How can I ever leave Nonna and Uncle Louie? Would they be willing to escape with me? God, I need to clear my head. I need my studio, I need to dance and get lost in the music. Maybe later, when the men are smoking and drinking, catching up with each other, I can retreat there without anyone noticing.

Papa stands, breaking me from my thoughts. "I want to thank each and every one of you for the respect and honor you have shown our Princess tonight. I request that you wear these armbands in memory of my late wife, the mother of my daughter and heir, until after the burial tomorrow. Her services will be held at Saint Barbara's, followed by her internment in the Family mausoleum here, and a dinner.

"This week will be tough on all of us but, as a Family, we will come out of these trials stronger. Our Princess, as you know, finally put an end to the Caza Family by delivering retribution on their Capo. She was heroic during the attack, took charge and gave orders. She saved many through her bravery. She showed no fear and didn't hesitate to kill those that got in the way of protecting the Family. Her only goal was to save as many as possible and put an end to this war with the Caza Family.

"Last night, after hearing her story, I realized my little girl is no longer a child. She will no longer be treated as one, either. Not by me, nor anyone. She has proven herself, has proven she deserves the respect and honors due to her. She has shown everyone that she is strong, intelligent, and brave and more than capable to lead."

The men stand, applauding loudly. A few call out in appreciation. My cheeks heat with a blush as I smile and nod. Papa turns, gifting me a warm smile and I give him one right back. He shifts his attention back to the men and continues.

"We no longer have to be worried about attacks from the Caza Family. Young Peter, Pietro's son, called me early this morning. While he's only sixteen, he's a real man. He apologized for his father and his Family's attacks on us. Pietro, he said, was a 'much-hated Capo,' adding the he and his mother both despised him. Peter told me of the promise he made to our Princess yesterday and that he plans on keeping it. He assured me our war is over. He, and the few men who abandoned Pietro are going to try to rebuild their Family. There are several women who were widowed and children who are fatherless that need to be taken care of. We will not abandon those women who were widowed by a fool's war or the children.

"The Caza Family does not have much power now. Pietro hated me and was determined to eliminate me for not marrying Olga. He wrongly placed that hatred on Sophia and Alessandra. Pietro Jr. assured me that his Family will be respectful and not cause any further problems for our Family. Those who do will be taken care of severely. Peter asked I convey his thanks to the Princess for giving them a fresh start.

"He is a smart man and is aware of how things work. He knows that his Family's holdings and businesses now belong to us. He has no blood relatives except his mother and two sisters. The men that are left work for us now, and they understand that. If they can't accept my rule, you men know what to do. It will take time to weed through the few remaining men. We must do our best to make this work. I will be assigning people to see to the merging of our Families and merging the Caza business ventures into ours. I will keep a close eye on these changes and make sure it's what is best for the Family.

"During this transition, I ask that you keep your eyes and ears open. If you have any suspicions about any of the Caza men, please let me know immediately. Thank you for all of your support and faith in me during these trying years. We owe this victory to our Princess. In the months to come, this will be very beneficial to us all."

The men applaud again, whispering amongst themselves, but Papa holds his hand up. "We still have other enemies, but nothing to be concerned with for now. The story of our Princess shutting down the attacks yesterday has spread. Your skills, and the Princess's have put real fear in them of retribution from us. However, I want everyone to keep the thought of future attacks in mind as we move forward. But, tomorrow is a new day and next week will be a new beginning for all of us."

Papa approaches me, placing his hand on my shoulder. "You will be the talk of all the Families for a while. But university is in your future, sooner than I'd like. We'll talk about that after you've had some time to grieve and heal. You've been trained to protect yourself and the Family, but you also need a business education. You are the future of this Family. I've never been prouder to call you my daughter. Thank you, from all of us, for what you did yesterday." He

163

kisses my forehead, then turns to the men.

"Men, feel free to stay and chat as long as you'd like. Chef made some appetizers and, as always, the bar is open. Remember, the second floor is off limits. I will either be here or in my office to discuss anything that can't wait until Monday afternoon."

The hum of conversation fills my ears as I stand. Uncle Louie puts his arm around me and whispers in my ear, "I'm going to chat with a few of the men. If you need me, don't hesitate to interrupt. I'm here for you first, Little One... whatever you need."

Throwing my arms around his neck, I hold him tight and breathe in his scent. "I know," I whisper. "I love you more than life itself. I wouldn't be able to deal with *any* of this without you. Go and visit. Do some back pounding, belching, crotch scratching, general guy bonding. I'll be okay, promise."

With my arms still around his neck, he wraps an arm around my waist and stands, lifting me from my feet. He gives me a gentle shake as I giggle into his neck, feeling safe. Setting me back on my feet, he pulls back and tweaks my nose. "I'll check on you later, Little One. If it gets too much, head upstairs. It's off limits so you can escape." He winks and walks away, heading toward Lorenzo.

Exhaling, I let out a deep breath and scan the crowd of men milling around. There are a several men lingering near me, casting glances my way. They're probably waiting to talk to me. Ugh.

"If at any moment you want to escape, just elbow me," Luigi whispers in my ear, startling me. "I won't leave your side for a second, okay?"

"Thank you," I mumble under my breath. Shoring myself up, I take a step toward the men waiting for my time. Man after man thanks me, some praising me, some asking me to join them at the shooting range. Luigi always answers the request with a firm, "No, not allowed. She trains here at the compound." Thank God. I don't want to train these men. They need to learn to practice on their own.

Throughout the entire hour and a half of men wanting my attention, Luigi sticks to my side like glue. I'm thankful he's there. Some of them try to flirt with me, to which he would shift slightly, turning me to the next man. I mentally noted which ones seemed to truly appreciate me and which ones appreciated my body. Stephen and Antonio posted themselves on either side of Luigi and I, giving us space.

"Okay," Antonio says loudly, "let's give the Princess a break. She's been talking with you for a while now, without anything to drink or eat. None of you have even offered her refreshments. Let's give her a second."

"You just want her to yourself," someone jeers, causing the rest to laugh at him.

"Princess, can I get you some wine?" another calls.

"Let me grab you something to eat!" yet another volunteers from the back of the crowd.

Laughing, I hold my hands up, quieting them. "Thank you for the offer, but right now I really do need a break. I also need to discuss tomorrow's plans with Luigi."

Placing his hand on my lower back, Luigi steers me away from my admirers. They nod as we pass, some brushing their hands on my arms. There were quite a few winks and coy smiles from the younger men. I swear I hear Antonio growl behind me.

Arriving in the study, Luigi requests that the few men in their leave to give us the room, and their

Princess, some privacy. They clear out, giving me respectful head nods. Luigi closes the door behind the last man and leans his back against it.

"Well, Princess," he says with a smile, "I think your Papa is going to have quite a few men requesting to be added to that secret list of his." He laughs hard.

"Hey!" I exclaim, swatting his arm. "That's not funny! Why would you say something like that?"

He tries to catch his breath and wipes his eyes. "Come on. You have to know that Antonio was ready to explode out there. He does not like competition when it comes to you. You were out there, all innocent," he cocks his head and blinks wide eyes, trying to mimic me, "just answering their questions, quietly thanking them with your gorgeous smile. It's why I didn't stop it, even though I knew you were tired. I wanted to see how long it would take him to break. He was beet red. Fuck, I'm shocked he didn't pee on your leg to mark you as his!" He trails off, laughing again.

"Luigi!" I gasp, swatting at him again. "Are you kidding me right now? Most of those men are your age and older! They were just being nice. They were *not* flirting with me. And they certainly don't want to be on Papa's stupid list," I declare, crossing my arms over my chest.

"Please," he says, rolling his eyes. "You've seen how many men have younger wives… much younger. They know that in four years your papa will be picking your husband. They're going out of their way to be noticed by you."

Panic grips me, and I blink hard, taking a deep breath. Letting it out slowly, I whisper, "Luigi… that can't happen. I won't be married off to some guy I don't even know and have zero chemistry with…" Looking into his eyes, I plead with him, "I can't."

"Hey, hey," he says, sobering. He grabs my shoulders and holds my gaze. "Take another breath. I'm just teasing you. Sure, some of those men are interested in you. Just be aware that they might have ulterior motives when they say those nice things or do something for you, especially if they want to hang out. You need to be aware of that. I'll always watch out for you, but you need to help me out. Hell, your uncle and I have already had to put some men in their place. I'm sure there will be more as you get older."

His hand drifts to my cheek, where he strokes his thumb across it. "There's nothing to worry about until you graduate. We'll figure this out. I'll never let your life be that miserable. I won't allow you to be stuck with someone who isn't right for you. Lou won't either. Okay?"

I nod, then face plant into his chest. Luigi wraps me in his arms as mine wind around his waist. "I believe you," I say into his chest. Straightening, I announce, "Okay, let's get back out there. I'll make my excuses, and then you can have some guy time too."

He smiles, leading me back to the door. Pausing, he gives me a wink. "Aless, I wouldn't have missed this for anything. It was way more entertaining than belching and crotch scratching!"

He bursts into laughter as he opens the door. Antonio and Stephen are leaning against the wall across the hall, and Luigi laughs harder. I elbow him, shoving him aside. Before I can say anything, Antonio wraps his arm around me and hugs me tight. He quickly releases me, and his hand finds my jaw. Tilting my head, he looks deep into my eyes.

"Are you okay, Aless?" he asks softly. "Really okay? A lot has happened in the last two days. I need to know you're okay."

I smile while Luigi snorts quietly behind me. "Yes, Antonio. It's been hard, but I'll be okay. Mom's in a better place. I'm comforted by the thought that she's with Elena and my brother, that she's relieved, happy and at peace now. I know she's watching over me."

"Alright, Romeo," Stephen interjects, bumping Antonio out of the way. He wraps me in his arms, just like Antonio did. "If you need anything, anytime... day or night, I'm here for you." His words don't feel like a come on. His voice lacks the feel of lust and desire that I get from most of the men. Seems he really sees me as a friend. I return his hug tightly.

"Thanks, guys," I say, stepping away from Stephen. "You're both amazing friends."

They both smile warmly at me. "I need a break from the testosterone show, so I'm gonna head upstairs. Thanks for helping tonight."

"We'll see you tomorrow," Antonio says.

Luigi again places his hand on my lower back and steers me to the stairs for my escape. At the top of the stairs, Luigi stops me and turns me to face him. Caressing my cheek again, he softly asks, "You know I'm only a call away too, right? Besides, I can get to you faster than they can. If you need anything, including cake and ice cream, I'm your man."

Giggling in response, I answer him. "Luigi, I know that and have already gotten you to bring me cake and ice cream. FYI, you'd be the one I'd call before them." I flash him a wink and kiss his cheek before turning and continuing down the hall to my room.

Finally, in the peace of my room, I change into my workout clothes. The night flashes through my mind when I freeze in my motion of pulling on yoga pants. OMG! Did I kiss Luigi on the cheek? What was I thinking? Oh well, I shrug. I mean, I did ask him to rescue me if Papa chooses Antonio for me to marry. God, knowing that there are more men clambering to be added to the list gives me the chills and not the good kind. I have four years, *four freaking years*, to get it together and plan an escape. University will be good, it'll be far away from here. Maybe I'll be able to use a degree when I do get out of this life.

Now that I've earned the Family's respect, maybe I'll have a little more freedom. Maybe they won't be watching me twenty-four seven. Maybe, just maybe, I'll be able to research and plan a safe escape, maybe figure out a way to get Nonna and Uncle Louie to join me. Sure, we'll probably live the rest of our lives on the run, but maybe they'll have some ideas, so we can figure something out later. Right now though, I need to clear my head. Getting lost in music and dancing is just what I need.

Knowing I'll never be able to sneak out the back door to my studio, I make my way to Uncle Louie's room and his hidden door that leads to the secret passageway that exits to the side of the house by the bushes. If I'm quick enough, I'll be in my studio before anyone spots me. I know my uncle won't be too happy if he finds out I used his exit, but only close trusted Family members know about our hidden passageways. He showed me just in case the house was ever attacked, and I needed to escape.

But tonight, tonight I need this break… time to myself, an escape from my thoughts. He'll get over it. I'll tell him when I get back. Anyway, I'll be safe in my studio because only Papa, Luigi, Uncle Louie and I have the alarm code. Reaching the exit, I peer out over the lawn. Seeing no one, I dash across the lawn to my sanctuary.

Chapter 14
MEETING THE OTHER WOMAN

*I*n my studio, a weight lifts off my chest, and I can finally breathe fully. I only turn on the small lights in the corner near the stage, leaving off the main lights, so the patrolling guards don't spot me. I turn to the sound system and hook up my iPod. Making sure the volume is down, I select my Gymnastics Playlist and hit play. I start by stretching but quickly move onto bridges which lead into back handsprings. Feeling limber, I move to my trampoline. I want to feel free for a change, so I just jump. Trying to get as high as possible, I bend my knees when my feet reach the trampoline and push up hard. Flying through the air is freeing. Mixing it up, I throw in a few flips, feeling the last of my stress flow from my body.

Feeling good, I stop jumping and change my music. Katy Perry's "Firework" flows through the surround sound speakers. I run to the stage, leaping to the first pole. Using my momentum, I swing from pole to pole then climb to the top of the last one. From the top, I descend the pole in a controlled fall, twisting and flipping down it.

Totally loose, I mix in some dance and gymnastics moves, making my solo performance a tad risqué. This is just what I needed. I giggle quietly, singing along to my music. Recalling what I saw that stripper do for Papa, I try some of her moves, but I'm sure I don't look as good as she did. Before the last chorus of the song, I leap from the pole, reaching for my aerial silks. Climbing the fabric, I wrap myself and spin carefully to loop the fabric around my arms and legs. As the chorus starts, I let go, falling and twirling. My feet hit the floor with a soft thud as the final notes drift thru the air.

Breathing heavily, I stand for a minute to control my pulse and blood pressure. God, that feels good. A thump from the back of the studio has me jumping off the stage and reaching for a bo staff. With the oak rod in my hands, I call out, "Who's there? I heard you back there. Come out and show yourself. I've killed enough people this week, and I'd rather not add to that number."

The back door opens, and a very nervous woman walks in carrying some garment bags folded over her arm.

"Well, well... looks like Papa gave you the alarm code to my studio. Are you here to deliver more clothes for me?"

She doesn't say anything, just nervously shuffles her feet.

"Are you the one who's been doing all the shopping for him - or rather, for me?"

Still frozen, she blinks rapidly, her eyes darting around the room.

"I'm not going to kill you," I continue. "Yet, at least. I didn't know who was there, or if you were a rival Family. I've had a bit of a rough few days," I finish, glancing at the floor.

The woman lets out a breath, nodding. "I know," she whispers. "I'm so sorry. I didn't know anyone would be in here, but I saw you through the window. I was curious and wanted to watch you. I've heard so much about you for so long, I wanted to see for myself. You're really great. In fact, I've never seen anything like the moves you did."

I realize I'm still holding the stick defensively, so I set the end on the floor and tap it to the rhythm of the music quietly playing.

"Thank you," I nod. "Now, will you answer my other questions?"

"Yeah," she smiles. "But, your father is going to be really angry when he finds out."

"He doesn't need to know," I answer quickly.

"Okay," she answers. "No, I don't do shopping for you, I make your clothes. I'm a seamstress."

"And a stripper," I interrupt her.

Her eyes bulge on a gasp. "Well," I shrug. "You're not the only one who gets curious. A few months ago, I snuck out here because I forgot my book. I heard music and peeked in the window, and saw you dancing for my father... and what happened after. Don't worry. I didn't tell anyone. When I realized what was going on, I left."

The shock of what I just said is clear on her face. I want to laugh, but I hold it back. "How long have you been having sex with my Papa?" I ask her.

She shakes her head, looking at her feet. I know I'm being hard on her, but I need answers. Taking a deep breath, she lifts her eyes to mine. "I'm sorry you had to find out that way. I had no idea anyone could see us in here. He'd usually tell Lou to make sure you don't come out when I'm here."

"Wow," I whisper on a chuckle. "So, Uncle Louie knows about you... WOW," I breathe.

"Yeah, I've met him a few times. I'm not a stripper, though. I only did that for a short time," she says softly.

"So, you make my clothes?" I ask, changing the subject. "I like them, thank you. Do you make and design all of them?"

"I've been making them since your first formal Family Meeting."

I chuckle as she continues. "I'm so glad you like my work. Making and designing clothes is what I do now. I have a little shop in town, thanks to your Papa." She extends her hand. "I'm Laura by the way. It's nice to meet you, awkward as it is."

God, I cannot believe I'm standing here talking to Papa's ex-stripper mistress. It's obvious she's scared of me. That's probably a good thing to keep in mind, in case I need to use it later. Papa's told her about me, certainly. Hmm, I need to get information that he'd never tell me.

I take her hand and shake it. "Hello, Laura. It's obvious you know who I am, so I'll just skip that part. How long have you been my father's mistress? I'm assuming you're exclusive with him, and no one else."

Her eyes snap to mine as a firm look crosses her face. I can respect that. "Yes, your Papa and I are exclusive. I've been with him for a little over four years. We're very close and in love. He tells me everything, we talk a lot. I'm very sorry about your mother. Al really did love her. I know all about her depression, and the breakdown she never fully recovered from. He felt he lost her, that she wasn't the same person he fell in love with, but he never stopped loving her."

Crap, Papa loves this woman? I never thought it could be that intimate of a relationship. She does know the code to my studio. That rankles me more than I'd like to admit. Feeling bitter, I question her further, "So, even though you were fully aware of my mother and her illness, as well as knowing all about me, you still slept with my father?"

"We were friends at first," she says softly. "I was a waitress at one of the clubs. Al asked for me to dance for him, even though I'd stopped doing that. I agreed, and we got to know each other. He opened up to me, sharing the struggles with your Mom. He was so kind to me, so sweet. One thing led to another, and, well, we've been sleeping together ever since."

She pauses, weighing her thoughts. The next words out of her mouth blow my mind. "I do love him. He thinks he's in love with both me and your mom. At first, he felt guilty for loving me, but he knew your mom would never really get better, be the woman he fell in love with. I'm so sorry. I really am, but I wouldn't change it. We both come from similar lives."

Rendered mute by her admission, I nod to acknowledge her words, but wonder how their lives are similar. Now it's question time. "How old are you?" I finally ask after a few minutes of silence.

Laura blushes. "I'll be thirty in two months."

"You do know how old he is, don't you?" I ask, taken aback by her age.

"Yes," she laughs lightly. "I know he's a lot older than me. But that's okay. I don't see age, and neither does he."

"Well, isn't that nice," I observe sarcastically, "that yet again, *he* can fall in love with someone outside the Family... but *he* demands that I accept whomever he picks and arranges for me. What a freaking double standard! Ugh. He's such a jerk."

"He is that," Laura chuckles. "We've talked about that, too. I gave him my opinion once, and he shut me down. I'm not allowed to discuss that topic with him again. I do agree with you. He shouldn't force you into an arranged, loveless marriage. But you know your father, he won't listen to anyone once he's made up his mind. I wish I could help you."

"So, umm," I start hesitantly, looking at my feet. "Does that mean, uhh, you and Papa will be getting married? Now that mom's been murdered?"

"Oh," she breathes softly. "We never talked about that. There was no way he knew your mom would be murdered. I knew going in that he would never divorce her. I was okay with that, okay with what we had. Marriage is a subject we never really talked about."

Looking back up at her, I ask, "Do you love him enough that if he asked, you'd marry him? Or are you just using him for his money?" I stop, letting my eyes wander her form. "Where are you from? America? You have an accent. And if you do marry him, do you know what you're getting yourself into? What's the American equivalent? Ah, he's the Godfather… controls a crime Family."

"Wow," she says, her eyes wide, "You don't beat around the bush, do you? And yes, I'm fully aware of what your father does. Yes, I'm from America, New York to be exact. The reason I don't have a problem with your Family is that I escaped mine in coming here. They had a falling out with another Family, and everyone was getting killed. I knew it was time to leave if I wanted to continue breathing. Now you understand our similarities, but you have a way more powerful Family then I came from, but that's a story for another day."

Laura takes a breath and looks down like she's trying to compose herself. I'm sure she's shocked at how much she's shared with me already. I watch her, waiting for her to continue.

"Alessandra, I know about your training and how good you are. Thank you for saving your Papa's life that day at the shooting range. You were really upset with him, yet you saved him." Her smile is knowing.

"Yes, he told me about that, too. I hope you still aren't thinking of killing me for sleeping with your father."

"Oh, Laura," I laugh bitterly, "if I'd wanted you dead, you already would be. I would have killed you months ago."

She gasps, but quickly gets the joke and we both laugh. "But, I'm not going to kill you. I couldn't do that to Papa, if, as you say, he loves you."

"Thank you. I'm so sorry you had to watch your mother murdered in front of you. If there's anything, I can do…"

Holding up a hand, I stop her. "Don't. It's okay. She suffered for over twenty years. I realize she's in a better place. She's with her sister and my brother, she's at peace. I'm dealing with it. Thank you, though."

Taking the stick, I put it back in its slot on the wall. "You might want to put those clothes in Papa's office. Then we can keep up the farce, and he can give them to Nonna and Camilla tomorrow to give to me."

"Yeah," she agrees. "I'll go put these away. I was supposed to text him when I got here."

I laugh, waving a hand. "Don't worry, I'm leaving. I've got to figure a way back into the house without being seen. One more question… does Nonna or Camilla know about you? Or am I the only one in the dark? Well, other than Mom."

She pauses on her way to the office and turns to look at me. "I've met your Nonna a couple of times. She's smart and put two and two together. Al got a long lecture from her. Camilla, well, she flat out refuses to acknowledge my existence."

"Can you blame them?" I ask. "You are the 'other woman.'"

"Yeah," she smiles, "you're right. But I'm nice to them when I do see them. I only see them when I'm dropping off clothes. But I think Al's mom saw me kiss him goodbye one day and she told Camilla. I've only seen her a few times in these past four years."

"Well, it was nice meeting you, Laura. I'm going to head back to the house. Thank you for being honest with me and telling me the truth."

She smiles warmly. "I'm glad we finally met. Maybe in time, your father will feel it's okay for us to formally meet. I know he's not ready for everyone to know about me, and I won't push him. He's mourning your mother and, believe it or not, he's having a rough time. I'd appreciate it if you didn't mention this to him."

She continues to Papa's office, and I call, "Bye, Laura." I sprint from my studio. Once outside, I hide in the shadows of the building and take a deep breath to collect myself. In a window of the house, I spot Uncle Louie drinking a beer, still talking to Luigi, Lorenzo, and Papa. I scan the yard. It's clear, so I make a mad dash, keeping low. I sneak back into Uncle Louie's secret exit, confident he'll never know I left.

Back in my room, I take a quick shower and climb into bed, praying no one checked on me while I was gone. Once I calm myself, I realize no one did, otherwise they would have raised the alarm. Lying here cuddling Fluffy, I think about all I learned tonight. Would Papa actually marry Laura one day? She seems nice enough. Maybe they could have another child or two… take the pressure off of me. That would be so helpful. I need that to happen, within the next four years preferably. Might have to sneak into their room and poke holes in Papa's condoms… hiding my face in Fluffy, I giggle uncontrollably. That would be perfect!

Footsteps in the hall silence my giggles. There's a soft tap on my door as it opens and light spills in from the hallway. I close my eyes and lay still, breathing evenly. Uncles Louie's steps come closer as he walks to my bed. Brushing the hair off my face, he kisses my forehead. He tucks the covers around me.

"Love you, Little One," he whispers. "Always will. I promised your mom I'd make sure you're happy and we'll figure this out." He kisses me again, resting his hand on my cheek. He pulls away, and I listen to his footsteps as they get quieter. Finally, he closes my door.

"Love you too, Uncle Louie," I whisper to the closed door. He's my world. But he's right. We have four years to figure this out. I know I can depend on him to help me. Now I just have to make it through the next few days. Once these armbands come off after the burial on Sunday, I'll be able to move on, to heal.

I just wish everyone would stop asking me every two seconds if I'm okay, and stop looking at me with sad eyes. That's one of the hardest parts of all this. If everyone would just act like things are normal, that would help me. I need to start planning for university… and my escape from this tragic life.

Chapter 15

BREAKFAST

I couldn't sleep last night. I tossed and turned, snuggling with Fluffy, trying to find sleep. I even tried thinking of Grayson, for the first time in forever, hoping that would lull me into a restful, happy sleep. It didn't work, though. It made my chest hurt for a completely different reason.

Around six in the morning, I gave up. Taking a long, hot shower released some of the tension from my shoulders. Applying my makeup, I use waterproof mascara and forego eyeliner on my lower eyelid… just in case I cry today. God, I hope I rid myself of all my tears during my meltdown two days ago. Better to be safe than sorry, though, and not be a black-eyed mess later.

I pull on the black shift dress and matching jacket that Laura made me. The pink belt and matching shoes are the perfect nod to Mom. I have to admit, Papa's mistress has skills. I love her style and the options she gave me.

By seven, I'm ready and pacing my room. Huh, I've picked up Uncle Louie's habit of pacing to calm myself. I chuckle to myself and grab my iPhone to check the Facebook no one knows I have. There's nothing of interest, so I delete the browser history and grab my book. Maybe a few chapters of my favorite day-walking vampires will help calm me.

A knock on my door startles me out of my fantasyland of hot vampires willing to do anything to keep their mates happy. I check the clock, noticing I've gotten lost, once again, in the fictional world of my book. Since it's later, no one would worry if I showed up for breakfast now. Knowing it's not Uncle

Louie, I get up and open the door.

Luigi stands there, wearing his signature smirk. "Good morning, Princess. I thought you'd be up. May I come in?"

Opening the door fully, I gesture him to come in. "Sure, come on in." He hands me a small gift bag with pink tissue paper sticking out of it.

"What's this?" I ask, taking it from him.

"It's nothing much, just thought you'd like it, especially today," he answers quietly.

Pulling the tissue from the bag, I giggle, pulling out a silver box with a red square in the center and white letters running through it.

I smile up at him. "Oh, Luigi! I love you! These are perfect! Now I won't feel left out when I'm with you guys."

Uncle Louie pokes his head in my room. "Excuse me. Am I hearing things? Did you just admit to being in love with Luigi? If that's true…"

I swat his arm, laughing. "No, Uncle Louie, look!" I shout, showing him the box. I carefully tear open the box to reveal an ivory case engraved with my name. I open the snap and reveal a pair of family issued tortoiseshell Wayfarer Ray-Ban sunglasses.

"Luigi!" I exclaim, throwing my arms around his neck. "They'll help so much today. Thank you so much."

"Knowing how much Al doesn't like you in black, I thought the tortoiseshell would appease him. We use them, so people can't get a read on us. They're custom ordered, with lenses darker than the ones in the store."

Putting them on, I check them out in the mirror. "Well," I call over my shoulder, "do I look as cool as you guys do?"

A huge smile breaks out across Uncle Louie's face. He slings an arm around my shoulders, saying softly, "Yes, you look just as mysterious, but more beautiful. I'm a bit let down, though, that you weren't serious about your declaration of love to Luigi…"

"Knock it off," I whine, shoving his hand off my shoulder. "Let's go downstairs and have breakfast."

They nod as I head for the door. Uncle Louie catches up to me and tucks me against his side. "I'm guessing you didn't get much sleep last night, what with you being up and ready to go this early."

"Yeah," I nod. "I tossed and turned all night, but I did get a few hours of sleep. I can't wait until Monday, so everyone can stop walking on eggshells around me."

Downstairs, we head to the dining room, where the sounds of people eating and chatting quietly come from.

As we enter, Nonna pushes up from her seat and rushes to me. Her arms wrap around me, squeezing tight. She steps back, grabbing my hands and holding them in her warm ones as her eyes travel my outfit.

"You look good… I mean, you look beautiful. The dress fits you perfectly."

"Thank you, Nonna," I smile, kissing her cheek. "I'm so glad you approve. I love the way it fits. The jacket is perfect, too."

"How are you feeling this morning?" she asks, tilting her head and watching my face. "Did you sleep well?"

"I'll be fine, Nonna. I just need to make it through Monday, okay?" I whisper, reaching out to hug her again.

Turning away from her, I head to Chef's table in the corner to request my favorite breakfast. It's quiet, and I feel eyes follow me as I move through the room. Taking a deep breath, I turn to face them.

"Look, I know you're all worried about me. I'm fine. I got a couple hours of sleep last night. Let's just eat and get through today."

God, I hope that stops them from asking how I am. I'm so tired of everyone looking at me with sympathy, like I'm fragile... like I'm going to break down again. I'm not. I'm strong, and I'll figure out some way to get through this *and* control my emotions. At least I hope so.

"Hiya, Chef. I'd love some of your amazing French toast. You know how I like them," I finish on a wink.

He smiles warmly. "Covered in lots of butter and powdered sugar. Coming right up, Princess."

Taking my seat, I ask Papa, "How are you today? Did you sleep well?"

At the question, the memory of meeting Laura last night flashes through my mind. Huh... did Papa spend last night in my studio? Did he have sex with her there last night? Or does he sneak her into his room here? My mind is a flurry of questions and thoughts. I wish I could shut it off!

"Are you okay, Alessandra?" he asks, patting my arm. Crud, I missed his answer.

"Yeah, sorry. I'm fine. My mind is elsewhere today. What were you saying?" I ask on a small smile. His lips tip up into a smile of his own, something he doesn't do often.

"Eat up, Princess. We have a big day ahead of us. Family will be arriving soon," he says with a wink as Chef sets my breakfast in front of me.

The clicking of silverware and the tinkling of cups and saucers fills the room as everyone focuses of fueling their bodies for the long day ahead. Not liking the silence as my thoughts gear up into race mode again, I try to fill the quiet void. There is no way I was going just to sit here and let everyone think they had to handle me with kid gloves, afraid to talk. I look over to Luigi and smile big, and wink at him. As he takes a drink from his orange juice, he wrinkles his brow at me. I'm sure he is wondering what I was up to.

"Papa," I ask, dragging a bite of French toast through the powdered sugar on my plate, "when will I meet the lady who makes my clothes? I love them and would love to thank her personally, maybe even collaborate."

Luigi coughs, pounding his chest. Camilla tries to cover her smile with her napkin. Nonna's head turns to Papa, and she cocks an eyebrow. Uncle Louie blinks rapidly and takes a long, long sip of his coffee. Oh yeah, everyone here knows about Papa's *big secret*.

Watching his face, I try to look innocent, with true intentions. He clears his throat, placing his napkin beside his coffee cup.

"Well, eh, Princess... I'll, umm, see what I can, uh, do about that."

From the corner of my eye, Luigi shakes his head, still trying to catch his breath.

"Why can't I meet her, Papa? Does she have a local shop? Maybe Uncle Louie and Luigi can bring me there next week. How did you meet her? Is she a member of the Family?"

Papa's nervous. His forehead glistens with sweat in the light from the chandelier. He might even be blushing. "Umm, I met her, uh, when Lou and I were out at, uh, dinner one night?" It almost sounds like a question. This is fun. "Right, Lou?" he asks in a firm voice.

Uncle Louie coughs and looks at me with big eyes. He nods, "Yeah, we, uh, we met her at dinner about four, maybe five years ago."

"Right… dinner," Nonna mumbles into her coffee cup.

"Did you say something, Nonna?" I ask innocently, giving her my attention. I heard her just fine. From the corner of my eye, Papa gives her a glare. I take a deep breath, trying to maintain my composure and not crack up. I'm enjoying putting Papa in the hot seat.

"What's her name?" I ask, putting the last bite of delicious French toast into my mouth.

Papa lifts his coffee cup to his mouth, mumbling into it, "It's uh… Laura, I think."

"Papa," I say, lightly laughing. "This woman's been making my clothes for almost a year now, and you *think* her name is Laura?" Shaking my head, I ask, "Did Mom know her?"

Nonna coughs, setting her cup down harshly on the table. "Are you okay, Nonna?" I ask, concern heavy in my voice. "Do you need some water?"

"No, sweetheart," she waves a hand, "I'll be fine. Thank you. The coffee just went down the wrong pipe."

Papa clears his throat. "Her name *is* Laura, and she does have a shop in town. I'm sure Lou and Luigi can take you sometime next week. Right, Lou?" he asks, raising an eyebrow at my uncle.

"Why sure, Princess, Luigi and I would *love* to take you over there next week." Uncle Louie says sarcastically.

"I can't wait," I beam at him. "Thank you."

Nonna stands, stopping my fun. "Well, let's finish our coffee in the sitting room. Company will be here soon, and I want the dining room cleared and cleaned before they arrive."

"Good idea, Mama," Papa says, looking relieved as he finds his feet. "I have to make a few calls first, but I'll join you there shortly. Promise," he says turning to me, "I'll be right back."

Standing, I nod. "Okay. I'll put on some soft music in the sitting room then."

"That's perfect, sweetheart," Papa says, kissing my forehead as he walks past me.

Huh. Wonder if he's off to call Laura. I mentally laugh to myself as I make my way to the sitting room and the sound system there.

"You did that on purpose," Luigi whispers from behind me, making me jump.

"Snuck out to my studio last night," I whisper under my breath. "Needed to clear my head, dance… ended up meeting Laura. You all knew about her," I accuse him, "and kept the secret. We had a long talk. And I'd like to discuss that with you later."

He nods, his eyes huge. "Okay," he says shakily. "We'll talk later. Just be prepared for another lecture about not going out there without someone. Your uncle is gonna kick my ass if he finds out I knew and didn't tell him."

185

Fiddling with the sound system, I bite my lip to stifle the smile that threatens to break free and don't answer my friend and guard. They all knew and need to stew in their own guilt for not telling me.

Chapter 16
NO MORE SECRETS

The sound of heels clicking on the marble floors of the hall breaks me from my study of the side lawn. Turning from the window seat, I see Annalisa running toward me. Rising, I meet her, and she throws her arms around me, hugging me tight. My arms wrap around her slim waist, and I held her just as tightly. There's nothing like a hug from your bestie.

"Hey, Annalisa," I say into her hair.

She steps back and reaches for my face, her hands shaking. Studying my face, she asks, "Are you okay? Mom kept telling me to give you space, told me Lou would send Luigi if you really needed me. I couldn't believe her though. I needed to see you myself, to know you're okay. It's been killing me that I couldn't be with you the last two days. Sure, you sounded fine on the phone and in your texts, but I needed to see your face and look into your eyes to see for myself."

My bestie, I love her and her huge heart. She didn't take a breath the entire time she spoke.

"Breathe, Annalisa," I instruct, taking her hands into mine. "Can I talk now?" Amusement laces my tone. She smiles, nodding, and I continue. "I'm fine, *chicca*. Yeah, I'm not sleeping much, but I think today will help remedy that."

Annalisa opens her mouth to say something but Gwen, her mom, steps between us and pulls me into her arms.

"Oh, darling. How are you doing?" Her voice shakes with emotion. "How can I ever thank you? How?"

Returning her hug, I savor the feeling of her arms around me. "You have nothing to thank me for, really. Nothing at all."

Gwen holds me, swaying slightly. Letting out a shaking breath, she gives me one last squeeze and steps back. "Your mom would be so proud of you. You're so strong and giving, so mature and beautiful."

"Thank you," I answer. My voice is steady, and I hope it conveys that I really am fine.

"You're like no one, man or woman, I've ever known," she says, shaking her head. "You're stunningly beautiful, full of grace and poise, yet fiercely protective of your Family, willing to kill for them. I've never seen anything like it. I've been in this Family all my life, born into it like you. I've witnessed Family fights… and wars. But I've never seen someone like you. Never, ever."

Gwen holds my shoulders, looking at me with awe-filled eyes. Papa, hearing the words of Mom's best friend, says, "Gwen, come on, let's find you a seat," just as the men come into the room. "She's fine, *cara mia*."

He gestures towards the couches, urging us to take a seat. Gwen grabs my hand and Annalisa's, leading us to one of the plush couches. Our living room is very large with two custom designed white couches that were in a semi-circle facing each other. They both are adorned with several throw pillows of varying shades of beige. We were used to having large gatherings, so there were also several different styles of chairs in the room, as well as a chaise longue by the window. I sat down between Gwen and Annalisa.

Spying the empty chaise lounge near the window, I recall how Mom loved that chair. She'd sit there for hours, looking over the lawn. She would pull the heavy drapes back, watching the wind blow through the sheers. When the wisteria was in bloom, she'd close her eyes, breathing in the sweet scent of the blooms. Pain lances my chest and I turn away from the chair.

Papa takes one of the winged back chairs to my left. Nonna, Camilla and Uncle Louie sit on the couch across from us. The rest of the people gathered take up the other various chairs throughout the room.

"Gwen," Papa starts, "Alessandra has been training with Lou since she was six. When she was twelve, Luigi and Lefty," he crosses himself at Lefty's name, "joined in with her training. I didn't want to concern Sophia," he crosses himself again, "with thoughts of her daughter needing to have this type of training. It would have panicked her, which is why I kept her in the dark, *and* everyone else."

Gwen sighs, nodding sadly. "That is true, it would have caused her undue stress. She didn't need that."

"Because of the future in store for Alessandra, she needed this training. Lou has done a superb job, as we've all witnessed. But then, she *had* to be that good, because she's a girl. She surprised us all. I couldn't be prouder of all she's accomplished. She's a gift to all of us. I've been blessed with the best daughter any father could want… or ask for. I have no doubt that she will be a capable and amazing Capo, when the time comes."

Heat suffuses my cheeks with each and every positive word out of Papa's mouth. When he finishes his little speech, Nonna asks Gwen, "Is there anything I can get you? A drink, wine perhaps?"

Gwen smiles at her, "I'd love a glass. By the way, I meant to tell you, I love your dress. Did you get it from Al's mistress's shop too? I always forget the name of it."

Camilla coughs while Annalisa sucks in a large breath, her hand flying to her mouth. My eyes study the people in the room. Shocked faces stare at Gwen's brazenness. I want to laugh but hold my tongue, not allowing my face to show any reaction. Keeping control, I wait to see how this plays out.

"Guinevere," Papa growls firmly.

"What?" she asks. "Oh, come on. We *all* know about her. If you think Sophia didn't know about your mistress, you have another thing coming. She was just glad that you weren't screwing your way through every woman at the clubs, like some of the other men here." Her eyes drift over to Vito, a sneer lifting her lips. "Al, she loved you more than life itself, but she knew she wasn't all there all the time. She knew you are a man with needs that she couldn't see to. Sophia ignored it because she couldn't imagine life without you, like a lot of the women in the Family do. I could tell it hurt her, but... she looked the other way. It wasn't like you had a different woman every other month, just the one woman all these years."

"ENOUGH!" Papa shouts, rising to his feet. "My daughter is sitting right next to you. This is neither the time, nor the place."

Standing, I intercept the glare Papa is directing at Gwen. The heat and anger in it almost has me faltering, but I recover quickly. His anger rises, the muscle in his jaw ticking. I feel slightly guilty about my little game this morning. Taking careful, measured steps, I approach him.

"Papa," I say softly, "it's okay. I already know about Laura."

The glare he was directing through me clears as his eyes fly to mine, shock and confusion replacing it as I continue. "I questioned you about her this morning because I wanted to see if you would tell me, and then it almost became a game as everyone coughed and choked, and I realized then everyone at that table knew but me."

Speechless, he stares at me. I've obviously stunned him. He's never lacked the ability to find words. His brown eyes are huge, I can almost see the confusion working its way through his brain. The room is so quiet, I probably could hear a pin drop. Deciding to take mercy on him, I explain.

"A few months ago, I'd left my book in my studio, and I wanted it. I snuck out to go grab it."

Uncle Louie growls, I knew he wouldn't like that admission and was probably pissed. But... the time for lies and secrets is over. I persevere, continuing.

"Once outside, I heard loud music playing. I snuck in there, wondering who was listening to Def Leopard's *Pour Some Sugar On Me.*"

Someone snickers and Papa's hard eyes return as he scans the room, delivering death glares. Taking a deep breath, his eyes snap back to my face.

"I looked in the little window... and," the next words I say in a low voice for his ears only, "I saw a lot more than I ever wanted to." Returning my voice to a normal level, I continue, "Luigi must have seen me, because he grabbed me and dragged me outside, and then back into the house. I questioned him, pressing for answers. He told me she was more than 'just a stripper' to you. I didn't want to hear it then."

"Oh, shit," Luigi mutters as Papa turns his head to him, moving to take a step.

Grabbing his arm and staying his movement, I beg, "Don't be upset with him."

A shudder works its way through my Papa. He looks at the ground, rubbing the back of his neck.

Slowly, he faces me and meets my eyes. "I wish you hadn't found out that way," Papa says on a whisper. "And I wish someone," he says pointedly, "had given me a warning so I could have made this better for you."

Sighing, I go for broke. "To be honest, I sneak out there a lot. It's an escape from the stress, and everything else, to let go and just dance. I don't go anywhere else, only my studio." I glace at my uncle. "I'm sorry, but I need it. I don't do anything dangerous. Only dance, use my silk ropes and the poles.

"You could fall," Uncle Louie shakes his head, growling. "You are not allowed out there by yourself, especially at night."

"Hmm," I murmur softly, tapping my chin. "I thought it was because of your *poker games* when they're really stripper nights. Yeah, I know about that too."

Nonna, Camilla and Luigi snicker, but poor Annalisa sits there, shocked. I can't wait for the bazillion and one questions I'll get from her later. Again, I press on.

"Papa, last night…" For the first time, I hesitate. "Last night was rough for me. I couldn't sleep, and I was stressed out. I needed the freedom of dancing. I snuck out there after changing my clothes. While I was out there, I heard a noise, and I flew into action. I grabbed a bo staff and demanded they show themselves. I'm sure you know who it was, Papa."

"This I have to hear," Nonna mumbles. Camilla just gasps.

"Oh," Gwen whispers, probably to Annalisa, "this is getting really good. I'm so glad we came early. Go on, honey, tell us who it was," she encourages.

The tick returns to Papa's jaw, and the skin of his neck turns red. He's getting angry, probably at the people watching his humiliation. Sheesh, getting caught having an affair by your daughter? Bad stuff. He's also probably angry at Laura. He's obviously blindsided by the news, which meant she kept her word and didn't say anything to him.

"It was Laura. She was carrying garment bags, I assume for me. When I confronted her, she was scared, of me... and probably of *your* reaction. It was clear to me that, as Luigi said, she was more than just your private stripper, and that she was the woman who has been designing and making my clothes. I told her how much I love the clothes she'd sent so far. But I'm not dumb, I took advantage of her fear and grilled her for information about herself and her relationship with you."

Papa turns and heads toward the bar. He pours himself a glass of grappa and takes a slow slip. A smile tries to break free, but I pull it back.

"Think I could use one of those," my uncle mutters. Luigi and Vito agree. They all join my Papa at the bar, getting their drinks.

My eyes scan the room. Antonio, leaning against the wall, snags my attention. His eyes ensnare mine. I could swear he's looking at me with encouragement. He gives me a slight nod, so I keep telling my story.

"Laura told me you've been seeing each other for over four years. Oh! And that you're in love with each other. Don't worry, though. She assured me, more than once, that you still loved Mom. You claimed to be in love with two people at the same time."

He looks down at the bar top, inspecting the grain of the wood. Papa turns, coming to stand in front of me again. "I am, I mean... I was. I loved your mother, but she wasn't getting better. Recently, her bad times were longer and more intense."

"You think I don't know that?" I ask, venom lacing my words. "I know you liked to drug her and hope I didn't notice. I'm not a child and haven't been one since I was six and shot at my birthday party!"

"You were too young to have to deal with or understand your mother's issues," Papa says angrily, raising his voice too.

On the verge of exploding, I say sarcastically, "Well, *ex-cuuuse me*. I knew a lot more than any of you gave me credit for. I knew about her doll, the one she dressed in Junior's sleeper. I knew she rocked it and sang to it. I knew that she slept with that doll, too. I was more a part of her life than you ever were."

"Oh, shit," someone says, amid gasps of shock. I concur, but I have no control of what slipped out of my mouth. I'm angry at him.

Papa takes a step closer to me, leaning down to look into my eyes. His hand lifts from his side, but, on instinct, mine raises to block him, in case he's thinking of hitting me. I glare into his eyes. "I wouldn't do that again if I were you. I told you once before that you'd never hit me again. I meant it, Papa… or Father… Capo, whatever you want me to call you right now."

He straightens, looking around the room with a smirk. "Well, well… my daughter has a set of balls now. I wasn't going to hit you. But, I do want to know what you told my girlfriend."

Exhales of relief sound from our audience. Once again, the room falls into complete silence. We stand there, facing off. "She said she was impressed with my dancing, and other skills. Guess you shared a lot with her, about Mom and me. Laura said you're the only one she dances for and hasn't danced since you became involved. She impressed that she only did it as a second job because she was new to Italy. She explained how she fled her Family in America because of the war they were involved in. She told me that there are no secrets between the two of you. I told her that if she valued her life, she wouldn't tell you about our meeting. Not until I was ready."

"You threaten to kill her?" Papa asks a wrinkle in his brow.

"I didn't say, 'kill...' I just wanted to get through the next three days in one piece. But, she was scared of me. I'm glad, she should be." My voice is smug, full of pride.

He throws his head back, laughing. "What have you created, Lou?" he asks my uncle. "Do you hear this girl?"

"Yeah, I hear her," he says from his spot by the bar. "And, for what it's worth, I agree with her. Laura *should* be scared of her."

Papa's eyes find me again. "Well, young lady, I'm not thrilled with your little game. Nor am I thrilled with you sneaking around and being nosey. At least I don't have to figure out a way to tell you. I honestly had no idea how to do that." His smile is depreciating.

"Papa, don't misunderstand. I'm not happy you were screwing around on Mom. And knowing she knew about this, pisses me off even more."

"Princess," Papa interrupts me, "I tried to be as discreet as possible. I had no idea your mother, nor any of the women knew. They didn't act like they knew, nor did they give Laura any indication they knew when they were in her shop."

"Well, excuse me," Gwen says, disdain dripping from her voice, "when a stripper only dances twice at the club then becomes a waitress with the best shifts, but that doesn't last long because all of a sudden she has a brand new clothing shop, a nice car and an apartment close to the estate... especially when *you*, and all the men of the Family, tell *us women* to get our clothes there, people talk. We were all very aware that the only man you ever sent there was Lou, and that you'd personally check on her. We'd never seen you take a personal interest in any shop, not even one of the Family's. You usually send the new guys. Oh, and let's not forget that her little shop just doubled in size last year, turning it into a high-end boutique."

Gwen turns to me. "Alessandra, sweetie, don't be upset with your father. He was faithful for years before he became involved with Laura, and only Laura. Your mom even liked Laura, as much as she wished to hate her. She'd had a few outfits that Laura designed. Don't get me wrong, they weren't friends by any means."

Shock hits me. "But, why? Why didn't she say something? Why didn't she stop it?" This information will take some time to digest.

She shakes her head. "Honey, you know your mother wasn't stable. She knew your Papa loved her. She also knew she wasn't enough and allowed herself to slip back into her fantasy. She couldn't imagine her life without him, so she didn't rock the boat. Her fantasy was her way of dealing with her losses. No one, not you, nor your Papa or even me, could really help her for long. She was here one moment and gone into her mind the next."

My eyes fall to the floor. "Still," I whisper, "it hurt her, and that hurts me."

Rising, Gwen pulls me into a hug. "*Cara mia*, give it time. You'll understand when you're older, trust me." Leaving me, she pours herself another glass of wine.

Sad, I look to the far wall, and Antonio catches my gaze. His eyes hold compassion, for me and my pain. He looks like he wants to approach me but is holding back through sheer force of will. Unable to stand the look directed my way, I find Luigi at the bar, sipping his grappa. He gives me a small nod. And I realize something about Papa.

"You're a two-faced hypocrite," I turn, pointing at Papa. "You know that, right? Once again, you've supposedly fallen in love with a woman who isn't a part of the Family. But still, *you* insist on picking my husband, denying me the same privilege of finding and falling in love with someone. You're a total hypocrite." Silence falls across the room as Papa marches up to me. He leans down, getting in my face again. "You are one brave young lady to talk to me, your Capo and Papa, like that." His voice is loud, his words crisp, clearly enunciated. "Let me make myself crystal clear. *Yes*, I will be the one to pick your husband. If you haven't noticed, I pick out mates for almost all of the men in the Family. Whether you believe it or not, I know what is best for you."

His eyes wander my face. "I see that fire in your eyes. I know that strong will you have, the one that doesn't need to be broken. I can see your strong spirit, it pours out of you. I know that the man I find for you cannot be a pussy. You need a man, a real man. One that can stand beside you, support you, while you run the Family... one that will listen and encourage you, not break your spirit. He will be strong, even with all the power you'll have from your position. It won't be an easy or simple job. I know, I live it daily, Alessandra. You need a man with a mind of his own, not someone you can control. Someone strong, because you need a firm hand to keep you grounded, and a hard *fuck* to let you know your place." Nonna gasps, as does Gwen.

"I will not allow some weak, pussy of a man who

knows nothing about the Family come in and try to take it over. I will not allow some asshole to come in and try to rule through you. *I know* what you need, and I will not pick someone who cannot meet the requirements. I know what is best for this Family and I will accept nothing less than the best for you."

"Enough, Al!" Uncle Louie shouts.

"Watch it, Alessandro," Nonna adds.

We stand there, glaring at each other for a while. My anger had risen with each word out of his mouth. 'A hard fuck'? Who the Hell says that to their daughter? Such a hypocrite. I cannot believe him.

"This subject is closed," he growls into my face.

"Vito, Lou, Luigi. My office. Antonio stays with the women," he says loudly, straightening. With his eyes still on me, he gives me a smirk, "And make sure Alessandra doesn't go roaming."

His face softens, just a touch, and he kisses my forehead. He whispers, "Hate me all you want for now, but know that I do love you and I only want what's best for you, and the Family. As much as you might hate me right now, I know I don't have to fear you killing me in my sleep… or do I?" He gives me a wink. "I don't really think I do. I know you love me, or you would have let that man kill me last year."

He leaves with Vito trailing behind. Uncle Louie catches my eye, mouthing, "I love you. We'll talk later," and follows them.

"Wish me luck," Luigi says with a crooked smile. "Hope I don't get shot in there."

I give him a half smile, watching him follow after my uncle. Luigi always knows how to make me smile. I love that about him. My heart still pounds in my chest, thinking over what Papa said. Oh God, everyone in this room heard him! Even Antonio, who finally sits in the wingback chair that faces the couch Annalisa and Gwen sit on. I collapse next to my bestie's mom, vowing I will not marry *any* man Papa picks for me. I will escape.

Chapter 17
THE MEN TALK
(LOUIE)

*W*e all walk in to into Al's office, as my brother continues to shake his head, rubbing his hands down his face. It makes me want to laugh since he brought this on himself.

Why did he call us into his office, though? Was he looking for a way out of Little One's piercing questions?

"What did you call us back here for?" I ask as soon as Luigi closes the door, unable to resist. "We have less than an hour before we have to leave for services at the church."

Taking his chair, Al weaves his fingers together and places his hands behind his head. "What the fuck..." he mutters.

Spearing Vito with a look, he asks, "Did you know your wife and the other women knew? Why didn't you fucking warn me?"

"How many times did I volunteer to check on Laura and the shop?" Vito retorts. "You wouldn't hear of it. I had a suspicion that they knew because of the questions Gwen asked. But what would have changed, what would you have done differently if you had known?"

Scrubbing his hands down his face again, Al says, "Damn..." Taking a deep breath, he stumbles over his next words. "I don't know. Maybe I could have talked to Sophia on one of her good days. I could have apologized, made sure she knew I loved her, always have and always would. I wouldn't be sitting here feeling like the biggest damn asshole ever."

He laughs sardonically. "I know you all probably think I'm an asshole, so don't deny it. But, fuck. I really do love two women. I love them both for different reasons, in different ways... or rather, *did* love two women. But because Sophia was murdered, I didn't get to tell her all the things I needed to. I don't have closure." He huffs. "Fuck, I'll figure this out though."

Al shakes his head, clearing it. A scowl replaces his melancholy look. "Lou, what the fuck is going on with Alessandra? Sneaking out of the house? Fuck, she's probably been sneaking around and eavesdropping on meetings."

Sneering, he turns his look on Luigi, looking ready to strangle him. "And you, Luigi... do you need to tell me anything? Or do I need to get my knife to cut off your balls? Have you been doing anything I need to know about with my daughter?"

"No," Luigi says adamantly, sitting up straight. "No, sir. At this point, there is *nothing* going on between Alessandra and me. We're friends, close friends, but nothing inappropriate. Sure, sometimes it's hard for me to remember she's only sixteen, but I try to think of her as a little sister. Nothing more."

"At this point," Al parrots. "What do you mean by that?"

"Sir," Luigi takes a deep breath. "We're close. Can, uh, I be honest without worrying about being shot? I want to be honest without that thought hanging over my head."

"As long as you don't tell me you've already fucked her, you have nothing to worry about. Speak freely," Al answers him.

What the fuck is he about to say? He takes another

breath.

"Look, sometimes, I look at her, and I don't see a sixteen-year-old girl. I see one hell of a beautiful, strong, intelligent woman full of sass and sweet. But then we talk, and it's like a switch flips. Big brother, protective feelings come over me, swapping out the, um, other ones."

Shit, I'd bet good money he's whacked off thinking about her. I'm going to have to keep a closer eye on these two. Al stares at him for a few beats.

"Should I take you off my list, or should I leave you there?" he asks.

"I'm not saying to take me off the list just yet," Luigi answers, meeting Al's pointed look. "I'm aware she's sixteen, and you won't be making any decisions for at least three to four years. I don't know if my feelings for her will change as she grows up... or her feelings for me for that matter. Right now, we get along great, we're good friends. But who knows how that will change, evolve in the next few years. But I vow to you and Lou, here and now, that I will *always* respect her and *never* do anything inappropriate."

"Okay," Al nods, leaning back in his chair. "Glad to hear it. I'm glad you admit to wanting to be on the list. You used to fight me about it. This is a step in the right direction. There's no guarantee I'll pick you, but Antonio is your fiercest competition for her hand... if he can learn to keep his dick in his pants," Al finishes with a pointed look at Vito.

"I'm not saying this to move up the damn list," Luigi interrupts him. "I need to tell you Alessandra has *no* interest in Antonio. She sees him as a brother, the same way Annalisa feels about him. Keep that in mind, for her sake."

"I'm very aware of how she feels about Antonio,"

Al says, his voice contemplative. "I also know that she protected him during the attack. I see the way he watches my daughter. But, I will keep that in mind in the coming years. Stephen's already off the list. I see the developing feelings between him and Annalisa. I've spoken to Vito and think they might be a perfect match. This stays here," he taps his desk, "but we'll see how it plays out. I do have a question for you, Luigi."

My eyes bounce between my brother and my protégé. "If Alessandra were to develop feelings for you, could you see yourself feeling the same way? In the future?"

Mimicking Al, Luigi scrubs his hands down his face. Lifting his eyes, his tone is serious when he responds. "I'll be honest with you because you promised it was safe. Yeah, I could easily have feelings for her. I have to remind myself that it's not possible right now, and that keeps me from allowing anything further. I know my place as it is right now, that's why I won't *let* myself feel anything for her now. Honestly, I don't think I'm worthy of all that Alessandra is. I would never do anything, ever, to hurt her. She's safe with me. If you were to give me the nod, that all would change, and I know it. If I ever feel like it's too much to be around her, I will come to you or Lou. I repeat, *she is safe with me*. I will guard and protect her with my life."

"I don't see you fucking around at the club," Al comments. "You got a girl on the side? Or are you saving yourself?"

Vito and I chuckle at the question. "No," Luigi answers. "I'm most definitely not saving myself. I don't hook up with the girls at the club. There's a girl up north I see off and on. She knows the score, and it's not serious."

"Just checking," Al smiles, nodding.

When the room is quiet, I speak up. "Al, what the fuck were you thinking saying your own damn daughter needs a good hard fuck? Have you lost your goddamn mind? You're fucking lucky I didn't lay you out right there. Hell, I think Gwen was ready to jump from her seat if it weren't for Annalisa's grip on her arm. You don't speak like that to an *innocent* sixteen-year-old girl... especially one who *just lost her mom!*"

"Dammit," Al groans. "This daughter of mine gets under my skin, and I need to put her in her place. Could you imagine the fucking pussy she would pick for a husband? She's too damn strong-willed, too powerful of a woman. She needs someone strong who will stand up to her and not give into her every whim. She might get a man that would try to beat her, but, and let's be serious, she would kill him. Or, she'd pick a man that she could beat and turn him into a fucking pussy."

Vito and Luigi laugh, but I nod, knowing Al speaks the truth. "Don't worry brother, I'll pick the right one. The list has dwindled from ten down to four. I'm still keeping the other two names to myself for now."

"And what about Laura?" I ask. "After the services and mourning period for Sophia, are you thinking of bringing her around? About coming out publicly with your relationship since everyone already knows anyway?"

"Shit," he says, leaning into his elbows on his desk. "I'm a bit pissed at Laura right now for not telling me. I knew something was wrong last night, but she denied it. I chalked it up to her not knowing where we stand right now. Alessandra probably did scare her. I can't say that I blame Laura though. But no, I won't be making this common knowledge right after I bury my wife. It's too disrespectful to her. That doesn't mean I'll stop seeing Laura. I will make it public though, someday. I do love that woman."

He chuckles lightly. "She's coming to the services today. I haven't decided yet if I'll tell her about our little conversation today. I might just let it play out and see what happens if Alessandra says anything to her or not. Keep your eyes on them. I'll try to keep them apart. This timing blows."

"What the fuck do you mean, 'she's coming to the services'? Talk about disrespectful! Not just to Sophia, but to your daughter too, forcing her to see *your* mistress at her mother's funeral. I do not want Little One upset today, do you? Fuck, you can see her after if you need to."

Al sighs. "Fuck, I do not want a scene. Nor do I want to hurt Alessandra more than I already have. I'll call Laura, see if I can't persuade her not to come."

Opening the humidor on Al's credenza, I pull out one of his hand-rolled Cuban cigars. After cutting the end, I light it and sit back down. Al watches me the whole time.

"Help yourself, Lou," he offers, sarcastically. "Ever heard of asking?"

"Are we finished here?" I ask, ignoring his comment. "Because we should rejoin the ladies. A cigar might just calm us all down before we head back in there."

"I could use one," Vito says. "Al don't go picking a husband for Alessandra right now. You need to keep my boy in mind, and at the top of the list. He's growing up nicely within the Family. Yeah, he's got a few problems, but he's really attracted to the Princess."

I chuckle, saying, "Vito, no ass kissing now, or pushing your agenda. We're just enjoying our cigars and shooting the shit."

Luigi laughs, and we enjoy our remaining few minutes of a quality cigar in friendly silence.

Chapter 18

THE WOMEN CHAT

*A*fter the men leave, I remain standing, rooted in place for a minute. Taking a deep breath, I try to cool off before I take my seat on the couch. Gwen puts her arm around me and tucks me to her side.

"*Cara*, I know your life is hard right now, and that sucks. But, you have to know your Papa does love you. Yes, it's sad that your Mom died, but she loved you so much. As for your father's mistress... well, I thought you were the strongest young lady I've ever seen for pushing through the secrets and getting the truth revealed."

"I know," I say sadly. "Life is so tough. I feel blocked in, shoved into Papa's little box. I have no freedom, no choice in my life at all. It's like I'm a prisoner and he's my warden."

"Look at me," she says, taking my hands. "Listen, okay? I'm going to be brutally honest with you right now."

Turning, I lift my eyes to hers. Her face is warm. Nonna and Camilla watch silently from their couch across from us. Annalisa shifts behind me. Antonio is still in his wingback chair, and I know, *I know*, his eyes are on me.

"I was in your shoes when I was your age. Your mom and I had these exact same talks because your Nonno had picked Vito to be my husband when I was younger than you are now. Sure, he was good-looking, a strong and powerful man. Some of my friends wanted him, and some had even slept with him. I wasn't sure I wanted anything to do with him.

My mind lived in a fantasy world most of the time, I dreamed of finding someone to fall in love with and marry. I wanted the heart-stopping moments your mom had with your papa, but I'd known Vito all my life.

"My mama encouraged me to spend time with him, chaperoned of course. He stopped sleeping around, and eventually, I did fall in love with him. Yes, we've had our problems, mostly because he was screwing around on me. I did it once, just so he would know how it felt, but I ended up feeling all the worse for it. It almost ended up destroying us because he still loves me and was so very hurt. He cherished me and explained that to him sex didn't equate to love like it did for me. He said that the knowledge that he was my one and only meant so much to him. When I admitted to sleeping with someone else, it crushed him. There is nothing in life I regret more. That was when he began drinking heavily because he felt responsible for my actions.

"It took us years for us to get past my indiscretion, and for him to forgive himself, and me. Now that we've worked hard to get through our trials, *and* that no one is sleeping with anyone else, we are deeply committed to each other. We talk about everything, and I'm once again married to my best friend. I can tell him off and make love to him later that night. He's the first one I want to tell any news to or simply what happened during my day. He's the first thought in my mind now. We'll be together until death. He's so much more than my best friend, he's my everything. I'm that for him, as well."

Annalisa's hand comes to my shoulder. Letting go of Gwen's hands, I turn to my best friend. Tears fill her eyes, and I wrap my arms around her as she does the same. "I want what Mom and Dad have now," she whispers into my hair. "Just like we talked about in Venice. They really have it, the kissing and hand holding."

"Yeah, they do," I answer her. "You're lucky. I'm sure you'll have the same thing one day."

She pulls back, catching my eyes. "Don't give up on wanting it too. You could have it. Come on, you are beautiful, and men love your sass. I trust your Papa. He wouldn't pick someone you hate. Give it time and don't give up. Okay?"

I look down, avoiding her eyes, and nod. I can't bring myself to answer her as a familiar refrain repeats in my mind every time my future is mentioned. I *will not* marry Antonio just because everyone thinks I should. Somehow, I'll figure out a way to escape. If Papa has Laura, maybe, just maybe, I can make this work.

"Little One," Nonna says, kneeling next to me. "I'm so sorry. I had no idea you knew about Laura. It wasn't my place to tell you, no matter how much I knew it would hurt you. I didn't have the vaguest idea that your mother knew."

"Nonna," I sigh. "I'm not upset with any of you, only Papa. But, I guess I kind of understand him. I don't know."

Taking a deep breath, I ask Nonna an important question. "Where is Mom's doll? I want to make sure she has it so she can have it with her forever. It's only right. I don't care what Papa thinks."

"I know where he is, sweetie," Camilla answers. "I'll get him and her favorite blanket for him. I'll put him in one of your oversized purses so no one will see him until you pull him out to place in her coffin. I agree he should be buried with her."

Nonna nods as Gwen sniffles behind me. My eyes flick to Antonio. "You need to keep your mouth shut about this. You're not in here as a spy. You're here to make sure I don't 'run off.'"

"Alessandra," he smiles, "my lips are sealed. I'd never say anything to break your confidence. I had no idea about any of this. I've learned more today, about both of our families, than I have in years. You do what you think is best."

"Thank you, Antonio," I say, returning his smile. "That means a lot." He nods, saying nothing further.

Gwen grabs my hand again, "Okay, girl talk. You have to tell me, what did you think of Laura? Honestly."

We all laugh. Nonna and Camilla practically speak over each other. "Oooh, Gwen, good question. Yes, what did you think?"

Smiling, I tell them jokingly, "Kicking her ass might have passed through my mind." Antonio coughs, trying to cover his laugh.

"Don't worry, I wouldn't. Papa would have had a heart attack. I really do love the clothes she's made me, she's good at what she does. I do want to go her shop and see about getting clothes for when I go to university. I couldn't find a reason to hate her, but she is young for him. I told her that, too."

I blush, remembering the first time I saw her. "I'll be honest. When I saw her dance for Papa, I was impressed with her moves. Then she joined Papa, and they got down and dirty, well, I was done watching. But I did take some of her moves, and I think I've improved on them."

"Oh!" Annalisa exclaims while the women laugh. "Can you show me? I want to know them, too."

"I wouldn't mind seeing those moves," Antonio adds.

Turning, I shoot Antonio a nasty look.

"Antonio," Gwen sighs.

"What? What's that look for? It's not like you'll be stripping or anything…" I just shake my head at him.

Ignoring Antonio, I turn back to the ladies. "I guess I'm more like Mom than I realized. If Laura can make Papa happy, then I'm willing to accept it. That being said, I'd prefer if he waited until I go to university to bring her into the house."

Everyone nods, agreeing with me. The men enter the room, and I wonder how much they heard. *Crap.*

Camilla stands. "I'll go fetch that purse, Princess. We'll be leaving soon for the church."

I smile, catching her meaning. "Thank you so much, Camilla. I'll wait here." She leaves, and I'm content in the knowledge that this will make Mom happy. It'll give me closure, too.

Uncle Louie gives me a wink, as does Luigi. It warms my soul. But… my nerves begin to stir and my stomach twists. Today will be the toughest day of my life.

After a few minutes, Nonna claps her hands and tells everyone to head to the cars. Uncle Louie tries to take my arm, but I pull away.

"Uh, I, um, forgot something upstairs." Fleeing, I run for the stairs.

Chapter 19
THE SERVICES BEGIN

From the window seat in Mom's wing, I watch as everyone gathers around the cars. I'm not ready. I'm not ready to say goodbye to my mother. I just can't get it together to go say goodbye to her. Nonna and Camilla picked out the lovely pink dress she'll be wearing, and I'm sure she looks beautiful, laying serenely in her casket. But I'm so not ready for this. So here I am, hiding in my favorite spot, the bench seat in the bay window.

Surrounded by Mom's pink throw pillows, I recall her reading to me when I was little. Happier times for sure. As she started slipping further and further into her fantasy and I grew older, I'd sit out here and read… just in case she needed me.

Staring out the window, the tents and chairs set up for her burial in the family mausoleum reinforce that this is really happening. The group below me starts shuffling around, and I can tell they're getting impatient waiting for me to come back from my supposed errand. God, I feel like a little girl playing hide-and-go-seek. Chuckling, I watch as Annalisa, Vito and Antonio get into their car. Gwen hovers, presumably waiting for me. My uncle encourages her to go, and their car leaves to head to the church for Mom's vigil. I still can't believe all of this is happening.

My nerves flare again, my stomach churns. The tents catch my eye again, and beyond them to the mausoleum. God, Mom's going to be put in there… in that cold, stone building. Don't get me wrong, the mausoleum is beautiful, covered in gorgeous purple wisteria and amazingly carved stonework, it's massive and imposing. But… it's so cold, not warm like a home. The garden surrounding the marble structure is a slice of peace. Nonna loves to sit on the benches there, Mom did too. They spent a lot of time out there, talking to Nonno and Junior. Now, Nonna will go out there to talk to Mom too.

I'm sure I'll be going out there to visit her, even though I know she's not there. But, I'll have a place to direct my thoughts, I guess. I'm sure it'll help me if I can talk through things, thinking she is listening. The garden is beautiful, surrounded by fragrant flowers and soft trees. Hopefully, it'll bring me peace when I need it.

Minutes pass as I'm lost in my thoughts. Suddenly, two big strong arms wrap around me, pulling me into a hard chest. I sigh, leaning back as the sweet, musky scent of Luigi reaches my nose. He always wears the same cologne.

"How did you find me?" I ask softly.

"Well," he exhales, "I checked your room. And, since you weren't there, I figured you'd be here. I know you liked to hang out here and read. Sometimes when I was on guard duty, I'd look up here and see the small light and I knew you were up here. I know it was a way for you to be close to your mom, without admitting you were keeping watch over her."

"You know me better than most."

"You okay?" he asks, slowly rocking us.

I shake my head.

"Thought so. Have you been in her room yet?"

I shake my head again.

"You want me to go in there with you?" he asks. He is so sweet, such a good friend. I take a deep breath and think for a few seconds before answering.

"I'm not ready. Maybe next week, okay? But… I do want someone to come with me." I finally answer.

"Any time you're ready," he replies, nodding. "Little One, all you have to do is ask. I'm there for you."

"Thanks, Luigi," I murmur. "You're too good to me."

"Alessandra, I'm always here for you. Now, you ready to go? Your Nonna and uncle are worried. They can't start the vigil without you, you know that, right?"

"Yeah," I nod slowly. "It's just harder than I thought it would be. She's gone now, and I know it's forever… but I can still feel her. I know when I look in that coffin, she'll look like she's sleeping and that hurts my chest… so, so bad." Taking a shaky breath, I continue in a whisper. "I don't want to cry again. I don't cry. When I lost it… that was the first time I ever really cried. God, my throat already hurts like I'm going to cry."

He squeezes me tighter, resting his chin on the top of my head. "Crying is okay. Like Lou said, 'Tears are just your heart leaking the love it's lost.' No one will judge you." Luigi pauses for a second, then chuckles lightly. "Besides, you have your standard issue Ray-Bans to hide behind."

I smile lightly, and my voice is a bit stronger with my reply. "Yeah, I do. Thank you so much."

"We can put you in a circle if you want, Me and Lou on your sides, Antonio and Stephen behind, your Papa and Nonna in front of you. You can avoid the possibility of anyone getting close," he suggests.

Turning, I lay the side of my face on his chest. Luigi's strong, steady heartbeat pounds in my ear.

"You would do that for me?" I ask softly.

In answer, Luigi pulls his phone from his pocket, and types with one hand. "It's done. Your uncle is coordinating everything. During dinner, you'll be on the usual raised platform so no one can get close unless you want them to."

"Thank you so much, Luigi. You're the best," I whisper, absorbing his strength.

"I promise not to leave your side today," he says quietly into my hair. "And, if you can make it through the next three or four hours, I'll even promise to help you escape to your studio and work out with you. And as a bonus, I'll even show you some of my gymnastic moves."

Shocked, I pull away to look him in the eyes. "You have gymnastic moves? Like what?"

He smiles, holding out his hand to help me up. "This stays between us, but as a kid, I trained to be a diver. I did a lot of trampoline work and floor work to perfect those flips and my entry into the water."

My mouth falls open. "How did I not know this?"

"Oh come on," he laughs. "You think I wanted to open that can of worms, being teased and called gay for doing gymnastics? Just so you know, there's not a gay bone in my body."

I giggle at his fierce defense, knowing he's far from gay.

"I was teased enough as it was, called 'flipper boy.' Just imagine what the Family would have said. This is our secret, remember that." He cocks an eyebrow, silently asking for my agreement. God, he is so good at lifting me out of a funk.

"Okay flipper boy, your secret is safe with me," I

tease.

Looking up to the ceiling he asks aloud, "Why, oh why did I tell her that?"

I laugh, and he quickly joins me.

I brush my dress and jacket with my hands, smoothing the light wrinkles. "I'm ready once I grab my purse," I sigh.

Near where I was sitting is the large purse Camilla prepared for me, including Mom's doll. Reaching in, I grab my glasses and put them on.

"Aless," Luigi says, "you don't need a weapon today. Nothing will happen, I promise. Anyway, everyone is scared of you."

"I'm not carrying."

"What the hell do you have in here?" he asks, picking up my purse.

I glance at the driveway, seeing Uncle Louie turn to come into the house. "Mom's doll," I whisper. "I want to give it to her, put it in her arms."

"Okay," he says, holding my eyes. "Let's do this."

Handing me my purse, he waves his other one to the stairs. "Ladies first," Luigi says.

I take a deep break, shoring my nerves. *I can do this.*

As I take my first step, Luigi's hand settles on my lower back. My stomach flutters, but not due to nerves. Every other man who does this with me places their hand either in the center of my back or between my shoulders. Luigi's hand is low, very low on my back, where my back meets my bum. It feels intimate. I like it… maybe too much.

As we hit the marble-floored entryway, Uncle Louie comes in through the front door.

"There you are. Are you ready to head over?" he asks, looking at me, then Luigi.

"As ready as I'll ever be." I give him a small smile.

Walking out the front door, I hear Uncle Louie mumble something to Luigi. They have to be talking about me. Increasing the pace of my steps, I hurry to open door of the waiting SUV and climb in.

Uncle Louie and Luigi catch up to me. Uncle Louie slides in beside me in the back of the SUV while Luigi climbs into the driver's seat.

"I love you, Little One. We'll get through this together. Your Papa is coordinating everything to make sure you're left alone." He turns his attention on Luigi. "Let's go."

As Luigi steers us to the church, I realize I haven't seen Mom's bodyguards since the attack.

"Where have Lucca and Rocco been? I haven't seen them. Are they okay?" I ask, concerned.

Uncle Louie hangs his head, shaking it. "They're taking this really rough. They blame themselves for allowing your and Gwen to go to the reception without them. Doesn't matter what we've said, that they saved a lot of lives during the battle. It's hard for them right now. God, after that first night, I think they drank for a full twelve hours. Since then, they've been guarding your mother's body."

"What?" I ask, surprised. "Are you serious? They've just been standing by her coffin for the last two days?"

"Yeah," Uncle Louie nods. "Al's told them more than once that it's not necessary, but they refuse to leave her side. I think they rotate so they can try to sleep. I'm sure your Papa will insist they take a week or two off after today."

"I should have talked to them yesterday," I comment sadly.

"You've had a lot to deal with yourself, Little One. It's okay."

Pulling up to the church, Luigi stops the car at the front steps. Vito, Antonio, and Stephen are waiting. Uncle Louie exits and holds his hand out to me. The parking lot is jam-packed, so the church must be too. There are a few people loitering outside, but they keep their distance. God, there has to be close to three hundred people here today… maybe more.

Vito greets me with a warm look and turns to walk in front of me as my uncle and Luigi escort me forward. Stephen and Antonio take up the rear. I hear soft music coming from inside the church as we step inside the front doors. In the narthex, even more, people stand around, and they silence their soft chatter as we move past them, watching our procession.

As we enter the nave, I spot Laura in the last pew. She gives me a weak smile, and I return it. Why is she even here? At my side, Uncle Louie stiffens, catching sight of my Papa's mistress.

Even though we've entered the church, I don't remove my sunglasses. I don't want anyone to see my eyes. At the end of every pew, there's a huge pink bow, artfully decorated with an array of pink wildflowers. If I didn't know better, I'd think we were attending a wedding or first communion, not a funeral. I have to admit though, Mom would have loved the way the church looks.

My heart warms, knowing Mom's looking down

on us right now. Continuing down the aisle, I ignore the looks of sympathy from the crowd. I don't have the energy to greet them, and I shore myself up for the heavy emotions and feelings today has brought.

At the end of the aisle, I freeze. Mom's coffin is pink, a light pale pink. Her favorite shade. The top half is open, and I see the side of her face. She looks beautiful, peaceful... as if she were sleeping. Just like when I would check on her late at night.

On either end of her coffin, Lucca and Rocco stand guard, just like Uncle Louie said. My heart hurts for them, for the blame they lay at their own feet. Ignoring my Papa's outstretched hand, I walk up to Rocco and wrap my arms around him. He engulfs me in a tight hug.

"Please, Rocco. This isn't your fault. Mom wouldn't be happy with either of you big oafs blaming yourselves. Believe me," I say softly.

Leaning back to look into his eyes, I continue, "You watched her all the time. She loved you both dearly. But you and I both know she's in a better place now, with Elena and Junior. She's happy and at peace. We have to move on, that would make her happy. Think of her fondly every time you see her favorite color. After her funeral, we start afresh. Okay?"

He sniffles but doesn't say anything. Giving me a stiff nod, he releases me. Moving to Lucca, I tell him essentially the same thing I told Rocco. Lucca though, grabs my face and kisses my forehead.

"Don't worry," he says, resting his forehead against mine. "We'll be fine, for the both of you. You know your mom loved you... more than life itself. If there's anything I can ever do for you, just ask."

Nodding, I kiss Lucca's cheek. "Thank you."

I pull back, taking a deep breath, to shore myself. Turning, I face her coffin. Placing one foot in front of the other, I approach it. As I look down at her, so restful, my eyes sting with tears. Uncle Louie and Luigi stand behind me, their focus solely on me, probably praying and hoping I don't have another breakdown. The pianist resumes playing, louder this time, prompted by a nod from my uncle, so no one can hear what I want to say to her.

Leaning over my Mom's body, I place my hand on her cold cheek. "I love you, Mom," I whisper, "and always will. I'll never forget you, or what you told me. I'll do everything possible to be happy and break out of my tragic life, and I will find real love, just like I promised you. Somehow, some way, I will."

I pause for a second, memorizing her face. "I brought you something," I continue in a whisper, and I reach for my purse. Opening it, I pull her baby doll out and cradle it as I lift her arm. Quickly, I transfer the doll from my arms into hers and kiss her cheek.

"Keep an eye on me, okay Mom? I'll probably need your guidance and help a lot in my life," I tell her softly.

Straightening, I take in a deep breath as my eyes fall closed. I'm willing the tears away, but it's not working. With my head hanging down, I stand here waiting for the tears to subside and trying to calm myself.

"You okay, Little One?" Uncle Louie asks, placing a hand on my arm. Luigi's hand settles on my lower back.

"Yes," I whisper. "Yes, yes... we should take our seats."

Uncle Louie turns me, escorting me to Papa in the front pew. He bends, kisses my cheek, and I take my place beside him.

On my other side, Nonna tucks me to her side. Uncle Louie takes a seat next to her. Luigi and Camilla seat directly behind us, and I feel him squeeze my shoulder lightly. Beside them is Vito and Gwen, with Antonio, Annalisa, and Stephen filling the pew with Lorenzo on the end.

Behind us, the church is full to bursting. Family, every last one. Many brought their children.

The music stops, and the priest begins the mass. I try to pay attention, but his voice fades into a dull hum in my ears. Prayers, songs, Bible readings, it's all wordless, just noise. I stand when everyone stands, I kneel, and I sit. My focus is on trying not to cry. I don't care that Uncle Louie said it's okay. I don't want to appear weak. Taking deep breaths, I glance at the huge picture of Mom next to her coffin. It's from my fifteenth birthday. I remember she was laughing at something Gwen said. Her head is thrown slightly back, her eyes bright and happy. But there's still an underlying sadness I can see.

Suddenly Papa stands, breaking me from my retrospection. Nonna takes his hand, and he escorts her to Mom's coffin. I slide over to sit next to Uncle Louie, who instantly puts his big arm around me, pulling me close to his side. I watch as Nonna leans in, placing a kiss on Mama's cheek. When she straightens, Nonna wipes tears from her face. She moves to speak with Rocco as Papa takes her spot beside Mom's coffin. He runs his hand over her hair then bends down to kiss her.

Nonna comes up behind him and rubs his back slowly, wiping more tears. His body is statue still, his head hanging. I can't hear if he's talking to her or not, but I think he might actually be crying. Glancing between Rocco and Lucca, I find tears glistening on their cheeks, having slipped passed their sunglasses.

Finally, after many long minutes, Papa reaches up and closes her coffin. His hands rest on the closed lid, his head still lowered, now swaying back and forth. Nonna wraps her arm around him and lays her head on his back. The sound of people sniffling, deeply inhaling comes from behind me. Papa takes a deep, shuddering breath, his body shaking. Seeing him so affected makes me feel a kick in my chest.

As one, her pallbearers, Rocco, Lucca, Lorenzo, Vito and two other Family members, move to take her coffin. They lift it gently and carry it through the nave and out the front door to the waiting hearse. Papa and Nonna take a step to follow but wait for us to join them. They lead the way with Luigi, Uncle Louie and I falling in behind him. Tears flow freely from my eyes, and I have no way to stop them. My breathing picks up pace, it's becoming harder and harder to catch my breath.

Vito, Gwen, and Camilla fall in behind us as we pass them. Ignoring everyone, Papa heads straight for the cars. We climb in, and soon we're on our way to the estate and the family mausoleum.

Climbing out of the car, I'm struggling to breathe. I still haven't been able to get control. Uncle Louie takes my hand, tucking it in the crook of his arm. I try to take a step, but my feet are frozen to the ground. Luigi joins us, his warm arm sliding around my waist.

"Little One," Uncle Louie whispers in my ear, "breathe with me, okay? Slow down and breathe with me."

I try to do what he says, focusing on him, trying to

tear my eyes away from the pallbearers lifting Mom's pink casket from the hearse. My breathing stutters as I lean into my uncle. Sagging, Luigi holds most of my weight. Together, they move me closer to the mausoleum, and I lose sight of the hearse.

People from the church soon arrive, gathering around us as we finally join my father and Nonna. Standing to the right of the open crypt, the heady scent of blooming wisteria on the light breeze fills my lungs. As everyone finds their place, the pallbearers carry Mom to the priest and stop. The priest says a prayer, and once again the words are just a dull hum in my ears.

The pallbearers pass me, and as they do, I make the sign of the cross on my chest. I blow her a kiss as they enter the mausoleum. Slowly, carefully, they slide the beautiful pale pink casket into the niche in the wall. Tears cascade down my cheeks and I don't even try to stop them. As Mom's pallbearers exit the marble structure, two men step forward. As they work on sealing her tomb, I find I can't watch any longer, my heart shattering again.

Mom is entombed right next to Junior, as she wanted to be. Papa takes a step forward, and my eyes lift from their study of the ground. He passes Mom, kissing his fingers and touching the stone that seals her in. Nonna and Camilla follow and do the same. When they exit, they stand outside the door to allow the other mourners to do the same.

But, no one moves. They're waiting for me, out of respect. I'm not ready for this. I can't find the strength to do it. It took everything I had just to get through her Mass. I can't, I just can't. I don't want to be here anymore.

Pulling away from Uncle Louie and Luigi, I turn and flee. My breath stutters in my lungs, and I can't get oxygen in fast enough. Panic surges in my veins as I pick up my pace. God, it feels like I'm suffocating. I have to get air. Dizziness overwhelms me, and I stumble. Spotting a bench, my shaky legs collapse and I lower myself onto it.

Within seconds, Luigi is beside me, his arm around me, holding me tight. Uncle Louie squats in front of me, rubbing my knees.

"Come on, Little One. Keep breathing. You've got this. You don't have to go in there. It's okay," he says softly.

Unable to find my voice, I nod at him. Luigi rubs my back, and Uncle Louie hands me a handkerchief. I gently wipe my cheeks.

"I can't," I choke out. "I can't face them, talk to the Family... I know it's rude, but I just can't."

My uncle leans forward onto his knees and wraps me in his strong embrace. Engulfed in his arms, I'm finally able to take a breath, to breathe fully. The scent of comfort and safety fills my lungs, and I sag in his arms. My uncle's net of strength and protection surrounds me. Just that hug alone fills me with peace, with tranquility. It anchors me, reminding me I'm not alone. My tears slow as I wrap my arms around him. My heart returns to its normal, steady pace.

"Thank you," I whisper in his ear. "I love you, Uncle Louie. I'm better now. You always know just what I need." Pulling away, I look into his sunglass-covered eyes.

"I love you too, sweetie. Always will," he answers, kissing the top of my head.

"Luigi, take her to the tent where we'll be having dinner. Don't leave her alone, though I doubt anyone will approach her," my uncle instructs.

Luigi nods and stands, bringing me with him. "You ready, Aless?"

I blink, looking up at him, his arm still around me. Shaking myself off mentally, I try to lighten the mood, to ignore the reason for today. "Why yes, I am. Would you mind escorting me, fine sir?"

"Look at that, Lou," he chuckles. "My favorite sarcastic girl is back."

"I'll meet you over there shortly," Uncle Louie replies through his chuckles.

Reaching out, I grab my uncle's hand and pull him to me and kiss his cheek. He gives me a warm smile and turns to walk away. Luigi, with his hand on my lower back again, escorts me to Mom's pink golf cart to drive us to the tents where dinner will be served.

"I'm going to talk to Papa next week. I can't be seen in a pink golf cart. What do you think, Luigi? Will he go for red? A sparkly red?"

"Hell yeah. I'll put the request in myself," he answers, climbing in the driver's seat. "Besides, the men hate taking this one because it's pink. Though, it was always available for your Mom because they avoided it."

"Hmm, maybe purple then…" I ponder out loud.

Chapter 20

UNIVERSITY, THE PLAN BEGINS

(ONE YEAR LATER)

*I*t's Monday morning… and my birthday was last week. I'd refused Papa's attempts to get me to have another party. I told him to his face that if he planned one, I wouldn't go. I refuse to celebrate my birthday. I have enough horrible birthday memories, I don't want to add to them. He treats it like a damn national holiday. He did talk me into an intimate dinner, with no more than twenty or so people. Papa wasn't thrilled when he saw my list. I only included people close to me, but he finally agreed when he saw my resolve.

Thinking back on this last year, so much has happened… burying my mom, applying for university, hours of studying with tutors and helping Annalisa to get early admission. The studying probably wasn't necessary. Papa could have bought our way in early if we needed it. We took our tests for early entry to university last week, and we should find out today if my bestie got in. I have no doubt about my status.

One of my tutors encouraged me to take Mensa tests, and I passed, easily. Even though my education was important to Papa, he didn't let me join, saying it would be a distraction. I suspected it was because of the ideas I would be exposed to, and these highly intelligent successful people would be able to figure out who I am. Annalisa is who I'm concerned about. She wasn't expected to get perfect grades and had a bit more of a normal schooling than I did. Hell, I studied with a tutor for an hour after private school every day.

For the last year though, her social life stopped.

She came here every day after school, and we studied for hours to catch her up. Since people usually finish secondary at eighteen, we have to test for early admission at seventeen. Luckily, Papa and I are in agreement that I should go early.

Life is finally settling down, and I'm beginning to feel 'normal' again. Hopefully, I'll be able to start focusing on my plans for my future now.

A chime from my phone interrupts my thoughts of the future. Swiping my thumb across the screen, I find a group text from Papa to Uncle Louie, Luigi, Antonio, Annalisa, Stephen, Nonna, Camilla and me.

Papa: Family meeting, my office, 10 AM. DO NOT BE LATE.

Ha, like anyone would risk being late. Stretching, I glance at the clock on my desk. I have about an hour. I consider just laying here, but no… I need to get a move on. I'm ready to start my new life, and I need to plan for it.

Getting up, I head to the bathroom to get ready for the day. Papa's text leaves me in a fantastic mood, and the smile that greets me in the mirror is bright. I have a fairly good idea what this meeting is about. I'll be going to university soon, to start the next chapter in my "training." Papa's going to lay out *his* plan for me. Little does he know that he's playing right into my hands.

Things are coming together, I can feel it. I hope he really doesn't send Antonio and Stephen with us. Well, Stephen isn't as bad since he found out about Annalisa's feelings for him. But I could use a serious break from Antonio, from his jealousy and relentless advances. I finish getting ready and head to my closet. One of the things I'm looking forward to is the new wardrobe I'll be picking out for university, and I'll be visiting Laura's boutique to fill it. God, I'd love a pair of jeans.

Searching my closet, I finally find the shirt Annalisa got me. Light blue with the words *UCLA Bound* in yellow, I laughed when she gave it to me. Papa would get a kick out of it. Since he didn't say anything about a dress code in his text, I pull on my yoga pants too.

Pulling my hair into a huge bun, I secure it with three clips. The picture of Mom on my nightstand catches my eye in the mirror. Excitement flows through me as I pick it up.

"Mom," I whisper, stroking her face in the picture, "it begins now. I'll make our dreams come true. You and Aunt Elena keep an eye on me, okay? I'm sure I'll need guidance and encouragement soon." I bring the frame to my lips and kiss the cold glass. Carefully, I return it to its place on my nightstand.

At five minutes to ten, I leave my room and head to Papa's office. At the head of the hall down from his office, I see Uncle Louie and Luigi talking. Annalisa stands nearby, wearing classy jeans and a cute tank top with a cropped blazer. Now I feel underdressed.

Spotting me, Annalisa runs to me and grabs my hands. "I think the Capo is going to send me to university with you!" Her squeal pierces my ears as she jumps up and down.

I can't help but smile and jump with her. "I think so too. But, I want to talk with you about something. I know you're in love with Stephen, but I really hope Papa doesn't send him and Antonio with us. I wouldn't mind just Stephen, but your brother watching over us for the next few years would be a pain."

"You're right," she says, laughing. "Maybe they're getting a different assignment, or maybe something up north. I do want to keep seeing Stephen, so you may have to bite the bullet and keep Antonio busy for me." Annalisa eyebrows waggle up and down, and I laugh at her.

"God, the sacrifices I make for you," I reply shaking my head.

Leaning against the wall a chatting Stephen and Antonio catch my eye down at the end of the hall. In the standard Family uniform of a well-fitted black suit, white shirt, and black tie, I have to admit they look good. At least six feet tall and with dark, well-styled hair, they'd make any woman stop and take a second look. Too bad I know about Antonio's extracurricular activities, and Annalisa's already claimed, Stephen.

Any time they knew they'll be seeing Papa, they always style their hair precisely, not a hair out of place. It always makes me want to go mess up their hair, just to see what they'd do. The thought makes me chuckle quietly.

Nonna and Camilla walk around the corner, nearly bumping into me. Lucca and Rocco are right behind them.

"Well, what are you all waiting for? He said not to be late," Nonna says as she knocks on Papa's door and opens it the same time. So that's where Uncle Louie got that habit.

Nonna enters Papa's office, Lucca pauses, extending a hand for Annalisa and me to precede him.

Once inside, Papa stands, shaking his head. Vito and Lorenzo stand up from their seats in front of the massive desk, taking their usual positions behind Papa's chair.

"Good morning, Mama," he says, bowing his head at her. "Nice of you to knock."

"I did," she says greeting him with a kiss on the cheek. "You're the one who said ten, and not to be late." Nonna points at the clock which shows ten sharp. "If we can't be late, then you should show us the respect by being on time too."

Papa chuckles. "Can't argue with that. The rest of you might as well come on in. Girls, take a seat in front of my desk."

Nodding, Annalisa and I take our seats. I smile at Vito and Lorenzo, who give me their signature head nod. Nonna and Camilla take the chairs to the left of Papa's desk. Uncle Louie stands against the wall behind me. He gives me a wink and a huge smile as I smile back at him.

Luigi takes a place next to my uncle and leans in to whisper something. He wears a small smile, making me want to know what he's saying. Noticing my attention, Luigi gives me a wink. He and Uncle Louie relax, leaning on the wall.

Antonio and Stephen, though, stand at attention on the other side of the door from my uncle and Luigi. Feet shoulder width apart and hands behind their backs, chins up. They look like copies of each other, wearing the same stoic expressions. They look nowhere near relaxed, and it's hilarious.

Wanting to tease them, I straighten in my chair and wipe my face of any expression. I give them a stiff nod and a salute. Annalisa giggles at me and follows my lead, doing the same thing.

"Okay girls," Papa says taking his chair. "Turn around. Men, you can relax."

Focusing our attention on Papa, I find his eyes

reading my shirt. He smirks, shaking his head.

"That, young lady, is not an option for you," he declares.

Annalisa and I both burst into giggles. "We knew you wouldn't allow it," Annalisa says. "But you can't blame a girl for trying."

Papa shakes his head, looking down at his desk. "Alright. Most of you know why we're here today, to discuss the next phase of Alessandra's life… university. I've decided you'll both be going together. Annalisa passed her tests, thanks in part to you, Alessandra."

Annalisa and I grab each other, squealing. I turn to Papa, a smile on my face. He wears one too, as does Vito. I'm so thrilled I'll be spending the next four years with Annalisa by my side. I'm so happy I'll be able to see the love between her and Stephen grow, hear her hopes and dreams for her future. She actually has some say in the path her life takes. Hopefully, they get married before I have to disappear.

I'm not holding my breath for that one. Papa probably has an idea for me to get married first, for Annalisa to be in my wedding, then me in hers, like him and Mom with Vito and Gwen. There's no way I could ever do that, no matter how much I'd love to see Annalisa get the love of her life. Hopefully, they'll be engaged before I have to flee, and then I'll know my bestie will get her happily ever after, and Stephen would be there for her when I'm gone.

"Alessandra," Papa calls.

"Sorry Papa," I answer, my face heating. "My mind wandered for a second. Please, continue. I promise not to miss another word."

He smiles indulgently. "As I was saying, you and Annalisa have until Friday morning to get packed.

Lou will have the men ready to load the trucks with all of the things you'll need for university. Your classes start one week from today. You'll be pursuing a major in business and a minor in accounting."

"Friday?!" Annalisa shouts suddenly. "Really?"

I can't help but laugh at her. She grabs my arms, shaking me. "Why are you laughing? That's in four days! We have less than four days to pack!"

"Oh. My. God," I mock her, snickering. "Calm down, girl. We've got this. Now, please let Papa finish so we can go do that."

"I know this is sudden," Papa says to her. "but we've been planning this for well over a year. After this meeting is over, you'll be taken shopping for new clothes." His face turns serious. "Annalisa, you'll be Alessandra's *dama di corte*, lady in waiting. You will acquire clothes appropriate to that role. When in public, you will dress the same way Alessandra does, with decorum and class. You will be representing her, and this Family, as her companion and assistant. This means no short skirts, low cut, tight fitting tops, or exposed stomachs. I will accept nothing less."

Annalisa's mouth falls open, her eyes huge. I want to laugh at her. Papa waves his hand, and she refocuses on him, snapping her mouth shut. "Annalisa, when you are not in class or doing your duties, you are free to be yourself. Remember though, when anyone outside of the villa sees you, you are a reflection of Alessandra, the Family's Princess. From now on, you are more than Alessandra's best friend. You have an official role. You've been given a position of high status, one that is highly coveted. Camilla can give you more details later, but when Alessandra is in public, you are not to leave her side. Being the Princess's assistant means making sure she looks her best in any situation. It's your number one priority.

It's also a paid position, one that I'm sure you'll have for life."

Flicking my eyes over to Vito, I find him looking at his daughter sternly. She won't push her luck, but I want to know what's going on in that head of hers. Luckily, she doesn't make me wait.

"Does that mean," Annalisa hesitates. "umm, can I still wear jeans?"

Papa throws his head back, laughing. "You girls and your love of jeans. Is that all you got out of this, Annalisa? Your best friend has never worn any type of denim, but I understand you're used to them."

Annalisa's head hangs, her face flushing in embarrassment. "I'll allow you to wear them around friends, both in the villa and at functions," Papa informs her. "Places where jeans are appropriate. Attending classes is not one of them.

"Alessandra," Papa continues, turning to me. "You've proven to be a mature young woman. I believe I can trust you with your clothing selections. I think you know and understand what is expected of you and that you won't cross the line. With that, there are no more limitations of colors or fabrics. Before you ask, yes, that includes jeans and the colors black and red. Bear in mind, you represent the future of this Family. Dressing with modesty is your first priority."

Thrilled at the news that I can finally wear jeans, a grin breaks across my face. Annalisa dances in her chair beside me.

"Can I really get a pair of jeans?" I ask, excitement clear in my voice.

He nods. "It was something your mom convinced me of, just before your birthday last year. The only rules, and she agreed are no ripped jeans, none of those skin tight ones, they must not be low cut so that when you bend over you flash the world, and you must always wear full undergarments. Remember, *modesty*."

I glance at Nonna and Camilla who snicker, smiling at me. Returning my attention to Papa, I say, "Thank you for finally having faith in me, and for allowing me the freedom to pick out my clothes without limits. There were enough limits for so many years that I'm sure I know how to represent this Family with both modesty and respect. But, the umm, *full undergarments*? Is that your way of saying I must wear panties under my jeans?"

There are coughs and chuckles from behind me, but I don't join them… no matter how much I want to. "Yes," Papa replies. "That's exactly what I'm saying. I've noticed that, as have our men, that girls your age don't like seeing… what do you call it? Ah, yeah, panty lines."

I crack up, unable to resist. This conversation is ridiculous. "Papa, most of the girls I know always wear panties. They're just wearing thongs, so they don't have panty lines."

Papa shakes his head, looking me firmly in the eyes. His brow pulls down as his hand shoots out to point at me. "*No thongs*, young lady. I want to see those panty lines," he declares, slamming his hand on the desk. Annalisa and I both crack up, laughing hard. We're not alone as others join us, their laughter more controlled.

"Okay," I breathe, waving my hand and trying to catch my breath. "No thongs with jeans. I'll save those for other outfits."

Papa stares at me in shock. I laugh all over again, holding my sides.

"I'm kidding, Papa," I say through my hilarity. "I don't have any thongs."

I still cannot believe we're talking about this in front of everyone. Especially Antonio. He doesn't need to know about my underwear choices. I feel his eyes on me as Papa raps on his desk for our attention.

"Enough now, I need you both to listen to me." The laughter dies away as we all focus on him.

"If Lou or Mama, or even Luigi for that matter, tell you to change your clothes, you're to do so without question. Agreed?"

"Yes, sir," Annalisa and I answer in unison.

Papa leans back in his chair, his hands resting on his stomach. "Moving on from your wardrobe, you've both been to the villa up north. It's been years, so you may not remember. While it is smaller than this estate, there is plenty of room for all of you. Alessandra, you will be running the northern arm of the Family. I've had the security up there updated and upgraded. Lucca and Rocco will oversee the grounds and house security. They have their own living quarters away from the main house. Those men are not allowed in the house, period. They are there to protect the grounds while you are there, not to be your friends. They've been personally selected for this assignment."

Papa glances around the room. "The six men in this room are the only men allowed into the main house, aside from me. You will be allowed to have meetings with them, as Lou and Luigi will be in attendance. The men working and guarding the grounds know and understand these rules."

"Yes, sir," I reply, nodding.

I relax, and Annalisa sighs as Papa's face loses its

fierce look. "Annalisa," he says, "your relationship with Alessandra is about to change. You'll be replacing Mama and Camilla's roles. You'll need to learn as much as possible from them. I know you've been close friends all your lives, and that at first, this might be awkward and uncomfortable as you adjust, but I have confidence in you. You are to treat this position with seriousness and respect. As much as Alessandra is your best friend, she is still your Family's Princess and will one day be your Capo. You are being groomed to be her right hand."

My eyes find my best friend. Her face is serious, and I wouldn't be surprised if she asked for a pen and paper to take notes. She's taking in every word, like he's standing over her with a sword, knighting her as Lady-in-Waiting Annalisa. Sheesh, Papa really has my entire life planned. I cannot believe this. I have no say whatsoever. I really am just a freaking puppet.

"Alessandra," Papa says, pulling me from my pity party. "Something else your Mom wanted you to be able to do, if you desire, is to cut your hair if you'd like." A smile lifts my lips, knowing how badly she wanted to cut my hair, but Papa never allowed it. I'll leave it for now, though. Instead, I'll cut it when I run. It's one of my most noticeable features and all the men obsessed with it may not recognize me without it.

"No!" Two voices cry out from behind me.

Papa's eyes dance as he looks first at Uncle Louie and Luigi, then at Stephen and Antonio.

"OH!" Annalisa squeals. "You can cut your hair short like mine! I already know how to style it!"

"NO!" The same two voices cry again, this time louder and firmer. Uncle Louie chuckles.

"Well, Princess," Papa says. "What do you say?"

Standing, I remove the three clips securing the huge bun on my head. My hair cascades down my back to my knees as I run my hands through it. Sometimes I feel like a brunette Rapunzel, as long as it is.

"Papa," I answer, "I've had long hair as long as I can remember. I can't imagine having it short like Annalisa's." I turn to her, "By the way, you need to let that grow out. No offense, but I don't know what you were thinking having it short in the back and long in the front. You look like an American soccer mom who wants to complain about every little thing. Besides, you can't do anything with it, not like I can."

Two relieved breaths echo through the room. Yeah, I know it's Luigi and Antonio. Turning back to Papa, I continue, "I'm pretty good at styling this without having to spend hours on it, like some people. I might get a trim, but only to clean up the split ends, nothing drastic."

"Hey," Annalisa cries. "It only takes me thirty minutes... well, maybe forty-five, tops. Not hours!" I laugh at her defense of her short hair, shaking my head.

Papa stands, coming around to my chair. "Princess, turn around," he says with a smirk. "Slowly. I want to see your hair. It's so beautiful. I've always loved it, as have most of the men in the Family."

Giving him a small smile, I do as he says, turning on my toes, excruciatingly slowly to let him examine my hair. Uncle Louie holds his hand over his mouth, trying to hide the smile I see in his eyes. Next, to him, Luigi's head is tipped down, but his eyes are locked on me, or rather, my body. It feels a little odd, but his eyes find mine and a slow, secret smile forms on his face.

Continuing my turn, my eyes pass Stephen who

gives me a friendly smirk. Antonio, though, is licking his lips, his eyes roaming my body. They pause shortly at my hips and then continue to my breasts. Finally, Antonio meets my eyes, his eyes smoldering. Grossed out, I give him a disgusted look and shake my head.

Completing my circuit, I stop, facing Papa. "How long does it take you to put your hair back up?"

"You want me to put it back up?" I ask. Papa nods. Bending over, I flip my hair in front of me. Twisting it, I wrap it around and around and around before reaching for the clips on Papa's desk. Standing back up, I secure the first clip and quickly finish with the other two.

Suddenly, a loud grunt fills the room, and I spin around. Antonio is bent at the waist, Luigi in front of him, his eyes blazing with fury. Stephen and Uncle Louie shake their heads.

"What the fuck?" Antonio complains in a strained voice.

Papa chuckles beside me as I look from Luigi to Antonio. Turning back to my father, I ask, "Did I miss something?"

Papa returns to his seat and sits, leaning back and looking relaxed. He shakes his head lightly. "So, you don't want to cut your hair?" he asks, ignoring my question.

"No," I answer him, shaking my head. "Not right now. I'm going to have a full load of classes, learning to run the Family business *and* continuing my training. I'll have a pretty full plate. I'd rather not have to worry about styling my hair for now."

He nods, his eyes focused over my shoulder.

A deep voice hisses, "Yesss," behind me. Once more, scuffles and shuffling fill the room. I spin on my feet to find out what's going on, only to find Antonio and Luigi fighting.

"Hey!" I call, marching up to them. "What is going on?! Stop this, right now. Did you hear me? I said *STOP IT!*"

"Stephen," Papa, shouts over me. "Get your boy. Lou, get yours." Stephen and Uncle Louie do as they're told. Antonio is clearly the loser, his hair is messed up, and blood trickles from his nose.

Luigi's hair is a bit of a mess too. Well, at least their hair looks better. But what the hell is going on?

Stephen has one of Antonio's arms bent behind his back, and Uncle Louie has Luigi pinned against the wall. Both scrappers are breathing heavy, glaring at each other.

"Look at her like that again, and I kick your balls into your throat!" Luigi yells at Antonio. His voice is scary, a tone I've never heard from him.

My eyes spring open in shock.

"Luigi, calm down," Uncle Louie says, shoving him into the wall again.

"Ladies," Papa says, "I'm going to let you go on up to your room to pack. I'm sure the men have delivered some boxes for you to get started. Princess, you have a lot of packing to do, I'm sure. I need to knock some heads together and deal with this shit."

"*This* crap?" I ask, turning to him. "What is going on? If this has to do with me, I want to deal with it."

Papa smiles, his eyes shining, something I rarely see. "Looks like there's a bit of a fight going on over you."

"Me?!" I shout, looking between Antonio and

Luigi. "I don't think so. This has to be something else."

"I'm sorry, Aless," Luigi says. "I was teaching *this pervert* some manners."

I'm confused, so I just stare at them, not knowing what to do.

"Little One," Uncle Louie calls. "You've been dismissed. You two head on out. Luigi and I will be up to take you shopping in less than an hour. Go on now."

I glance at Papa, then Nonna and Camilla. They stand, motioning for us to follow them. "Come on, girls," Nonna says. "Let the men get this testosterone fest under control."

Walking from the room, I'm still trying to wrap my head around what just happened. And I will figure this out, that's for sure. I'll definitely be talking to Luigi later when no one else is around.

Annalisa laughs as soon as we're out the door. "Looks like my brother has some competition."

"What? What are you talking about?" I ask.

"Luigi has a thing for you," she says winking at me.

"Oh no, he doesn't," I announce, shaking my head. "If anything, he was protecting my honor from Antonio's stares and comments. But I will find out what's going on tonight, that's for sure."

"I don't know," she says. "I wouldn't be so sure Luigi isn't developing feelings for you. He went after Antonio the second my brother checked out your bum, when you bent over to fix your hair."

Nonna and Camilla chuckle behind us as we hit

the stairs.

"I don't see anything funny," I declare. "Luigi was just doing his job, teaching Antonio that he needs to respect me and not constantly stare at my body. I'm sick of the way he always stares at me. How will I ever get the respect of the men in this Family if Antonio is a walking hormone? I may just have to handle this myself and put him in his place with a nut punch."

"Alessandra," Nonna says, raising her voice over Annalisa's giggles. "Watch your mouth, young lady."

"Nonna," I complain, "saying I'm going to nut punch Antonio isn't foul, it's just stating facts. Do you really think he says that I have nice 'breasts and bum'? No, he talks about my *tits* and *ass*. You have to accept that I've put the little girl you want to believe I am aside. I must convince these men that I'm a strong, capable woman and I deserve their respect if I'm ever expected to lead the Family."

"I suppose you're right about that... but you don't need to stoop to the men's foul-mouthed level. You're still a young lady. Demanding their respect is one thing, but swearing like the soldiers is another," Nonna admonishes firmly.

"Am I not one of the best soldiers? Did I not kill one of our worst enemies, as well as many of his men? I think I've earned the right to use whatever language I feel necessary to put our men in their place. Don't worry, Nonna, I'm not making it part of my normal speech. But, if needed for shock or to gain their attention, I will use it, if only to get them to see me as more than the Capo's daughter."

"You are that. I think the men will always remember what you've done. You've earned your place. I'm sure most of the men respect you, if not fear you just a little bit," Nonna declares as we reach my room.

"Let me just state here and now that if I see any of the villa security staring at my body like I'm just eye candy, I'll put them in their place. I'm going to demand respect," I state with confidence.

Annalisa rubs her hands together. "I can't wait for this. There just might be some excitement in our future. Oh! Does that include Luigi? I've seen him checking you out... more than once." Her face is alight with excitement at the thought of me knocking Luigi to next Tuesday.

I sigh, wiping my face. "Yes, I'm aware Luigi's checked out my bum. He's told me he's an ass man and has even told me to cover it when it draws too much attention. It's also why he walks close behind me, giving death glares to other men trying to check me out. He does it to protect me."

"Aless," Annalisa says. "I don't care what you think. That man has a thing for you. You should kiss him! He might die of shock!"

"No!" Nonna shouts.

"Are you nuts?!" I cry.

Annalisa and Camilla crack up, but I ignore them.

"There is *no way* I will kiss Luigi... at least now. First of all, he's told me I'm too young right now. Second, he'd never do anything to lose Uncle Louie or Papa's respect. They trust him. He'd probably run so fast to confess that he'd leave burn marks on the ground. It's not worth it. Luigi and I are friends, and yes, we do tease and flirt, but it's safe. That is it."

"So, does that mean..." Nonna shakes her head, trying to ask her question. "Is Luigi someone you might actually consider as a husband and partner in the coming years?" She lifts an eyebrow, and I laugh at her.

"Nonna, I'm only seventeen. No, I'm not in love with Luigi, nor do I even have a crush on him, but I'd gladly take Luigi over Antonio any day. I'm still praying for a miracle that Papa will allow me to fall in love and not arrange a marriage. Unfortunately, according to Papa, the 'subject is closed.'"

"The lady doth protest too much, methinks," Annalisa says, quoting Hamlet and making me laugh.

$Chapter$ *21*

TESTOSTERONE FEST
(LUIGI)

$\mathcal{A}$s soon as the door closes behind the ladies, Al points to the chairs in front of his desk. I take the one to the left, and Antonio collapses into the other one. Lou stands behind me as Stephen does the same with Antonio.

"Okay, *boys*, we're gonna have a little chat," Al says.

Antonio gives me a nasty look which I return. *Asshole.* Lou squeezes my shoulder, encouraging me to keep my seat.

Behind Al's desk, Vito glowers at both of us, whereas Lorenzo looks like he's enjoying this. He's fighting a smile, but I don't see what's so fucking funny. That pervert was licking his fucking lips.

Lucca and Rocco, though, look like they wish I'd done more to Antonio. Actually, they look like they want to tear into him themselves. I knew I liked them.

"Antonio," Al says, breaking my study of the men behind him, "you missed our meeting before Sophia's services last year because I asked you to stay with the women. I asked Luigi if there was something going on between him and Alessandra and if I needed to cut off his balls."

Antonio snaps his head around, glowering at me. Stephen grips his shoulder, keeping him in place. Al smirks.

"Relax, boy. He's not touched her inappropriately. I trust him with my daughter. I've been watching them for some time now, the way they tease each other and

Luigi's protective nature of her. You should know he's on my short list. But *you*, Antonio, I do not trust. If Luigi hadn't intervened when you were ogling and drooling over my daughter's ass, you would have me to deal with."

Antonio shrinks in his chair, hanging his head. *Yeah, asshole, you weren't as smooth as you thought.*

"I'm sorry, sir," he says and looks up at Al. "I have such strong feelings for Alessandra. I just couldn't help myself. I'll try to control it better."

Lying fucker. "Yeah, just like all those *feelings* you have for every other girl with a slit in this town," I mutter.

"You say something?" Al asks.

Taking a deep breath, I meet Al's piercing gaze. "I did, sir. I'm sick of this punk kid fucking anything and everyone - including Aless's own friends- then professing his *feelings* for her."

Antonio's voice turns cocky. "Come off it, you're just jealous because you can't get laid. I've got them all begging for me."

Rage, white-hot rage, simmers in my veins and I move to stand. Lou's hands on my shoulders squeeze hard, forcing me back into the chair.

"Antonio," Al growls, "saying shit like that right after you tell me you have 'strong feelings' for my daughter makes me think you only want to fuck her, not be her partner."

Yeah, fucker. I relax a bit, knowing Al isn't an idiot.

"No sir," Antonio says contritely, "I definitely want to be her partner."

"When hell freezes over," I mutter.

Al smirks, rubbing his chin. "Luigi, I hear you mumbling over there. If you have something to say, say it loud enough for everyone to hear. Don't just sit there and mumble."

Sitting up, I point at Antonio. "Hell no. Only when hell freezes over will you be Aless's partner in *anything*."

Antonio explodes, rash and unthinking. Ah, this is perfect. "What the fuck? Just because you're her guard doesn't give you a say in anything. Find your own woman and leave *mine* alone!"

I snort, "If I leave 'your women' alone, I'd have to leave town to find one! When was the last time you got an STD test? You might want to do that. I've seen the women you fuck. You need to get tested cuz I hear some of those bad ones can make your little dick fall off, and we all know you can't live without your tiny friend."

Antonio tries to get up, but Stephen shoves him back down. "Let me assure you, my dick sure as fuck isn't little! Why don't you ask any girl down at the club?"

I smirk. "Ha, I don't have to go down to the club. Those girls are paid to tell the guys they fuck that their little winkies are the biggest they've ever seen."

"I don't have to pay for a fuck!" Antonio cries defensively.

"Well shit," I say, flicking my eyes at Al. "Does that mean you're taking advantage of the bottom line, not paying for their services while they're working? And you're on the list? What advantages will you take if you marry Aless?"

Al waves his hand, but I know I've given him a lot to think about. "You two need some time in the gym, under supervision. We're Family. We can't have this animosity hovering over you two. Luigi be assured I've heard your points and I will be following up on them. I had thought," he glares at Antonio, "he'd gotten it under control. But it doesn't seem he has."

Al leans back, a muscle ticking in his jaw. "Antonio, it appears you're still fucking anything with a slit you come in contact with. Obviously, all the talks we've had fell on deaf ears." Al leans forward, his eyes hard. "You fuck any girl in the club, you fucking pay for it. Do I make myself clear? There is a Family rate, but those girls are working girls. If you're fucking one, you're taking her time and money. She could be making good money with a *paying* client. Do you understand?" Al's voice is controlled, but rage laces through it.

Looking at his lap, Antonio mumbles, "Yes, sir."

"You're about to turn twenty-one. If you're still fucking every woman in this town, and Family, you'd better get a fucking test. That's an order. I want to see the results before I allow you to help the girls move this weekend. Do I make myself crystal clear?"

"Yes sir, I'll get tested soon," Antonio nods, mumbling again.

"No," Al shakes his head. "You'll get tested *today*. If I haven't seen the results, you aren't going anywhere, period."

Antonio shrinks in his chair, his head hanging low and shoulders slumped.

Al turns back to me. "Now son, whether you want to admit it or not, I believe you're developing feelings that are more than just brotherly to 'Aless,' as you call her." Al smiles warmly. "I know you protect her as a brother at times, but I see more in those eyes of yours when you look at her. I hear it in your voice when you

247

two are talking. I'm pretty sure Lou would agree with me on this." His eyes lift to Lou over my shoulder. Fuck me. Damn it.

"You're probably right on that one, brother," Lou says, a smile in his voice. "I see it too. I've asked 'Aless' if she is crushing on Luigi and she turned bright red, denying it over and over. She constantly reassures me that they're 'just friends.' She might be protesting just a bit too much."

He chuckles lightly. "I don't think either one of them honestly know what they feel for each other. But I am aware of it, and like you, I fully trust Luigi. Should I ever doubt him, you'll be the first to know… after I beat the shit out of him. They're good for each other right now."

"I've said it before, and I'll say it again," I announce to reassure my mentor and my Capo, "I would never touch a seventeen-year-old girl. She is safe under my guard. And no one else will ever touch her either, that I vow to you," I finish, flicking my eyes over the slumped form of Antonio.

"Luigi, Antonio brought up a good point. Are you getting laid?" Al asks, shocking me. Antonio perks up, looking at me with a smirk.

I can't help but chuckle at him. "I'm not a virgin. It's like I told you before, there's a girl up north I visit. We've had an on again, off again thing since we were in school. Sandy just finished university and has a good job. She knows the score, doesn't want anything permanent right now, just some fun. I also have one down here as well. I'm not an asshole who has to look like the big man with his conquests. I respect them and their desire to keep it quiet. I'm a big boy, I can handle it myself."

"Bet you 'handle it' yourself a lot… probably while you're thinking of Alessandra," Antonio pops off. Turning, I slug him in the arm.

"Oh, I think he protests too much," Antonio says laughingly, mimicking Lou's earlier words.

"Stephen," Vito whispers and Stephen smacks Antonio upside his head. Vito delivers the death glare only a parent can while Antonio rubs his head. Lou snickers behind me and I almost lose it.

"Thank you, Vito. He deserved that. Now you two, this bickering and fighting needs to stop." Al turns his attention to Antonio. "If Luigi or Lou catch you looking at Alessandra like you want to fuck her again, you deserve the shit-kicking they will deliver. Capisce? Get control of that wild cock of yours. You aren't a seventeen-year-old *boy* trying figure out how to use it anymore. You're a man and a member of the Family, start acting like it. And remember to wear a fucking condom. I don't want some bastard running around out there, and neither does your father."

Al turns his attention to Lou. "Keep an eye on Laura while they're shopping. Let me know how that goes. I've told Laura not to push too hard to befriend Alessandra, but you know how women are. Laura is aware of the guidelines for Alessandra's wardrobe and has been working on clothes for both girls for a while now. I want Alessandra to try everything on to make sure it's appropriate before she brings it home."

He looks around behind him, "Lorenzo, Lucca, Rocco, hope you enjoyed the show. You're all dismissed. Antonio, test results on my desk by Friday."

I stand up, and Antonio does too. I glare at him, ready to just walk out.

"Play nice," Vito calls, coming around the desk to stand behind Antonio. "Shake hands, boys."

Continuing to glare at him, I extend my hand to

shake his. Yeah, I might have squeezed his hand hard, and judging by the wince in his eyes and the fact that he released my hand first, I won.

As he walks out the door with Stephen and Vito, I lean into Lou. "I'll never let that punk-ass forget it if he turns up with a fucking STD."

We both crack up. "Believe me, none of us will," Lou replies.

In the hall, Lou stops me with a hand on my arm. "Luigi, I want to ask you something while we're out of hearing range."

His voice is imploring so I stop, giving him my full attention. "Are you going to jam me up too?" I ask, trying to joke.

"No, I'm not going to jam you up," he replies. "I just want to say you know how Little One feels about Antonio. But since my brother is hell bent on picking out her husband, I'd much rather it be you. I like you enough that I would bless that union... and encourage Al to choose you over that punk."

I freeze in shock. Did I hear what I think I heard? I blink, watching Lou carefully. "Really?" I ask, and he nods. "Thank you. I'm so honored you feel that way about me. Fuck, I need to tell you something."

Lou's eyes harden, but I push on. "I'm breaking a promise I made to Aless, the night of her first Family meeting. She asked me if Al was determined to marry her off, and if she couldn't find a way out, she asked me to put myself higher on his list. She asked that I request our Capo choose me for her husband. She feels that, as friends, we would have a better chance at making it grow into real love. In a way, she asked me to marry her. She wouldn't let me give her an answer then, but to think about it and take the steps if I was agreeable and she needed me."

I snort. "Her fear is that she'll kill Antonio, literally, if she's forced to marry him. She doesn't think he could ever be faithful to her. Besides, she thinks of him as a brother and doesn't feel 'chemistry' with him. I was shocked and honored that she asked me, that she would think of me like that."

Seeing Lou's face, I continue. "Don't worry. She's indicated that she's not in love with me. We haven't talked about it since, but it haunts me." I take a step closer, lowering my voice. "But if our Capo gets serious about Antonio being her husband, I will step up and ask for her hand. Do I love her right now? Not that way. Could I love her as a husband one day? I do believe that is possible. Absolutely. She's amazing. Aless told me to keep looking for my true love, to not give up. For her, me finding love and being happy would make her happy. She doesn't want to interfere with me finding 'heart pounding, stomach dropping real love.' You needed to know where I stand, and I hope you don't share this with her. She asked me in confidence and wanted me to keep it to myself."

I can practically hear the gears turning in his head as Lou tries to work through what I've said, that Aless asked me to marry her when she was fifteen. He shakes his head in confusion. Finally, he extends his hand. I reach out and shake it.

"This conversation stays between us," he vows. "I'm confident that you and Antonio are the front runners on Al's list. There are a few others, but I don't think they are even close to you two. Unless some miracle happens, you're her best option. And the best for her, I might add. We have four years to figure this out, though."

Lou turns, heading for the stairs. "Thank you for your honesty. I fully trust you with Alessandra. I've never doubted that. Now, let's go get the girls and see how Laura and Alessandra get along. This might be fun." He chuckles and pounds me on the back.

At Aless's door, Lou does his signature knock and open. He walks in, and I follow him. Aless shoots up from the floor where she was sitting crisscross applesauce.

"One day, you're just going to walk in here and catch me in my birthday suit," she says. The image of her in that bathing suit two years ago flashes through my mind. God damn it.

Lou laughs, "Oh, Little One. I brought you up better than to walk around your room naked. You change clothes either in your closet or on the other side of the dressing screen. I have plenty of time to cover Luigi's eyes. You don't have to worry about him seeing you nude."

"Well," I say, winking at Aless, "I was kind of hoping to see her naked to help me sleep at night."

"You want a nut punch too?" Lou whirls on me.

Raising my hands, I reply, "I was just messing with you knowing you'd get bent out of shape. Aless's virtue and nudity is safe with me."

"Alright, alright," Aless interrupts, "enough with the jewel jabbing and testosterone fest. It's time to take me shopping and tell me all about what happened after we left."

"No," both Lou and I declare in unison.

"But we will take you ladies shopping," Lou says.

"Not fair," Annalisa whines.

"I agree," Aless answers her, grabbing her purse and heading for the door. The whole way to the SUV they whine and complain about how we won't share. Lou and I just smile, not saying a word.

Chapter 22

SHOPPING AT MY FATHER'S GIRLFRIEND'S BOUTIQUE

*I*n the SUV, I feel an odd sense of relief and even some happiness. I've been looking forward to this next step in my life for so long, and I'm not sure I can contain my elation at being able to move forward with my plans. I'm taking the first steps to my freedom, and I'm fully committed to figuring out a way to escape. Having Papa trust me in picking out my clothes, without color limits and allowing me to wear jeans for the first time, is a step in the right direction. Going to university and learning to take over the northern branch of the Family businesses is another and will give me information that I can use to facilitate my escape.

My mind moves to the realization that I'm actually on the way to go shopping at my father's girlfriend's shop, Laura's Boutique. Those are words I'd never thought I would say. Pulling up to the shop, it's bigger than I thought it would be. Recalling Gwen's words the morning of Mom's funeral, I remember she mentioned that Laura had expanded.

Uncle Louie opens my door but blocks my way as I try to leave the car. Looking me in the eyes, he says, "Little One, if at any time you feel uncomfortable and want to leave, we can. You're in charge of this."

"I'm good," I smile, patting his arm. "I've got this. Let's go check out my new wardrobe," I say climbing from the car. I wiggle my bum as I take a few steps. "This bum is looking forward to some jeans!"

"Enough of that, young lady," my uncle admonishes. "No giving Luigi a show." I giggle in response and meet Annalisa as she comes around to our side.

Annalisa hooks her arm in Luigi's. "I don't know, I might just steal your boyfriend," she says, winking at me.

Smiling, I link my arm through his other one. "Does that mean I get to watch the big, strong Luigi beat up Stephen when he checks out your bum? That's something Stephen does. I don't think Luigi would stand for that."

Luigi laughs, glancing between us and Uncle Louie joins in from behind us. It's all the encouragement I need to keep going as we make our way to the front door.

"Girl, Luigi doesn't share or play well with others. I guess that means Stephen is free to roam. I can give him a call and let him know," I say.

"Nope, no thanks," Annalisa says, dropping Luigi's arm and reaching to open the door. "Now that you put it that way, there's no reason to tell Stephen anything. You can have him, I'll keep my secret boyfriend for myself."

"Hey, hey," Luigi calls. "It's my job to open doors, young lady." He takes the door from Annalisa.

Uncle Louie and I both laugh at Annalisa's quick dismissal of Luigi.

"Annalisa, I hate to be the first to tell you, but there is no secret about you and Stephen." Uncle Louie teases her.

"Fine, and who told you about Stephen? And who else knows? Please tell me my parents don't know?" Annalisa quickly drills us.

Everyone just laughs as we all walk into the boutique. I shake my head at them and release Luigi's arm. "See," I say to Annalisa, pointing at Luigi, "he just can't play well with others. He won't even let you open a door... so domineering. Sheesh." My uncle and my bestie both laugh with me.

Looking around the beautiful, very large boutique, you can easily tell no expense was spared. Laura walks out of a back room. Her eyes trail over us, and she smiles.

"Oh, it's so nice to see all of you laughing," she announces walking over to greet us. She stops in front of me and looks me over. "I'm sorry," she says seconds before throwing her arms around me. "I've wanted, no needed, to do this for so long."

Confused, I stand there for a second before hesitantly patting her back. "Umm, it's okay." My eyes find Annalisa, whose jaw is practically touching the ground.

Laura steps back, releasing me. She twists her fingers nervously. "I just wanted to tell you again, like I did the night we met, I've heard so much about you, for years. You've had one hell of a year. I don't want to replace your mother, not by any means, but I'd like to be your friend. If you hate me and want to call me your Papa's whore, that's okay too. Go ahead, I won't mind."

I raise my hand, stopping her. "Laura, I've never called anyone, erm," I pause, clearing my throat and continue quietly, "a whore." I smile sheepishly. "I will admit, when I first found out about you, I referred to you as Papa's stripper. Frequently though, I call Annalisa a tramp on a regular basis, well, because she likes to dress like one. But I love her anyway."

"Hey," my bestie calls out, "that's just because I call you a wannabe hooker with all your stripper dance moves."

I swat her hand, both of us giggling.

Uncle Louie clears his throat. "I've never heard you call each other such names and I'd better not. Aren't we here to look at clothes, and not this girly chit-chat?"

Laura puts her arm around me and her other around Annalisa, steering us to the back. "Okay girls, Lou is getting grumpy so let's get this show on the road. I've had my crew working on quite a few selections for both of you. I'm dying to see what you think."

She pauses, calling over her shoulder, "Men, you stay out front. I promise there's no one back here but me. I gave everyone the day off, so I could focus on the Princess. Besides, if anyone were waiting back here, I'm certain she could protect Annalisa and I."

My uncle sighs. "Laura, Al told us that no outfits can come home without approval from me and Luigi."

"What?" Laura stops, turning to face him. "Are you telling me that the Neanderthal I'm dating doesn't trust me to dress these young ladies with decorum?"

Luigi stifles a laugh, coughing. Uncle Louie shakes his head, rubbing the back of his neck. "I'm not getting in the middle of this one, Laura. We're just following orders. You'll have to take it up with Al."

"Fine," she sighs. "You two take a seat in the viewing area over there. I'll call Al while the girls try on their first outfits. And believe me, he won't be happy when I'm done with him either."

Uncle Louie heads towards several chairs, taking one facing the front door. Luigi gives me a wink before taking one facing the back. He'll be first to see me, and his smirk tells me he's looking forward to the show.

Laura opens a door, revealing a huge dressing room with two racks of clothes. There's a tri-fold mirror with a small platform and a small table with sewing accessories near it. Walking to the first rack, Laura waves her hand over it. "Alessandra, these are for you. You're more than welcome to find something off the racks out front too. They'll have to be altered to fit your unique figure perfectly."

Motioning to the other rack, she continues, "As you can guess, Annalisa, these are for you to try on. Your mother gave me your sizes but didn't know your measurements, so we tried our best. I've included suits, both slacks, and skirts with jackets and blouses, like Al, requested, along with business dresses and some casual things as well, for your time off."

Laura points to a table behind the racks. "Al wanted me to include anything you might need for a full wardrobe. You'll find shoes, and accessories like scarves, jewelry and purses there. You're more than welcome to look in the store, too, for more. I'll step outside, so you can try things on if that makes you more comfortable. Or I can stay and assist you, whichever works for you."

Annalisa's eyes are huge, just as mine are. "Wow," Annalisa breathes. "Our Capo said I need a whole lot of things to look the part for the new job I've been assigned in the Family since I'm now her helpmate," she throws a thumb over her shoulder at me, "or maybe it was assistant… or was it her shadow?"

My poor friend is overwhelmed by everything that's happened today. Trying to lighten the mood, I joke, "You could always say no, you know. But I think you like the idea of hovering over me all the time."

"Oh, yes," she says rolling her eyes, "that's always been a dream of mine. To be by your side, twenty-four-seven, 365 days a year," she sighs dreamily, batting her lashes. "And I'll get to know and see everything you do and guess what your next needs are, so I can be ready to fulfill it happily."

Smirking, I retort pompously, "I'm so glad you already know your job and what's expected of you."

Laura watches us, her expression changing from awe to dismay at Annalisa, to complete surprise at my response.

"Oh, Laura," Annalisa says softly, "we're just teasing each other. Don't let this bother you. We don't mind if you stay and help. Heck, Alessandra has had people dressing her for most of her life."

"Hey!" I cry. "Be nice. You know I wanted that to stop ages ago."

Laura shakes herself. "Okay, girls. We have a lot to try on and a fashion show for the grumpy men waiting out there… I'm sure they're enjoying all the fashion magazines I have. Let's get busy."

We've been trying on clothes for well over two hours. Uncle Louie's approved all of the slacks, blouses, and skirts I've shown him, the more business attire. I'm currently in my third shift dress. He rejected the first two, saying they were too tight. This one is just as tight, so I can only imagine what will come out of his mouth.

"Still too tight. I can see your panty lines. What would it look like if you bend over? What do you think, Luigi?"

Luigi, stunned, stumbles over his words. "Uh, I'd rather not imagine that right now, thank you." He shifts in his seat. "But yes, they are too tight for our seventeen-year-old Princess. They're too alluring."

I laugh, giving Luigi a look and rolling my eyes. He's talking about me like I'm not even there. Laura's not happy with their criticism either.

"I can alter them to fit looser, making sure there're no visible *panty lines* showing if she should bend over. God forbid the sight of *panty lines*. You do know most women wear thongs, so they don't have *panty lines*," she says, walking back to the dressing room.

I bite my lip to stifle the laugh that threatens to break free. Annalisa wears a similar expression. I shouldn't, but I can't pass up the chance to comment about thongs.

"Laura, you'll have to talk to Papa about that. Thongs are forbidden undergarments for me..." I trail off, laughter escaping. Annalisa joins in, her gleeful chuckles filling the shop.

Uncle Louie shoots me a stern look. "Laura," he calls. "since Annalisa's here, take her measurements to make future fittings easier. Her dresses and skirts should only be two, maybe three inches above her knees."

"You do know these girls are seventeen, right?" she asks, surprised.

My uncle stands, and walking around, he says, "I'm more aware than you know that they're only seventeen. I also know the Princess looks much older than her years. And, as of today, where she goes, Annalisa goes too. The both of them will constantly be in rooms with *men* of the Family. I don't want any of them to get any ideas, period. I also don't want these two to hear lewd comments. When the men look at them, they need to see professional, modest women. It will help ensure their safety, and grant them the respect they're due. Do you understand?"

Laura nods, looking chastened. "Yes, I understand. I'll keep that in mind when designing their clothes."

"Thank you for understanding the importance of this. I didn't mean to come off so harsh, but I got the impression that Al didn't fill you in on the reason for the modesty guidelines," Uncle Louie replies, his voice softer.

"No, he didn't," Laura sighs. "I didn't think of that. I was thinking the girls will be in university, not of Alessandra's place in the Family, nor of the meetings. Thank you for explaining it to me. I'm still new at this side of things and to thinking about such things."

To lighten the mood, I announce, "We've saved the best for last! I'm sure you'll approve of my last dress. It's my favorite style too, *retro*. Then you only have to suffer through the jeans!" Grabbing Annalisa's arm, I do a little dance. "Come on, girly! Get those giraffe legs moving!"

"Hey! I don't have giraffe legs, shorty," she jokes back. Everyone smiles as I continue joking with my friend.

"I'll have you know, the best things come in small packages... like jewelry!" They chuckle as we walk into the back room, thankfully.

After Laura measured both Annalisa and I, we quickly change into our last outfit and head back out for Uncle Louie and Luigi's approval. Facing the mirror, our backs to them, we admire my vintage dress. I love this one, black with red polka dots, and the short, cuffed sleeves are perfect. The square collared bust is just the right amount of loose, and it's tight from below my breasts to the waist, where it flairs out in a full skirt that falls below my knees. It accentuates my tiny waist, and I love that.

Annalisa wears black pleated pants with a fitted, red blouse and a short, black jacket with two red buttons. It looks absolutely adorable on her and fits her long, slim figure perfectly.

"Well?" I ask, looking at my uncle in the mirror. "What do you think?"

"He *has* to like them," Annalisa says, catching my eye. "We look like we could fit in on *I Love Lucy Show*."

"You're right, Annalisa," Uncle Louie says. "I love these two even though it might bring some attention to your chest by making your waist look tiny. It's not for meetings, though. Classes will be fine because Luigi and I will be there with you. Right, Luigi?"

Watching Luigi's face in the mirror, his eyes travel up and down my body. His eyes meet mine in the mirror, and he finally replies, haltingly. "Yeah... she, uh, she's not wearing that dress alone without one of us. Period. Depending on how the male students respond, I'll wait to see if it will be a dress she can wear regularly."

Frustrated, I roll my eyes at them. "I can't help that my boobs are this big, okay? But I *refuse* to hide them by wearing baggy dresses for the rest of my life!" I cry, throwing my hands up.

Luigi slides his eyes to my uncle, who shakes his head. "Calm down, Little One. He didn't say you couldn't wear it, just that we have to wait and see. You wouldn't want us to have to shoot someone for touching you, now would you?"

"I could use some help down here," I cry, looking at the ceiling. Annalisa giggles at me.

The front door dings announcing a customer and interrupts our bickering. Uncle Louie and Luigi shoot from their chairs, turning to face the front. I roll my eyes again, and my best friend laughs at me. Most likely it's a woman coming in to shop.

"Wow," a small, male voice breathes behind us. "Mom, look, look! It's Mr. Lou Canzano and Mr. Luigi Gallo."

I smile at Annalisa, "Ready to start your job?" Her jaw falls open as I turn around.

"Mom," a little girl squeals. "It's da Pwincess! Look... look!"

"You're a star," Annalisa whispers, giggling.

Uncle Louie looks at me, and I give him a small nod. Looking back at the boy in a small black suit with plastic sunglasses, Uncle Louie crouches down and gives him a smile.

"Tito, don't bother them," a woman holding a baby admonishes. She looks embarrassed. Laura puts her arm around her, saying something that relaxes her. They start talking about the baby, chatting and smiling.

I search my memory, trying to find the little boy's name, but come up blank. The little boy walks right up to my uncle, awe clear on his face, and sticks out his little hand. My heart warms at the sight.

"Hello, sir. I'm very pleased to meet you. We fought together at the pirate ship." Uncle Louie shakes his hand, and the boy continues. "My name is Tito, and I'm almost six. This is my sister Mia, she's three."

"Dat's da Pwincess," Mia says as little Tito pulls her hand, so she stands next to him.

Tito points to the woman holding the baby, still talking with Laura. "That's my Mom, Raisa, and my baby sister, Sofia." At the baby's name, my stomach takes a dip. "And I'm gonna grow up and be a soldier, just like you," little Tito finishes.

"I can see you're already a good soldier," Uncle Louie says, patting his shoulder. "You take excellent care of your little sister. And you're right, we did fight at the pirate ship, young man."

"Yes, sir," he answers my uncle excitedly. "I was up there protecting the Princess from the Wigi Monster and you."

His smile brightens even further, showing a missing front tooth when Luigi pats his back. "And you did a great job, too."

Turning back to my uncle who's standing again, he leans his little head way back to look up at him. "Can we go shake the Princess's hand, too? We didn't get to do it at her party because we had to go underground with Miss Annalisa. Our grandparents took us to the party because Mom was having Sofia."

My heart drops to my stomach. Did his mom give birth to his sister the day my mom died? Mia grabs my uncle's finger, shaking it, her eyes never leaving me.

"Pwincess!" the adorable little three-year-old squeals again.

"Go ahead, you can say hi to her," Uncle Louie says softly. Tito and Mia toddle over to me, and I squat on the edge of the platform, so I'm level with them. Tito takes my extended hand, shaking it.

"You're a Warrior Princess. I watched you and saw how good you are. You didn't miss one shot," he says.

Placing my other hand on the side on his little face, I reply, "How I wish you hadn't seen that. You should have been hiding and not watching. I pray it hasn't given you nightmares."

"Oh, no, Princess," he answers, smiling. "It doesn't give me nightmares. You protected us from the bad guys. And when all the shooting stopped, you took over, even telling the great Mr. Lou Canzano and Mr. Luigi Gallo what to do. And they listened to you, did what you said. Girls can't tell men what to do, but you did. Miss Annalisa helped us get underground. Thank you for keeping us safe and for ordering the men to fight and keep my Nonno and Nonna safe too."

His words pierce my heart and fill my eyes with tears. Wrapping my arms around this brave little boy, I hold him tight. With one arm, I reach over and grab sweet Mia too.

"Mommy, Mommy! The Pwincess hugs me too!"

Giggling, I release them. "You're so welcome, Tito," I tell him. "I was only protecting my Family, so you don't have to mention it again. Now, let's go meet your mom and that baby sister of yours."

As I stand up, Mia grabs my hand, and Tito grabs the other, leading me to their mom. Glancing behind us, I find Annalisa smiling and following us.

"Oh, my goodness, children. Don't bother the Princess. Can't you see she's busy buying clothes for university?"

Mia pulls my hand to get my attention. "You come back from unidersdidy?"

"Oh yes, darling girl. Uncle Louie and Luigi won't let me run away for at least a few more years," I smile at her cherubic face.

If only they knew, I think while everyone laughs at my joke.

"Raisa, the children are fine. Now, let me see this baby of yours," I say, smiling warmly at the nervous woman.

"Would you like to hold your mother's namesake?" she asks, stepping toward me.

I suck in a breath, glancing over her shoulder. My uncle and Luigi watch me closely.

"I'd love to hold her," I assure her softly. "What do you mean, my mother's namesake?"

She places the sleeping little girl in my arms. Her face is content, her light brown curls absolutely adorable and I kiss the top of her head.

"She's gorgeous. I love the pink bow in her hair," I whisper softly.

Raisa holds her phone up and takes pictures of me holding her daughter. Squatting down, I call Tito and Mia to stand next to me. Raisa snaps more pictures of the three of us.

Carefully standing back up, I notice tears in Raisa's eyes. Forgetting her earlier hesitancy, she wraps her arms around me and the baby in my arms. "Tito talks non-stop about that ugly day. He calls you the 'Warrior Princess.' I think all the boys call you that, and some of the men. Thank you, thank you so much. From the bottom of my heart. My husband and I are forever in your debt for protecting our children."

"No, no... please don't thank me. It was my honor to protect my Family. I've trained my entire life for this," I whisper in her hair. "Now, tell me more about this beautiful angel." I'm praying that'll get her to forget about that horrible day.

"No one told you?" Raisa asks, looking over her shoulder at my uncle who nods at her while staring at me. She takes a deep breath, her words stopping my world.

"I went into labor just as we were getting ready to leave for your party. My husband's parents decided to take Tito and Mia to the party, knowing it could be a while before I delivered. Since it was my third birth, it went rather quickly. Only hours after your tragic loss, my little angel was born. I wanted to honor you and your mother. I'd met her several times, and she was always wonderful. It was an honor to me to name my baby Sofia Alessandra."

Sucking in a breath, I will myself not to cry. An arm slides around me, and I look up to find Laura shedding her own tears as she hugs me close.

"Thank you, Raisa. This is an amazing tribute, and I'm truly blessed by your choice. It's the reverse of my name, Alessandra Sophia. I will always remember her, and I'm proud to share my birthday with her as well." I kiss the sleeping baby on the top of her head and hand her back to her mother.

Needing to change the mood, and quickly, I squat down to the children at my feet. "You two must take really good care of little Sofia, okay? You love her and play with her as she grows up, And make sure you help your mama with her, too. She's special to me." I quirk a smile, "You're both lucky. Do you know why?"

"Why?" Tito and Mia ask in unison, their eyes big.

"You not only have each other forever, but you also have a baby sister. You have a big family. I've always wanted a brother or sister to play with, but I never got one. I only had Uncle Louie here, and he didn't fit inside my little playhouse too well. I have to give it to him, though, he throws some of the best tea parties ever."

"He pwayed tea parties with you?" Mia asks in

awe, her mouth forming an O. I want to laugh at her expression, but I bite my lip.

Uncle Louie joins me, squatting down. "Yes, precious Mia, I did. I had to make sure the Princess had nothing but the best, so she got real tea and pastries."

"Weally?" she asks. "Wow. Will you be my uncle and come have tea parties with me?" I laugh because she is too cute.

"Oh, I'm sorry, *Piccola*. Uncle Louie and I still have tea parties, but I'm sure Tito will have tea parties with you. Since the great Mr. Lou Canzano does it for his niece, surely Tito can do it for his sister... can't you Tito?"

Tito looks like he tasted something sour. "You really played tea parties with the Princess?"

"Of course I did," my uncle nods. "I also played house with her and her bear, Fluffy.I played dress up, we did our nails, and a bunch of other things. We men have to keep our Princesses happy."

The little man smiles. "Okay. If Mr. Canzano can have tea parties, I can too," he says to his sister.

Biting my lip, I try to stifle my laugh. There are a few snickers, telling me others have failed in their attempts to not laugh at Tito.

"It may not be too late for those brothers and sisters you've always wanted," Annalisa says loudly.

My eyes bulge and I look at Laura, who's face shows shock. Luigi and Uncle Louie sound like they're choking with all the coughing they're doing.

"Come on," Annalisa says, studying us. "Laura's still young, and Aless wants a big family. What's the problem here? Don't act so shocked." She throws her hands up in exasperation.

"Sorry, Laura," I say putting an arm around my best friend to shut her up. "You'll learn Annalisa has a chronic condition called *foot in mouth* disease. She's suffered a lot because of it, but she's totally clueless."

Laura laughs nervously, Uncle Louie and Luigi howl at my joke. "Mind you, I would be totally thrilled if you decided to have babies one day and give me the brother or sister I've dreamed of my whole life, but please don't feel pressured by my big-mouthed friend over here… or by me."

"Hey," Annalisa protests. "I do not have a big mouth. I was only saying what you were thinking,"

Leaving my friend, I grab Laura and hug her. "Please don't feel pressured, Laura. And please don't mention this to Papa, it might make him pull Annalisa from her new job."

Laura laughs. "This conversation will not be repeated to anyone. I'm not bringing this up, that's for sure." Lowering her voice, she whispers, "But I do dream of that, of having Al's children one day. Don't you say a word, though. This is our secret." Pulling back, she winks, and me and I give her a smile in return.

A throat clears behind me, reminding me that Raisa is standing behind me, and I turn to her. "It was so lovely to meet you and your beautiful children. Can you do me a favor and not repeat anything you heard here today? Specifically what Annalisa said."

She makes a motion like she's zipping her lips. "Laura and I go way back. I swear to never breathe a word."

"Thank you so much, Raisa. Now I have some jeans to try on, so please excuse us." I shake her hand, then bend to kiss the baby in her arms. After a final hug and kiss to Tito and Mia, I grab Annalisa's hand and drag her to the back.

At the doorway, I turn and watch as Uncle Louie steals Luigi's sunglasses from him. He bends down and puts them on, Tito. "Now you look like a real soldier in training. Be a good boy and listen to your mom and dad." My uncle shakes his hand one last time in farewell.

"You know," Luigi says as we cross the archway into the dressing room, "you could have just given him your shades instead of stealing mine."

I hold off on closing the door to hear my uncle's response. "Could have, but didn't. It was way more fun to give him yours. And we both know you have a spare in the SUV. I've had mine for years."

Closing the door, I chuckle at their bickering. Turning, I realize that I'm actually about to try on my first pair of jeans. Lord, I hope I haven't built them up too much in my head.

Grabbing the first pair, excitement builds in my belly as I pull them on. They're a nice blue, not too dark nor too light. High waisted, they have a wide leg that's loose from the top of my bum. The dual rows of gold buttons on the front of the waist are a nice touch. The denim isn't stiff, but moves with every step I take. There's no way Uncle Louie can find fault with these, so I try to contain myself as I move to the viewing area to show them off.

Standing on the platform, I twist and turn, showing off my new jeans. A slow smile spreads across Uncle Louie's face. Turning my back to him, I bend slightly and wiggle my bum at him.

"See!" I cry. "They don't even slide down when I bend over."

Luigi and Uncle Louie crack up. "Okay, Little One," Uncle Louie says through his laughter, "you proved your point. The jeans are fine, and you can have them. But, if you don't get your bum out of my face, I'll swat it."

"You know," Luigi says, "if that's something you can't handle, I'll gladly volunteer for the position of 'bum swatter.'"

My back shoots straight, and I turn, pointing a finger at him. "I don't think so, mister!"

He laughs during my entire trek back to the fitting room.

I end up with three pairs of jeans. I'm thrilled with all of my clothes. More importantly, though, is the seed that was planted, the idea that Laura might give me a baby brother or sister. God, I wish I knew a way to make that happen. It would take the pressure off me and leave the Family with an heir. This is going to work out. My free life is coming, it's just a matter of time.

Chapter 23
ONE LAST LOOK

I'm so excited about the next step in my life, university, and more importantly, the official start of my escape planning. One thing dampens my elation. Papa told me he needs closure about Mom, so he's going to get rid of everything, and if I want anything I need to get it before I leave. It makes me sad, but it makes sense. Thankfully I don't have to do it alone, Luigi is keeping his promise and going with me.

Nonna's already gone through her room, packing sentimental things like jewelry, pictures and nick knacks. It's just... I need to go in there one last time. I need to see if I can still smell her, feel her presence- and to steal her perfume. Mom had a scent created for her, a soft, fresh smell with a hint of wisteria. We jokingly called it 'Mom' because it was a scent that was all hers.

At seven in the morning, I'm ready to go. I'm wearing my first pair of comfy jeans and a pair of soft brown leather boots. It's amazing to pick out my own clothes and dress more like a girl my age. Skipping down the steps, Luigi's voice stops me.

"Look who's the early bird this morning!" he calls. "You must be more than ready for today," he observes as his eyes wander up and down my body. "You look great. Do you want to join Lou and I for breakfast?"

Smiling at him as I reach the bottom of the stairs, I lace my arm into his. "That would be lovely, thank you, kind sir. Would you please escort me to the dining area?" I reply, affecting the accent of a proper woman from the southern part of America.

"You're getting good with those accents," Luigi laughs.

"Thank you," I say resuming my normal voice. "In time, I want to lose any accent I currently have, but be able to pull any one out when I need to."

"I'm sure you'll master it in no time, even though I think it's silly. To me, you don't even have an accent. You sound like the beautiful Italian woman you are." Luigi shakes his head, placing his large, warm hand over mine resting on his arm and leads me to the dining room.

As we walk in, Chef places Uncle Louie's breakfast in front of him. My uncle, spotting my arrival, says, "You're up and ready. The jeans look nice, I might add."

"Thank you," I answer, smiling. "I need to eat breakfast and then I have to finish a few things before I'm ready to leave for university."

"Figured you'd be too excited to do anything else... but, this is a big move. Mama and Camilla left a few hours ago with Lucca and Rocco."

"What?" I ask, surprise in my voice. "And here you talk about me being up early. They had to be up before the sun." As I laugh, Chef places my favorite breakfast in front of me, French toast with lots of butter and powdered sugar. He also included delicious crispy bacon and tall glass of orange juice.

Looking up to thank him, I find him looking at me with glassy eyes. "I had to make your favorite," he says in a soft voice, "for the last time. We're going to miss you a lot, Princess. The house will be empty and quiet without you. Come back and visit, please."

My eyes grow wet with his words. I climb from my seat and throw my arms around him, and he hugs me back. "If you want to come, I'm sure someone else can cook for Papa. I'll miss all of the special treats you make just for me. Thank you, Chef, so much. You've been the best." Standing on my tip-toes, I kiss his cheek. He kisses the top of my head and heads back to his cooking area.

After a few minutes of devouring our food, I have to ask, "Why did Nonna and Camilla leave so early?"

Taking a deep breath, Uncle Louie stares at the ceiling for a second. He's deciding just how much to tell me, but what he does share will be the truth. It's how he always acts when he shares details without giving everything away.

"Mama and Al got into a bit of a disagreement last night. She told me that she and Camilla would be leaving as soon as possible this morning. I don't know what it's about, and I didn't ask, but I have an idea. I won't tell you my suspicions in case I'm wrong. I'm sure she'll fill us in when we arrive. She also wanted to make sure those moving our stuff put everything in the right place."

I drink the last of my orange juice and place my napkin on my empty plate. "I'll find out what's going on later. I'm off to call Annalisa to make sure she's gotten those guys up and that they're here in plenty of time before we leave."

Dashing up the stairs, I mentally plan the text I want to send to Annalisa. Once in my room, I grab my purse and pull out my phone to send the text. Before nerves overtake me, I leave the house and head to the mausoleum to spend some time with Mom.

The scent of wisteria fills the air as I walk through the gardens that surround the Family tombs. It's so beautiful and peaceful out here. Instead of sitting on one of the benches outside scattered here and there, I enter the marble structure and head directly to her niche. Placing my hand on the stone that marks her tomb, I notice the fresh wildflowers in her vase and those spread throughout the open space. It has to be Papa, he knew how much she loved wildflowers. While every other man gives roses to their wife, Papa always gave Mom wildflowers.

Closing my eyes, I lean my forehead against the cold stone door to Mom's crypt and start talking to her in my head.

I don't know if you can really hear me, but it makes me feel better to talk to you. I'll probably be doing this a lot in the years to come. Mom, you'll always be in my heart, a part of my soul. I won't be visiting you here very often after today.

It starts now, Mom. I'm planning my escape. Papa is sending me to university, so I'll be getting the education I can use later in life to support myself. I'm determined to keep my promise to you. I love you, Mom, and always will. I'll make you proud of me, I promise.

Running my finger over her name etched in the stone, I kiss it lightly. A noise from outside startles me, and I turn, finding Luigi walking in, a warm smile on his face. He's always checking up on me and making sure I'm okay.

"I saw you walking over here. I gave you a few minutes, but I wanted to check on you… just to make sure you're okay."

"Yeah, I'm okay. I needed to come see her one last time before we leave," I say quietly.

"Looks like someone added a bench and has been bringing a ton of flowers out here," Luigi observes, looking around.

"Yeah," I nod. "Wildflowers were Mom's favorite. I think it might be Papa, but that might be hopeful of me. I don't know who else it could be... except maybe Lucca and Rocco."

Luigi nods, putting his arm around me. "It's a possibility. They did love Sophia. But I have a gut feeling it's your Papa. I bet he's been spending a lot of time out here, trying to find his own closure."

"Yeah, maybe," I concede.

Luigi puts a finger under my chin, making me meet his eyes. "There is one last place you wanted to go before we left. Do you still want to go to your mom bedroom room?"

"Yes. Let's go now, before Annalisa, and everyone else gets here," I mumble.

"Milady," Luigi says in a horrible British accent, bowing slightly, "may I escort you to the west wing?" He offers his arm, and I lace mine through his.

"Why yes, good sir," I mimic him. My accent is better than his but still needs work. "Lead the way, young man."

Chuckling, we leave the mausoleum. I look back over my shoulder, memorizing the beauty of the cold building. Luigi leads us across the yard to the house... where I'll go to Mom's room for the last time ever. After today, Papa will clear it out, and it won't be *hers* anymore.

At the door to Mom's room, I hesitate slightly. Luigi places his hand on my lower back, quite low, giving me strength enough to open the door. Twisting the knob, I give it a little push, and it swings open. I jump a bit, seeing someone sitting in Mom's rocking chair. Light from the doorway illuminates Papa, reading what looks like one of Mom's journals.

"I'm sorry, Papa. I didn't know anyone was in here," I say, ready to leave him there.

He looks up, startled from his reading.

"Aless," Luigi says quietly behind me, "I'll be right outside if you need anything." He pushes lightly on my back, forcing me into the room.

"You don't have to leave, Luigi," Papa calls. "I was just surprised. I got lost in reading."

"Aless wanted some company, so I agreed to join her."

Papa smiles. "Luigi, it's okay. I was just getting the rest of Sophia's journals. I sat down for a minute to read and got engrossed. I'm just trying to understand her... and her struggles. Alessandra, if you'd like to read them yourself, I'll give them to you when I'm done."

"No, Papa," I answer him quietly. "Those are too personal for me. But you should read them all. She's been writing them since before she met you."

"Yes," Papa nods. "I've already read a lot of them. After Junior's death, God, her pain, and misery, I could feel it. I'll box them up for you, in case you change your mind.

"Mama and Camilla packed up a few things for you over the last few days," Papa continues, closing the book in his hand and standing. "I don't know what's left that you might want but take whatever you want. Tomorrow morning, I'm having the room cleared and redecorated."

He walks towards the door and kisses my forehead

276

as he passes. "I'll give you a few minutes to yourself."

He turns to Luigi, a smirk on his face. "Can you let Lou know that Antonio will not be coming with you, nor will he join you for ten days? He didn't pass the tests I required of him." Papa pats Luigi's shoulder as he leaves.

Frozen, Luigi's face is a mixture of emotions, shock, surprise, and finally giddiness.

"Holy shit!" he cries, shaking himself. "Antonio failed. He actually failed! Oh, this is going to be good!"

"What?" I ask, confused. "What did Antonio fail?"

In answer Luigi picks me up, swinging me around. Setting me on my feet, he places a quick kiss on my lips, leaving me speechless.

"Remember our little clash the other day? The outcome of that was your Papa ordering Antonio to get tested for STDs before the trip, because of his promiscuous ways. And that cocky son of a bitch has an STD! Bet that took ol' Antonio down a notch, in life, *and* on the Capo's list. God, we'll have some fun with this knowledge, as well as ten days of peace and quiet."

Oh my God! This is fantastic! Ten days without Antonio... it'll be wonderful. Shoot, I hope Antonio hasn't given an STD to anyone I know... Luigi pulls out his phone, texting someone. It's probably my uncle.

He confirms that a second later. "Your uncle is having a field day with this. I kind of feel sorry for all the harassment Antonio will be facing with this one." He pauses, rubbing his chin. "On second thought, no, I don't feel the least bit sorry for that bastard. He deserves everything he has coming to him."

Luigi laughs again, continuing to text. Turning from him, I refocus on my reason for coming to Mom's room. With a quick look around, I head to her bed and grab a pillow. Bringing it to my nose, I inhale deeply. Her scent is faint. It's been a year, after all. Wrapping my arms around it, I decided I'm taking it with me. Finally, I turn to her dresser and grab her custom perfume.

"Mom would laugh at this knowledge, Luigi," I say, smelling the bottle and giving mom's pillow a squirt of her perfume. I turn to face him. "I'm done in here. I got Mom's perfume and her pillow. Let's go."

At the door, I turn and face the room, taking a mental photograph. After today, this room won't be the same. It hasn't been the same since Mom died, but it'll no longer be hers. I close the door, and Luigi places his hand on my lower back again. I lean into him as we pass the bay window where I spent so much time. Outside, wisteria blows in the breeze. I wonder how they'll grow in America. When I get settled, the first thing I'll do is plant them… lots of them.

Chapter 24
LETTING MY LIFE BEGIN

*W*e're minutes away from the Family villa. I'm starting my new life at university in a few days. I'm even more excited about the start of planning my escape from my tragic life.

The ride up has been great, with Annalisa beside me telling jokes at her brother's expense, Uncle Louie, and Luigi joining in. It's been a long time since I've been here, at least five years. The last time was with Mom and Papa. Neither are with me this time.

Since I'm to be Papa's assistant regarding the northern branch of Family business interests, I've been informed that the master suite is now mine and has been redesigned for me. Mom did a lot of it before she died, and Nonna and Camilla have been working on it as well. Uncle Louie told me he had some input too. I'm so excited to see it, but no one will tell me anything, only hints that I'll no longer have a little girl's room full of pink and toys.

Mentally, I snort at the thought of how appearances are everything. Papa informed me that due to my new position, I'll be head of the house. In the eyes of the Family, I'm an adult and responsible for a full staff, including the security, maids, and cooks of the villa.

"Well, what do you think?" Annalisa asks, placing her hand on my knee.

"What?" I ask. "I'm sorry, I was daydreaming, and I haven't heard of word you've said. What do I think about what?"

"About all of us getting T-shirts that say, 'I'm Clean' on them and wearing them when Antonio shows up in ten days," she says, filling me in.

"Oh, my God," I laugh. "That would be the best! And not just us, I want everyone to wear one, from the villa staff to the guards on the property."

Luigi and Uncle Louie laugh from the front seat. "I don't think it'll take much to get them on board with that plan, at least for a few hours," my uncle comments.

"He asked the Capo to keep this between them," Annalisa informs us. "He'll be so embarrassed when he realizes everyone knows. But come on, he earned this one. Maybe he'll learn from it and keep *it* in his pants for a while."

"Hate to break it to you," Luigi says, shaking his head, "but your brother isn't the sharpest when it comes to thinking with his big head. He spends too much damn time listening to his little head, if you know what I mean. Some guys need a bigger scare than an easily cured STD to stop them from roaming, trying to get any piece of ass they can. I'm fairly confident that he'll at least suit up from now on… err, wear a condom. Hopefully, you won't have to worry about becoming an auntie before you want to."

"Eww." Annalisa and I both laugh in unison.

Luigi slows at the gate, and the guard there nods at him, entering a code to open the huge doors. While waiting for them to open, I observe several men lining the driveway. They carry AK-47s on their shoulders and wear a pistol on their hips. Once the gates swing open, Luigi continues up the lane to the villa. As we pass, the men nod at the SUV. I wonder if those are for Uncle Louie and Luigi, or for me. Will I have to let them know who's really in charge? Hmm…

Several of the men I recognize from Family functions and meetings, some I'd only recently met in the last few weeks. All of this protection, though, makes me uncomfortable. It seems more than at home, which is ridiculous. But I need to find out.

"Uncle Louie," I ask. "Are there more guards here than at home? It sure seems like it. And why are they carrying big guns? Are we under threat that no one's informed me of?" I open my mouth to ask more questions, but he cuts me off, turning around in his seat.

"No, Little One. We're not under a new threat. But, you are the Family's most precious item, and everyone knows that. We're going to take every precaution to make sure you, and Annalisa, are safe at all times. As you're aware, there're still a lot of other Families and business partners that would give anything to get to you or cause you harm. The Capo would rather be on the safe side and give a show of strength, to let anyone who might consider attacking a reason to reconsider than to appear weak and vulnerable."

"Great," I mutter. "Let the fun begin." Uncle Louie's face makes me wish I'd kept my sarcastic comment to myself.

"Now Alessandra, whether you like it or not, you *are* the Princess of this Family. With that comes power, responsibility, and the possibility of threats. You're an adult now, and you must handle yourself as one. You will not show any of these men that sarcasm or lack of respect for your position. These men look at you as their leader and the future of this Family. You will respect that and them, and be honored to receive the respect they show towards you... Capisce?

Taking a deep breath, I realize he's right. They're only doing their job. "Yes, sir. You're right, and I'm sorry. I'm fully aware of my role. I'll watch my mouth when it comes to my protection and the security that entails."

"Your Papa has spent the last year showing you the ropes, introducing you to the men of the Family. He's shown you a lot about how things are done. You've attended meetings and planning sessions. You'll be making decisions on behalf of the Family while we're here. You need to get yourself into that mindset. When you're in the house, around us and the house staff, you and Annalisa can be your normal selves, speaking freely and joking around. The moment you walk out that door though, you need to flip a switch. You are the Princess of the Canzano Family and will behave as such."

"Don't worry, Uncle Louie. I understand my place and my role. Am I allowed to call you Uncle Louie, or should I refer to you as Lou like the men do? Will I still get tucked in by you?"

"Smartass," he chuckles. "No, you may not call me Lou. Has there ever been a night in your life when I haven't tucked you in and kissed you goodnight?"

There was once, but I decide not to mention that night in Paris where I upset him so much he went out and got drunk, needing to be carried home by Luigi and Lefty. "No, Uncle Louie, there hasn't."

"And there won't be until the day I give you away to marry the man chosen to be your husband. Now shut your sassy mouth and leave it at that."

Luigi stops the SUV in front of the huge water fountain. When I was little, I loved sticking my feet in there. Uncle Louie would grab me and tease me, pretending to throw me in it. I smile at the wonderful memory. Nonna and Camilla stand at the front doors, waiting patiently... or maybe not so patiently as Camilla is almost dancing in place.

My door opens, surprising me. Rocco holds his hand out for me, and I take it.

"Where did you come from?" I ask, smiling at him.

"I was on the other side of the fountain, making sure the men were in their assigned places. There's some new, younger men up here and I wanted to make sure they weren't lurking around to get a peek at your beauty," he tells me with a wink.

"Well thank you for protecting my virtue," I reply, laughing at him. "How are things going up here? Any problems with the men I need to be aware of?"

Rocco releases my hand, walking beside me. "It goes quite well, Princess. All the men have been briefed on their positions and responsibilities. I've assigned rooms for them to bunk in and made sure they're aware how things will be run up here. I've informed them each of the standards they must keep while under your service. If there's anything you or Miss Annalisa need, let me or Lucca know. We'll send one of the men out to get it." His words are formal as if giving me a report.

"Thank you, Rocco. I'll make note of that. By the way, you and Lucca are required to join us for dinner. You're family, and unless there's something that requires your attention, I expect to see you both there."

"Thank you, Princess," he smiles warmly. "We would be honored. Now, if you'll excuse me, I need to check with Lucca as to the men's schedules for the upcoming week."

"Don't let me hold you up, Rocco," I say, freeing him up to do his job. He delivers a head nod, bow type of move, takes three steps backwards, turns on his heel and moves to where Lucca is standing on the side of the driveway. How odd…

Uncle Louie replaces him at my side, and Annalisa

comes up to my other side. My attention moves to my Nonna who smiles at me. It's a beaming, radiant smile. She waves her hand, beckoning us toward her.

"Come on! We've been waiting all day for you to get here. We cannot wait for you to see everything, and to get your approval on the changes, Alessandra. There's only an hour before dinner."

"Mama," my uncle chuckles as she wraps me in her arms, "you just saw us last night. By all means, lead the way. I'm excited to see these changes you've made."

Releasing me, Nonna swats at her son. "I've been here preparing and making sure everything is perfect for my granddaughter, so excuse my enthusiasm for Alessandra's opinions."

The villa is as beautiful as I remember. It's the embodiment of a traditional Italian home. Lots of paintings and statues, huge arching windows with flowing, sheer curtains, and the smell of wisteria from the back garden greets me as I walk through the foyer.

On the foyer table is a wildflower bouquet, including the tiny purple flowers. In the sitting room, the couches have been adorned with animal print pillows, instead of their usual red and black ones. Nice touch. Examining the room, I'm surprised to see a leopard print chaise longue near the window. I'm claiming that right now!

"Alessandra!" Nonna calls, breaking me from my inspection of the sitting room. "For the first time since you were born, your uncle won't be sleeping just across the hall from you."

"Why?" I ask, my eyes bulging. This is a surprise.

Uncle Louie smiles at me and throws his arm around me. "Here's the deal, Little One. We've been talking, and we want Annalisa to become comfortable in her new role as your assistant. Her room will be across from yours. Luigi will have the room at the top of the stairs, so no one can get to your room without passing him." He slides his eyes to Annalisa, "That way we won't have to answer to Vito about Stephen taking advantage of his close proximity to a certain young lady."

Annalisa blushes prettily while everyone laughs. "Don't you worry about that. Stephen knows my room is off limits. Not only has Antonio warned him, but Dad threatened him with bodily harm if he did anything 'untoward.' Something about using his, ahem, 'cock as a decoration for his rearview mirror.' Poor Stephen was white as a sheet." I crack up imagining Stephens face during that conversation.

"Little One," my uncle says, getting my attention again. "We're not that far from you. Camilla, Mama and I will be down here on the first floor. It's where we used to stay when we came here while your parents were upstairs. Remember?"

"Yes, but there's so much room upstairs, you don't have to stay down here anymore," I argue feebly. I don't think I like this change.

Uncle Louie gives me a squeeze and leads me to the stairs. From the bottom of the huge staircase, I spot a new painting at the landing where the stairs split. This one is gorgeous, a view of the town near our home in spring. Thank God they replaced the portrait of Papa, Mom and me when I was crowned Princess. I would have hated looking at that every day.

At the landing, Uncle Louie turns into a tour guide, waving his hand to the stairs on the left. "This leads to the guest wing. It's where all male guests will stay, including Stephen and Antonio."

Taking the stairs to the right, he continues with his tour guide ways. At the top, he opens the first door.

"Here we have Luigi's room. I trust him to make sure no one comes past this point without his knowledge."

Luigi goes into his room and stops in front of what looks like an alarm panel.

"Lou, take a few steps down the hall," he says. My uncle does, and there's a loud beeping from Luigi's room and the lights inside start flashing on and off.

"Oh, deviously smart," Annalisa says, laughing. "I'm convinced no one will come up here without permission or they'll end up being shot by Luigi." Damn, now I'll have to include Luigi when I need an escape, I realize.

Continuing down the hall, Uncle Louie explains, "The alarm is also there to make sure that a certain young lady doesn't sneak out at night to work out in the studio we just had built."

A studio! Awesome! I keep that to myself and give my uncle some grief. "Wow, you two will go to any level to keep me on a short leash but thank you for the studio."

My uncle ignores me. "There are four additional rooms in this wing, should you have any female friends stay the night. We wouldn't want to expose them to Antonio."

"Got to protect my friends from the STD laden player," I add laughing. Everyone joins in, but Annalisa howls, holding her stomach.

Nonna steps forward, taking over the tour from her son. "The room to the left of your room is Annalisa's." She opens the door, revealing a large, beautifully decorated room. It's much larger than Annalisa's room at home. There's a solid oak queen size bed with lavender linens and dark purple throw pillows. On the wall is a portrait of a ballerina dressed in purple flowing fabric. Next to the life size painting is a floor length mirror and a ballet barre.

My best friend squeals and runs into the room. "Oh my God! It's perfect! I love it. Thank you! Thank you so much!" She twirls on her toes then runs to a door which she swings open. "Look at this, Aless," she cries. "My bathroom is as big as your old one!" She dances to another door, opening it. "And look at this closet! I actually have a walk-in closet! And all my clothes are in here and unpacked! I so wasn't looking forward to that part of the move."

I can't help but giggle at her excitement, knowing how thrilled she is at not only having a walk-in closet but not having to share a bathroom with her brother.

"Come on, girlie! Let's go see my room!" I call. Instantly, she's by my side. With a nod of agreement, we bypass the tour and run past everyone.

Stopping at the French doors, we each grab a handle and turn, throwing them both open and freeze. Before me is the master suite. There's a sitting area around a fireplace with an over-stuffed, winged back chair and two love seats in creamy white leather. Over the fireplace is a huge flat screen TV. We run to it in awe but are stopped again at the sight of my bed. My massive four poster *king* sized bed is made of gorgeous mahogany. The bedding is a satin burgundy with loads of burgundy and black pillows. In the center of it all is Fluffy.

Leaping onto the bed, I grab my bear, hugging it. I bounce on my knees, saying, "We love it! It's amazing!" I fall to my belly and bend my knees, swinging my feet behind me.

"Nonna, is Papa aware of the colors in my room? That it's red and black?" I ask curiously.

Nonna laughs lightly. "Yes, he's aware of the color scheme. Your mother had everything custom made for you, just over a year ago. He's approved it, saying 'She's a young lady now. I hope she likes it.'"

Sitting up, I survey my room. My eyes stop on my nightstand. Crawling over to it, I lift the picture that just this morning was on my nightstand back at home. "Thanks, Mom," I whisper to the photo of her. "You've made my dreams come true." I kiss the glass and carefully put it back.

Standing on my bed, I walk to one of the posts at the foot. Swinging around it with both hands, I say loudly, "This is it! I'm letting *my* life begin!"

"Now do you understand why I wanted to live downstairs?" Uncle Louie asks with a sigh.

"Why? Because you've *finally* accepted that I'm an adult?" I question, rolling my eyes.

Everyone smiles at me, almost indulgently. "Follow me," Uncle Louie says. He walks out of my room, and I leap from my bed to chase after him. Across the hall, he opens the door that faces mine, revealing an office.

"This is *your* office. You have direct access to all Family businesses and records. It's linked to your father's computer system back at the main estate. You have complete control up here. There's a desk for Annalisa, but no one, and I mean *no one* aside from those living in the house are allowed in here. No friends from school, nor from back home. The only reason anyone else is allowed in here, in the event it is required, is to be reprimanded."

"I understand," I reply, nodding.

Nonna takes my hand. "Little One," she says seriously. "This is *your* villa to control as you see fit. In the end, everyone here answers to you. If there's anything you want changed or added, just say the word, okay?"

I'm stunned. Mine to control? Everyone answers to me? I didn't realize how big of a deal this was, how huge the changes were.

"Thank you, Nonna, but I love everything you've done. It's perfect." I wrap my arms around her. Feeling overwhelmed, I hug everyone in the room, finishing with Luigi.

"Be warned," I whisper to him. "I'll be testing your high-tech security system." He chuckles in my hair and gives me a squeeze.

Releasing me, Luigi says, "I accept your challenge, sweetheart!" Grabbing my waist, he lifts me up and throws me over his shoulder. I pound on his back as he makes his way back to my room. Bumping his shoulder, I bounce into his arms, and he tosses me onto my bed.

"I can't wait to see you try it," he says laughing at my shocked face.

"Care to share with the rest of us?" Uncle Louie demands, a scowl on his face. Annalisa smiles, but her cheeks are red.

Scrambling to my knees, I answer my uncle. "Since you're all so nosy, I guess I will. I just warned Luigi that I'd be putting his high-tech security system to the test. That's all."

"Young lady," Uncle Louie cautions, "that studio of yours is off limits without one of us with you. Capisce? The men here also use it for training. You are not to go there unattended. Do I make myself clear?"

"Yes, sir!" I stand on my bed, saluting him. "I understand and agree with you, especially if the men will have access. Don't worry about that. I just want to see if I can get past it and call him from downstairs. Is that okay?"

My uncle smiles as Luigi shakes his head at me, likely thinking there's no way I can get past his security measures. "That's fine, so long as neither you nor Annalisa leave this house without a proper escort. That means one of the five of us, Rocco, Lucca, Luigi, Stephen or myself... preferably two of us."

"Okay, okay," I sigh, swinging around one of the posts of my bed. "We know the rules. But, as you're fully aware, I'm more than capable of kicking anyone's ass if they try anything." I move to the other post and swing around it.

"And since, as Nonna said, this is *my villa* to run, I'd like to make my first declaration. Unless we have company or it's a special occasion, we don't have to dress for dinner. Business casual will be fine. No need for ties and jackets unless you want to. I want us to be a family here, able to relax with each other. Do I make myself clear as Princess of this villa?"

Everyone nods enthusiastically while some chuckle. Nonna grabs my hand. "Glad to see you already taking charge. Your first decree is a good one since we only have about fifteen minutes before dinner. I, for one, am thrilled I don't have to run and change. See you at dinner, Little One." She squeezes my hand and leaves. Everyone trails out after her, leaving me alone in my massive bedroom.

Taking advantage of these precious fifteen minutes, I check out my room. This is my first real chance to absorb everything in it. My bathroom is twice the size of my old one, and the shower is huge. Annalisa would probably drool over this thing. It's bigger than the one we had in the hotel in America. My clothes and accessories are unpacked and neatly organized. The closet is more like a dressing room with an ottoman in the middle and a three-way mirror in the corner. I'll be able to see every angle when I'm deciding what to wear.

This is really it, Mom, the beginning of my life. With that computer connected to Papa's and all of the Family dealings, I'll be able to collect information to gain my freedom. I'll need a USB drive to store it on. I'm relieved to have a working plan. Gather information, get my education, and play the part. By the time I turn twenty-one, whether I'm finished with university or not, I'm making my escape.

Thoughts of planning my escape invariably lead to thoughts of Grayson Riggs. I'll have to do some researching on him as well. I grin at the thought. Let the good times roll!

Chapter 25

NO MERCY FOR ANTONIO

My y first week has flown by. We quickly fall into a daily routine. The staff Nonna hired is competent and well trained. They mostly stay out of the way, focusing on the house, the grounds and making excellent food. I'll have to work on them being more relaxed around me, though. Annalisa is coming along nicely in learning about her role as my assistant. She's up at least an hour before me, making sure everything is ready for my day.

Our first outing was Sunday Mass. Uncle Louie informed me that every time I leave the house that I'm to wear my Family ring and Family necklace. Everyone needs to be able to see them, to know who I am and my position within the Family. For years, I'd just been the Family Princess, with no real role other than to look pretty and maintain appearances. Now though, I run our northern interests and carry heavy responsibilities.

Today, Antonio and Stephen are due to arrive. I've planned a bit of fun at Antonio's expense. He texted Uncle Louie last night saying that after a round of antibiotics, he'd passed a new test and Papa agreed to allow him up to begin his guard training under Rocco and Lucca. My uncle told him to wait another day, informing him that we were busy on Saturday but to be here after Mass on Sunday. He did it partly to make Antonio squirm, but also because I was still waiting on the shirts I'd ordered.

Before we left for Mass, the shirts arrived. Lucca said he would distribute them to the guards while we were gone. When we arrived home, I was pleased as punch to see every single one of them wearing their

'I'm Clean' t-shirts under their jackets as we drove up the driveway. They all smirked at the SUV as we drove past, so I know they're loving this.

Not only are the guards wearing them, I've ordered that the house staff wear them too. I ordered V-neck shirts for the women, and they seem to love being out of the stiff, white button-up uniform blouses they usually wear.

After Mass, Annalisa and I change from our dresses into jeans and our own 'I'm Clean' shirts. I'm on pins and needles, anxious to see Antonio's response to my little joke. Annalisa and I are pretending to read, but every few seconds one of us looks up and giggles in anticipation.

"He just passed the gatehouse," Luigi announces, making us both jump. Snickering, we try to get control. We lay back on the couches trying to appear relaxed.

The doorbell rings. Unfazed by it all, Luigi calmly says, "Game on. I'll get it."

"Shit, not you too," Antonio complains from the foyer. *"Does every fucking man in this Family have to rub this shit in my face? I thought we were supposed to be professionals."*

"Stephen, here's your shirt," Luigi says, ignoring Antonio's whining. *"That is if you're clean? The girls are in the living room to your right."*

Stephen laughs, joining Luigi. *"Thank you, sir."* He's always so respectful. I'm so happy he feels the same way about Annalisa that she does about him.

Three sets of footsteps sound on the marble floor, one hard and heavy, almost angry.

"I swear that if you put that T-shirt on, I'll kick

your ass… and you can forget all about those five minutes alone with my sister."

I rise from the couch as they enter the room, my back straight and my face stern.

"Stephen, if you've never had a sexually transmitted disease, you damn well will wear that shirt and show your pride in that fact. If Antonio so much as lays a finger on you, I want to know about it. And don't worry, you'll get ten minutes with Annalisa, but only downstairs."

"Thank you, Princess,," Stephen bows his head. He pulls off his jacket and sets it over the back of a chair. He shrugs on the shirt and looks at his best friend.

"Sorry, dude. You did this to yourself. I warned you something like this or worse could happen. Gotta glove up or keep it in your pants."

I laugh internally at him. Sheesh, he has almost the same sense of humor Annalisa does. They're going to be so great together. The thought pierces my heart because I'll never see it.

"Whose wonderful idea was this?" Antonio asks. "And how in the hell did you get everyone in on it? No one was supposed to know."

Annalisa stands from the couch and pulls long, yellow gloves from her back pocket. Why didn't I think of that?! Stephen cackles with glee as she puts them on. Tentatively, she pats her brother's shoulder.

"Sorry, Ton," she says in a remorseful voice, "we just can't be too careful around you."

I crack up just as Uncle Louie walks in, wearing his own shirt. Nonna and Camilla are right behind him, wearing medical masks. This is going so much better than I expected! I'm so happy everyone is having fun with this... well, everyone except Antonio.

"Boys," Nonna says. "Lunch is in about fifteen minutes. You need to wash up... especially you, Antonio."

"Aw, come on!" he whines turning to face them. His body rocks back at the sight they present. "Now I know this is all your doing, Alessandra," he accuses, pointing at me. "You're getting them to humiliate me, and that is something you'd totally do."

"Well," I say in delight, "I did order and buy the shirts. However, it was your sister's idea. I just ran with it. She's already a great assistant, coming up with marvelous ideas. But the gloves and masks are their own personal touches."

The corner of Antonio's mouth lifts, probably in admiration, just as the doorbell rings.

"Good afternoon, young ladies," one of the staff says. *"May I take your things? The Princess and Annalisa are in the living room."*

"Thank you," three voices say in unison and Annalisa, and I squeal in excitement.

Gigi, Lola, and Lilith come into the room. I tackle my girls, and we end up in a big group hug. As we break apart, Lilith approaches the man who opened the door for them and retrieves a gorgeously wrapped box from him.

"Thank you," she nods and turns, handing it to Antonio. "This is from the girls in town back home." She gives him a smirk and kisses his cheek.

"Uh, thank you... I guess." Antonio looks confused, holding the huge box as he watches Lilith walk back toward us. "But um, when did you start hanging out with our Family?"

"Well, Ton," Lilith laughs lightly, "while you were out of contact due to your... slight problem, I learned Alessandra was about to start attending the same university as me. So, I made a trip home because I wanted to thank her for saving my mom, brother, sister and me from my evil sperm donor. It wasn't something that should be seen at school. We hit it off and, since we'll have two classes together this semester, she invited me over today."

Antonio and Stephen's jaws hang open in surprise at her little story.

"Okay... but what's in the box?" Antonio asks, shifting the unwieldy thing.

"Open it!" Gigi grins. "Come on, don't be a spoilsport. I can't wait for everyone to see it."

Antonio's eyes dance around the room nervously. Lilith and Lola clap their hands in anticipation. I'm dying with curiosity as he slowly peels the paper away.

"Okay, enough is enough," Antonio says gritting his teeth as he lifts the flaps of the box. "I get it, joke's on me."

"What is it?" Lola asks excitedly. "We can't see! I've been dying since we picked up Lilith. She wouldn't tell us."

Antonio grimaces as he folds back the flaps of the box. Crowding around closer, I see there are a colossal number of condoms in the box, in an assortment of colors and types.

Unable to resist, I say, "Well, I've heard how much you like to get down and dirty. Is that enough for you?"

"This is great!" Luigi comments, laughing.

Everyone laughs at Antonio. "Come on, Antonio,

hold up your present!" Lola calls out holding up her phone to take pictures.

Antonio smiles at Lola and dutifully does as she asks, hefting the box up and propping it under his arm so we can see it. Reaching inside, he grabs a handful and poses for a picture. We all laugh as he hams it up, shoving some of the condoms into his pockets. Lola turns into a professional photographer, moving to get different angles. Before I know it, I'm holding my side and tears are leaking from my eyes.

"What the hell is going on in here?" Papa asks loudly, startling us.

We all fall silent as Papa scans the room. Laura, by his side, also looks around the room. A smile grows on her face until she cracks up.

"I hope you have extra shirts for Al and me," she says through her hilarity.

Papa's stern face morphs into one of amusement, and he finally chuckles. For the first time, Antonio blushes at our teasing. Papa's eyes fall on Antonio's hand still holding a handful of condoms, and the box he set back down on the table.

"Boy," he says, "I sincerely hope you use those ncxt time. If you need someone to show you how to put one on, I'm sure Luigi here can help." Papa laughs, pounding Luigi's back.

"Shit," Luigi moans. "Can I request to be left out of his sexual education? I doubt he'd listen to me anyway." He turns to Antonio, "Just remember, those go on your *penis*. They're not fuckin' balloons."

"Sir," Antonio says in a firm yet quiet voice, ignoring Luigi, "I know how to use them. I'll never touch another girl without one."

"Do you think," Uncle Louie asks, joining the

conversation, "you can leave the *girls* alone and stick to grown ass women?"

"Here, here!" Papa calls. "Make sure every woman you touch is an adult."

Antonio's face gets redder, his cheeks bright with embarrassment. We all laugh at him. I can't believe he's so embarrassed by this. I mean it's his own dang fault.

"Lunch is ready," Nonna calls from the foyer. "Would you please move to the dining room?"

We continue ribbing Antonio as we walk into the dining room. The staff has already prepared the table, adding extensions so it'll seat all fourteen of us. Papa takes the foot of the table and Laura sits to one side of him. Uncle Louie escorts me to the head and pulls out my chair. I look up at him, rolling my eyes.

"Behave, Little One," he whispers to me. "Your Papa wants and needs to see how well you're handling your new responsibilities."

I sigh but know he's right. Papa needs to see that I *can* do this. Uncle Louie sits to my right, and Luigi takes my left. Everyone else takes chairs along the length of the table and begins chatting.

Turning my attention to the head chef, Carlo, I give him a nod. Within seconds, the rest of his staff come out of the swinging door that leads to the kitchen, carrying trays of steaming soup already ladled into bowls.

"Papa, what are you doing up here anyway? Checking up on me?" I ask with a smile. "You didn't mention a trip when we spoke yesterday."

"Yes, that's exactly what I'm doing," he answers, smiling. "Also, Laura wanted to deliver some special items she made just for you. She said they couldn't be delivered and wants to make sure they fit correctly. Lucca took the packages up to your room when we arrived. After lunch, you and the ladies can go check them out while I have a meeting with the men. Laura and I will be flying home later this afternoon. Does that meet with your approval, Princess?"

"What kind of meeting will you be having with *my* men? If there something I need to be aware of?" I ask and casually start eating my soup.

"I do like the way you're taking control up here," Papa observes, like we're the only two people in the room. "As for the meeting I'm having with *your* men, I just want to see the grounds, make sure Lucca and Rocco have everything under control. I also need to put the fear of God into Antonio and Stephen, explain what's expected of them and what will happen if they cross any lines. Does that meet with your approval?"

"That should be fine, then," I reply, smiling. "I'll go with Laura and my girls to see what she's come up with and you can meet with my men. Lucca and Rocco have done a wonderful job so far. You'll be pleased with them."

Realizing we're putting on a show for everyone, I decide to change the subject. "Excuse us, we'll talk about business later. Let's enjoy our meal."

"No, no," Gigi giggles. "That was quite entertaining, Princess. I've never sat at a table where you were at the head. It's impressive, very business-like." Her eyes hold admiration, and I smile at her. Everyone relaxes at her words, chatting and eating.

There's no way I'm going to allow Papa to take charge up here. He put me in this position as head of the villa, and I'm keeping it… for now. To be honest, I actually enjoy it. The responsibility of directing and planning with the men is invigorating. Hearing their ideas gives me points of view I hadn't considered or even though of. Without Papa constantly around, I've been able to acquire more information. It'll all come in handy when I finally make my move to escape this life. But there's no way he's speaking to *my* men alone. I'm showing up to that damn meeting. The fitting with Laura can wait until later.

Chapter 26

SOME IMPRESSIVE UNDERTHINGS

*A*fter lunch, the girls crowd around me and practically drag me to the stairs.

"I can't wait to see your room," Gigi says.

"Me either," Lola agrees.

Lilith kind of hangs back, observing us as we approach my doors. Taking a deep breath, I swing them open. Gasps sound out behind me.

"Damn," Lilith breaths.

"Lucky bitch," Lola says.

"You know, my parents' room wasn't even this big, and my Papa was a Capo too," Lilith declares.

"Yeah," I answer her. "Your Family was never as powerful as ours. It could have been if your Papa had just let his animosity toward our Family go and had focused on building up his businesses."

"Oh, I know. He wasn't just a vindictive son of a bitch, he was an idiot to boot," she jokes with me. It warms me that the fact that I killed her father doesn't bother her, nor impede what looks like will be an amazing friendship.

"Ladies," Nonna interrupts, "I know it seems like a lot has changed, and it has. Alessandra will always be your friend, but you need to come to terms with the fact that she is also your Princess. A lot of responsibility comes with that title. As you just witnessed at lunch, she's more than just a pampered little snot sitting in a villa. She runs this estate, as well as the Family interests up here. She's fully responsible for anything that happens up here, and your Capo is preparing her for the day she takes over the Family from him."

As Nonna speaks, my girls find seats in my sitting area and absorb everything my Nonna says. I'm dying at every word that passes her lips. More and more of my life is being controlled, and I'm being dragged into it whether I want to be or not.

"Annalisa's discovered how much pressure Alessandra carries on her shoulders in the last week," Nonna continues. "Since she's become the Princess's assistant, their relationship has evolved too. While they still joke and have fun, Annalisa becomes more professional and assists her in any way she can when Alessandra is required to be 'the Princess.' Your relationships with Alessandra will evolve, too. A day may come when she gives you an order, and you will obey without question. She is second in command of this Family. Think about what I've said and remember it."

Damn it, I need this conversation to end. I don't want my friends to start looking at me differently. Sure, Annalisa's taken it in stride, but she grew up with my father's second as her Papa. She's more familiar with the inner workings of the Family. Lola and Gigi aren't. Lilith gets it though. She was a Capo's daughter.

"Hey, I'm still me, okay?" I say, stopping Nonna's speech. "Let me go try on whatever it is that Laura's brought. I'll come out and model for you."

"Okay, girl," Lola adds her two cents. "We know you're the Princess and all, but you're going to have to give us a break and show off that closet when you're done. I might want to borrow something, you know... friend to friend."

"Oh, just wait till you see the bathroom," I call, playing along with her. "You'll forget all about the clothes and want to take a bath!"

Nonna, Annalisa, and Laura follow me into the closet. Camilla stays with my friends to keep them entertained and to keep an eye on them to make sure they don't go wandering where they shouldn't... especially, Lilith. Even though the Canzano Family has taken control of everything her Papa used to control and her brother, Pietro Jr, has been helpful in facilitating the takeover, we're still watchful.

Laura opens the large suitcase Lucca put on my ottoman, revealing a case full of 'underthings,' as Papa calls them. My jaw drops in shock and I glance at my best friend. Annalisa's eyes are huge as she stares at the bras, panties and even garter belts.

"Papa couldn't wait or just ship me these underthings?" I ask Laura.

"Oh, honey," Laura answers. "We're women, we don't have to hide behind non-provocative terms like your father does. Come, girls. These are underwear... panties, bras, and garters." I giggle at her bluntness. "But, Alessandra, these are much more than that. I also have some for Annalisa."

Carefully, Laura sorts the organized bras, selecting a beautiful red and black lace one and holds it up. It's the sexiest bra I've ever seen, never mind worn. Carefully, Laura reveals a hidden pocket and pulls out a throwing star.

"Oh my gosh," I breathe in awe, touching the lace covered bra. "That is the coolest thing ever. But... did Papa approve of these?"

"Well, he asked me to make them. He didn't specify what I could and couldn't do. He just said 'something pretty, but it needs to hide these weapons' and handed me a box. Because I know what colors are in your wardrobe, I went based on those. I'm sure that as long as you don't show your Papa the more risqué ones, he'll be fine. What he doesn't know won't hurt him."

"And no one else," Nonna adds.

"Well yeah, Nonna," I agree. "Trust me, you have nothing to worry about there."

Laughing, I move to get a closer look at the suitcase Laura's brought.

"Uh, you made some for me, too?" Annalisa asks.

Laura shakes her head. "Not like this one. I made you some really cute underwear sets with matching garters. There's a gun holster on the garter because I was told you're to begin training to handle a gun. It makes sense, especially after what happened last year."

"Did you know about this?" she asks me.

"I did," I nod. "I actually suggested it last year when Papa decided you'd be coming with me to university. He decided we should focus on studying to get you accepted early before we started. And, since you're the Robin to my Batgirl," Nonna and Laura laugh, but Annalisa's face warms. "You need to be prepared too."

We try them on, and they're magnificent. They fit perfectly. Nonna puts mine away in my underwear drawers as I confirm they fit perfectly. Annalisa's are put back in the suitcase to be taken to her room after we're done.

Annalisa's bras give her a little lift, with the help of some thin padding. Mine, though, lift my breasts, giving me more cleavage that I really, really don't need. But the lingerie is beautiful and oh-so-sexy. Just trying them on, I feel sensuous and confident. Knowing that I'll be wearing such provocative, yet deadly lingerie under my clothes will boost my self-esteem when dealing with Family matters. Who am I kidding? I feel badass and sexy. I don't say that though, because of Nonna. These will be coming with me when I leave though. The hidden compartments might, sadly, come in handy.

Turning to my new clothes, I try to decide what to model for my friends. I grab my favorite new acquisition, the black retro dress with red polka dots. Unable to resist, I put on the matching bra and garter set. It's time for Lola and Gigi to learn that I'll probably always be carrying a weapon of some sort or another. Lilith will get a kick out of this.

My last stop before leaving my dressing room is my hidden safe. After it scans my fingerprints, I pull out something a bit fun. Tucking them away, I pull on my dress and face everyone. Annalisa's eyes are bright and excited. Laura nods, seemingly satisfied with her handiwork. Nonna gives me a playful glare.

Walking out, Nonna whispers in my ear, "Be nice, young lady." She, along with Laura and Annalisa, are right behind me.

"I'm always nice," I whisper on a huge smile as I re-enter my room.

Throwing my shoulders back, I spin on my toes for Lola, Gigi and Lilith.

"Well," I ask smirking, "what do you think of my new dress?"

"Wow," Gigi declares, "you look like a sexy pin-up girl in that dress!" She turns to Laura. "Do you sell those in your shop? I need me one of those!"

"No, sorry." Laura replies smiling. "That one was made just for Alessandra. I have some similar ones in assorted colors at the shop."

"We'll be there next weekend," both Gigi and Lola say in unison.

"You won't find one like this," I say mischievously. "This outfit is special because it gives me the ability to defend myself at all times." I slide my hand into the hidden pocket of my bra and finger one of my matte black throwing stars. It's perfectly balanced and flies through the air like a hot knife through butter. As I pull my hand out, I quickly fling it across the room. With a *thunk*, it embeds deep in the wooden door to my bathroom.

"Oh my gosh!" Lola giggles, covering her mouth.

"That was awesome!" Gigi squeals.

"Well look at you, you pint-sized badass," Lilith says, smiling at me.

Lifting my skirt, I show off my new garter, complete with my purple P238 Sig Sauer in its holder.

"You'll always be safe with me when we're out and about," I tell them.

Lola whistles and Gigi claps. She looks at Annalisa in surprise.

"Do you have awesome lingerie like that too?" Gigi asks her.

"I got some gun holster garter belts because I'm starting shooting lessons tomorrow. But no, I didn't get flying-knife-star-fighting-thing pocket bras. I'll pass, thank you. Anyway, my boobs are small enough that I don't want to risk lopping one off!" Annalisa giggles, grabbing her B-cup breasts. We all laugh at my silly friend.

Lola grabs my hand as we catch our breath. "Alessandra, even before I'd heard about your secret killing-machine abilities, I've always felt safe with you. I mean, your uncle's always with you and that *hot* Luigi. They always have one gun each, probably more. But never mind that. I have you now, and please tell me the truth... tell me you've noticed how hot, H. O. T., *hot* that man is, or are we going to have to hold a girl meeting to remind you that you're female? We need to get your mind off guns and knives and onto the more devastating weapon on Luigi's body."

I chuckle, rolling my eyes. "Lola, I'm neither blind nor stupid. I'm fully aware of what Luigi looks like. I see him every day. And before you ask, no, we're not involved in that way. He's a great guy and a really good friend."

Almost as one, my friends roll their eyes.

"Uh-huh," Lola mumbles in disbelief.

"Suuu-re," Gigi says sarcastically.

Lilith's mouth just hangs open in incredulity.

Annalisa waves her hands, getting their attention. "No, no, she speaks the truth! I've seen it. I don't know what's wrong with her, but there's nothing going on with them... for now." Nonna and Camilla smile, as does Laura, but my friends all start chatting excitedly at the idea of me and Luigi. Ugh, I do not need this from them.

"Alright, ladies," I call trying to get them to shut up. "Let me show you my closet and bathroom. If you don't start playing nice with me, I might just end up getting some target practice in today."

"Alessandra," Nonna admonishes me. "Is it nice to threaten your friends like that?" The sparkle in her eyes gives away her amusement, and I play along.

"Okay, okay," I say in a placating falsetto. "I promise not to shoot to kill... maybe just scare them. Is that okay?" I can't contain it, I start laughing as

I watch my friends' faces. "But, if you ladies stop picking on me, I promise not to shoot anyone. Now, let's finish up this tour. I know Annalisa is dying to show you her room and the guest rooms for you guys. I also have a meeting to get to."

After showing them my closet and bathroom, which they all fawned over, I leave them with Annalisa and head downstairs with Laura. As I reach the bottom of the stairs, I meet up with Papa, Uncle Louie, and Luigi coming in the front door.

"All done with the new additions to your wardrobe?" Papa asks.

"Yes, Papa," I tell him with a smile. "They fit perfectly. Thank you for asking Laura to make them. And thank you, Laura."

"Oh, *cara*," she says, "it was my pleasure."

We head to the living room where we find Stephen, Antonio, Rocco and Lucca waiting, along with a few other men. I guess it's okay because Papa's here and he invited them in the house.

Antonio whistles a cat call and Papa snaps a glare in his direction.

"Are you already starting with that shit?" he growls.

"I'm sorry, sir. I was trying to express how beautiful Alessandra looks in that dress, and I was speechless," he responds smoothly.

Walking over to Antonio, Papa pulls him out of his chair by his shirt and gets in his face. Everyone is silent, and Laura presses close to my side. In a quiet voice, Papa berates him.

"We've already talked about this, so this will be your final warning. Listen and listen good. If you *ever* want to be in my daughter's presence again, you will never whistle at her like she's a whore. I will personally knock those teeth out of your thick fucking skull if you do. Do I make myself clear?"

"Yes, sir," Antonio replies quietly.

"I don't care if it was a joke or if you were playing around. As of today, you will treat her as your Princess and show her the same respect you show me. She has more power and authority over you than anyone else in this room besides myself. She deserves to be treated honorably and with respect, not like one of those cheap girls you dip your cock into. Now apologize to your Princess and boss." Papa releases his shirt and shoves Antonio towards me. The poor guy stumbles before finding his footing and shuffles over to me.

"I'm very sorry for disrespecting you, Princess," he starts, his head hanging down. "I'll never do it again." When he finishes, he lifts his eyes to mine and winks. Fucking winks! Laura gasps at my side.

That's it. I'm so sick of his constant flirting, his cock-sure attitude that he's God's gift and every woman wants him. My hand snaps out, and I grab his crotch, twisting his junk.

"Damn straight, you'll never treat me like that again. I've had enough of you and your flirting and you thinking you're the best thing since sliced bread. Next time, not only will I slap the shit out of you, but I'll rip these *little* jewels right from between your legs," I say, squeezing hard and twisting a little more. Antonio whimpers, breathing hard. "I'll deliver them to your parents, with my apologies for taking away their grandchildren. As of now, I demand not only your respect, but that of every man in this Family.

Am I understood?"

The men in the room gasp, and their clothes rustle as they shift in their seats. Releasing Antonio, I give him a little shove. He bends at the waist, grabbing his crotch and coughs. Turning to the other men in the room, I decide that now is the perfect time to make sure they're all on the same page.

"It seems I need to set some things straight. I am not a sexual object for your entertainment, and I will not tolerate you staring at my tits or ass. I demand that you respect me as your boss while you are in my employment. If you have a problem with that, you will find yourself either nut punched, or I will rip your balls off and hand them to you, unless I want to keep them in a jar on my desk." Uncle Louie snorts, as does Luigi.

"There is a world of difference between admiring someone with a quick glance or openly staring at them and licking your lips and winking. It sullies your admiration, making it something crass, cheapening the woman you're admiring. It repulses me, it's not a turn-on in the slightest. It's insulting and makes me feel like a piece of meat. I've never ogled or gawked at any of your asses, chests or even cocks. I may have noticed a few of you, but because I'm a grown ass woman who knows how to act in public, I would never demean you like that. I would appreciate the same courtesy from all of you, since I am the one in charge here."

The soldiers nod, some of them have their hands in their laps. I know they're shocked at what I just said, including the cursing. Lucca and Rocco smile warmly, though. I'm just relieved and thankful that neither Papa nor my uncle stopped me from saying what needed to be said.

"Do we understand each other a little better?" I

ask Antonio, patting his cheek.

Antonio coughs. "Yes, ma'am," he says in a soft voice. "I understand both of you perfectly. I will control myself and show you the respect you deserve."

"I'm glad to hear that," I nod, acknowledging him. "Now, Papa. I'd like to make some changes. Antonio and Stephen are trainees. They should move to the bunkhouse with the other soldiers. Lucca and Rocco are my head soldiers, and I would like them to live in the house here. They've earned their place in the Family and deserve that favor. Don't you agree?"

Papa blinks, looking shocked at the scene I just made. He clears his throat. "Princess, this is your villa to run as you see fit. If that is how you want it, by all means, I support you fully. And on that note, I think you've made yourself perfectly clear this evening."

Papa approaches me, and Laura moves to his side. Her cheeks are pale, and her eyes are wide. I'm sure I've shocked her more than anyone else tonight. "And may I add that you look just beautiful in that dress. Wonderful job, Laura."

He turns to Luigi and Uncle Louie. "Make sure the both of you stay by her side at this university. I wouldn't want our Princess to castrate any of the young men there… or for any of them to get ideas. Make your presence well known. If you need to make a more definitive statement for the first few weeks, take Lucca and Rocco with you."

"You have nothing to worry about, sir," Luigi responds. "We're not letting her, or Annalisa, get more than ten feet from us. We'll be in the back of their classes during the entire class. Everyone will know she's protected."

"Papa," I whine, shaking my head. "you're fully aware of how well I've been trained. You've seen first-hand that you have absolutely nothing to worry about."

"No, darling daughter," he says, looking me up and down. "I have absolutely everything to worry about. With a body like yours and your beauty, I would feel so much better knowing you're fully covered and watched over even if you could probably kick all their asses. I'd rather you not be in that type of situation."

"Whatever," I mumble, rolling my eyes.

Several men chuckle, but Papa ignores them. "I've talked with Lucca and Rocco, as well as my brother, and approve of the way they're set up and running things here. You're doing a spectacular job with the house staff as well. They've had nothing but compliments for you. I can rest easy now that I know you have things under control. Laura and I will be leaving now, knowing you can take care of anything that might come up. Feel free to kick anyone off your team if needed. I'll find them a much less comfortable assignment."

Papa's eyes flit over to Antonio. I smile and lean onto my toes to kiss his cheek. I know it always makes him uncomfortable, but his words of confidence in me leave me floating. I give Laura a hug and whisper another 'thank you' in her ear. She squeezes me in return.

"Oh, don't you worry about my men," I say winking at Papa. "I can make their life a living hell all by myself if I need to. They know the house is off limits and will be leaving right behind you."

As one, the men stand and follow my Papa through the door. Stephen and Antonio linger, though, with Lucca and Rocco right behind them.

"I'm sorry Antonio was such an ass to you." Stephen punctuates his statement with slapping the back of his best friend's head.

"Hey," Antonio complains, "I've taken enough abuse today."

"But I need to know," Stephen continues, ignoring his friend, "now that we've been kicked down to the bunkhouse, does that mean we're banned from this house like the others?" His eyes plead with me to say they're allowed here. Besides, I can't do that to Annalisa... she might just use her forthcoming firearm training in retaliation.

I shake my head. "Stephen, you and Antonio are expected to be at all meals in this house, just like Rocco and Lucca when they lived in the bunkhouse. You're more than welcome here, but only on the first floor. There's no reason for either of you to be upstairs unless invited by myself, Uncle Louie, Luigi, Rocco or Lucca. Those living quarters are earned, and you never earned them. Papa arranged it that way based on your association with our Family. That wasn't fair, so I corrected it."

"Thank you, Princess," Stephen says, hugging me. "We left our stuff in the car when we arrived, so we'll just drive down to the bunkhouse and unpack. I'm sure Antonio doesn't feel up to walking anywhere right now anyway."

He walks to the door, leaving Antonio standing in front of me. His head still hangs down as he cups his crotch.

"Good night, Antonio. If you need some ice, please go to the kitchen and get some. I don't want you to suffer any permanent damage."

Looking up, his eyes find mine. "You surprised the shit out of me tonight, Princess. Never in a million years did I think you'd ever grab my dick and nearly twist it off. But... you're right. I deserved it. I think you also took the chance to make an example of me, make sure the other men got the message to not stare at your fine-ass body." He turns his lower body away from me when I take a step forward. "I'm kidding, totally kidding. Can't I tease you? As long as I'm not openly lusting after you, right? It'll be hard… well, maybe not that hard after you nearly took my cock off."

"You should probably shut up while you still have *something* to play with. Next time you won't be so lucky," I say, crossing my arms.

"Okay, okay. Good night, Alessandra." Antonio bends, hugging me. He limps out the door with Rocco and Lucca trailing behind him, giving him grief.

Uncle Louie stands behind them. "You made yourself crystal clear tonight. I didn't like hearing some of those words coming out of your mouth, but you said what needed to be said." He gives me a look filled with pride as he leaves.

Luigi leaves behind him, but the look he gives me is different. His eyes sparkle, maybe even smolder. What in the world is going on in his brain?

Chapter 27

SHARING SECRETS AND DISCOVERING NEW THINGS

*A*fter dinner, Annalisa gets her alone time with Stephen. They're downstairs in the library, and I'm sure they're not reading. Well, maybe Stephen's trying to read how far Annalisa will let him go tonight… I giggle at the thought.

Stretching out, I put my feet up on the arm of the couch near my fireplace. Propped in my lap is my second iPad. It looks just like the one my Papa gave me, but it's not. Annalisa got this one for me on the sly. I gave her cash for it and continue to give her money to pay for the internet. I explained that I just wanted something to myself, something that wouldn't be tracked by my uncle or father. She understood and was willing helped me out. I'm so glad she understands my need for a little secrecy.

I've created a Facebook profile under a false name… well, not so false. I picked Alexa Bellamy, part of my Nonna's maiden name before she married my Nonno. Before she married him, her name was Valentina Alexa Bellamy. Her father was the Family accountant. I'm fairly certain no one, other that Nonna herself, would figure out that I'm Alexa Bellamy.

My profile states I'm nineteen. The picture I chose is a black and white one of me, where I'm peeking around a wisteria tree. Uncle Louie had taken it on one of our picnics back at the compound. My hair was down, swirling around my shoulders, but you can't see just how long it really is. And because it's a black a white picture, you can't tell my hair or eye color either. I love how much a black and white photo can hide.

A notification pops up telling me Sarah Riggs accepted my friend request. Oh, my God! This is it. My hand shakes as I comment on her wall.

"Thank you so much for accepting my friendship request. I'm hoping to move to the states after university. I would love to make new friends ahead of time."

Clicking over to her *About* page, I see she's living in Los Angeles, CA now, not New Jersey like when I met her. Unable to resist myself, I click on her photos. The most recent album is titled "A Visit From Bro." Pay dirt! The pictures were posted a few months ago, and I quickly flip through them. The caption reads:

Visit from the greatest brother of all time. He's here for a week on leave. It's been TWO long years since I've seen him. He's all hush-hush about what he does in the Army, saying "it's classified." I'm going to enjoy the heck out of having my brother home while he's here. Love you, Grayson!

A few months, hmm… he's probably twenty-two or twenty-three here, but I'm not sure. I never really did ask how old he was. He said he finished high school early and that he went straight to university. Studying him in the picture, I notice his hair is shorter, but his eyes are still the mysterious dark blue, almost purple. A huge smile makes his dimples pop. Sarah must have just jumped on his back, and his hands reach back to hold her legs. God, they look so happy. My heart swells seeing him smile.

Sarah's hair is lighter than Grayson's and hangs just past her shoulders with gorgeous highlights. She's so beautiful she could easily be a model. Recalling how tall she was when we met, I know she could totally do it.

I scan the other pictures in the album. He must have visited around Christmas. In one, he's sitting in a recliner, reading something. In the window over his shoulder, snow falls, and the multi-colored lights shine on the tree. With his stocking feet propped up, Grayson wears jeans and a black turtleneck. The shirt is tight, defining each and every muscle in his arms and chest. The person who took the picture must have called his name because his eyes aren't on the book in his hand but instead focused on the camera. His head is still tilted down, and my heart stutters. He's heart-stopping gorgeous, my Greek god.

With each new picture I look at, my heart pounds harder in my chest. Now that I know where Sarah is, I'll have a better chance of reuniting with Grayson. He'd said she was going to NYU, so she must have transferred to UCLA, and she'll be graduating in the next year or two. With the snow, she must have gone back to New Jersey to see him. I mean, it doesn't snow in sunny California, does it?

Clicking on the next one, my breath catches in my throat at the sight before me. They're at the beach. I vaguely notice Sarah in a blue string bikini, my eyes are on Grayson. Black swim trunks hang low on his hips, revealing the deep cut V of his hips. His eight-pack abs are on glorious display, as well as a trickle of hair that disappears into the waistband of his trunks.

My eyes trail from his belly button down that strip of hair to his waistband and a little lower. My lower abdomen quivers as I reverse the path, following it up to his chest. His dark hair fans out from a patch at his sternum, dusting over his large pecs. I feel naughty looking at him like this, but damn, I can't help it. He's a Greek god, total perfection.

Settling on his face, I memorize every inch of his stunning beauty. His chiseled jaw, kissable lips, strong nose... and those eyes, dark and mysterious. My eyes flutter closed as I remember kissing those lips, the heat and pressure against my own. The way his eyes on me made me feel like I could fly. God, please let me find my way to him again.

I flick back through the pictures and save each and every one to my iPad. Thank God I chose to have a full password on this, not just a four-digit passcode. No one will be able to hack it. I'll fill it with every picture of Grayson I can... and any information I can find on him. This isn't something I'll ever share with anyone. This is just for me.

I continue scrolling through the pictures, but one stops me. Seven other guys pose with Grayson, each one of them insanely hot. They're all shirtless, showing off their defined chests and arms. Dang, what is in the water in America? The guys hold Sarah horizontally in their arms, like she's a log. The one on the end is in a wheelchair and holds her feet. Score, she's tagged each and every one of them. I'll have to friend request them too. The caption reads:

Some of the Brothers of Camelot LOL! Always holding me up and supporting me. Fitz, Carpenter, Jackson, Hunter, Spencer, Stevens and Bishop! Love these guys!

Holy cow! That *is* Stevens! Yup, just like Grayson told me, they all use their last names. Before I lose my nerve, I quickly friend request each and every one of them. Oh God, am I acting like a crazy stalker? What will they think of me? Ugh. Hopefully, they'll see that I'm in France and just a university student... and friends with Sarah. I bet a ton of Sarah's friends have asked to be friends with them on Facebook. What girl wouldn't?

Huh, what does Sarah mean by "Brothers of Camelot?"

A knock on my door startles me from my sleuthing. My finger flies to the lock button. Looking over at the door, I find Luigi, his hands stretched up and holding onto the door frame.

"Whatcha reading?" he asks cheekily. "Maybe a hot… steamy… romance?"

"Well, jeez," I answer, smiling. "I can't hide anything from you, can I?"

"Nope," he replies, coming in and lifting my feet. Taking a seat, he places them in his lap. "You can't hide a thing from me. You're an open book."

My smile grows as I tease him. "Mm-hmm, is that so? Since you think you know *everything* about me, let me ask you this. Who was my first kiss?"

His eyebrow raises, and he chuckles. "Oh, come on. Are you going to try to lie and tell me you've let someone kiss you already? I haven't heard of your uncle killing anyone, and I know I haven't killed anyone for touching you… so I'm going to say you haven't been kissed yet."

Pulling my feet from his lap, I sit up and lean toward him. "Well, Luigi," I say quietly as I stand up, "I hate to be the bearer of bad news for you, but I'm sneakier than you can guard. I've allowed three different guys to kiss me."

Luigi shoots to his feet. With his hands at my waist, he hoists me over his shoulder and walks to my bed.

"Luigi," I hiss, "don't throw me on my bed!"

He ignores me, bumps his shoulder up and tosses me to the center of my bed, making me squeal.

"Stop throwing me on my bed!" I admonish him. "That's the second time you've done that." Giggling, I scoot up the bed until my back meets my mountain of pillows and I'm sitting upright.

"Holy fucking shit," Luigi mutters, staring at my legs. "What the hell are you doing wearing a red and black garter? What the fuck? It's a goddamn holster?!

That's your Sig strapped to your leg!"

"Oh," I smile at him, looking innocent. "I forgot I was wearing it." Snapping the release, I remove it from the garter holster and set it on my nightstand. Slowly, I slide the garter down my leg, then repeat the process on my other leg, laying them both next to my gun. I was careful to keep myself covered, never revealing more than a few inches above my knee. Looking up at him, he appears to be in a trance.

"Hey… hey Luigi," I call, snapping my fingers. His eyes fly to mine. "This is what Laura brought me today. She made me several different sets, and you should see the little pockets she added to my bras. Some can hold throwing stars and others are narrower for my throwing knives. They're so cool. She complained about having to use this super strong, uncuttable fabric, and how it almost broke her sewing machine."

Luigi still looks a little dazed, so I persevere. "She said Papa asked her to make them, so I'll always have protection. Please don't tell anyone you saw that. I'm not supposed to let any of the men see. But *someone* likes to throw me on my bed. Laura was hoping Papa wouldn't find out that she made them so risqué. She just wanted me to feel pretty underneath my clothes. You and I both know Papa would never understand that."

Luigi jolts from his shock-induced statue impersonation and scrubs a hand over his face. He takes a deep breath. "I agree with them. I don't give a flying fuck who it is. Unless you need to pull that gun out and use it, never let that skirt go above your knees. Never let anyone see what's hidden under there. Those need to stay completely hidden. At. All. Times. You got me?"

His voice is firm, possessive and I can't help but

laugh at his complete turnaround. "Well, if you hadn't thrown me on the bed, you wouldn't even know that I was wearing them. And, since no one else likes to throw me on my bed, no one else will see them either."

Luigi just shakes his head, plopping onto the corner of my bed. "That was one sexy as sin visual I didn't need to fucking see. Damn, girl."

"Oh," I tease, smiling at him. "So you think that was sexy, huh?"

"You know, that innocent teasing could get you into a lot of trouble one day," he chuckles. "Now tell me the truth. Have you really kissed three guys? I need names, so I can kick their asses. If one of them is Antonio, I might just have to kill him… after I throw up. As much as you can't stand him, there's no way you'd willingly have allowed that."

"Geez," I laugh again. "It wasn't that bad, nothing that would cause you to vomit. I'd get more enjoyment out of kissing Fluffy than kissing Antonio again. It wasn't from his lack of talent, that wasn't bad at all. It's just… there wasn't that zing, that spark. There was zero, and I mean *zero*, chemistry. Not even a little twinge."

Luigi's hands shift through his hair, slightly pulling on it. "When? Where? How did this happen? Where were Lou and I when this kiss fucking happened?"

I howl at his reaction, "Oh my God, you *really* want details? Fine, if it'll make you feel better. You don't have to kill him because he didn't force himself on me. I would have taken care of him myself if he had. It was the right after Annalisa's birthday last year when I stayed at her house. I'd forgotten Fluffy in her game room. I'd stayed up reading, and you know how I can't sleep without him, so I went to get him. When I opened the door, I saw Antonio asleep on the couch. I thought if I could tippy-toe over to the chair, I could grab my bear and get to bed. When I turned to the door, Antonio was sitting up, checking me out."

"Shit," Luigi mumbles. "Were you in your pajamas?"

"Yes," I say, laughing lightly. "I was wearing shorts and t-shirt. Anyway, I told Antonio to stop looking at me like that. He came over to me and asked why I always fought him off, why was I so against him. I told him the truth that he'd been with too many girls I know and that he doesn't *do* anything for me like that. I said I loved him like an annoying brother, explained that I never got butterflies in my tummy, no sudden stomach drops. I told him that I want those feelings before I give myself to someone, that I deserve it."

I laugh, remembering everything I said that night. "I also told him that the only reason he thinks he feels anything for me is because of the way I look, that it's just a physical attraction... and because I tell him 'No' when most girls don't. He denied it up and down, like I knew he would. I was shocked when he said it was because of who I was, as a person... how I gave away my toys and how I treated his sister. He said he admired me."

Luigi hangs on my every word. Taking a breath to fortify myself, I explain the actual kiss. "At that point, he's inches from me. He asked if I never let him near me, how would I really know that we don't have chemistry, and damn it, he was right. So, I stood there and allowed him to kiss me. It was nice, but then the faces of all the girls he'd slept with flashed in my brain. I pulled away, explained there wasn't anything on my end, no stomach drops or butterflies, and what I *felt* of his reaction was purely physical. I let him know that there would never be another kiss between us and if he told anyone, I'd deny it to my grave. I grabbed Fluffy and went back to Annalisa's room where I locked the door. We haven't spoken of it since."

Luigi looks stunned as his stares at me with wide eyes. Finally, he takes a deep breath. "But come on, Aless, you can't be blind to the fact that Antonio has not given up on you. Yeah, in your mind he doesn't have a chance, but he *thinks* he can change your mind. When he's around you, you keep yourself armed if I'm not by your side."

"Okay Luigi," I giggle, rolling my eyes. "I'll do that."

He falls to his back, laying across the foot of my bed and puts his hands under his head. I flip to my stomach and turn my head to the foot of the bed with my feet resting on my pillows.

"The other guy isn't even worth mentioning. It was totally gross and barely lasted a second. The end."

"That's only two," Luigi observes, turning his head to look at me. "Who was the third?"

"Oh, you don't know him," I smile. "And there's no way I'll ever share those moments with anyone. Our time together is sacred to me. What I felt with him is what every other man will be measured against. I'll judge every kiss in the future against the ones I shared with him. Luigi, when we kissed... the world, everything around me just came to a complete stop. It was amazing and incredible. My heart was pounding so hard and so loud that I could swear he heard it. My stomach dropped and tumbled like it was on a roller coaster. I had butterflies so powerful it felt like a herd of buffalo stampeding. The chemistry was off the charts explosive. And that's what I want. That's what I deserve."

Luigi rolls to his side and props his head in his hand. He studies my face for more information, but I don't give him any. "The only time you've ever been alone where something like that could have happened is at that party you went to in America."

Without looking away, I mime zipping my lips and throwing away the key. He shakes his head and moves a little closer to me until we're inches apart.

"As much as I would really, really love to blow your fucking mind right now," he says in a low, gruff voice, "and kiss the living hell out of you, I won't. I made a promise and an oath that I wouldn't touch you until you're eighteen and of legal age. I'm a man of my word, and you're only seventeen. But… one day, Aless, I want to see if we have that chemistry."

My jaw falls open in utter shock as he gives me a smoldering look.

"What the hell is this?" Uncle Louie yells, breaking our stare down. We both start laughing and roll over and climb from my bed and approach my uncle.

"*Nothing* is going on. We were just talking, Uncle Louie. As you can see, I'm clothed, Luigi is clothed," I say, waving my hand's in Luigi's direction. "But if I decided to jump on Luigi and have my dirty way with him, don't you think I'd have closed and locked the door?"

Luigi, now at my side, laughs and cocks an eyebrow at me. "Have your dirty way with me? Not gonna happen, Little One. We just discussed that. Your secrets are safe with me." He taps my nose with the tip of his finger, still laughing.

Uncle Louie smiles. He pats Luigi's back, a little harder than necessary, and says, "I'm so glad to hear that… but, Little One, we don't have secrets, do we?"

I give my uncle an innocent look.

"Fine... I'll let that slide. But I'm making a new rule. Any time Luigi is in here, that door stays open," he declares firmly.

I laugh hard, clutching my waist. "Hate to say it, Luigi," I say between laughs, "but I don't think it's you my uncle doesn't trust. I think he really believes I might try to jump you."

Luigi wraps his arms around me and whispers in my ear, "Just you wait until you're eighteen, young lady." Pulling away, he delivers a kiss to my forehead. Mocking a proper Southern woman from America, he declares, "I'm strong and can resist your temptations, I'll fight you off, you sexual fiend."

Uncle Louie howls with hilarity. "Good night, Luigi," he says in a stern voice. "The girls have class in the morning."

Luigi pounds my uncle on the back as he moves to the door. "Good night," he calls over his shoulder. "I'll see you both in the morning. I just have to make sure your assistant isn't still in the library, studying how far she can go with Stephen without getting caught."

When he's gone, I flop back onto my bed. "Am I about to get a lecture?" I ask.

"Do you need one?" he chuckles.

"No," I sigh. "And to be honest, Luigi is never anything but respectful. He's never tried anything or made me question him. He really is an amazing friend. We enjoy each other's company, and we like to tease each other, but it never goes any further than that. Okay? There's nothing to worry about."

He puts his hand on my cheek and turns my head, so he can see my eyes. "Are you developing feelings for Luigi?"

"Why does everyone keep asking me that? I don't think either of us would allow that to happen. I'm scared of ruining our friendship Uncle Louie. I *need* him. He always knows how to bring me out of a funk, without fail."

"Okay," he mutters. Bending down, Uncle Louie kisses my forehead. "Good night, Little One. I love you. And if we don't figure out things with your Papa, I'll make sure you'll never marry Antonio. We still have a few more years yet, okay?"

I nod and kiss his cheek. "Just so you know, I'm not marrying anyone in the Family, Uncle Louie. I promised Mom that I would find real love, and I'll keep that promise if it's the last thing I do. But now's not the time to talk about that, okay?"

He nods, inspecting my face. After several long seconds, he releases my face and turns to the door. When he's halfway there, he stops and looks at me over his shoulder. "You're right, now isn't the time… but please keep in mind that there is a great alternative to Antonio- your great friend, Luigi. That's all I'm going to say about that. Good night, *Piccola*. I love you more than life itself. We'll work this out, I promise. Sleep tight."

I shake my head as my uncle walks out the door, shutting it behind him. I lay there, thinking about what happened tonight. The biggest revelation is that Luigi thinks I'm sexy. Heck, he looked positively stupefied when he saw my legs, and he wants to blow my mind with a kiss when I turn eighteen. What if we have that chemistry? What if it's hot? Could I stay here?

"No," I mumble to myself, getting up to grab my iPad on the couch. Luigi and I are great friends, but that's it. Besides, it would mean staying here, running a crime family and always looking over my shoulder, always being ready to kill at a moment's notice. I don't want that. I don't want to raise a family in this world. What this Family does is illegal, no matter how much they want to candy-coat it. Most of it isn't moral either.

I want to be good. I don't want to be a killer. I want to be on the side of what is good. I don't want to do evil. No matter what happens, I can't marry Luigi either. I've got to stick with my plan to escape to America and see if Grayson is in my future.

Changing into my pajamas, I settle in on my bed. Pulling up the calendar, I enter the date Grayson, and I officially met with a little heart emoji. Bringing up my Facebook, I continue flicking through the pictures on Sarah's page, saving them all. Two of his friends accepted my friend requests, which encourages me.

To give myself credibility, I shared some silly memes and posted some of the scenic pictures from our trip to Paris. Going back to Sarah's pages, I realize she responded to my comment, obviously having stalked my fake profile.

Oh, to live in France with all those romantic French men. You must have them all over you, reading your poetry, LOL. And the food! I spent a month there after I graduated high school. I loved traveling Europe and all the sights.

I look forward to seeing your posts and getting to know you. If you ever make it out to California, let me know. A girl can never have enough friends. See you around, girlfriend!

I respond:

I can't wait to see all of your posts and share with you. And WHEN I make it to California, I'll be sure to connect with you! Thanks!

I power down my secret iPad and hide it in a hidden compartment under my nightstand, knowing it's safe there. I turn to my window and look to the full moon and to all the stars in the sky and hope, Grayson is looking at this same night sky, as I say a little prayer.

Grayson, please wait for me. I promise I'll help fate along and find you in a few years. Mom, if you can hear my prayers, help me figure out the perfect way to escape so I can find real love and have my free life.

Want to know what happens to Alessandra? Does she escape and find her way to America? Does she stay and marry Luigi? The finale in the My Life series, "My Free Life," is coming soon!

I'd love for you to follow me on Facebook at: NecieNavone

Twitter: @NecieNavone

Instagram: necienavone

Sign-up for my newsletter: necienaove.com